It Just Wasn't Done

B B Campbell

A Novel

Book design by Beverly S. Maxton, MC, NCC

Published by SoulRaz Unlimited
Prescott, Arizona

ISBN: 979-8-9930859-0-6

Library of Congress Control Number: 2025921787

For inquiries: blove9now7@gmail.com

About the Author

Dr. Betty Campbell Henderson

In May 2004, Dr. Betty Campbell Henderson, mother of four children, grandmother of nine, and great grandmother of eleven, retired her position as a college guidance counselor for "at-risk" college students in Phoenix, AZ and moved to Prescott, AZ.

She activated her metaphysical ministerial license, married Dr. Bob Henderson and dedicated herself to writing, teaching, and facilitating personal growth and self-enhancement workshops and spiritual counseling. It was from a journaling workshop this book was selected. An experience that exceeded all expectations.

This book is dedicated in honor of José Irizarry, without his expertise in writing and publishing, this book would not have been possible. Thank you my dear friend.

In honor of my parents, Melvin and Tresa Campbell whose love and faith in me never faltered; Mom and Dad, I am eternally grateful.

To the Great Masters, whose unconditional love and dedication to Truth Principles throughout history, taught and modeled kindness, compassion, Brotherly/Sisterly love and the Oneness in all Creation.

I am blessed because of your loving gifts of guidance. Words. do not express my deep gratitude.

INTRODUCTION

*D*o *you get up , so fearful of what lies before you? Are your memories filled with abuse, hatred, and distrust; that it has become too difficult to risk or trust life, or hope that it could be any different?*

Do you question yourself about what is constant and never seems to change? Where is the light, if all you see is darkness?

There are some of us who were born privileged, but are ignorant of others who have to struggle. What happens when there becomes an awakening, an awareness to pain and struggle all around you regardless of how much money or things you have or give? Where do you go? Who do you confide in, or as to why? And then, how do you get help?

What if your efforts to help, to serve, or teach, or love are rejected by fear and misunderstanding? What happens when you find yourself in the same hole as those you believe needed your help?

Do you wonder and maybe ponder at great length, as to your purpose here at this time? Does sometime, feeling grateful---seem hypocritical?

Have you laid in bed trying to reconcile forgiveness and resentment as being closely related? Does your heart hurt and your brain curse what you see and ask the same question, Why? And do you dodge your soul's greater question? "What do you plan to do about it?" Or do you choose to "just wander along" as your whole insides become a mass of solidified thoughts and feelings that never seem to move forward?

Lillian Rose Somerset questions these and many, many more......

LIST OF CHARACTERS

Chadwick Nicholas Somerset I

Born 1740 London, England married Victoria Amelia Campbell 1772

birthed Chadwick Nicholas II, died 1775

Chadwick Nicholas Somerset II, married Mary M. Shawnessy

1798, emigrated to Philadelphia,

birthed Chadwick Nicholas Somerset III, 1818

Chadwick Nicholas Somerset III

married Mary Maud Murphy 1855, birthed Lillian Rose 1861

Lillian (Lily) Rose Somerset-Huffman

married Martin Huffman 1890, birthed Mary Therese 1891

Louis Phillipi Beaumont, born in France 1827

bought land on Mississippi River, father of Jade Nichole

Jade Nichole, aka Bess, daughter of Louis Beaumont and slave Missy,

wife of Desmond Lafayette aka Jeb Dominican,

Medical Assistant to Dr. Chad in Dayton, Ohio

Jean Michel Beaumont, born in France 1829

Owner of High Stepper Plantation

father of Phillip and half slave Desmond

Phillipi Beaumont, born in 1864

Son of Jean Michel and wife, Marion

Desmond Lafayette aka Jeb, born 3 weeks after Phillipi

run away slave son of Jean Michel and slave concubine, Rochelle

Jack Tom Jones, Kentucky farmer, evil slave seller
married Jenny Sterling, fathered Gunnar and Maxwell
Jenny Sterling, devout abolitionist, Presbyterian
whose father and uncle are conductor's on
Underground Railroad, Mother of Gunnar and Maxwell
Rev. Henderson Sterling, father of Jenny,
along with brother, Benjamin, are devoted
conductor's on Underground Railroad.
Elder Brock Burns, a Scottish emigrant
assisting Rev Sterling at his church in Cincinnati
married Jenny Sterling, opens a Center for Homeless
Gunnar Sterling, son of Jenny and Jack Jones
after Jack dies, Jenny has her son baptized,
Gunnar Benjamin Sterling
William Lincoln Bailey, raped son of Bess,
adopted by Quakers; Obadiah and Martha Bailey,
conductor's on the Underground Railroad
Sister Therese Anne, French nun, served as
a Sister/Nurse in the Civil War, LilyRose's music teacher.
Opened Home for Mother's and Children in Philadelphia, PA
Sister Jade Nicole aka Bess, wife of deceased Jeb,
Medic at Battle of Ft. Donelson. Bess is Medical Assistant to Dr. Chad
Co-founded Home for Mother's & Children, Philadelphia, PA
Allen Moses Huffman, successful owner mercantile in
Wilmington, OH, devout Jew, believes in giving
respect, compassion, and his best service to community.
Eva Stein Huffman, wife of Allen, birthed Martin ,
their only son in her late 30's, insists on celebrating
Shabbat, delights in spoiling their grandchild, MaryTherese.

Martin Stein Huffman, perceives himself a political genius
and card shark. He is an abusive alcoholic, thief, sexually
cruel and evil abuser to both his wife and child.
Mary Therese Somerset-Young, daughter of LilyRose and Martin,
wife of Jonny Young, died three months after birthing Lily Kai
when their bi-plane burst into flames over St. Louis, MO.
Franklin Mitchell, handyman to Dr Chad and Harmony Village
married to Mildred Grace, has a grandson, Lukas, aka Junior, who
joined the U.S. Navy during Civil War
James Black, Sr. a merchant captain sailing from France to America,
married a Russian born French citizen, birthed James, Jr. on board ship
in the port of Philadelphia.
James, aka Jimmy Black, after death of both parents, became
Captain of his own barge, working with Underground Railroad
transporting slaves across the river at Cincinnati, and Indiana.
Annette Black, half American Indian and daughter of a French aristocrat
captured by a tribe. After's mother's death ran away and
stowed aboard Jimmy's fathers ship. Jimmy's mother allowed
her to stay on board, thus growing up with Jimmy.
BethAnne Black, daughter of James and Annette Black. Whose parent's
married, with his mother's blessing when he was nineteen and she,
eighteen. BethAnne grew up at Harmony Village, Ohio
Donald Denlinger, widower, father of Amanda Sue,
twelve year old soloists at the Christmas Musical Concert.
Penelope Ann Symthe, housekeeper, and clerk at mercantile, married
Donald Denlinger,
supported his dream to be a minister.
James Patterson, CEO OF NCR Dayton, OH. During 1913
flood, organized employees to build boats which saved

thousands of lives around Dayton's flooding rivers.
Lily Kai Somerset-Joseph, daughter of Mary Therese Somerset-Young,
graduate of WC, Harvard Law School, married Native Am. Artist,
Ardon Morning Star Joseph, professor of Art History, curator of
Wilmington's Art Gallery; parents of twins.
Joanna Dorene and Jonathan David twelve year old twins
of Lily Kai and Ardon Morning Star Joseph.
Lillian Rose Somerset, daughter of
Dr. & Mrs. Mary Maud Somerset III, of Dayton, Ohio
graduate of WC, mother of Mary Therese-Young and grandmother
of Lily Kai Joseph, great-grandmother of Joanna and Jonathan Joseph.
Suffragette, Trustee of Somerset Music & Fine Arts Trust,
and Children's Science Center of Clinton County
William Lincoln Bailey, a former slave,
rescued by the Underground Railroad, adopted by
Quaker's; Obadiah & Martha Bailey, soloist for
Christmas Musical, graduate of WC,
creator of Gunnar Memorial Garden,
& Children's Natural Science Center of Clinton Co..

An Aboriginal Australian, Hylius Maris Affirmative Poem
I am a child of the Dreaming People
Part of the land, like the gnarled gumtree.
I am the river, softly singing,
Chanting our songs on my way to the sea.
Rages that dance on the snow,
I am the snow, the wind, and the falling rain
I'm part of the rocks and the red desert earth
Red as the blood that flows in my veins,
I am eagle crow and snake that glides
through the rain forest that clings to the mountainside,
I awaken there when the earth was new
There was emu, wombat, kangaroo
No other man of a different hue.
I am this land, and this land is me,
I am Australian

BOOK SECTIONS

SECTION I

Freedom Calling

When the heart can no longer shut off the pleadings of the body,

the mind must dig deep to find courage to take action.

SECTION II

A Call to Serve

The mind and heart are in constant battle until

the heart recognizes that love is stronger than the ego.

SECTION III

Closets Running Over

Hatred grows bigotry: incest, rape, and abuse. become

societal norms until the heart takes courage and risks change.

SECTION IV

Summary and Epilogue

Sources Used

Author's Comment

Group Questions and Acknowledgments

HOME OF GRANNY ROSE

WILMINGTON, OHIO

On a cool September afternoon, Lillian Rose Somerset-Huffman is seated in the parlor on a worn rose brocade love seat waiting for her family to arrive. The room is filled with family portraits and memorabilia saved over the many years that Lillian Rose lived in this family home. Memories of birthing her only child, Mary Therese and nursing her husband, Martin and his parents, flooded her consciousness. It was during the nation's terrible flu epidemic that they all died; first her beloved mother-in-low, then her protective

father-in-law and two days later, Martin passed, never awakening from his coma.

Lillian Rose scanned the room. The highly waxed mahogany panels were vigilant to the many secrets the elegant and well kept home hid in protective silence. "I've waited long enough," surprising herself that she spoke out loud. "Abuse can kill the soul, I must tell the true story to my family!"

That morning, after her traditional breakfast of orange juice, boiled egg, dark toast, and black coffee; she began to contemplate the story her soul was called to share.

Climbing the curved carpeted staircase, pausing to catch her breath, she thought about her upcoming 94th birthday. "Ninety-Four Years! Sounds like a lifetime away, but it seemed just like yesterday." Realizing her many blessings; wonderful parents, grandfather, classical education, children, and grandchildren, she sighed in gratitude.

For more than 30 years, she has been a trustee for The Children's Nature Center just outside the city limits of Wilmington. Remembering made her heart beat faster anticipating what must be shared.

Opening the large cherry armoire with carved swirls of inlaid gold etchings, her eye caught sight of the beautiful rose velvet jacket and wool grey skirt she wore opening night of the first All County Christmas Concert sponsored by Wilmington College and local churches of Clinton County. Tears flowing, she opened her grandmother's French music jewelry box. Taking a deep breath, she retrieved the hand carved rose to pen on her jacket lapel. It was then her eye caught sight of the black smooth nut that belonged to William. Kissing the nut, she whispered, "It must be told," as she tucked the nut into her skirt pocket.

Exiting the stairs, she heard a young voice calling, "Granny Rose," Silently asking spirit for guidance, she responded cheerfully, "I'm coming, Granny is coming." "Oh, my dear, I'm so happy to see you. Please come into the parlor." "Oh, here's your Mom and Dad!"

As Ardon removed their coats, she embraced her grand-daughter. "Lily Kai, I'm so pleased you found time to answer my call and pay me a visit. I've a story I'm anxious to share and it makes me happy you are all here. Please have a seat while I pour some tea. I made ginger cookies with walnuts and raisins, they're my great grand's favorite!"

Whispering, lady-like, Jody shrugged her shoulders and sighed , "GrannyRose! you spoil us like babies, you know we'll soon be thirteen!" "Of course you will, I sometimes forget. Please forgive your old Granny-Rose."

Rising from her seat to get more tea, Lily Kai asked her Grandmother about the beautiful velvet jacket and skirt she was wearing?. "Isn't it beautiful? It was the ensemble I wore opening night of the very first all county musical performance in Wilmington. I dug it out to share with you," as her thoughts drifted for a moment to the past.

Opening the drawer to the walnut inlaid end table next to the settee, Lillian Rose caressed affectionately, an old leather diary she kept in the drawer. Looking up to her family seated anxiously, she spoke softly. "My grandfather Somerset gave me this diary when my mother died. I was almost six years old. Mother wanted to return to Philadelphia so that she could live her final days among the roses in my Grandmother's garden on the Somerset Estate. We traveled many days by buggy and train in order to grant mother her final wish. While on the trip, Father and I took turns feeding her and making sure she was warm and comfortable. Father called me, his little nurse, but even then, I knew music was my passion. Mother lived just three days after we arrived. She was able to spend time with her large Murphy family, visit Sister's of Charity of the Blessed Virgin Mary Convent and School, from which, she graduated."

"It was a beautiful warm spring day, my mother asked Father to please take her to the Rose Garden. She wanted to sit on the bench beside the statues of the Virgin Mary and St. Francis. Covered in Father's mother's Tartan plaid and wearing her Irish green beret, both she and father chanted the rosary as she passed on to be with our Heavenly Father. My distraught Father was with her to the very end, while I napped in my grandmother's sewing room. Grandfather, intuitively knew that this would be her last day. When I awakened, Grandfather kept me entertained by feeding me peppermint candy sticks and allowing me to look through Grandmother's box of pictures, her drawings of Father as a child, family portraits she painted of personal favorites: Father's christening, confirmation, college graduation, and taking the Hippocratic Oath as a physician, Grandfather had a large portrait of Mother and Father's Wedding Day, and a small tin type of me as an infant."

The funeral was held the following day. Father returned to Dayton as soon as all the details were completed. He left me with my wonderful, kind, and patient Grandfather who never left my side. He allowed me and Fluffy Ball, his ancient black long haired cat, to sleep with him. Every night as we said our prayers, we blessed Father and the poor children everywhere, then he would sing an old English lullaby as his beautiful Irish tenor voice lulled me to sleep. I knew he loved me deeply, but I missed Father, my True North Star. Grandfather promised to take me home as soon as plans could be arranged."

I couldn't sleep on the train, because of my excitement. I wore my poor grandfather out by constantly chatting about my friend BethAnne, the Free Clinic, Bess, handyman Frank, and my pony, Billy.

Before we left Philadelphia, Grandfather gave me this leather journal with instructions to "write while feeling the experience." Pausing for a moment, she turned to speak to Lily Kai, "I'm so sorry Lily Kai for not sharing my journal, as I promised on the eve of your wedding. I must confess, as the kids say today, "I just chickened out." Everyone was silent, never remembering Granny Rose being so serious as she was this day, She continued:

"I never met my great-grandparents Somerset, as they died before my father was born. My grandmother Somerset also passed away before my father married my mother, Mary Maud Murphy. Father always regretted that he never knew his Somerset grandparent's. They too, passed away long before my father was born."

"While in Philadelphia with my dying mother, I was privileged to become familiar with my Murphy grandparents, Sean Murphy and Anna Marie McCullom and my Murphy cousins. It is my hope in telling this story, to stimulate your interest into learning more about your ancestor's; their lives, personal accomplishments, and contributions to society."

"I know there is an art to researching one's family history; however, I've tried to record what I know from the stories I heard, read, and experienced with family and friends. I've tried to document facts and dates as soon as I came to know about them. I admit to not being as organized as you or others might be. My hope is that as I share, you will feel an appreciation and maybe a greater understanding for the struggles of those who went before you."

"The story of our ancestors began in England. My great-grandfather, Chadwick Nicholas Somerset I, was born in 1740. My great-grandmother, Victoria Amelia Campbell was from the lineage of the Clan Campbell in Scotland. My grandfather, Judge Chadwick Nicholas Somerset II, of Philadelphia and my father, Chadwick Nicholas Somerset III, are responsible for what little I know of my Somerset ancestors."

"My story begins at my great-grandfather's home in London, England and then progresses to the day before my father was to marry my mother, Mary Maud Murphy, of Philadelphia, Pennsylvania. I invite you to just relax and allow your imagination to picture my grandfather's home filled with the excitement of the next day wedding between Mary Maud Murphy and Chadwick Nicholas Somerset III. The Murphy's organized a hunting expedition to provide pheasant and rabbit to be served at the huge Irish wedding ceremony with dinner and dance to follow." Picking up the old journal, holding it to her breast, Granny Rose shared the stories with her own voice and emotional inflection.

Rest satisfied with doing well,
leave others to talk of you as they will.
-Pythagoras-

SECTION I

Freedom Calling

When the heart can no longer shut off the pleadings of the body,
the mind must dig deep to find soul courage to take action.

London, England

Chadwick Nicholas Somerset I, was born in London, England in 1740. Chadwick was the only living heir to the Somershire-Anglo Saxon tribe from Northern Great Britain that defeated French invaders in about 550 B.C. He was educated at Oxford University, became a barrister for the Crown of England at the age of twenty-six years.

At the age of 32, he married Victoria Amelia Campbell, daughter of William James Campbell, chieftain of one of the Campbell Clans in the Scottish Highlands. At the age of sixteen, she was betrothed by her father to another clan chieftain twenty years her senior. On the eve of her wedding, after finding her father passed out drunk, she executed a plan to escape. An excellent rider, she stole her father's favorite steed, Lightening, a prized stallion from his stables. Kelling, the cook, who raised Victoria after her mother's death, helped Victoria steal her dowry from it's secret hiding place behind the fireplace. She packed a satchel, then kissed Kelling goodbye. She quietly led Lightening out of the stable onto the dirt road which headed south towards London. England.

Victoria rode all night through a cold rain, until she came to a Catholic Convent just outside of London. Soaking wet, she begged entrance. She told her story, offered her dowry to the convent as payment to stay under their protection. Delighted, Mother Superior accepted Victoria's desire to be converted and immediately found a vacant room with a cot. She began her studies to become Catholic and a governess,

A few days after turning eighteen, a wealthy Duke came to the convent in search for a governess for his two children. She was immediately approved for employment. After packing her few belongings, she fell to her knees begging Mother Superior to allow her to take her horse, Lightening. Hearing the conversation, the Duke offered to pay for the horse. Mother Superior happily agreed to the sale. Immediately, they set off for London, hoping to arrive before dark.

Victoria met the children the next day. The Duke's children, a four year old girl and six year old boy.were very spoiled. Demonstrating bad manners, they refused to follow Victoria's directions and do their studies, Victoria approached the Duke concerning the matter. She said that if he wanted his children to grow up ignorant, ill mannered and misbehaving, then he, the parent could continue as he is doing. But if he wanted his children to be educated, kind and well mannered, then he must give her full reign to carry through with their education and discipline. Startled at her confidence in speaking her mind, he listened and said, "Well, of course, we'll give it a try."

"Sir, I do not believe in any form of spanking or belittling a child. There are more positive ways to teach and model responsibility and good manners. I think in time, you'll be quite pleased."

It was at a dinner party at the home of the Duke's, that Chadwick I, met Victoria. He had stepped out into the garden for some fresh air when he heard her with the children. She was telling them a story about the "wee people" and how they are not happy when children pester frogs, pulling blossoms off the stalks of flowers, and hurting each another. Chadwick did not stay to hear the ending of her story, because knew he due for after dinner for drinks and cigar in the Duke's library.

After about six months of constantly thinking about Victoria, Chadwick traveled to the Duke's home to ask if he would have any problem with him asking Victoria for permission to court her.

Surprised, the Duke laughed, "Chad old boy, she'll be a handful. In her short time here, she has taught my children that bedtime is after their dinner, to draw and paint what they are feeling, to sing and play happily together and, this is a really big one, to be kind and mannerly to all people." "But of course you know it is against protocol to entertain or court below our social status. But knowing you, it never seems to brother you what people think." Reaching out to shake his hand, "Would you like for me to invite her to join us for tea in the front parlor?"

A year later Victoria and Chadwick I, were married. But first, before accepting his proposal, Victoria insisted that he must agree to: (1) Marriage must be in the Catholic Church, (2) As a married couple they must share all family economics, and the rearing of children and their education. Chadwick had no idea what all that would entail, but quickly agreed. They were married May Day, 1772 in the Roman Catholic Church in London and honeymooned in Paris, France.

In the Spring of 1773, Victoria gave birth to their only child, Chadwick II. In 1774, after becoming very ill with consumption, she died in her husband's arms, begging him to promise he would not send their son away to private school. Broken hearted, he swore to her he would raise the child to respect all people, be courageous about life, and to learn to respect the world's various cultures.

After months of grieving, and with the help of their cook and housekeeper, Sir. Chadwick I, began little Jugan's studies. He nicknamed him Jugan, Old English for Judge, because of his manner in negotiating what he wanted. An eager and excellent student, he devoured the Classics (Latin & Greek) Poetry, Geometry, Astronomy, and Music. He became quite proficient playing the violin and loved debating politics. Jugan was accepted on his own merit to Oxford University. Graduated 1791 with honors.

In Spring, Chadwick Nicholas Somerset II, married Mary Margaret Shawnessy. They met while she was a maid at the college. She came from a very poor Irish family, for which she sent all her earnings to help support her large family in Dublin . They emigrated to Philadelphia in the Spring of 1791. Jugan's father had developed a good friendship with Benjamin Franklin, while Franklin was in London representing the American Colonies. Chadwick I, believed the couple would love the American Colonies and the freedom their founding principles supported.

Chadwick II was accepted into the largest law firm in Philadelphia. He loved his work, especially defending the poor. He felt they deserved a chance, even if not able to afford it. On Christmas Eve, after believing Maggie was barren, she delivered a beautiful baby boy. Following tradition, they named him Chadwick Nicholas Somerset III, and called him Chad.

He was educated at home by both parents. His father, like his father, taught him all the formal courses necessary for higher education. Maggie taught him to love nature, to grow vegetables and flowers, roses her favorite, and to be a gentle, caring, and sharing young man. She shared her poor life as a child in Dublin and how during the potato famine the family almost starved to death. She was a very devout Catholic, always busy knitting blankets for little children and taking baskets of food to the poor and needy.

Chad announced early in his youth, he was going to become a doctor. Both parents were thrilled. He attended Kings College in New York and graduated Harvard Medical School, and was accepted as an intern at Pennsylvania Hospital in Philadelphia. His parents were overjoyed to learn Benjamin Franklin was its founder.

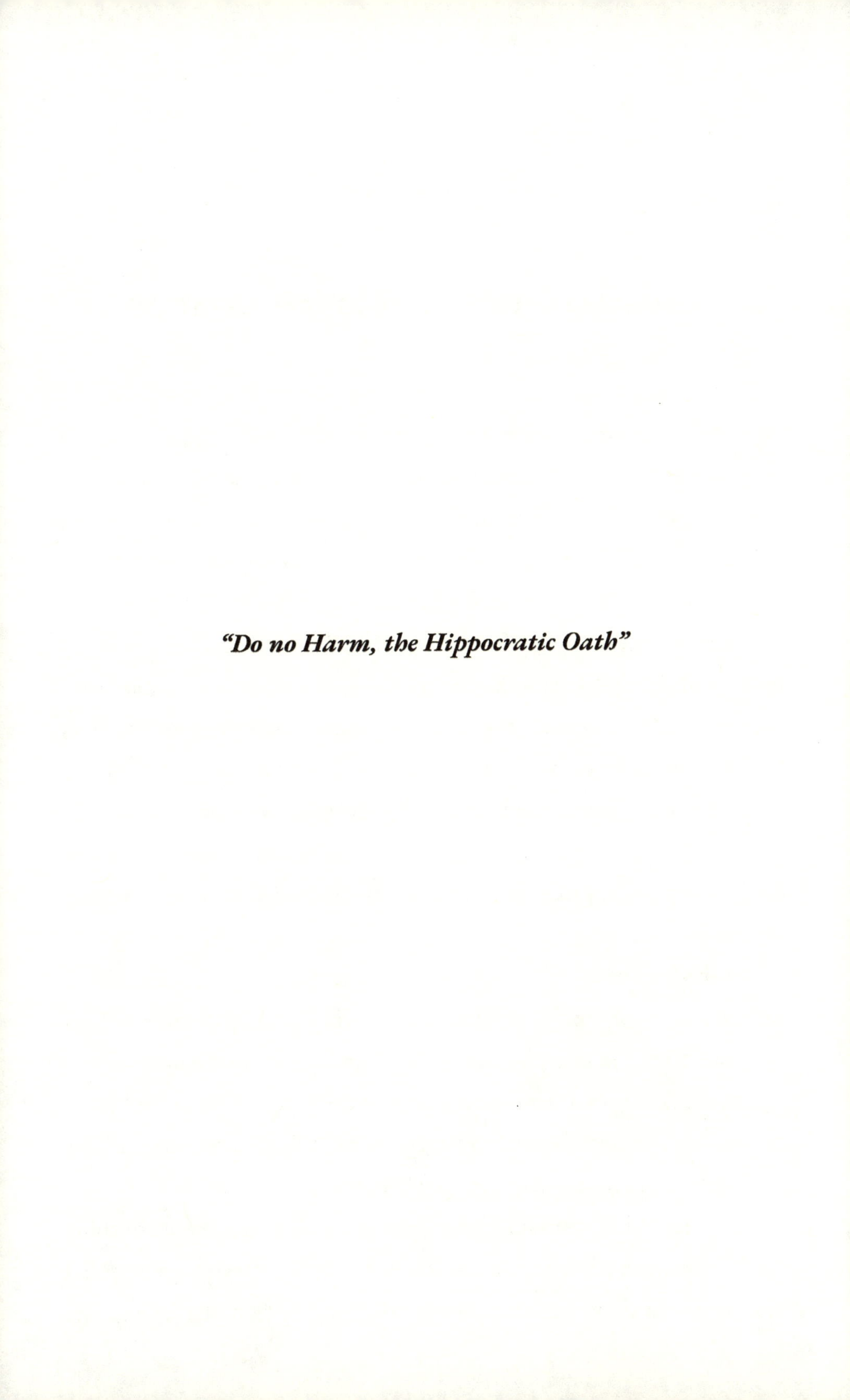

"Do no Harm, the Hippocratic Oath"

MAGNOLIA GROVE BEAUMONT PLANTATION

Missy, a young kitchen slave grabbed her stomach while holding on to the back of the oak chair by the old chopping table. Water was streaming down between her legs. She knew better than to scream as the Master's kitchen overseer, Big Bertha would surely slap her senseless No slave got any special help from Big Bertha.

Coming into the kitchen from the garden, Big Bertha grabbed Missy by her arm. It didn't matter to Big Bertha when and where slave babies were born. They all got the same treatment. A pregnant slave had just three days to deliver the baby before returning to their job on the planation. Missy would be no exception, just because her baby was seeded by the Master.

Missy was a rape child by her mother's former master. Master Beaumont took a liking to her green eyes and light skin and paid a good price for her at the slave auction.

"Hush yo mouth, I tell yo girl, yo mo truble thn yo worth to me. Git yo bad self out of here and git yo old Mammy to hep yo drop de chile. or I tell da master to put ya sum plac else. Git!" Shoving her out the door.

Big Bertha's rag tied around her head was dripping wet from the heat in the cooking shed. She began chopping onions, still disgusted about Missy, she yelled at OldTom, "yo git me sum hep, rite now."

Missy, scared and trembling, looked around the inside of the old birthing shed. There was a pile of rags in one corner, a big pot for water, a dirty pallet of straw on the floor, and some dried herbs hanging from the ceiling. She felt another pain coming. Pacing around the perimeter of the room, she took deep breaths and held her engorged belly. She wondered if the old healer, a midwife, would come? She was ancient, squat, and wild looking. Some thought she was at least a hundred, with a puckered wrinkle mouth, dripping a stream of burgundy snuff. She could draw two fingers together to her mouth, and shoot a stream of snuff clear across a room, kill a fly while not blinking an eye, nor offering an apology for who or what stood in its way. The Master bought her in New Orleans. She was advertised as a good Creole cook, but her cooking days were over. Folks believe she to be a voodoo witch, which kept most of the plantation away from her.

Master kept her on because when his daughter, Josephine was born, she saved his wife's life with an herb that stopped her bleeding to death. In the midst of that thought, a pain hit Missy as she fell to the floor moaning. The door flap opened, in walked Mammy and the healer. Mammy had a pitcher full of cool water with some herbs in it. "Heh," she said, "drnk, y'll feel better."

The healer pointed to a pallet for her to crawl to. Mammy had laid a tattered quilt on the top of the pallet making it to look a bit cleaner. The healer reached into a pouch she had hanging by a rope at her waist. Pulling out the object, she raised it over Missy's head. Up and down, over her whole body, walking and clapping her hands she chanting. Squatting down beside Missy, she instructed her to get on all fours. She poked her fingers into Missy's woman parts, then laid her ear on her belly and then raised two fingers, smiling. Indicating that Missy had two babies. Mammy brought in another bucket of hot water, as she began to pray, "Oh, Lawd! Hep her, hep my lil one, hep her Lawd!"

Missy willing herself not to yell, tossed and turned on the pallet. The healer motioned sternly for her to get back up on all fours, squat, and breathe deeply and to push. Very quickly, a head appeared, Missy yelled just as a tiny skeleton of a child dropped into the healer's hands. She handed the baby to Mammy who sighed. "A grl chld," Disappointed, she cleaned the tiny baby girl and wrapped her in a blanket. She then heard another yell coming from Missy as another baby fell into the arms of the healer. The healer shook her head, the baby was not moving as the healer massaged it, shook it, but the boy child did not move.

Exhausted, Missy fell back on the pallet as the healer delivered the afterbirth. Then consciousness hit Missy, she cried, "My babies, I want my babies." Her Mammy laid the baby girl on her mother's chest, and sadly whispers, "Duh Lawd wntd him in heven, he no mak it." Missy sobbed and sobbed. The healer took the man child while Mammy cleaned up the birthing shed. Then, Mammy helped Missy and baby to her shack to recover. Missy knew she had to be back in the kitchen in two days. She was determined to take care of her baby herself . She believed her child to be the most beautiful baby she'd had ever seen. But of course, all mothers felt that way.

Two days later, Missy, with her little girl nursing on her breast, bound by a cotton piece of fabric around her neck and back, was standing at the oak chopping block when Miss Josephine, Master's ten year old daughter entered into the kitchen for some sugarcane candy. She rushed to Missy's side when she saw the bundle on her breast.

"Oh Missy!" She is as light as me! Oh, look she has green eyes. I'm going to call her Jade, Jade Nicole. She'll be my very own baby doll!"

"But, Miss Josephine, she needs to be nursed and changed. Don't you think you should wait for her to get a bit bigger?"

Miss Josephine responded. "Oh yes, Missy, but I'll visit her everyday and dress her up."

Thus began, the confusing life of Jade Nicole. She was neither a privileged white child nor a totally abused slave girl. She was somewhere in between; but alway lonely, without understanding and never to be free.

Every Ending is a New Beginning.

Free Medical Clinic

Dayton, Ohio

After completing his requirements to become a full-fledge Medical Doctor; Chad chose to move to Dayton, Ohio where the city was in dire need of doctors of all kinds. He travelled to Dayton to meet with the mayor and city counsel. Chad advised them that his goal was to open a medical clinic

After his appointment with city dignitaries, he visited Mother Superior of the Sister's of Charity. He asked her the same question he asked the mayor. "In what area would you recommend for me to open my clinic?" She looked him straight in the eye and asked, "Dr. Somerset, are you here to serve or to make more money?" Surprised by her direct question; he immediately responded with a smile and an assuring touch.

"Mother, I am a privileged young man, reared to serve and care for those less fortunate. I want to build a medical clinic to serve all types of people. I intend to have a "free clinic" once a week, to hold free classes on cleanliness, nutrition, growing and preparing food, budgeting and child bearing and rearing.". He was still talking when Mother Superior grabbed his hand and shouted enthusiastically! "Let's go. I know of a house for sale in the perfect neighborhood."

She could have been a real estate salesman, spouting off all the possibilities she saw in the run down neighborhood of poor immigrants, mixed races, and unemployed lost souls. He starred sympathetically, as he watched filthy children playing in dirty water, some naked, others playing a stick and stone game. Several pregnant women were hanging clothing on rope lines, while chickens and pigs ran after children. It was then, something inside of him shifted, as he saw the sign. FOR SALE *take any offer.*

He asked Mother Superior to excuse him for a few minutes. He knocked at the door. An old man with a cane came to the door. Chad asked, "Is this house for sale?" "Yep." "Could I look around?" "Yep." Chad stepped inside.. Immediately he could see that in the past, this was an elegant and well built home. "Are you the owner?" "Yep" "How much do you want for it?" "What do you have to give?" "I need to take Mother Superior back to the convent, then I'll come and get you. We can do our business at the bank. I'll be back in about an hour. Is that alright with you?" Reaching out his hand, "My name is Dr. Chad Somerset, what's yours?" "Frank Mitchell, are you serious?" "Yes, I am. See you in an hour. Have your deed ready," as he went out the door.

About an hour later, Frank opened the door before Chad could knock. "Doctor, if you're for real, why in God's green earth do you want this place?" "Did you find your deed?" "Doctor, I'm sorry, but the banks got a lien on it." "Don't worry about it, I think we can work something out."

Chad escorted Frank to his rented buggy. They headed to Dayton National Savings and Loan Bank. They were greeted by the president, Mr. Luther Columbus. He was surprised to find Frank with Dr.Somerset, a wealthy doctor from Philadelphia. To the stares of staff and customers, he escorted them to his office, closed the door, then offered both a glass of water. "Well, how can I be of service to you?"

Dr. Somerset responded. "Frank tells me you have a lien on his home. I'd like to buy it. My intention is to open a Medical Clinic. I've been told there is a need in this city."

"Dr. Somerset, I can show you many more properties that are certainly more conducive to your liking and in a far better neighborhood." "No thank you, I find Frank's home and neighborhood perfect for my clinic."

Now how much do you need to clear this lien. I'm eager and I believe Frank can use the money."

After the bank president excused himself to find a teller to handle the transaction, Chad told Frank that he wanted him to open a bank account at the bank. He also stated he would like to hire him. The teller returned with the paperwork for both to sign. Chad advised the teller he would like to open a bank account and that Frank would as well. Chad signed the papers, gave the teller a check and Frank handed him $50.00 to be deposited in his new bank account. Gazing with disgust, the teller does as asked.

Walking to their buggy, Frank posed a statement to Dr. Chad. "Sir, I could certainly use that money!" "I know Frank, but I'm going to hire you and you'll be earning money weekly."

"Doin' what?" "What kind of work can you do?" "I used to lay bricks, but can't do that anymore. Mostly I work in construction building houses, sheds, privies, barns, that sort of thing. But my leg is pretty bummed up " "Perfect! When we get to your house, I'm going to examine that leg to see if there is anything I can do to fix it. Is there anyone else living with you?" "My grandson. He's fifteen and gets into lots of trouble. I can't take the strap to him, he's a lot bigger than me." "Where's his ma and pa?" "Don't know, he said they told him to go live with me, and then took off."

They pulled up in front of the house, Chad took down the sign, and walked up on the porch that had seen better days. Inside they smelled something burning. Frank called out, "Junior, you're burning down the house. Get your lazy ass out of bed before your supper burns up." Barefoot and running like a scared rabbit, Junior removed the skillet from the wood stove. Seeing Chad, he stopped dead, skillet in one hand and a rag in the other. "Whose he?" As he laid the skillet on a large stone near the stove.

"My name is Dr. Chad Somerset, the new owner of this house." "Does that mean we're out?" "No, that means you are about to be employed or you'll be out."

"Doing what and for what?" "That depends. First job is to go to the market and pick up a dozen boiled eggs, a loaf of bread, a quarter pound of tea, a watermelon, six potatoes, some fresh greens, and if they have a fresh pie or cake get that too."

"What with?" Reaching in his pocket of his vest, he pulled out some coins, "With these." "Mister, if I go in there with those, the constable will get me for stealing." "Oh, you do have a point. Let me write a note to the grocer and the constable. What are their names?" He began to write.

Dear Mr. Green and Constable Smith,

I have just purchased Frank's home in which I intend to open a medical clinic as soon as we can get it good as new. I asked Junior to purchase us some food for supper as I intend to meet with both he and Frank about employment.

If you have difficulty in believing this, please send a runner to talk with Mother Superior at the convent for verification as to my intentions here in Dayton.

Most humbly and sincerely,

Dr. Chad Somerset.

Handing the letter to Junior, he paused to say, "Junior, I'm putting my faith in you to do this errand. I believe you don't want to disappoint me, Do you hear me young man? because, I'm mighty hungry?" "Yes Doctor, I'm on my way."

"Frank, let's look at that leg. Pull your trousers down." Seeing an open wound by his left knee cap, seeping pus and partly scabbing he asked,

"How did you hurt your leg." "At the mill, I got a day job unloading grain. A draft horse with blinders knocked me over into a pile of trash. Cut it on a broke bottle."

"When was that?" "About a month ago, I keep putting vinegar on it, but it ain't healed yet. Keeps me up most of the night." "Well, we are gonna fix that."

Dr Chad left to go to the buggy to find his doctor's kit. Just as he was walking back in, Junior came back grinning all over himself. "I got all you ordered. At first they were rude but after reading your letter and Mother Superior's visit, they treated me like a gentleman. Store keeper actually gave me free, two loaves of day old bread. What do you think of that?." Dr. Chad responded, "Day old is better for you anyway."

"What are we going to fix up for him Grandpa?" Dr. Somerset answered, "First things first. Help me by boiling some hot water. Be sure you clean the pot real well. I will wash the wound, cauterize the infected skin, and bandage it with some salve. You'll be good as new in no time. Then we'll fix our supper, I'm starved!"

During supper, Dr. Somerset advised that he must return to Philadelphia in a couple of days. He shared that Mother Superior would be put in charge of the project. He asked Frank if he thought he could oversee the workers and report their progress and order supplies needed to complete the remodel by May. He informed them that when he returned, he would be living in the building until his wedding which was scheduled to take place in Spring. Frank and grandson smiled and nodded. "Dr. Somerset, asked Frank," why do you believe we can do the job? And why do you trust us to do the job?" Smiling from hear to hear, Dr Somerset replied, "Because Frank, I'm an excellent judge of character." Pausing he continued, "The mill will deliver materials as needed, and you are welcome to live here until I return from Philadelphia in about a month. Mother Superior is no dummy to building convents, so always feel free to ask her anything you're not sure of. Nuns are capable of doing the work most men and boys do."

He walked them through the house explaining why the lab was to be located in the kitchen, the importance of cleaning out the well of any debris and the need for two outhouses, one for females and another for males. He emphasized to Frank, after the remodel was complete, he'd like to employ him as his full time handyman for the clinic. Frank still in shock, nodded affirmatively, unable to speak up. Then he excitedly slapped his hand on the table exclaiming, "Might be, Doc by saving my wages, that I can buy me a home in the neighborhood." Doc replied, "I don't see why not!" Junior excitedly shared that after the clinic was completed, he'd like to go north to become a seaman on the Great Lakes. Maybe see the world, nothing is impossible, right?"

Two months later, Dr. Somerset arrived at the door of his new medical clinic. Frank was delighted to see him, as he proudly showed off all the craftsmen's handiwork. The well was totally re-dug by Junior, a roof put over it to keep out animals, rain and snow. A free flowing spring was discovered at the far end of the property. Frank used his cement finishing skills to build a pond with gold fish and frogs. Dr. Somerset was thrilled beyond measure! Everything was falling into place. His imagination pictured he and Mary Maud seated by the pond after a day in the clinic. It was at this point, GrannyRose interrupted her story to say:

"My father returned to Philadelphia in June to marry my mother. Excited about his up and coming marriage, their five day honeymoon in New York, and finally to bring his lovely bride to Dayton, Ohio."

GrannyRose took a long deep breath, laid the leather bound journal on the table next to her chair, then announced. "I think we all need a little break. The tea pot is cold and mother nature is calling. I also could use some exercise, these old legs are feeling kind of stiff." "GrannyRose, allow me to take the pot to the kitchen to refill while you and Jody take a little walk. Don't forget your cane. Jody, please help GrannyRose with her jacket and be back here in twenty minutes. If you go to the stables, be sure to turn on lights before entry, GrannyRose's eyes are weak." Lily Kai motioned for Ardon to come into the kitchen."Ardon, she's a lot weaker than the last time we were here. We need to check the house to make sure everything is in working order. I'm glad we chose to stay a couple of days, she's so independent, and won't ask for help."

"I can see she has already fixed dinner and is in the oven. I want us to honor her need to tell her story, but we also don't want to tire her out. Joey can help me feed the animals and muck out the stalls. Her handyman is very useful, but he could probably use a day off." He opened the refrigerator to find petite egg salad sandwiches already made for lunch, and sliced cucumbers, onions, and tomatoes with sliced cheeses arranged on a salad plate. "Lily Kai, the lady is amazing. She thought of everything! She even has a big bag of potato chips and more homemade cookies."

Just then GrannyRose and Jody came in. They were giggling like teenagers. Following behind was Joey caring a baby bunny. "Look Dad, they are new born, probably yesterday. Aren't they cute? I wanted to show you and Mum before I return it to its mother." Everyone oooooed and ahhhhed, then shooed him out the door as it was time to clean up for lunch.

The Somerset-Joseph family enjoyed the wonderful lunch prepared by their grandmother. Ardon put another log in the fireplace by the front parlor while the children organized the massive box of family pictures. Lily Kai apologized to her grandmother for missing many opportunities to visit the only home she ever knew. They now live in the old Huffman Mercantile Building. Ardon remodeled it into a beautiful first floor classroom and Art Gallery. The second floor was their living quarters. Three bedrooms, huge kitchen, and living room. The attic was divided in half. The front half was Lily Kai's law office, conference room and legal library with a huge copy of the Declaration of Independence and U.S. Constitution hanging on the walls. The other half was Ardon's creative art space. Half of his ceiling was all glass to capture the light at various times while painting and sculpting. He had reinforced the floor with oak timbers 12 inches wide and 4 inches thick. Over these studs, he laid marble tiles in a patch work pattern of earth tones. In one corner was a kiln for firing clay with a huge 6 ft chimney to vent fumes and smoke. Everything was safety approved by the Fire Department and in pristine condition.

"Just three miles from here!" Lily Kai thought. "I just let myself and family get caught up in stuff, not realizing how much we are missing by not spending time with GrannyRose. This has got to change!"

After all their chores were done, they once again, gathered into the front parlor to be an attentive audience for GrannyRose's Story Time. She sat serene and beautiful as she continued with her story:

"I have only fond memories of living in Harmony Village, helping Bess and Father in the Free Medical Clinic and taking music lessons. I loved playing my great-grandmother Somerset's baby grand piano that traveled from London to Philadelphia, then from Philadelphia to Dayton, and is now in the music room of this old home. It is truly a miracle that it holds it tune and has all the ivory's intact." Just then Joey raised his hand to ask a question. "GrannyRose, if the clinic was free, how did great-granddad afford to buy medicine, bandages, and medical equipment?"

"Joey, that is a very excellent and intelligent question. First of all, Father allowed for all of his patients to pay in the best manner they could. Some days we got eggs, a live chicken, some coupon's for any work we needed, and I remember one farmer brought us a live piglet. Father knew, most people felt it was shameful to take charity. The Somerset's have made a lot of money. My great grandfather was a lawyer for royalty in London, England. My grandfather was a Judge, who inherited his father's wealth, but always shared his wealth with less fortunate. Father followed the same principle his grandfather and father taught," "Make good and unselfish investments, always share where you are inspired, and support the poor, abused, and less fortunate souls by showing them respect and dignity." "Joey and Jody, I too, have inherited great wealth from both my father's family and the Huffman's. I have most of my money in a trust. I share my wealth in many ways. I learned at a very young age, that money doesn't bring happiness. Loving service has always brought me happiness. Some day you will have great wealth. I pray you will have learned the joy in being of service. Your father is a great example of giving service by sharing his God given talent as an artist and your mother serves on many charitable boards and gives of her time and legal services to those unable to pay."

Both grandchildren were excited to share their goals and ambitions to help people. Jody began, "I love horses, they are very smart and sensitive. I want to become a psychologist so that I can help children with emotional disability problems to trust horses to help them with their fears. What do you think of this, GrannyRose?"

"I think that's wonderful! Your passion for animals, especially for horses was exactly what your grand mother, MaryTherese dreamed of doing. She was killed in an airplane crash when your mother was only a tiny baby. Tomorrow I'll share with you some pictures of her. She looked exactly like her Grandmother Huffman, jet black hair, big round green eyes, and a tiny little feminine body."

"Joey, what is it you want to share about your goals and aspirations?" "GrannyRose, I love plants, rocks, and minerals which means I love biology and chemistry. I want to go to Stanford University in California to become a medical researcher to find a cure for diseases like polio. I just love researching in laboratories. I believe that this is a career that serves and helps people, don't you?"

"Absolutely! My father would be very proud to know that his great, great, grandson found a cure for leukemia, the disease that killed my mother." Silence, total silence, as her family pondered what to say or not say. Wiping her eyes, Granny Rose continued:

"When the James Black family moved into our village, they brought laughter, joy, and new possibilities. James Black, an importer of expensive French wines, made many trips to Cincinnati to pick up his shipment. Most of the time, he hired a transport to deliver the valuable cargo. It was on one of those trips that he witnessed a family of three, a mom, dad, and baby, riding a bicycle built-for-two. On his return, he stopped at the Wright Brother's Bicycle shop to order one. When it arrived, our village was so delighted to be treated with delight to watch he and Annette riding with daughter, BethAnne in her basket. The last time I saw BethAnne was when they all joined Father to attend my Christmas Musical Concert. They moved to Columbus the following year. I lost track of BethAnne when she was a graduate student at Ohio State in Science. James became a self-taught chef and manager for one of the finest restaurants in Ohio." After a long pause, GrannyRose continued, "We best get on with the story, there's a lot to be told."

A man must elevate himself by his own mind,
not degrade himself.
The mind is the friend, the conditioned soul,
and the enemy as well.
-Bhagavad Gita-

When life gives you lemons,
Make Lemonade.
It's just that simple!
-Lillian Rose Somerset-

Home of Judge Chadwick Nicholas Somerset II.
Eve of Dr. Chad's Wedding

Philadelphia, Pennsylvania

Chadwick awaken with jar! Lying on his stomach, his face buried in the feather pillow, he raised his head, arched his back and yelled out loud, "What the hell?"

Male voices were laughing downstairs; dogs were whimpering and yapping outside his window, when suddenly Chad remembered, "Oh, bloody hell! Hunting! Damn! I'll never live this down!"

He reached at the foot of the bed to gather his robe and house slippers to head down the back stairs to the outhouse before making an appearance to his cousin, Calvin and best friend, Herb. They both were dressed for the hunt, planned months ago, as their last bachelor day with Chad. Herbert Longfellow, a fraternity brother at Harvard was in town from Maine to serve as Chad's best man. Not being a Catholic, they had to get special permission from the Bishop. It was granted since Calvin, a Catholic would be standing at the altar as well.

Returning to his room, he was met by Oliver, a man servant employed by his family since his birth. Oliver and his wife Mable are devoted to Chadwick II, especially since the death of his wife, Mary Margaret. Together, they work diligently to make sure everything runs smoothly on the large estate. Mable keeps the calendar for both his office and the estate. Since becoming Judge of Philadelphia, he is called to travel some distance to hold fair and just trials. Oliver is often needed to drive the buggy so that he can relax and prepare himself for jury selection and overseeing the conduct of both attorneys. Judge Somerset believes the 'letter of the law applies to everyone.

Appearing at Chad's bedroom door, Oliver approached saying, "My Mable sent up some hot tea and one of her pecan buns. I'm sorry Sir, but you do not have time enough for a full breakfast. May I help you get ready? The young men are rather rambunctious; and certainly don't appear to enjoy waiting." "Yes, Oliver, I don't believe patience is one of their virtues. If you could locate my guns and equipment, I'd surely appreciate it. I'll head down the stairs and make my apologies,"

At the foot of the landing stood Calvin and Herb looking like two pigs at the feed trough ready to bounce on anything that just might get in their way of the feed schedule. Calvin teased, "Chad, Old Boy, are you being deprived of your precious shut-eye on the eve of the big event?" Herb chimed in, "Or maybe he's too weak to walk in the wood looking for wild turkey?"

Just at that moment, Judge Somerset pointed to the kitchen door, re-minding the hunters they needed to bring home at least two turkey's and at least a couple of rabbits, as requested by the parent's of the bride hosting the meal after the wedding. The Murphy's announced that their kitchen must have the game by two p.m. in order to properly prepare for the wedding feast. "Now get going, and for God's sake, be careful!"

As the young men gathered their equipment and headed towards the wood, Judge Somerset wiped a tear from his eye, remembering how much his Maggie would love to be here for their son's wedding. They would cry together, His sensitivity was her attribute she most chrished about her husband. "Oh, how I miss her!" Memories flooded his mind, as he opened the door to his study.

Maggie never regained consciousness from the sudden stroke that took her life three years ago. It happened just two weeks after Chad moved to Dayton, Ohio to open his medical clinic. His graduation from Harvard Law School and finishing his internship at Pennsylvania Hospital which was founded by Benjamin Franklin, thrilled both of them. It was her greatest joy to know that he followed his heart, instead of tradition to become a lawyer. From the time he was a little boy, he tried to heal every bird, butterfly, and puppy he found sick or hurt. He'd go around addressing himself as "Dr. Somerset."

Maggie was crushed when he announced he was moving to Ohio to set up his practice. She shed a few tears, then bravely hugged him with encouragement to remember that The Somerset's are dedicated to serving those less fortunate. "I know Mother, you and Father taught me well. I'll always hold true to your faith in my honor and ability to serve others with kindness and compassion,"

Then quietly, hugging his mother and shaking his father's hand, he made his exit through the big double doors, on to his new adventure. After his buggy pulled away, Maggie ran into Jugan's arms. Both parents weeping quietly, as Jugan wrapped his arms around her.and whispered in her ear. "We spent his youth teaching him to believe in his dreams, but today, as he leaves to achieve them, letting go is so damn hard."

After she caught her breath, she exclaimed sadly, "Jugan, your father never met our beautiful son!" "So sad. but how proud he would be to see that his grandson is carrying forth principles he admired about his friend, Benjamin Franklin. Do you recall the three of us at home in London, reading together "Poor Richard's Almanac? Father believed in the American Dream so much, he encouraged us to emigrate to Philadelphia, The City of Brotherly Love. Any regrets my love?"

"Oh no Jugan! I love our home, family, our loyal servants, and God for making this life possible." Jugan swept her up into his arms, hardly believing they had shared twenty plus years of wedded bliss. They met when he was a student at Oxford and she an Irish maid working in the home of the Chancellor. They both were warned of the danger courting a commoner below his social status. Jugan spoke to his father about the situation. He advised the couple to take a month off from courting each other. If after the separation, they both felt the same way, he would give his blessing. After a month separation, they were to join together at Jugan's home to discuss their future after Maggie had her meeting with the Chancellor.

As Jugan became concerned as he waitedMaggie to arrive. Then the front door chime rang. The butler opened the door to Mary Margaret's presence. Carrying a satchel, wiping her eyes, she asked politely to see Master Chadwick II. Hearing the sound of her voice, Jugan hurried to the foyer. Pulling her into his arms, softly whispering in her ear, "What happened, my love? Why are you weeping so?"

"Jugan, he, he fired me! Made me leave immediately. I didn't have a place to go, so, so, Oh, Jugan I'm so ashamed."

Just then Jugan's father entered the foyer asking if he might be of some assistance?" Jugan blurted out! "The Chancellor fired her, threw her out in the street like a bundle of rubbage!"

Immediately aware of the need to intercede into the emotional outburst by the couple, Mr. Somerset guided them into the parlor by the fireplace. "Now, Miss Mary Margaret, tell me in your own words what just happened. And Jugan, please allow her to talk and you and I will listen."

Wiping her nose, placing her soiled handkerchief in her skirt pocket, she started, "It's like I said to Jugan, I politely told me employer, that Jugan and I were seeing each other and we had your blessing. He jumped up, slammed his pipe on his desk and told me I was terminated immediately, to get my stuff and go. He shouted out he was disgusted with Barrister Somerset for falling into the gutter with his son."

Jugan stood up with his fists drawn yelling that he'd call out the Chancellor for his slanderous words. His father gently urged him to be seated. Jugan sat down and gathered Mary Margaret's hand into his, then once more opened his mouth to speak, "Forgive me Father, but I can't bear that she is being treated this way. She's a good girl! Such archaic rules, treating women as though they have no intelligence, no feelings, and not trustworthy. Tomorrow I will withdraw from Oxford, I've had enough of their old foggy attitude." All at once, Mary Margret stood up, reached for her shawl and hat, and said, "I'm so sorry, it is all me fault, Jugan must finish his schooling, and I must go home to Ireland to help me family."

"Please, both of you!! Be seated, I think I can help." "Mary Margaret, if you return to your home, will that put a burden on your family living conditions?" Dropping her head, she nodded. "Do you send most of your wages to your family," Again she nodded, not once looking up, while all the time rubbing her hands together. "Me Mum has three wee ones. They need me money to help out. I'm sorry Jugan, I never told you how poor me family is."

Looking up at the clock on the mantel, Mr. Somerset announced that it was almost dinner time. Mary Margaret was to be their guest for dinner. After dinner they would discuss the solution for their predicament. He called for Millie to set another place at the table, and to take Miss Mary Margaret to the powder room to freshen up for dinner. Mary Margaret froze, not believing what she was hearing, Jugan helped her up, as Millie escorted her to the Ladies Powder room.

Relieved, Jugan went upstairs to his room to change for dinner. Mr.S omerset went into his study to write a letter. He called for his servant to deliver the post right away. He then went to the dining room. As Jugan came bouncing down the stairs to join his father in the dining room.

Anxious, Jugan waited at the foot of the stairs for Maggie. Millie escorted Mary Margaret into the dining room for dinner. She looked relaxed, as Chad and his father showed her to her seat. Her only concern was table manners. She was taught to be a personal maid, but never had the opportunity to dine formally. She also realized how through all of her emotional outbursts, she had reverted back to her Irish slang. She was horrified that she embarrassed both herself and Jugan. She thought, "Oh Mary, Mother of God, please help me."

All seated at the dining table, Mr. Somerset offered a blessing. He then started the conversation by sharing the joy of rearing his son. As a toddler, together, they flew kites, paddled the Thames, and studied Mother Nature. He said that Chad was such an eager student, that he couldn't wait for his father to catch up. They all laughed. He then directed a personal question to Mary Margaret. "My dear, what do you dream of doing or becoming?" So relaxed, she found herself opening up her heart to share, "Sir, I dream of playing piano." Her cheeks glowed pink while her feet shook under the table.

"Mary Margaret, that is a very beautiful dream. Jugan plays the violin, I believe a duet is manifesting between the two of you. My dear, never be embarrassed to dream. All worthwhile accomplishments began with a dream. So nourish all your dreams with love."

Just then the chauffeur returned. Mr. Somerset excused himself. Jugan reached across the table to touch her hand. She never moved, nor looked up. Mr. Somerset returned to the table. Unfolding his napkin in preparation for dessert, he address the couple,

"Well, just as I believed, we have a solution to Mary Margaret dilemma. Mother Superior of St. Mary's orphanage has a need for a girl with your experience. She requires someone who is good with children under age five. The older children are educated at the parish; but the little ones need some sort of structure to both entertain and educate. She can offer a private room, three meals a day, and a monthly stipend. She is anxious and hopes you will accept her offer. I personally know she has a piano that she'd love for you to play. Is this the type of work you would enjoy? Mother Superior is anxiously waiting for a response this evening." "Oh yes! I'm good with children! I love telling stories and especially Bible stories about Jesus and his mother, Mary. Do you think she will like me?"

"I'm sure she will! I'll send a response back to her this evening. But for now, let's have dessert. Millie prepared a beautiful strawberry torte. We have a lot to accomplish tomorrow."

"Miss Mary Margaret, for the night, you are our guest. Everything is being readied for your comfort. We will need to leave by nine in the morning as Mother Superior is anxiously awaiting your arrival. Millie will show you to your room and where to prepare for your bath. Goodnight my dear." "Good night Sir, and goodnight, Jugan."

"Son, may I have a quick word with you? I would like to speak with you in my study." They adjourn to Mr. Somerset's study.

Once inside, Jugan took a seat. His father began by asking, "Son, please let go of your anger about the Chancellor's prejudice and ignorance. You have earned your education. Don't throw it away because you feel put-on by a system that is very old and will take generations to change, if it ever does. I will speak to the Chancellor. We've had words in the past, but I have faith in a higher power and feel all will end well. Monday morning attend your classes as if nothing has transpired. Make no mention of Mary Margaret to your chums, unless they ask. Many are guilty of the same actions, only they are not serious about the young women and are just using them. I'm proud of you, my son. Your mother is looking down smiling her approval. God Bless you, and get some sleep. Tomorrow is another day.

Mary Margaret and Chadwick II, were married the week after Chadwick's graduation from Oxford University. They emigrated to Philadelphia, Pennsylvania the following year. With his excellent credentials, he had no problem finding a firm eager to hire him. He was employed by the largest legal firm in Philadelphia as a junior partner. After two years, he would be accepted as a full partner with a caseload addressing the courts. He loved being a defense attorney because of his love to serve those less fortunate. He had proven his ability to make the firm money while he gave his services to the poor.

Once the couple was firmly established in their new home and Jugan had a fair size case load he could comfortably manage, he felt it was time to write his father of their good fortune. Seated at his desk, with quill and ink, he gathered together his thoughts.

From the desk of:

Master Chadwick Nicholas Somerset, II, Attorney at Law

Dear Father,

Maggie and I were so pleased to receive your Christmas letter and beautiful silver tea set. What a lavish gift! However, we realize your generosity as coming from your heart to your only son and beautiful daughter-in-law. We are grateful. We use it almost every day. However, finding good tea in the colonies is quite a challenge these days

Maggie's creativity in embroidering the quote of Benjamin Franklin was a labor of love. She loves quoting Old Ben and knew you'd like to have a sampler to hang on the wall in your study.

As you can see by my stationery, our latest news is that I've passed all that is required by Pennsylvania to be an attorney and am penning this letter from my desk on the second floor of a rather new commercial building in downtown Philadelphia.

Father, I know how much you admire American's; however, I must inform you, the chaps here could take some pointers from you and old Oxford. My opinion is they're lacking in knowledge and skill in presenting their cases before the courts. I do believe in time, they will come up to par. Harvard College is making great strides in both law and medicine.

What are you up to these days? Please don't tax Millie's patience with your tales about Scotland Yard. She's too valuable of an asset to be sacrificed for a good laugh. Seriously, Father, please take care of yourself. We are hoping, one day soon, you will choose to come and visit the country you so admire.

We hope to be able to start a family very soon. Maggie dreams of a flock of children to care for along with her beautiful rose garden. I'm such a lucky man. Your love and devotion for Mother rubbed off on me. You are the greatest father anyone could ever have. I appreciate everything about you.

I(we) love you,

Jugan and Maggie

Judge Somerset gathered his pipe and tobacco pouch as he entered into his study. Still thinking about Maggie, he sat down in the old leather chair behind his father's old oak desk. After his father passed, he inherited several items that were familiar furnishings growing up in the Somerset Home in London. Opening the middle drawer, he found the last letter his father wrote before his passing. "I must gather all these items for Chad to read about his grandfather. I regret he never met his wise and talented grandfather. He was so admired for his character and wise counsel."

Carefully opening the letter that was over twenty-five years old, he settled in to read the letter written beautifully in old English script, penned on Somerset stationery with the ancient Somerset Crest. His father was very proud to be of the lineage of Anglo-Saxon tribes that ban together to defend their lands from French invaders in late 500 year B.C.

The letter was dated March 20th, just one month after Jugan had penned his New Year's letter to his father. Amidst the sweet and comforting aroma of Virginia tobacco and Indian ink, familiar in the old library, Judge Chadwick Nicholas Somerset II could almost hear his father calling him by his pet name. "Jugan, Jugan come out from behind those draperies. It is time to study Greek. Do you recall the last myth we were reading?" The sound of his father's soothing voice from long ago penetrated Jugan's heart and consciousness. No one called him Jugan anymore. Maggie began calling him Jugan after learning what it meant. Now that Maggie was gone, the pet name disappeared into the lonely chambers of his heart and soul. Mission in hand, he carefully opened the letter and began to read the message from the only parent he ever knew, as tears flowed down his face.

Dear Chadwick and Mary Margaret,

I was delighted to read of your passing the bar. I know this is the success you both desired. I too, am pleased. Mary Margaret, I am so appreciative to receive the Benjamin Franklin Sampler. It is beautiful and hangs right above my desk. Mr. Franklin became a dear and devoted friend. He was such a kind and intelligent gentleman, of which we both learned from each other. I confided my detest for English caste system. He agreed as he shared his solutions to the matter. He said that unfortunately, it would probably be another century before there would be any agreement in changing the system. He was a very independent, out spoken and a wise gentleman. I admired him greatly. Thank you Maggie, if I might pen your affectionate nick-name.

My news on this side of the Atlantic is that my old body is beginning to show wear and tear. My physician has advised me that my lungs are damaged by London fog and lack of sunshine. He prescribes retiring to the countryside. You know that will never do. I like living in our home, being fussed over by

Millie and Ned. How I love those two devoted souls! They make me laugh with their antics. *Wouldn't trade them for a castle full of gold. Besides, I like my daily routine. Even with their constant nagging to drop my smoking jacket into the laundry bin. I do confess how difficult it is to part with that old tattered garment, if only for an hour, I'm hopeless, I know.*

I still enjoy now and then, meeting with some Oxford chaps; bright, idealist, and eager to make a go of it in the Crown's legal system. They remind me of myself, and of course, you, my son.

My fondest memories were listening to you mediate with Nellie your bedtime schedule. I knew then, Jugan, an Old English term for judge, was the perfect nickname for you.

I am enclosing a copy of my Last Will and Testament. I'm sure I will not be around much longer. I've been away from your beautiful mother for far too long. No one could take her place. I had to make it very clear throughout English Society, that I was content with being your devoted father and teacher, while tending to my client's needs.

Since you emigrated, both Millie and Ned received an education as well. Millie has a paper stating she is a qualified Nurses Assistant and Ned is a certified carpenter. We can be proud of their accomplishments. I hung their certificates in my office besides mine and yours. They are kept clean and shining.

In the future, should you and Maggie be blessed with children, I'd be thrilled if you chose to name a boy after me to honor my lineage, and a girl, after your mother, Victoria Amelia. That would certainly please us both.

My second request is concerning Ned and Millie. I have provisions in my will for them to receive quite a large sum of money. I asked if they might want to emigrate to the American Colonies, but they choose to stay in England. They both feel they are too old to make that big of a change. Neither have any idea of the amount of money they will receive from my estate. I would like for you and Maggie to help them find a modest cottage, two horses, a buggy, furnishings, and to set up a monthly stipend for their living expenses above the norm as perceived in London's society for the working class. I would also hope that they may be able to have medical, as needed, and burial plot and grave site maintenance.

I've deeded our home to Oxford as a library and student lounge. I would like it to be dedicated in honor of your mother and called, "Victoria Amelia Campbell-Somerset Student Friendship Center." Any book, memorabilia you might like to have, please remove before the home is emptied. There are personal portraits, scrap books, your mother's piano, my violin, my gold watch, your mother's jewelry, to be handed down to Maggie and your heirs. Please take your mother's treasured family Scottish Crest and tartan and all of our certificates, the Somerset Crest, and Mr. Franklin's Sampler. The old boy would not rest in peace if it were left in England. I also gave Millie your Mother's gold crucifix and Ned a silver watch of mine.

Jugan, my son, soon you will be very wealthy. Much more than you ever believed possible. I've invested wisely, lived frugal, but not stingy. You will learn that some of my investments are in Philadelphia, and that in the future will benefit your city and country. I know you and Maggie will be generous to those less fortunate, teaching basic life principles, "What you give will always come back increased tenfold." We, who have much, have a responsibility to model life's many life principles by showing kindness and compassion. My heart overflows with joy and humility knowing you are giving legal services to help those in need and cannot afford good legal counsel.

In closing, please understand, I have no regrets, just gratitude. Your mother and I had just a few short years together, of which, we lived joyfully, enjoying our servants as our family and friends. You brought such happiness to me; as a baby, an adolescent, and a young man. I've been blessed. Your mother was a saint sent from Heaven. She was a beautiful courageous, and caring soul. Blessings to you my son and Maggie, my beautiful daughter-in-law. I've been truly honored and blessed to be your father.

As for my funeral, make it simple. My close friends have mostly departed. Millie will know those who are left. Father Jeffer-Smith will guide you with the formality of the event. I choose to be laid at rest next to your mother. The gravestone will need engraving and the plot tended.

By the time you receive this, I will be gone, I feel it in my bones. If you look up into the night sky, and see a star's light grow brighter, then you'll know once again, Victoria and I are together.

Always and forever,

Your Father,

Chadwick Nicholas Somerset I

Jugan placed the letter back into the drawer. He heard the young hunters in the kitchen laughing and reliving their hunt. Chad called out for his father, "Father, we have two turkey and two rabbit. You can rest in peace, we've done our job." Chad and his father met face to face in the hallway. His father slapped him on his back with a big smile on his face then asked? "Did the Chaps leave? Chad nodded. "Good job," said his father, I had faith in your hunting ability."

"Yes, they needed to prepare for the evening dinner and Calvin said he'd drop the game off at the Murphy's on his way home. He's concerned that Herb's attraction to Maud's younger sister, Peggy could be a problem. She's a very attractive young girl, I think Calvin's a little jealous." His father paused for a moment then said, "Chad, could we share a pot of tea before going upstairs to prepare for this evening's dinner?"

Thinking his father seemed a little nervous, he calmly asked,"Is there something bothering you, Father? You seem to be a little on edge." "No, just wanting some alone time with you, my son."

Chad was rather surprised at his father's soft tone and he actually appeared shy. This was quite unnatural as his father was a highly respected attorney and never at a loss for words. His father rang the tiny bell on the table by the divan. Right away Mae appeared. He told her they'd be having tea in the parlor.

His father started their conversation with an inquiry into how Chad's new medical clinic was doing? Chad was thrilled to share he was open six days a week, with a free clinic for the poor on Saturday. He shared that sometimes he received a basket of eggs, a lot of fresh produce, and once-in-awhile, a few coins. His patients had the regular complaints; pleurisy, gout, rheumatism, hay fever, cuts and bruises, as well as many simple farm accidents to repair. Delivering babies is still a novelty for a male doctor; as most still think it is a woman's job; a midwife, to deliver babies. As he portrayed his vocation as the greatest, he looked at his father, and asked? "So what is it you wanted to talk to me about?"

His father cleared his throat and said, "Son, I know you are an excellent physician, well educated in your profession, but,.do you feel confident in knowing what women want?" "In what area do you mean? Women love beautiful things, wonderful music, and being admired. Is this what you are referring to?"

"Yes and no," he replied, "You see Chad, before I married your mother, my father had a man to man bit of advise for me that I've been eternally grateful to have been given. He told me that a real woman, and he emphasized "real', desires to be loved, honored, and respected above all the jewels, latest fashions, and place in society. They are often seen as naive and ignorant children and property that is owned!".

"My father told me that my mother refused to marry him unless she was treated as a full partner in their marriage. That meant open communications about where they lived, how money was spent and the rearing of children must be a shared responsibility. She also insisted their bedroom be a sanctuary for sharing love's greatest intimacies. She also,confessed that she and most women know very little about their own body, and nothing about a man's."

"So you see, my son, you've got a big job ahead of you. Your sweet Irish lass is innocent about everything involved in being a woman or being in a loving marriage. Be patient with her, as you allow her to get to know you, your body as she becomes familiar with her own body with its many different feelings She will learn the art of sensuality; in doing so, a reciprocal response will heighten your marriage bed with joy and sur-render. Most marriages, unfortunately, take years to heal the honeymoon nightmare of the groom behaving like a bull in a china store; ramming and forcing themselves into their loved one. A good motto to remember: Most everything about a woman is on the inside, everything about a man is on the outside. Patience my son is the best attribute to develop a loving and life long relationship."

Judge Somerset, wiped the tears from his eyes; emotionally drained, he finished.. "Son, I'm not embarrassed to say I love you with all my heart. I wish your mother could be here to see our son be joined in happy matrimony."

Embracing his son, wiping his nose, heaving a deep sigh, he released Chad as he started up the long stairs to prepare for the evening's festivities.

Chad still recouping from his father's open heart and wise advice, was also equally surprised to hear his father remind him from the top of the stairs, "We must prepare for dinner We're the hosts and cannot be late. I asked Oliver to check with the Union League to be sure they are prepared for a wedding party of about forty, which includes at least ten children." "Okay Father, I'll be ready and Father, I love you too, and I truly appreciate all of your wise and loving counsel."

While engaged in his toilet, Chad thought of his father's marital advice. He reflected on how his mother was always involved with the management of the home, promoted him to attend public school, and often times their dinner conversations were around Father's legal defense strategy with Mother freely giving great advice. Now, as he thought about it, his mother was always independently involved in projects that did not involve his father. Wasn't that true in other homes? No, he could remember staying at Herb's home in Northern Maine during Spring break. While at dinner in Herb's home, his father totally controlled the conversation. His mother said nothing unless his father directed a personal question to her. Certainly a double standard. Hmmmm, he thought, "I certainly want a partner, not an object that must be managed."

Just then Oliver arrived to assist with his formal attire. Chad still felt uneasy accepting help in getting dressed; but Oliver would feel he neglected his duty if he didn't assist Master Chad in his formal attire. The Union was the oldest establishments in Philadelphia, still demanded a high standard for dining in the evening. He hoped by holding the function at such a high end establishment, it did not put the Murphy's in an embarrassing situation. Oliver handed him his gloves and cane, Chad thanked him sincerely for helping find all of the necessary studs, spats, and crisp starched handkerchief needed to complete his evening attire. He knew Oliver and Mae were paid very very well, but it still unnerved him to be waited on. He was happy Maud did not expect to have this luxury in Dayton. In fact, she excitedly stated that she was eager to help in the medical clinic. He thought joyfully, "Yes, I'm ready to be a married man and all that goes with it!"

Descending the stairs, he met father and Oliver at the door. As he and father were getting seated in the buggy, he felt sadness because Oliver and Mae turned down their invitation to this evening's event. Both felt it was a family affair, unable to embody, "That they were family!" They said they would attend the wedding and the festivities that followed. Chad thought, "A cast system. Prejudice, the basic cause, of which I detest in any form!"

Both men sat silently as the horse shoes beat a cadence on the cobble stone street that had been paved when Philadelphia was the Nation's first capitol.

The elder Somerset's thoughts were on Maggie and her love of being a wonderful hostess. Her specialty in creating a feeling of congeniality and joyful conversation would put the Murphy's at ease. Oh, how he missed her!

Oliver pulled the carriage up to front of the Union League ancient establishment. Oliver stepped down to open the carriage door for Judge Somerset, "Watch your step, Sir." Taking the Judge's arm.

Chad, needing no assistance, stepped down just as the Murphy carriage arrived. He strolled over to assist the Murphy's. Maud looked absolutely beautiful in a purple velvet cape and matching satin gown. Her radiant auburn red hair and sparkling green eyes always caused him to feel a bit shy and speechless. She held out her gloved hand. "Good evening, Chad. I was concerned we might be late."

"No, no, you're right on time." His face aglow, feeling embarrassed as a young school chap with his hand caught in the cookie jar.

Judge Somerset led the family into the establishment's foyer. Arriving a little bit later was Chad's mother's brother and his family. Their son Calvin and friend, Herb were demonstrating their best behavior. No Harvard antics tonight.

After all guests were gathered in the dining room entry way, Judge Somerset introduced the Union League's Manager and staff. Chad blushed when his father introduced him as "Dr. Somerset." The title still felt a little foreign to him.

Judge Somerset and Mr. Murphy were seated at each end of the long table. The Somerset Family on one side and the Murphy's on the other. Judge Somerset stood to welcome everyone.

"Tonight, we are gathered together as two families united together to bless the marriage of my son, Dr. Chadwick Somerset III to your beautiful daughter, Mary Maud Murphy. Mr. Murphy, If you please, would you offer grace before we partake of our meal?"

Mr. Sean Murphy stood up, his face shining red. A shipbuilder and prominent citizen in both the Irish community, as well as the City of Philadelphia. He had worked long hours to achieve the prestige and economic status he now enjoyed. During the Revolutionary War, he provided ships and supplies to the Union Navy that was greatly needed. Mr Murphy cleared his throat, then began to speak.

"Judge Somerset, I have always respected you as a man of honor, with the courage to do the right thing. Thank you for asking me to offer the blessing tonight for Chad and Mary Maud, on the eve of their wedding." Let us pray. Blessed Mother of God, whose son, Jesus Christ, in whose name, I ask humbly for your blessing for Chad and Mary Maud's wedding Bless their future life together as husband and wife. Bless them with good health, loving children, and prosperity from this day forth. Thank you for this family gathering and the wonderful food we are about to eat, In the name of the Father, Son, and Holy Ghost, Amen."

As he sat down, his nervousness left and his joyful personality came forth. Judge Somerset rose with a wine glass in hand to offer a toast: "May God and all His Heavenly Angels, Bless us this beautiful evening with good health, loving thoughts, and safe keeping." As a seasoned attorney, Chad knew his father could deliver a long and elegant toast, but he chose to honor Sean Murphy by offering a simple and heartfelt blessing instead.

Menu chosen for the evening, was a simple, tasty and elegant meal. The long dining table had two large plates of French cheese, Italian olives, and an English sugar loaves with a French white wine. The first course was a mushroom soup with red wine and raisins. The main course, a roast pork with dried apples stuffing, surrounded by braised baby potato's, carrots, and cabbage with home made biscuits and corn muffins, red wine and Indian black tea. For dessert, the chef prepared the Union League's famous Chocolate Cherry Cream Cake with bubbling champaign for the adults.

Everyone was very pleased with the evening festivities. During the meal, a gentleman played soft classical music on his violin.

After the dessert was served and eaten, Mr. Murphy announced it was time to call for the carriages as the wedding ceremony would begin with an early Mass. He advised everyone needed to get some sleep, to be dressed and at the church by 7:30 in the morning.

With hand shakes and hugs, they all boarded their carriages and headed home. Herb shared his desire to enjoy conversing more with Margaret Ann, the Murphy's seventeen year old daughter. Slapping Chad on the back, he assured him that he would always be an honorable and perfect gentleman. He shared, "Chad I've enjoyed observing your courtship with Mary Maud. Old Boy, believe me, someday, I hope to be blessed to have the same type of loving relationship. You inspire me.

Upon arriving home, Oliver asked about the evening's menu. Judge Somerset knew Oliver felt great pride in Mae's cooking skills. Pondering what to say, and how to say it, "Oh, the pork roast was good, but nothing like Mae's. She makes the best!" He caught Oliver smiling and swelling up like a pumped up ostrich.

Both Somerset's wished Oliver a Good Evening and headed up the staircase. Chad, paused, then said to his father, "Father, thank you again for all that you have done for Mary Maud and myself. This evening was awesome. I want you to know that I am the most fortunate man in all of Philadelphia. Mostly because I had you and Mum as my parents. I pray I can be as loving a parent as you have been to me. Grandfather must have been a wonderful man to have raised a son of your calibre "I love you." Hugging his father and wiping a tear, he went to his room.

What things so ever ye desire,

when ye pray,

Believe that ye receive them,

and ye shall have them.

Mark 11:14

Magnolia Beaumont Plantation

Merci, Mississippi

Louis Phillipi Beaumont, owner of Magnolia Grove, is the largest sugar plantation in Mississippi. The plantation is over 2,000 acres. Within its perimeter is a small town called Merci, Mississippi, population 112 white folks, a sugar mill, mercantile, feed and grain store, bank, and a Catholic Church. Master Louis and his brother, Jean Michel moved to this area from New Orleans. They emigrated from France. After many travels up and down the Mississippi River, they decided on this area due to its proximity to New Orleans and north to St. Louis. Their enterprises are selling liquor, sugar cane, horses and slaves..

Jean Michel began importing and breeding the Southern France Mernes breed. Unlike most French horse breeds; they are stocky in build, can be ridden easily by women and children, excellent in pulling buggies and wagons, and dependable show horses.. Jean Michel's plantation, "High Stepper Plantation" breeds, shows, and sells this unique breed which is popular with the elite and political wealthy gentlemen. Jean Michel demands and gets top dollar in every aspect of his horse business.

Once a month, the brothers host a huge town picnic, horse show, and auction at the boat dock on the Mississippi River. Plantation owners, small farmers, and merchants congregate before sunrise on Saturday morning to look over the slaves, horses, and the many items for sale by the locals. Slaves; male, female, young and old, purchased by the Beaumont brothers in New Orleans, arrive in chains by the Bella Beaumont River Boat. They come from Cuba, Bahama, Haiti, and Puerto Rico. There are also some mixed breeds, a combination of Negro, Caucasian, East Indian, Asian, and Native American that can bring top dollar to their enterprise. Tradesmen come prepared to buy, sell, or trade animals, molasses, hard liquor, grain and building supplies. This is a time to get acquainted, swap stories, politics, and possibly get married.

The small Catholic mission church is the only parish available for plantation owners and river boat crews to attend. The nearest is about two hundred miles north at St. Louis. Since the Beaumont Brothers built the town and church on their land, they choose to ignore the Catholic priests opposition to gambling, heavy drinking and auctioning slaves on Sunday while Mass is being served. The elderly priest worries how his Bishop would handle the priest's slave woman that cleans his room, the church, does his laundry, vestments and prepares his meals? His heart is heavy knowing he has no one to hear his confession. "Forgive me Father, for I have sinned, Hail Mary Full of Grace."

Jean Michele Beaumont has two sons. Phillipi Louis named after his godfather, Louis Phillipi Beaumont and Desmond Lafayette, named after Jean Michele's French groom and General Lafayette, the famous French general much loved by American's during the Revolutionary War. His son Phillipi was born by his wife Marion, and Desmond by his house slave, Rochelle. He purchases her when she went on the auction block in New Orleans. Her beauty and defiant nature as she stood on the slave block intrigued him to pay twice as much for her than he paid for any slave

She claimed to be a descendant of an African King, fluent in Spanish and French with knowledge and use of medicinal herbs.. The boys were born two weeks apart. Marion knew of her husband's infidelity, but did not care. She gave him a son and as far as she was concerned that was her only duty as his wife. She chose to have her own suite of rooms in the mansion, and Jean Michele had his. Rochelle was invited to his suite and lived with him most of the time. He showered her with all kinds of gifts and called her his "Ebony Queen." Marion was happy being mistress of the large mansion, entertaining dignitaries, and drinking French Wine. She rarely visited the nursery where the boys were being raised. Jean Michele heard Rochelle refer to Desmond as "Jeb" short for Jebanizee, a famous African King. It made his stomach sour with fire! "Why?" he wondered, "Did it bother him so?"

Rochelle captured his heart. She was so intelligent! After he taught her to play chess, she beat him most of the time. She could speak French and Spanish fluently and was an excellent story teller. After Jean Michele built her a small cabin on the edge of the woods, the boys, Phillipi and Desmond would go there for daily story telling time about Africa, sailing the seas, and growing plants for healing.

She would ride with Jean Michel overseeing his stable of valuable horses. He taught her to ride. Often they rode together in the vast wooded areas by the river. He rode his mare Champaign and she rode an older mare, TeaCup. One moonlit night, as they lay watching the stars and listening to the crickets, he asked, "My sweet, Ebony Queen, what would you like for me to give to you as a token of my love?" as he stroked her long jet black tresses and kissed her beautiful body. With a long pregnant pause, she spoke, "Jean Michele, there is only one thing I want or will ever want, and that is my freedom. You'll never grant me that, so that's all there is to that."

He sat up, looked into her eyes, turned his head as the tears streamed down his cheeks, breathing deeply and in quiet contemplation, he put on his breeches, shirt, and riding boots. Walking towards the door of her cabin, he turned to her, "Yes, you are correct, I'm a coward, I lack the grit it takes to follow my heart, to go against society, my family and religion. Rochelle, I no longer will be a burden to you, my beautiful lover. I will no longer call you to my bed. The only freedom I can give you, is your own home, the joy for you to have visitations with our son, and to no longer be burdened by my desire for you. Please forgive me, I will always love you. Goodnight."

Rochelle lay there smelling his male scent, feeling the vacant spot where his huge muscled body had lain, and remembering how her words broke his spirit like a young colt exhausted by the rope he was tethered by, to finally drop his head in surrender. She wept the night away. The next day, her thoughts ran wild; wanting to die, then wanting to live. She even gathered the herbs to make the tea that would end it all in a few minutes. Suddenly realizing it took more courage to live knowing he was close by, then to just end it all.

"I need a purpose," she said out loud. Gathering various different types of weeds, she began to weave a tapestry that told a story of bondage and freedom. "I must be grateful, most slaves never see their children again after birthing them. Life goes on, and just maybe Jeb someday might find his way to freedom."

The boys, Phillipi and Desmond were receiving an excellent education from the professor who came weekly to teach proper English, French and Latin. Both were excellent in mathematics, and astronomy. They also took their religious lessons from the priest at the mission. Desmond love these classes, Phillipi hated them. The boys looked almost exactly like twins; but their personalities were very different. Desmond was kind and patient and loved all animals and Mother Nature. Phillipi hated to lose at chess, horse racing, or in story telling. He would embellish the truth and dare Desmond to correct his interpretation. He always reminded Desmond that he was and always will be, Phillipi's personal servant.

On their visits to Magnolia Grove Plantation, Uncle Louis' home, the boys were free to explore the Magnolia Groves, stage horse races with the town kids, and teach the kitchen and house slaves how play cards,. On the day the boys first saw Jade Nicole after becoming a young lady, they couldn't stop talking about the miracle they witnessed. Phillipi was smitten. Desmond warned him that she was the Master's child and had decreed "hands off" to all males in the community. Phillipi took this personally, and stated egotistically, "You'll see, my father will open the door for me to play around with Miss Green Eyes Jade Nichole." Galloping away, he whipped his horse mercifully. With great sadness in his heart, Desmond followed. He feared for Miss Jade, he knew Phillipi's evil conniving ways when challenged with not getting what he wanted." "A slaves life is hopeless!" He thought about the Nanny Slaves who nurse white babies and then had to let them go when they got older. Slaves like himself, who really don't know who they are, struggle to stay alive and feeling they have no real purpose. Women like his mother, who loved their Masters, but could not be free "Why?" He thought with a heart as heavy as a lead ball.

Upon Desmond's arrival home, the Master came to greet him. He asked Desmond if what Phillipi conveyed about Jade Nicole was correct? "Yes, Master, that is what I heard." "Well then, I guess I must talk to my brother." As he headed to the house.

Taking his horse to the stables, Desmond found Phillipi's stallion still needing attention, but no where could Phillipi be seen. Desmond unsaddled both horses, brushed, fed and watered them both. He prayed. "Please Father, don't let Phillipi hurt Jade. Lord, show me how I can protect her. She's innocent to the evil's he does so freely.

You may call God Love
You may call God Goodness
But the best name for God is
Compassion.
-Meister Ekhart-

CHADWICK NICHOLAS SOMERSET III AND MARY MAUD MURPHY'S WEDDING DAY

PHILADELPHIA, PENNSYLVANIA

Six-thirty the next morning, Oliver knocked at both the Judge and Chad's door. He had hot water, tubs, and hot tea for both. Judge Somerset instructed Oliver that he and Chad would take care of their own baths. He wanted to leave the house by seven fifteen in order to be there fifteen minutes early for the Wedding Mass. He reminded Oliver that they would take the carriage with the large sorrel mare.

At exactly 7:15 in the morning, Oliver announced the carriage was ready. Both the Somerset's, father and son came down the stairs in full morning formal attire. Mae and Oliver applauded and cheered. "Oh, me Lord, ye are both so handsome," Mae singing like a bluebird.

"Mae, you look beautiful in your pink hat and dress, and just look at Oliver, sporting a new suit and tie, Why, I barely recognized you, Old Boy!"

The wedding was being held at St. Phillip Neri in the Southwork area of Philadelphia. The same Irish Catholic area, according to local Protestants, that were allowing the Pope to take over America. The protest was short-lived and peace was restored.

The Somerset carriage arrived just as the big double doors were being shut. The doorman escorted Chad to the priest's office while the family took their seats in the church. Herb and Calvin were already in the priest's office. The aide to the priest instructed where each would stand, then followed the priest to their place in front of the altar. The music began as the bridal attendants walked slowly down the aisle, each smiling as marionettes; all Murphy children. Five to seventeen years of age, wearing flowing silk dresses the color of garden spring flowers; yellow, pink, green, blue, and lilac. Their wicker baskets were filled with colorful spring flowers with little loose petals to be thrown at the end of the wedding reception.

Chad's heart was pounding so loud he thought everyone could hear the extent of his nervousness and his joy. This is the day he long awaited. He met Mary Maud when she was just a child, fell in love with her when she was sixteen, and became betrothed when she was seventeen. He father approved the engagement as long as Chad understood they were not to be married until she was eighteen. While still in college, he learned she loved being out-of-doors, listening to birds sing, and growing flowers. Her special flower was a red rose. Her bouquet today was made of red roses and lily's of the valley. While in medical school, they communicated weekly by long letters. She learned he loved medicine, the opportunity to serve, and his Somerset heritage.

The string quartet orchestra started playing Bach's Ode to Joy, as Mary Maud Murphy, escorted by her father, walked slowly down the aisle. Her eyes totally focused on Chad. Watching her, his mind kept thinking of the things she shared in her letters, her love of playing the harpsichord and writing little songs for her younger siblings. Arriving at the altar, her father lifted her veil, kissed her cheek, then gave her hand to Chad. Her father stepped back to join her mother at the bride's side of the sanctuary. As both faced each other, the priest began by asking the following question of the couple, Chad's knees were shaking so hard:

Priest: Chadwick Nicolas Somerset, will thou take Mary Maud Murphy here present for thy lawful wife, according in the rite of our Holy Mother, The Church?

Chadwick: I will

Priest: Mary Maud Murphy, will thou take Chadwick Nicholas Somerset here present for they lawful husband, according in the rite of our Holy Mother, The Church?

Mary Maud: I will

Priest: Have ye not read that he who made man from the beginning made them male and female? For this cause shall a man leave his father and mother and shall cleave to his wife; therefore, and they shall be one flesh. Now they are not two, but one flesh. What God hath joined together, let no man put asunder.

"In the name of the Father, Son, and Holy Ghose, Amen"

And so concluded the marriage vows, the exchange of wedding rings, and the Holy Eucharist. In total, the marriage ceremony and mass lasted for two hours. Children began to squirm, nursing babies whimpering and howling like a den of canine pups, while adults, both men and women struggled to keep their stomachs at rest. The priest then completed the wedding ceremony with a blessin

Holding his hand over the couple, He prayed:
"May the God of Abraham, the God of Isaac, and the God of Jacob
be with you,
and may He fulfill His blessing upon you, that you may see your
children's children unto the
third and fourth generation, and thereafter may you have life
everlasting,
by the grace of our Lord Jesus Christ, who with the Father and the
Holy Ghost
lives and reins in God for ever and ever, Amen.
The organist began to play, Bach's Ode to Joy as the couple led the wedding party down the aisle to receive their guests loving blessings at the entry of the

Church's front door.. Flower petals were showered over the couple as they left the church for their wedding breakfast celebration.

The wedding breakfast was an elaborate feast filled with delicious food, joyful laughter, and Irish Songs and Jigs. The Murphy's, all singers, entertained the wedding party to seasoned Irish Folk Ballads. Tommy Murphy, the bride's sixteen year old brother with a magnificent tenor voice, serenaded the couple with Thomas Moore's classic love song, *The Last Rose of Summer.* Tommy finished his beautiful rendition with a confident and deep bow. Everyone responded with great appreciation with cheers and a standing ovation. Immediately following, a bagpiper dressed in an Irish traditional kilt began to play a jig. Mary Maud's young five year old twin sisters, Coleen and Carrie pulled up their skirts and started dancing an Irish jig while everyone enthusiastically clapped in rhythm with the music. Chad caught his father's eye, smiling. Chad felt his father missing his mother's presence. She loved family gatherings, music, story telling and having a jolly good time. With so much gratitude, he reflected, in silence, "Thank you Mother for all your blessings, for believing in me, and teaching me to follow my own heart. I've always known that medicine is my true path!"

Seeing that everyone had eaten, the orchestra leader announced that it was time for the bride and groom to have their solo dance. Chad froze. He and Mary Maud had never danced together! Mary Maud reached out her hand to Chad, and immediately he felt at ease. He took her hand, joining together in dancing a waltz. His father bowed to his new daughter-in-law, inviting her to dance. Mr Murphy followed suit by dancing with his beautiful wife, then cut in to dance with his daughter. Soon the who party joined in waltzing, then doing a fast step. The wedding celebration was a huge happy and joyful success!.

Chad and Mary Maud strolled around the ballroom greeting all their guests; thanking them for their attendance and generous gifts. It thrilled Chad that Oliver and Mae were having such a good time After giving them a hug, Chad and Mary Maud very discretely left the party by the side door for their honeymoon reservations at The Morris House on Independence Square in the heart of Philadelphia.

Chad had reserved the Wedding Suite for early dining. They were scheduled to catch the morning train for New York City. He was so excited to share The City and its modern conveniences to his new bride. For five days he would treat Maud to great dining, museums, musical and theatrical events and the latest in fashion. After their honeymoon, they would return to Philadelphia to bid their family goodbye to leave for Dayton, Ohio. In Dayton, they would begin their new adventure as husband and wife, physician and help-mate. Both eager to open the newly rebuilt medical building in the heart of the city's disadvantaged poor and immigrant citizens. Eager to serve, they both believed in their new adventure! Life is good!

The couple were greeted by the manager of the Morris House and the maids assigned to serve the newly wedded couple. Shown to their Honeymoon Suite, the couple were advised that dinner would be served at seven pm. The couple were anxious to freshen up and be relieved of their wedding attire.

Behind an Oriental screen, Maud changed into a pink taffeta gown with an overlay of sheer crimson silk and tiny rose buds encircling her bosom. She let her fiery red hair fall in long curls tied by a velvet rose ribbon which hung softly to the left side of her shoulder. She wore the pearl necklace Chad had given her for a wedding gift. The pearls were originally a wedding gift from Judge Somerset to his bride, Mary Margaret on their wedding day. Maud cherished the pearls and vowed to hand them down to their first daughter on her wedding day.

Chad chose a pair of dark trousers, a white shirt with a ribbon tie, and a soft beige swede jacket. He wore black leather boots that fit snugly below his knees. They both smiled as they critiqued each other before dinner. A gentle knock at the door interrupted the admiring moment. Chad opened the door to Everett, Morris House maiter'de. "Sir, I wanted to personally announce that dinner will be ready in about fifteen minutes." "Thank you Everett, we will be down shortly," as he politely closed the door.

Turning to Maud, he asked, "Well my beautiful bride, are you ready for our first dinner alone as man and wife?" "Oh, yes Chad! I'm so excited!" Taking his arm, they descended down the carpeted stairs. Everett met them as they entered the dining room. He called for their waiter to escort them to the table in the corner by the glowing fireplace. The table decorated by a single pink rose, was dimly lit, creating an ambiance of love and romance. After assisting Maud with her wrap, the waiter seated her. She graciously thanked him as he assisted Chad to be comfortably seated, he explained the menu: An appetizer of stuffed clams, Red Bordeaux Wine, followed with Roasted Pheasant w/red wine gravy, wild rice w/petite apricots, string beans and button mushrooms, and a petite wedding ring of puffed rolls with hot butter, and for dessert the house speciality, A dark chocolate cherry mousse with whipped crème and French Champagne. After explaining the menu, he proudly bowed to the couple,"Madame, Mousier"and left them to begin with their appetizers.

"Chad, you spoil me. I've never dined like this, hope I don't embarrass you." "My sweet, you are just perfect, believe me, I'm not accustomed to dining this formal, but it's our wedding, so let's enjoy it while we can."

The waiter brought a white wine with an appetizer of stuffed clams/olives/cheese canape. He poured a small glass of wine for Chadwick to test. After slowly swirling the wine, taking a sip, he nodded in approval. The waiter then poured a glass for both Chad and Maud.

After he left, Chad explained the ritual was to make sure the wine met the customer's approval. He confessed to know nothing about wine tasting. He trusted the establishment to offer only good to excellent wines. He raised his glass to toast a happy, healthy, and prosperous marriage. Maud, feeling a little shy, raised her glass to add, love, children, and peace. Chad urged them both to go easy on the food and wine. "I believe we are not accustomed to such rich foods and alcoholic beverages." They laughed teasingly while sipping their vintage wine, a little too much for their unaccustomed drinking pallets.

Their first dining experience was glorious and memorable. Half way through the main course Maud got the hiccups. Blushing, she covered her mouth with the napkin as she whispered, "Oh Chad, I'm so sorry," taking her hand he whispered, "Its okay, it happens to the best of us."

He raised his hand to the waiter to order two coffee's with crème to be served with their dessert. When the waiter began to serve the champagne, Chad asked that it be delivered to their room. After finishing their dessert, Chad assisted Mary Maud with her chair, took her arm and began to ascend carpeted staircase. Filled with food and drink, Chad very carefully escorted Mary Maud to the top of the stairs. She stopped to admire the beautifully decorated tapestries and paintings. She hugged Chad and said, "Is this a dream? Am I really married and on my honeymoon?" "Yes, my darling, we are married and enjoying our honeymoon!"

Arriving at the door of their suite, Chad picked up his bride and carried her into their room. "I think this is a tradition I will love," as his massive well built, six foot two inches frame easily picked up her petite barely five foot body; light as a feather while both laughed and looked around.the hallway. She reached to give him an endearing affectionate kiss ."And this, my love, is a tradition I know I will always love!" "Oh, my darling Maud," looking into her glowing blue eyes. "I love you with all my heart, and now my dear, "if Madame Somerset, will excuse me, I must prepare for my toilet."

Leaving the room for the men's room located in the back of the building, he paused to reequest the maids to bring a chamber pot, bathing tub and linens for Mistress Maud. Respecting her privacy, he thought about his father's loving advice. As a medical doctor, he thought he knew a lot about himself and a woman's body. But he is learning; patience, kindness, and compassion were the most important ingredients for a happy marriage bed. He was determined to encourage and support his wife as an equal partner in their life journey as husband and wife.

Maud looked around the room for what she might use as her own privy. Just then she heard a tapping at the door. Thinking Chad might have forgotten his key, she was surprised to see two young maids delivering a chamber pot, a soft cotton robe, linens, and toiletries. "Madame, as they curtsied, we have your toilet. The bellboys will bring a large tub with hot water. Do you want it placed behind the screen? Knowing your married and such, we need to ask your preference?"

Two men arrived with tub and hot water. Following the suggestion of the maids, they placed it behind the screen. The maids filled the shelves with scented soaps, perfumes, sponges, oils, brushes, and combs. After completing their well rehearsed jobs, they excused themselves. "If you need more water, please ring the bell and we'll be quick to serve you." Maud closed the door behind them.

Maud quickly relieved herself, then placed the crockery cover over the chamber pot. As she was undressing, she heard Chad come through the door. He encouraged her to relax and enjoy her bath. She could hear him humming. She thought, "He is surely is a happy and caring gentleman. How did I get so lucky?"

Chad approached the screen asking? "May I be of service in washing your back?" Startled, she shyly said, "Yes," She immersed her body into the deep water so that it covered her breasts and shoulders. "Where are the bathing cloths? Oh, never mind, I see them," as he gently began to scrub her back. Gathering a bar of French soap and a brush, he said, "Sweetheart, have you ever thought how your beautiful head is placed on your neck? How your head can turn to the left and then to the right?" He gently massages her neck, gently turning her head. "The human body is such a miracle, how it can grow such beautiful red hair. In our Anatomy classes we would preserve dead bodies and make artist's renderings of all body parts. This was necessary to learn how everything is connected, their movement and functions. However, it is not the same as observing the miracle of a live human body doing what God created it to do." "Notice the rise and fall of your shoulders by the emotions you are feeling. Madame, may I wash your beautiful hair? I will be gentle." "Yes, of course, .my long hair becomes difficult to rinse, I often use vinegar water to help in removing the suds," she responded nervously. "No worry, I shall call for a cup of vinegar. That should be an easy request." Chad rang the bell for the maids. Two came, taking the request, then hurried to the hotel's kitchen to fill the couple's request. Upon returning, Chad gave them a coin and requested another large bucket of hot water to be delivered in about thirty minutes. They curtsied as they closed the door. Maud safely hidden behind the screen, smiling nervously.

Chad asked if she mixed the vinegar with water? "I mix it in a water pitcher and add enough water for at least two rinses. I pour the vinegar water slowly through my hair." "Now my lady just lay your head back into my hands so that I can better shampoo your hair, scrub and massage your scalp."

Shy but excited, Maud, relaxed as Chad shampooed her hair, rinsed it, and dried it with a large Turkish towel. Speaking very softly, Chad explained the benefits of being completely relaxed. "Do you trust me enough to relax as I massage your arms and back?" She immediately replied, "Chad, I trust you completely."

He began by asking her to take a deep breath and to close her eyes. "Now picture yourself in your rose garden, the beginning of sundown, crickets are chirping, birds quietly nesting, and the sweet fragrance of a sweet rose fragrance permeates the air. Quietly, you follow the scent. Standing before the budding and blooming bush, you inhale its aroma, to bask in its sweetness. You are now relaxed and at peace with yourself and your surroundings."

When Maud was completely relaxed, Chad described the purpose of each extremity as he massaged it. He explained how the shoulders were connected to her spinal column, how the muscles and tendons help shape the body and serve as protection for the bones, and are also connectors to the nervous system. He demonstrated how the fingers and hands were strong enough to crush an animal bent on harming a child and tender enough to hold a precious new born babe and an emerging butterfly from its chrysalis. These functions are controlled by signals from the brain, some conscious and others unconscious. All the while educating Maud, as he gently washed and massaged her back, shoulders, arms, hands, and fingers. She was so relaxed, he could hear purring like a kitten that had its belly full after nursing.

The door knocker startled them both. He rose to answer the door, then explained to Maud, "My beautiful bride, while I answering the door, you will need to finish your bath because it is almost time for me to enjoy mine."

He laid a large bath towel and robe by the tub for her to use. Smiling and feeling content, he opened the door. Addressing the maids, "Thank you for being so prompt and efficient, we will need about another hour before being served our wedding champagne."

"Sir, we hope the bath was to your expectations. When we return, the bellboy will remove water, commode, and tub. We maids will remove used linens and toiletries to be restocked with fresh linens, oils, and soaps. Either a bellboy or the dining room waiter will set up your lovely evening champaign table. It has been our pleasure to be of service to you and your bride on your wedding night." Two red faced young maidens curtsied and hurriedly closed the door behind them.

Chad rang the bell for another bucket of hot water to be delivered immediately. Mary Maud stepped out from behind the screen wearing a beautiful cotton and lace dressing gown, brushing her long wet hair, looking radiant and refreshed. "Thank you my husband, I enjoyed my bath and massage," she teased.

Chad added the hot bucket of water into the copper tub, then began to strip naked while Mary Maud immediately turned her back. Smiling, he requested, "My love, could I request that you wash my back?" "Of course, I may not be as proficient as the good doctor, but I will give it my Irish best."

She gathered soap and a wash cloth. Allowing the water to flow from the cloth down his back, she then lathered his back with the bar of soap, scrubbed his back with a big brush while singing an Irish song. She doubled her fists, then pounded on his back and shoulders to relieve the tension from their long wedding day.

She marveled at how the muscles were defined, and how the veins protruded when making a fist. She loved massaging his long fingers and strong hands; like poetry in motion. She shared how exciting it will be to watch him in surgery saving lives by his carefully learned skill. He thought to himself, "she had no idea how gruesome surgery could be, but of course, it is beautiful as well." Saving lives is always a glorious blessing.

Asking if she might hand him a bath towel, he stood naked except for the towel wrapped around his waist as he rang for the bellboy to remove the tub, commode, and toiletries. He also advised them that they would be ready for their champaign in about 20 minutes.

After they left, he removed the towel. Displaying a well defined muscular body, he donned the white monogramed robe the hotel provided. Maud stared in amazement. She was completely in awe as to all the preparation Chad orchestrated to make this evening so perfect. She found herself anxious, but not afraid.

Opening the door for the waiter, Chad instructed him to set up their wedding evening champaign table in front of the window. After the table was properly set with linen tablecloth, lace napkins, champaign flutes, tiny pastries, and candies, the waiter placed a chilled bottle of the finest French Champaign the hotel had to offer. After opening the bottle, he poured two glasses half full, bowed to the couple, then closed the door.   .

The couple held hands as they prepared themselves to have a wedding toast and a piece of strawberry sugar cake and crème. They admitted to being full from dinner, totally relaxed from their baths and massages, and dog tired from their wedding festivities. They decided what they really needed was a good night sleep.

They removed their robes and crawled into bed. Chad took his bride into his arms, kissed her passionately, then spoke lovingly and gently, "Tonight, we just lie in bed and share. It's our time to get to really know one another. If you like, I'll begin." Chad looked deeply into her radiant deep blue Irish eyes, "I've loved you from the time you were a young adolescent. I couldn't wait for you to grow up. You did and now we are here. He kissed her forehead. "I grew up an only child of affluent parents.

However, they did not spoil me like many of my rich friends. I had many chores to do. I was not allow to pay anyone to do them for me. My allowance came from extra jobs I did, not my regular chores: like mucking out the horse stalls, chopping wood, and gardening. I was sent to public school. However, I was required to learn more than what they taught. My father taught me French, Latin, and some Greek. He also required that I learn astronomy, geometry, and physics. I'm so grateful, because of his tutoring, I was far ahead of most of my peers at Harvard.

My mother came from Dublin, the oldest of ten children. Their family was almost wiped out during one of the potato famines. She came to London to work as a servant girl at Oxford. My father was from an elite social class. He hated being perceived to be higher than the servants. He just did not believe in the traditional English aristocracy."

"My grandparents paid their servants very well and treated them like family. When my grandfather passed, he left them a nice home, a life-time living allowance. She became a nurse and he a carpenter. He taught his life principles to my father and he taught and modeled these to me. My grandmother was Scottish from the Clan Campbell, and a traditional Presbyterian religion of most Scots. She broke tradition by choosing to be a Catholic. She ran away from her home to be educated in England. She became a governess to a wealthy Duke with two children. She met my grandfather and married him. She told him right up front, she would not marry any man unless she was treated as an equal. She taught him how that might be accomplished. He was an English Barrister for the Crown; he relied on her wisdom in trial for many difficult cases. He was admired and respected by both the legal and society as an honest and fair jurist. I am proud of my family. Not for their money, but because of how they chose to serve their fellow human beings and share their wealth. Maud, it is my desire as a doctor to carry forth their legacy. My basic values are: love of

God, family, humanity, and to share my talent, time, and wealth in support of my country and freedom for all." "I hope this gives you some insight into who I am. Please ask anything you want to know. I will always tell you the truth, regardless of how difficult it might be." He held her in his arms under the covers of the cool night. They both breathed heavily, allowing the quiet of the moment seep into their conscious minds. "My darling, I want to know who you are at the depths of your being. I'm anxious to hear from your own lips who and what you feel about life, and your secret desires. Anything you want to tell me, I'm happy to listen with love and understanding."

Maud was very quiet for a moment as she worked to contain her emotions. "My love, I can feel your deep honesty coming forth from the deepest part of your heart. I've had such a different growing up, but like yours, it was filled with love."

"My parents were very young when they married, but they always knew what they wanted. They chose to emigrate to America, work hard to provide for their growing family, and to be of some help to their family back in Ireland. I am very proud of my father. He worked diligently to own his ship building business, to sponsor his brother and some of his workers to come to America and to take care of our growing family. I was in my mother's womb on the long ships voyage across the sea. But, she did not let her sickness defeat her great desire to be an American. Her dreams of being an accomplished pianist carried her through the worst of times. She delivered me two months after arriving in Philadelphia."

"I too, dream of being very good at playing the piano, growing beautiful flowers, roses are my favorites, and becoming a good parent and helpful wife. I love what you shared about being your partner. I'm not sure I could be a good nurse; but I have good ciphering and organizational skills, and love meeting knew people. Chad, I love you more deeply than I ever believed I could love anyone."

Embracing for a long endearing kiss, Chad said reluctantly, "My love, we both need to get some sleep. Tomorrow will be a long train ride to New York. We will have a five day honeymoon in New York to finish what we started here. Goodnight sweetheart, sweet dreams." "Goodnight Chad, you're right I-am-so-very tired. Pleasant dreams"

Kahil Gibran, "Secrets of the Heart"
Will you accept a heart that loves, But never yields?
And burns, but Never melts?
Will you be at ease With a Soul that quivers before the Tempest,
but never surrenders to it?
Will you accept one as a companion
Who makes not slaves, nor will become one?
Will you own me, but not possess Me
by taking my body and not my heart?
Then here is my hand- - -grasp it with Your beautiful hand;
and here is myBody- - -embrace it with your loving Arms,
and here are my lips, bestow
Upon them a deep and dizzying kiss.

Magnolia Beaumont Plantation

Fourteen year old house slave, Jade Nicole is summoned to the Master's office. Nervous, she looks into the mirror on the oak dresser to see if her hair is properly coiffed and her stocking pulled tight. Since Mistress Josephine, the Master's daughter married and moved to New Orleans, Jade wasn't always sure if she was looking and acting as the Master desired.

Mistress Josephine loved her like a baby doll, as a child; then as a little sister when she grew up. But of course, she was only a half sister and part Negro, that was never ever addressed. Jade attended all classes Josephine had with the professor. He assumed she was Josephine's younger sister, and treated her as such. Since Josephine's marriage, the professor was to continue teaching her all the lessons a young girl should need to become a lady in proper society. Jade loved her classes; playing the piano, studying about plants and their medicinal value, and story telling. Her birth mother, Missy died when Jade was five years old. Since her death, she did not feel welcomed in the kitchen or out in the gardens with the other slaves. She was so lonely and could not understand her purpose or what was to become of her.

Checking once more in the mirror, she walked quietly down the hall to the Master suite and knocked on the door. "Come in," answered Master Louis. She opened the door and curtsied to the tall handsome figure she knew to be her father, but was never acknowledged as so. He smiled, "Come, come over here, have a seat by my desk. My dear, you are looking lovely this morning. Did you do well in your French lesson?" "Merci, " she teased, starring into his jade green eyes with a wisp of red hair slipping out from bottom of his white powdered wig. "Master, I always do well in all my studies. But I do miss Mistress Josephine. It was so much more fun learning together."

"Yes, my dear, Josephine is now a married woman, that will make me a grandfather in the near future." "Oh, Master, I'm not complaining, it's just that I get lonely sometimes." "I'm sure that is true, and Jade Nicole," trying to get control of his emotion "Thats's part of what I want to discuss with you. If my calculations are correct, you soon will be fifteen years old. You are a beautiful, talented and accomplished young lady who speaks two languages fluently. The professor tells me your French is excellent and your ciphering is outstanding. And little lady, your good at chess, you've beat me a few times." Smiling, lowering her head and peeking through her long luxurious eye lashes, she asked? "Does that make you happy Master?"

Remembering Josephine's request the last time she visited her home, he cleared his throat, leaned back in his chair, and said, "Yes, yes it does, You make me happy just the way you are." Stumbling for words, and clearing his throat, he said, "Jade, you are approaching womanhood, and with a terrible war on the brinks to head our way, and as your guardian, I feel it prudent that I send you where you can be safe. I have written a letter to The Bishop at the Basilica of St. Louis, King of France in St. Louis, requesting he be your guardian until you are eighteen. He has accepted the honor to guide you into maturity and also assist you in gaining employment as a governess." "You'd like that wouldn't you Jade?"

Tears streaming down her cheeks, wiping her eyes with her lace hand-kerchief, "Merci Master, yes, but, I'd miss you, and my kitty, Fluffy" "I understand Sweet Girl, but sometimes the decisions that are made for our protection, can hurt, I'm sorry."

"I've sent word to my brother, that I'ld like to engage his son, Phillipi and his servant, Desmond to escort you to the dock where they will row you to the Bella Beaumont River Boat. Captain Flint, my employee. will see that you are given a state room and safe passage to St. Louis where the Bishop will meet you, to escort you to the family I've arranged for you to live with until you are eighteen years of age. The Bishop has assured me, the family is of highest moral standing in both the Church and Community of St. Louis. He is the owner of and president of the local bank. The Bishop will continue to tutor you with your formal classes and all that is required to become a governess. After you meet all the requirements, the Bishop will assist you in gaining employment as a governess to a family of means. How does that sound?" A long and quiet pause, "Master, I appreciate all you have done for me, but Fillipi scares me, by the things he says, and way he looks at me. He makes me feel unclean."

Master Louis stood up, walked to where Jade is seated, helped her stand to be embraced, then said, "Oh, Oh, I see," Raising his voice to a loud crescendo, "Trust me, I'll make sure no harm comes to you on your journey, leaving this plantation, then continuing up to the dock, on the river boat, and your trip on up to St. Louis!"

"Jade Nicole, my sweet dear girl, do you not understand that this letter makes you a free woman when you're eighteen? I personally would escort you to the Bishop, but I'm due to have a meeting with the Governor, and cannot leave at this time." Their eyes meet, frozen into their gaze. For the very first time, Louis Beaumont felt a stirring in his heart. One he has never felt before. He is fond of his daughter, Josephine, but the sweet purity of spirit he felt emanating from Jade Nicole, is a love he cannot explain. At last finding his voice, whispering with assurance, "It's going to be just fine. I swear to you, I will not allow anyone to hurt or harm you. I promise to visit you on your eighteenth birthday in St. Louis. Until then, we will write each other; you will share all the wonderful happening in your new life." And even more softly he whispered, "Jade Nicole, my precious sweet jewel, I wish things could be different, but I honestly don't know how." Kissing her on the top of her auburn red hair, "Now go and prepare for dinner, then after dinner, pack your trunk for your new exciting journey to St. Louis."

After dinner, Master Beaumont called for his sorrel mare to be saddled He rode by moonlight to his brother's plantation. The stable groom, helped him dismount and led the mare to the barn for grooming. With a warm greeting, Jean Michel joined his brother, welcoming him into the front parlor of the mansion.

Jean Michel inquired, "Louis, why am I being blessed with my brother's attendance on such a beautiful moonlit night?" Louis responded by asking that his godchild and his servant be able to join them as he has a favor to ask of them. Jean Michel rings for the butler to notify his son and Desmond to please join them in the parlor.

The boys could be heard leaving the game room laughing and teasing each other about the chess game that Phillipi just won. They enter the room as Phillipi offers his hand to his uncle saying, "Uncle Louis, what brings you out this evening?" "I have a little job I'd like to entrust you and Desmond to do for me tomorrow. As you know, the Bella Beaumont River Boat is presently anchored in the river about 200 yards from the our dock and boat house. It delivered the forty-seven slaves that were auctioned this past weekend. I've employed Captain Finch to take Jade Nicole up river to the Cathedral of St. Louis where she will be in the care of the Bishop until she is old enough to be hired as a governess for an affluent parish member."

With a questioning and obstinate posture, Phillipi looked first at his father, then to Desmond and shouted, "But Uncle Louis, Jade is nothing but a slave! Why are you giving her such good treatment? I know she's pretty, but for God's sake, no nigger deserves that kind of treatment!"

Louis Beaumont slowly, but with great purpose, walked toward his nephew, speaking directly into his face while shaking his fist in anger, said, "JUST WHO MADE YOU the AUTHORITY as to WHAT I CAN or CANNOT DO?" Then turning to address his brother, "Jean Michele, your son has just insulted me, and I fear embarrassed you with his adolescent and stupid opinions." Turning back to look at young Phillipi, "If I cannot depend on you, my God Child, to do this job for me in a gentleman like-manner, with both honor and respect as to my desire and authority, then I shall look elsewhere for someone I feel will honorably and trustworthy do my bidding." As he turned around, headed toward the door, Phillipi jumped up and called out, "No, please Uncle Louis, please wait. Yes, of course you are right, I was out of line and in no way do I want you to believe that I am unable or unwilling to escort Jade Nicole in a gentlemanly manner to her appointment with Captain Finch on the Bella Beaumont tomorrow. I humbly apologize for my rash and ugly comments." No one said a word, heavy breathing filled the air, "Sir, what time do you want us to pick her up?" "Jean Michel, I would not ask this of your son if I could do it myself. I have an appointment with the governor tomorrow concerning the tariffs charged for exporting molasses and cotton. If I could arrange it for another time, I would, but I can't." Jean Michel responded, "What time do you need them, Louis? I'll see they are there?"

"They need to be at Magnolia Grove at 2:00 p.m. "And Gentlemen, I expect by this time tomorrow, the Bella Beaumont's horn will blare a signal she is heading north to St. Louis. Join me in praying for good weather and happiness for all. Good Evening Gentlemen."

As he left the room, the silence in the parlor was thick with residue from Master Louis' masterful executed purpose with specific instructions for tomorrow's mission. Breaking the silence, Jean Michele warned his son, "That is the most anger I have ever witnessed from my brother. Phillipi, you acted like a small school boy caught with hand on his cock!" "But why Father, didn't you defend me?" "Why, you ask me , why? Because Phillipi, Louis was correct! You not only embarrassed me, you brought great shame to your own soul. I pray you learned a valuable lesson tonight, and that Jade is safely on The Belle headed to St. Louis tomorrow, because if you ever lose my trust," Red faced with anger, Jean Michel left the parlor without finishing his statement and saying goodnight.

At 1:35 in the afternoon, Phillipi and Desmond arrived at Uncle Louis' plantation driving their best carriage with two of their best horses. They were very careful to arrive at their appointed time so that they could be sure to have Jade Nichole on time for her appointment with Capt. Finch on the Bella Beaumont. She was dressed in a beautiful emerald green velvet riding habit, hat, gloves, and boots. Her trunk was beside the long front porch with her travel bag and basket lunch. Everyone on the plantation was gathered around Jade to wish the best for Jade Nicole.

Phillipi inquired as to the where was of his uncle? The head butler, Morris informed him that the Master left before breakfast for an appointment with the governor. Phillipi instructed Desmond to load her trunk and to help her into the carriage. Morris whispered softly in Desmond's ear, "You watch out for her, do you here?" Desmond got Morris message loud and clear.

Jade Nicole was hugging her friends goodbye, when Desmond advised her, "Miss Jade, it's time to go" "Oh please Desmond, I forgot my parasol!" "I'll get it," As he assisted her into the carriage, he then ran to get the parasol. Phllipi, already seated in the carriage whispered to her, "Well

Princess Jade, you won't be a precious jewell by the time I get through with you. You'll be tarnished and of no good use"

Desmond arrived with the parasol, handed it to Jade, then observed both fear and anger radiating from her. She spoke defiantly. "Thank you Desmond, I think it will be quite hot by the time we arrive at the dock." She opened her parasol and looked straight ahead.

Desmond knew Phillipi must have said or done something to cause her to flash such a look. Desmond knew he must appear casual, but to stay aware of Phillipi as he could not be trusted. Desmond climbed up, took the reigns. He could not hear what Phillipi was saying to Jade, but knew it was not anything appropriate. "Please Lord Jesus, I'm a needing you on this journey."

They arrived about an hour later at the dock's hitching post. Stopping the horses, and before he could hitch them, Phillipi started yelling like crazy person, ordering Desmond to unlock the shed, water, brush down, and feed the horses and to unload the trunk and place it on the row boat.

Jade climbed down, refusing any assistance from Phillipi. He just stood, flashed an egotistical grin, in a most evil like manner. Desmond thought, "Has he gone crazy, he surely cannot be trusted. "Desmond was tying the horses to the hitching post, when he saw out of the corner of his eye, Phillipi pull out a knife from the back of his breeches under his vest. He was speaking low to Jade, as they walked to the shed.

He yelled for Desmond to unlock the shed. "Hurry, the young lady needs some shade and cool water? Walking slowly, as if not paying atten-tion, Demond opened the door, walked in and started sweeping out the spider web's in order to kill some time, as he thought about what he must do. Spotting a knife laying on a stone used for cleaning fish, he picked it up and put it in his vest pocket then left the shed to finish grooming the horses, acting as if he heard nothing and was deaf and dumb to Phillipi's mumblings to Jade.

Phillipi picked up the basket of food as he shoved Jade into the shed He carried his knife in his right hand as a constant reminder as to what he could do if she didn't follow his orders. He closed the door.

Desmond sneaked around the backside of the shed to listen. He heard Phillipi tell Jade to remove her jacket to her dress. Resisting, she slapped his face. He then held her arms tighter and told her, "Get with it, show me those titties, as she opened her mouth to scream, covering her mouth, he threatened her, "Princess, don't you bother yourself by trying to get help from that "boy" he belongs to me and does what I say and when I say it."

Desmond hearing Phillipi's words, saw life as it was. What good is it to wear fine clothes, have a good education, but to never be able to dream?" A dream is to have hope, and there is no hope in being a slave. Just then he heard Phillipi say, "Now damn it! Show me what you have or I'll slice that pretty little face until it looks like a fish fillet." She began to weep and beg. "Please, I beg of you, I can't do this." "But, bitch, you will do it." At that moment Phillipi heard a sound in the far corner. A big black water rat come running towards him. He turned to find something to kill it with, tripped and fell flat on his face. His fearful acrobat performance caused him to drop the knife. Groping in the darkness to fined the knife, he realized Jade had escaped. Cursing his clumsiness, a voice out of nowhere said, "Is this what you are looking for?" "Thank God, Des, go get that girl! Then get a rope out of the boat, we're going to have to tie her up to deliver her to Captain Fink."

Desmond found the rope in the boat. Then walked towards Phillip and said, "So you own me? I'll do anything you tell me? Right? So, instead of me tying up Jade," he grabbed Phillip from behind, holding his knife to his throat, he told him to drop his knife. Phillip threatened, then he pleaded,

"Des, you know you better turn me loose, Father will have you strung up if you do anything to me." Desmond told him to take off his jacket, pants, shirt, stockings, shoes, then Phillip started pleading like a squalling baby. "Please Des, you're my brother, we'll tell Father Jade tried to escape that'd why she had to be tied to be delivered to Capt Finch."

"You are so pitiful! You can rot in hell as far as I'm concerned." He finished tying his arms, legs, and placed his sock in his mouth. After he was securely tied, Jade took the fish knife and held it to Phillipi's throat and said very politely in her best slave dialect. \ "Masta Iz noz one way to stik ta nif, so plz move, iz itchn to stik it." Phillipi cried like a baby starving for its bottle.

Gathering up Phillipi's clothes , the knife, his gun out of the carriage, the lunch basket, the lantern, oil, fishing pole, coffee pot, iron pan, and ammunition, he turned around before leaving the shed, "Phillipi, you're a liar, cheat, and an almost rapists. You are a devil. Goodbye!" He slammed the door shut and threw the key into the river. Pausing as he saw Jade pin a note to Master Louis on the door.

"Jade, I want you to trust me. I promise to God I will not harm you. If you want me to take you to that river boat so you can go to St. Louis as your daddy planned, I will. But after I deliver you, I'll be rowing up river, hiding in the woods, running for my life, because that boy in that shed will have every law man, slave trader, and hound dog looking for me so he can string me up a tree."

"Yes, we are brothers. We had a lot of fun growing up, but today, I learned a very hard lesson! He'd sell me as quick as a pat of butter melts on a hot biscuit. So Jade, what do you want me to do? It's your choice, to the river boat or to wait here until your daddy comes for you?"

Jade starred at this tall courageous, kind, and honest young man. Breathing deeply, she said, "Sir, if you don't think I'd be too much trouble, I'd like to go with you. You see, I've learned freedom is not having things, freedom is being someone, and dying for something you believe in." Desmond could hardly believe his ears, then he shouted, "Well come on woman, we've got a lot of traveling to do." as he took her hand, helped her into the boat, and started rowing as the evening sun was about to go down. Both were very quiet, choosing to be with their own thoughts and feelings. They both knew the severity of this journey, but still, so excited to be on the journey of a life time. Two run-away slaves of mixed blood, house slaves, well educated, but having nothing but themselves and their dreams.

Master Louis Beaumont arrived back at his plantation at about five p.m. He took his gelding to the barn to be cared for. His cook asked him if he was ready for dinner? Feeling rather uneasy and missing Jade, he looked at his watch. The Bella Beaumont had not blared its horn, the signal that both their cargo and passenger was on board and they were on their way. "Something is amiss," he said to himself as he turned right around to ask the groom to saddle him another fresh horse. "I fear Phillipi has done the unforgivable." as he rode the mare as fast as he could to the boat dock.

Finding Phillipi naked and tied in the shed, he cut his ropes, as Phillipi tried to give Louis a lame excuse. "Shut up, you fucking liar! I will see to it that your father does not allow this to go unpunished. Until then, you can walk home like a slave, see how it feels to be stripped of your clothes, shoes, and dignity. The only light was from the moon. It was cold and filled with many unrecognizable sounds. Louis felt guilt and remorse; his whole being started to shake. "What is happening me?" he asked himself. He could hear Phillipi dragging behind, begging for him to let him ride. Then Louis felt a warmth going from his feet to the top of his head. He could feel a light, but not see it, he then began to pray. "Heavenly Father, I've been selfish, greedy, and abusive. Help me, guide me to live a life filled with goodness and mercy. I promise to strive to do right for all people. Show me how, and I will do it. Please Father, take care of Jade and Desmond, they are innocent children of your love. Thank you Father, Amen"

Suddenly, he saw up a head, a figure. He held his horse back as his eyes focused to see a man hanging from a tree by the side of the road. Phillipi frightened, started screaming, "Please Uncle let me ride." He helped Phillipi to ride behind him. They rode in complete silence.

As they pulled into Jean Michel's barn, Phillipi was so tired, cold, and fearful of what laid ahead that he said not a word. Jim, the old groom was startled to see Louis with Phillipi, but no Desmond, worried he said nothing. Louis asked, "Jim, I'd appreciate if you could take care of my horse, I might have to go home tonight."

They entered the mansion from the porch by the side parlor. Jean Michel was seated by the fire reading. He looked up to see both Phillipi and Louis, he asked? "What happened? "Phillipi, your father has asked you a question. I'm waiting to see the accuracy of your story."

"Father, Desmond overtook me, tied me up, took my clothes, and kidnapped Jade. I think he is rowing up the river. We need to get a posse and hang him." Jean Michel looked to his brother with mixed emotions. His eyes filled with tears, his heart beating wildly, then he asked, "Louis, I need some clarity?"

"Brother, I gave your son the opportunity to tell the truth. He did not know I found this note written by Jade tacked on the door of the shed. Shall I read it out loud so that both Father and son can be enlightened?" Jean Michel nods.

"Master, Phillipi tried to rape me, Desmond stopped him, Des was going to take me to the river boat, but I knew Des would be punished, and not Phillipi. I begged Des to take us to freedom. If you send dogs I'll gladly hang too. I love you, Jade"

So, on the way home, I allowed your son to feel how a Negro slave feels, stripped of clothing and self esteem. Also my brother, along side the road, we saw terrible sight! Probably a gang of white youth, looking to have some fun, hung a poor young Negro to a tree."

Louis took a seat on the divan by the fire, then continued. "Jean Michel, this may be hard for you to believe, but I felt a light, going up from my feet to the top of my head. I felt a loving and nourishing voice inside my head that said, "Louis, you have lived a greedy, and abusive life, thinking of no one but yourself in order to gain more wealth. I have given you the power to choose, choose wisely."

"Jean Michel, In that moment, I saw my whole life right in front of me. My selfishness and urging that caused you to follow me to America. You loved your life in France. My beautiful, loving Jade, who was a joy and loved by all, I even sent her away to protect her, and all she wanted was for me to claim her as my daughter. I failed her and you in so many ways."

"It just this minute, dawned on me what I must do. I'll be going home to begin dismantling my life. We're on the brink of a terrible war. All slave owners will be fighting for their own greed. They will come and take our horses, livestock, slaves, and land. I'm going to free my slaves, encourage them to cross the river and go to the northwest. Jean Michel, I'm so sorry it has come to this, I failed you, and I'm so terribly sorry." He fell to his knees and sobbed.

Jean Michel shouted to Phillipi, "Go get cleaned up and get something to eat. And, then stay out of my sight, Your lies and disgusting behavior makes me sick, and what's worse I feel responsible for it."

He turned to his distraught brother, speaking so softly and lovingly, as he helped his brother to his feet. "Louis, I don't know what tomorrow will bring, but tonight, I want you to stay here, take a long hot bath, eat, and try to sleep. Right now, I need to go to Rochelle and tell her our beautiful and loving son escaped to freedom. She will be happy for him, but sad for me. Because I never acknowledged Desmond. He never complained, not once, God forgive me, I pray they get to freedom. Ohio is a long way for two house slaves to travel without getting caught. As we both know, they are much more valuable then field slaves." Jean Michel led his brother to the guest bedroom, called for the butler to get him hot water, clean clothing, and food. He said he'd return in about an hour.

*The energy that expresses itself in the form of evil is the same energy
which expresses itself in the form of good,
and thus the one may be transmuted into the other.
-Charles Henry Mackintosh-*

The next morning, the couple awakened to a gentle rap at the door. Chad grabbed his bathrobe as he headed to the door. The maid apologized for waking the couple, but the manager said they had to catch a train in a couple of hours. She didn't want them to miss it. Chad thanked her and asked if she would order a carriage to take them in about an hour and half to the train station? And if possible, could you please bring some breakfast to the room while we get dressed and packed" "Yes Sir, right away."

As he closed the door, Maud was already putting things in her valise. Laughing as she quickly folded her clothing and gathered her personal items. She disappeared behind the screen as Chad rushed down the back stairs to use the privy.

When he returned, he found the maid had already brought their breakfast. Maud was dressed, packed, and fixing her hair. He quickly put together his valise while asking the Maid if the carriage had arrived? "It's waiting for you at the front entry, I'll let him know you are on your way."

The couple wrapped the hot apple pastries, boiled eggs and cheese slices in linen napkins and placed them in Maud's knitting bag Chad laid some coins on the table for the maids, gathered their bags, opened the door and followed the Maud down the stairs to the waiting carriage. Laughing like little children caught in mischief, they arrived at the station just fifteen minutes before their scheduled departure.

They enjoyed their breakfast as the countryside past their vision from their window seats. The sound of the train rolling over the rails was hypnotic, like a dream she never imagined possible. Maud didn't want to miss a thing. She longed to write in her journal that Peggy gave to her, but felt she'd miss something if she did. The sky began to turn from light hazy blue to a dark navy blue black. She reached for her shawl just as loud thunder clap roared, shaking the moving train. Chad stirred from his slumber, grabbed his coat from the hanging rack to wrap around Maud. Seeing the lightening flashes and hearing the thunder, he remarked, "Looks like we're bringing heavy rains to the city. For sure, we'll need parasols for the next couple of days." Seeing that she had fallen asleep, he placed his coat over her, thinking, "I guess with the thunder storm there is nothing to keep your interest, Rest my sweet love." As he joined her in catching some needed sleep.

They both awakened as the train pulled into the station. As they departed, a porter hailed a carriage, to load their luggage, and told the cabby to take them to St. Nicholas Hotel on Broadway, the newest and finest hotel in New York.

Judge Somerset surprised the couple with a wedding gift of the luxurious honeymoon suite at the St. Nicholas Hotel. Chad had planned a honeymoon trip to New York, but his father gifted the couple a trip they could only dream about. Chad purposely did not inform his bride the type of accommodations they would be enjoying. He could hardly wait to see her face when they arrived at the grand entrance.

Listening to the downpour on the carriage roof, it reminded him of an orchestral staccato drum beat, a poetic crescendo to announce the magnificent unfoldment of a great mystery. Startled! A voice announced!

"Sir, we are here." As he stepped down to unload the luggage, then opened the door to assist the couple with large umbrella's, as they hurried to the grand entrance. The driver carried their luggage to the door; Chad handed him some coins, the doorman quickly guided them to the registration desk, while he had their luggage sent up to the honeymoon suite. Everywhere they looked, the initials SNH were engraved or embroidered. A visual constant reminder of the hotel's abundant ambience. Once inside their room, the couple just stared in awe! Blinking her eyes in wonder, she sighed, "Never, ever could I imagine such luxury! Furnishings with velvet and gold, Valuable paintings hanging on all the walls!"

Chad gently took her arm as they walked through the various rooms of their suite. She ambled along as if in a trance. The walls were layered with white damask, the marriage bed had a mattress with springs, light flowing feather coverings, and a bathroom with a huge bathtub, shower, white marble sink, and flushing water closet. As they both continued to be in awe, the bellman announced that they would be serving tea in one hour. Chad immediately turned to hand the gentleman a coin in appreciation. After closing the door, he enjoyed watching his bride turning on and off the water in the sink. He opened the cabinet doors to find it fully equipped with scented soaps, oils, perfumes, brushes, combs, lotions, and tooth brushes. Linens of all sizes,, fluffy robes, slippers. He turned to Mary Maud and said, "They certainly have thought of everything for the marriage bath! Father certainly out did himself in giving us the wedding gift of a lifetime!" She smiled nervously, then he spoke softly, "I'll leave you to use this beautiful room in private."

He closed the door as she sighed in relief! After using the bathroom, she washed her hands, removed her hat and shoes. He feet were tired after their long journey from Philadelphia to New York. The the marble tiles felt cold, but after leaving the bathroom, the thick pile white carpet in their bedroom felt just wonderful.

She found her husband at the window seat looking out on Broadway at the pouring rain. Maud silently walked up behind him, embraced him and said, "Will we wake up tomorrow to find this has all been a dream?" "If we do, then my father will sue them for false advertising." he teased.

I think I'll use the bathroom before I unpack. They will be bringing our tea in about twenty minutes. So we best be ready. Maud began to unpack as he returned whistling an old English folk song about a young fair maiden.but was interrupted by a rap at the door. She opened the door to a young bell boy pushing a tea cart on tiny wheels. Another bellboy was carrying a vase of pink roses. He set everything on the little round table by the window. The china teapot was snuggly wrapped beautifully in a crocheted tea cozy of gold silk threads. The Havaland china dishes were gilded with gold. Everything was engraved **SMH** in gold The linens and napkins embroidered with the St. Nicholas Hotel symbol in gold and silver threads. Maud's eyes sparkled as she exclaimed! "It's so beautiful and elegant, I'm afraid to touch it!" Chad in his sweet calm manner, pulled out her chair, said, "My Dear Lady, please be seated, for it's time for tea!" After she was seated, he sat down, laying his napkin on his lap, "After you my dear. Eat up and enjoy, 'cause in Ohio we don't have running water, flushing toilets, and servants to serve tea, I'm afraid my dear, it's just you and me." "Why Chad, among other talents, you're also a poet," she teased.

One hour later, the bellman arrived to take away their tea tray. They were still unpacking, when Chad asked what time was dinner. The bellman replied, "Eight p.m. Sir, will there be anything else I can do for you?" "No, nothing that I can think of. Thank you." After closing the door, Chad remarked, "How does one get any rest with all these eating interruptions?" Both doubled over laughing. Chad still chuckling said, "If we want to have a nice bath before that bloody bellman comes back, we best get to it," as he turned the water on in the bathtub, he gathered the oils, soaps, brushes, and towels.

Noticing Maud had changed into her luxurious bath robe, Chad began to gather his toiletries; shaving soaps and razor. When the tub was half full, he invited her to enter. Turning his head as she disrobed to enter the huge copper tub, he asked if he might join her. "If you would like, I'd be obliged" She turned her head as he undressed and wrapped a bath towel around his lower body, then turned on the water and waited for it to add another two inches, he then climbed in. Using the big bathing sponge, he began washing her shoulders, while all the time staring into her hypnotic blue eyes. She began to wash his shoulders and hairy chest. He asked her to turn around so he could wash her neck, back, shoulders, and breast. When the nipples harden, she began to moan. Whispering in her ear how beautiful she is and how much he loves and adores her, all the while licking her neck, her ears, while massaging her breasts, and then her tummy. He guided her hand to touch her breast while sharing how important it is to know her own body and how to use and enjoy it.

Suddenly! she turned around, threw her arms around him; began kissing his neck, ears, and nipples; panting erotically she asked, "May I, may I please, Oh, I love you so much, may I see you fully, my husband?" Quite surprised, but fully enjoying her sensual request, he rises from the tub, as his cock grows, she gasped! Reached to touch it, then wilts back into the water.

He grabs a towel, dries himself, then lifts her up, dries her and takes her to bed. After laying her on the huge marriage bed, he put on his bathrobe, went into the other room and returned with her beautiful silk and lace dressing gown she received as a wedding gift from her mother. Chad reminded her, "In a few moments, the staff will be bringing our Wedding

Dinner. After enjoying our meal, receiving its sustenance, we will be better prepared for what we just started in our marriage bath."

A few minutes later, the hotel waiter assigned to serve them, rapped at the door. "Good evening Sir, Madam, I have your Honeymoon Dinner. I believe the window area over looking Broadway is perfect, what do you think?" Both speaking at once, they concurred.

Seated together on the white satin settee, they observed every detail of the waiter's precise preparation. After lighting the candles, he turned to the couple, bowed, "If you need anything else, please call. Our maids are on duty all night, and do you wish to have our DO NOT DISTURB sign placed on your door with a desire for a WAKE UP call for breakfast to be served at 9 a.m.?" Chad smiled, "Yes, to both, Thank You for your excellent service, here's a little bonus," The waiter bows again, and leaves immediately, closing door behind him.

Dinner was beautifully presented, even more so than afternoon tea. Wine, Onion Soup, Jellied Salad, Prime Rib with Julianne Potatoes, Hard Roles and butter, Boston Creme Pie with French Champaign. Both agreed, Elegant Dining!!!

Chad lead Maud to the side of the huge marriage bed. The coverlet was beautifully tatted with a gold fringe. Two large satin pillows with the St. Nicholas monogram inviting Chad to lay his head down by his beautiful wife, "My love, as I've shared before, our bodies are instruments, capable of making beautiful music. An instrument must be understood, examined and practiced in order to perform to its maximum potential. Tonight is our time to explore, and examine intimately our instrument's so that we can create beautiful music together. Unfortunately social norms have prevented the art of sexuality to become perfected. Do you trust me to take you on this journey? While on this journey together, you will have the opportunity to learn about my body as well as your own. Are you willing?

My Beloved, I will not do as most men do on their wedding night. By demonstrating a lack of patience, they take their brides virginity without knowing first who she truly is, what her body is capable of doing, and how they can so easily blend together when love, gentleness, and compassion are felt."

Not a sound, just heavy breathing, permeated the marriage bed, finally the bride grabbed her beloved and cried out,

"Oh yes, please, I trust you with my heart, body, and soul. I want to learn, I want to know all about me and all about you. Yes, I am ready to be filled with the joy of being connected to you, my husband, as one body, one soul." And so, the sensual and sexual anatomy lesson began.

"Home Builders"
The world is filled with bustle and with selfishness and greed,
It is filled with restless people that are dreaming of a deed,
You can read it in their faces; they are dreaming of the day
When they'll come to fame and fortune and put all their cares
away.
And I think when I behold them, though it's far indeed they roam,
They will never find contentment save they seek for it at home.
JUST FOLKS by Edgar A. Guest

Benjamin Sterling's Home. Underground Railroad Station

Hopkinsville, Kentucky

Rev Henderson Sterling and his young daughter, Jenny arrived by wagon to the home of his brother, Rev. Benjamin Sterling of Hopkinsville, Kentucky for a visit.

Uncle Ben and his wife Lizzie have two children close in age to Jenny. The two families have not seen each other for about four years. Both men are conductor's on the Underground Railroad, moving slaves from the deep south to northern cities.

Rev. Henderson Sterling is a minister of the Presbyterian Church of Cincinnati. Since the death of his wife, he and his daughter have not left their home for any type of visits. Moving slaves north and preaching in church takes up most of his time. He is determined to escort his daughter for a little visit with her cousins.

Rev. Sterling and Jenny arrive at Uncle Ben's late on Saturday evening. Aunt Lizzie had prepared a big meal for their kin folk, their son had made a chessboard for entertainment, and daughter, Beth was anxious to share her library of books she has been collecting since last several years.

Tired from their trip over bumpy roads, watching out for straggling rebel soldiers, and hungry from lack of food and drink, they both apologize for their lack of energy. After dinner, their visitors asked forgiveness, but were just "plum tired" and in need of a good night sleep.

The next morning, Jenny awakened to the smell of coffee and bacon frying. Her cousin was already dressed and in the kitchen helping her mother fix breakfast. Uncle Ben was in the parlor studying his Bible in preparation for his sermon in about two hours. Rev. Henderson Sterling was with BJ feeding the livestock and gathering eggs. BJ had already milked the cow and brought the full pail in to be strained. Jenny very quickly dressed, plaited her hair so that she could be of some help. She started straining the milk through some muslin fabric. Aunt Lizzie was making a pan of biscuits, while Beth whipped eggs to scramble. The guys were in the Summer Kitchen washing up and tending to their old dog, Tuff. Soon, everything was ready! Jenny's tummy was growling. She laughed and asked forgiveness.

Uncle Ben asked his brother to say Grace, just as he was finishing, his stomach made a big growl! Everyone laughed as they handed out plates of bacon, eggs, biscuits, and gravy around the table. Aunt Lizzie was busy filling coffee cups when they heard a knock at the door. Uncle Ben went to the door.

A gentleman with a silver star on his coat asked who their visitors were? Uncle Ben invited him in for a cup of coffee and biscuit, He introduced Jenny and his brother as their kin from Cincinnati, Ohio. The sheriff warned that a band of rebels were seen raiding farms, and to be prepared. He left with two biscuits smothered with blackberry jam in one hand and gun in another. BJ quickly said that he'd stay home from church to guard the farm. Ben looked at his brother and asked, "Henderson, could you honor my little church with your presence to preach this Sunday? My subject is on the Sermon on the Mount. I feel the message Jesus taught to his disciples is very much needed today. Our country continues to kill their brothers and sisters because of the color of their skin? I believe BJ and

I are needed at home, and I'd be very grateful for your kind service to our little congregation. This war has folks scared. Attendance is low."

"Of course, the Sermon on the Mount is one of my favorite reminders of what it means to be a true Christian. I'd be happy to be of service, to my brother. May I borrow your Big Bible, I brought only my small New Testament. The print is kinda small for my poor eyesight?"

The ladies gathered the dishes and put them in a pan with hot water, BJ hitched up the buggy for his Uncle Henderson. After gathering their heavy shawls, the ladies climbed into the buggy and covered their laps with a heavy blanket. The church members were concerned for their minister, but was told he had a special project that he and BJ needed to finish before winter set in. He asked forgiveness for working on the Sabbath and would see them Wednesday evening for prayer meeting.

Rev. Sterlings message was filled with many examples as to how each of us, as children of God can be of service to our brothers and sisters in Christ. He shared that Jesus did not serve just the white folk, but that Jesus was color blind, he saw only God's love in all people. After the service, he greeted everyone with a hug, not just a hand shake. He said, "Hugs are free, Love is free, get rich on Love."

Arriving back at the Sterling Farm, they found BJ stationed at the upstair window with a rifle, and Uncle Ben in the barn loft watching for anything suspicious. He confided in his brother that he felt something was about to happen and he wanted to be prepared. Especially, if tonight they received some slaves to hide. Henderson unloaded his duffle bag and pulled out his hand gun to get ready.

There are always risks in freedom
The only risk in bondage
is that of breaking free
-Gita Bellin-

ABOUT TWO DAYS SOUTH OF MEMPHIS, TENNESSEE

MISSISSIPPI RIVER

It was a hot, and a beastly humid day. Both Jade and Desmond were soaked in perspiration. Desmond had removed his shirt, and Jade removed her jacket to her traveling suit. They had rowed almost an entire night, without saying a word. Both contemplating their escape, present situation, and dream of being free. Desmond whispered softly, "Jade, we need to find shelter behind some tall reeds or trees. River boats might spot us out on the river in broad day light." Just as he finished speaking, Jade spotted a huge bed of water lilies and reeds. She pointed to that direction.

Putting his finger to his mouth to shush her and to be very still, he stood up in the boat, his eyes surveying the whole perimeter, then said softly. "This is alligator territory, they could tip us over, we must be careful they're not laying on the bottom sleeping or just watching and waiting." In just a few moments, Desmond made his decision.

"Jade, we need to go farther up north before we stop for shelter. I'm certain there are alligator's close by. Please lay flat in the boat, if a river boat spots me alone, they will probably assume I'm out fishing. If you will, please hand me my hat and shirt, no one in their right mind is on the water without covering their body."

Again, Desmond rowed for another two hours. Their food and water supplies were getting mighty low. Jade had sifted the river water threw one of her petticoats to remove sand and dirt. As it settled, it tasted pretty good.

They had one hard boiled egg, a biscuit, and a large slice of thick ham that Mammy, the cook had sneaked into Jade's lunch basket along with a couple of apples. Jade said, "Desmond, because you are working so hard, you've got to eat and drink water."

He pointed to a clump of tree saplings growing along side the river. He spoke in a low commanding voice. "You stay down, while I row towards those saplings to see if we're alone or if there are others docked there." He slowly rowed, then using his oar as a stick, he pushed the boat through the shallow water. No one was around. Relieved, he sighed, "I think we're alone, be careful getting up, just in case I have take off again." She slowly sat up, looked around, then handed Desmond the jug of water. He gladly accepted it. Drinking very slowly, then he handed it to her, as she drank from the old crockery jug they found in the shed.

"Desmond, I've cut a piece of the ham, half the biscuit, and apple for you. Please eat, I can't afford for you to lose your strength, my Prince Charming." "Is there enough for you?" Yes, I'll eat a piece of the ham and half of the biscuit. Laying on the floor, doesn't take much energy." She smiled teasing him, as she observed him slowly eating, bit by bit, as if each morsel was mana from heaven. Finally he said, "Jade, we need to get some sleep. Do you think you could stay awake for a couple of hours, while I sleep?" "Oh, yes I know I can. I'll wake you if I hear or see anything." Desmond turned on his side, then fell fast asleep. Jade looked at her watch, a beautiful gold lapel watch pen, Master gave her for her birthday. When the two hours were up; Desmond was sleeping so soundly, she decided to allow him another hour's sleep. About 30 minutes into the next hour, she heard voices, she silently touch Desmond, he awoke instantly, motioned for her to lay down, he began to silently row from their place in the saplings, when a voice called, "Hey Son, catch anything?"

Desmond answered, "Naw, just some too little, tossed 'em back. Think I'll try deeper water. You take care, ye hear?"

After they were safely out of sight, Desmond told Jade she could get up. "Oh, Desmond, you were so cute talking to that fella about fishing. You're quite an actor." "Yes, and so are you. We'll probably become even better before we reach Ohio or Canada." He found another grove of thick trees of which Desmond believed would be safe to dock and leave the boat in search for some food. He hoped to find some root vegetables, nuts and mushrooms. Rochelle, his slave mother, taught him what was good and what was poisoning. Jade grabbed her basket as they waded to the shore.

Soon Desmond had filled the basked overflowing with greens, mushroom, and some nuts. Jade volunteered her skirt to carry more nuts, greens and mushrooms. Just as they were about to leave the forest, they found an apple tree with fruit still on it. They grabbed as many as they could carry. When they returned to the boat, thoroughly exhausted with only about a couple of hours of daylight left, she commanded Desmond to sleep until dark." He saluted her and said, "Aye, Aye Ma'am, I am happy to serve you." Then turned over to sleep the rest of the day.

Back at the High Stepper Plantation, Jean Michel and his brother, Louis decided to hold Phillipi accountable for his inappropriate behavior at the dock and for his lies and deceit to his Uncle and Father. They called him to the front parlor. It had been two days since either father or uncle had laid eyes on Phillipi who had been ordered to stay out of his father's sight.

"Father, you called for me?" "Yes, Phillipi, your godfather and I, have decided to give you an opportunity to redeem yourself by making amends to those persons you have offended and then to determine how you might correct your offensive behavior. Do you understand what I've just stated to you?"

"Yes, Father, but Jade is gone, how do I make amends to her?" "Do you not see there are others you have offended?" "Not really, Oh, yes, Uncle Louis, who trusted me to deliver Jade to the river boat." He rested his focus on his Uncle then said, "Uncle, I'm sorry I disappointed you." an apology sounding very robotic. "And, what about Rochelle? She is Desmond's mother?" "Father, she's a slave, I did her a favor, I sent her son free!" "Phillipi, how are you going to correct this behavior so that it doesn't happen again?"' "By promising not to do it again." Jean Michel turned his attention to his brother, Louis, then asked, "Louis, my brother, what have you to say about Phillipi's apology?" "I'd love to believe it, but he made a promised to me once before, his words do not merit trust." "I hear your frustration, Louis, what do you suggest should be done to help Phillipi gain personal integrity?" " I think Phillipi believes he is better than other folks; therefore, I propose he learn to be humble, by serving those he offended. I would like for him to muck out your stable daily for a week, then afterwards, share with you, his father, and me, his God Father, what he learned from this humble act." Jean Michel responded, "As Phillipi's father, I feel this action is a result of reaping what one sow's. Therefore, as the power vested in me, as your father, Phillipi, the job of mucking out my stable shall begin right after we have our lunch." Phillipi started to complain, when his father said, "Son, complaining will bring on an additional week of mucking." Phillip stomped out of the room. Louis complimented, "Jean Michel, I believe you'd make a fine and fair legal judge. I truly pray my godson has learned his lesson."

Two day later, after mucking out his father's stalls, Phillipi Louis Somerset, left a note in his room advising his father, "I've gone to join the rebels, with my education, I will probably be an officer. Pray for me, Love, Phillipi"

When his father found the letter, he called for his brother to share the note. "Jean Michel, I'm so sorry. Do you blame me for this?" "No, of course not, Phillipi has chosen a hard road, very much like you and I, to learn the lessons that he must learn and be accountable for. Louis, I believe we're learning our lessons, but the difficult part, which lies ahead with a war at our back door, will be the many decisions we need to make now. May God Bless us in doing the right thing."

A month later, Louis found a rebel army on the plantation. Only a few slaves, all very old and devoted to Louis were left. The other's took his advise. He gave them papers saying they were free, horses to ride, and food for their trip. The rebels were furious. Nothing much was left for them to steal. They took Louis last horse, his buggy, and the food stuffs left in the root seller. Before leaving, they enjoyed themselves drinking his liquor and making the old slaves dance as they wasted their ammunition shooting around their feet to make them dance. After they left, dead drunk, their officer warned Louis that they'd be back, if he was hiding anything they needed. When there was no sight of them, Louis did what he could for the poor old slaves. Some had been shot in their legs that he meticulously dug lead pellets out with only a little cider to heal the wounds, His heart was breaking as he soothed old Granny, his cook. "Granny, I'm so sorry. Their devils, and worst yet, I used to be just like them." Granny said, "No Masta, uzed neva lik dem." Louis cried like a baby as she rocked him in her arms he said, "God forgive me, God forgive me."

After gaining some control of his emotions, he told Granny that he needed to check on his brother, but he'd be back." She nodded as he left walking to High Stepper plantation. About a mile out, he saw a great dark cloud of smoking rising in sky. "Oh, My God No, the devils have burned High Stepper Plantation.!" Running as fast as he could, he found the mansion burning, slaves here and there, Old Tom holding Jean Michel as he sobbed like a baby, "Tom, what happened to Jean Michel?" Old Tom looked up, he too crying, then said, "Masta done had a big shock, they killed his lady, Miss Rochelle." "Where, where is she?" "Over by her shack." Louis took off running, her little home was burned to the ground, she was beheaded, and nailed to the tree behind the shack with her latest piece of art hung beside her. It was a collage of slaves journey to freedom. They hammered a large nail through her right breast, with a piece of paper scrawled in her blood, NIGGER WHORE. Louis fell to his knees, "Mary, Holy Mother of God, pray for us sinners." as he heard footsteps, he looked up to see Old Tom helping Jean Michel to his brother's side, "Louis, may they rot in hell, all she ever wanted from me, was freedom, and I was too much of a coward to give it to her."

"We were both cowards. Now, all we have is each other. Will you join with me, in doing what we can to correct this evil? Let's bury Rochelle, and any dead slaves, then if my place is still standing, we will ask God to guide us to making a difference. "No, Louis, Rochelle would not want to be buried. She told me once how in Africa, they burn their bodies, and allow the smoke to go to the Creator, and their ashes return to the earth."

And so, they spent the rest of the day, preparing the dead slaves for cremation, piling sticks, dried leaves, and rocks on their bodies. When finished, they set fire; while those who lived, danced, sang, and watched the smoke return to their creator. Louis thought, "And my people, have called these souls savages. The true savage lies in the weak man's evil selfish heart."

Desmond rowed all night, his palms were filled with blisters. Ashamed of his thin skin, due to never truly doing any hard work, he did not allow Jade to hear him complain. Finally, it would soon be day break. He knew they needed to find a safe place to hide for the day. Desmond's calculated that they must be getting close to the Tennessee state line. But, he had no way of knowing for sure how far they rowed. Finally he found a bed of tall reeds. As they watched a school of water fowl diving for food, they believed this might be a place they could replenish their food supplies and remove their boat from the water. They noticed a little leak, and knew they needed to repair it before going much farther. It was the third day and fourth night, covered in filth, sweat, and looking like a soaked wash rag, Jade said to Des, "Soon we're going to need to take a bath and change these clothes." "I know Jade, but we need to be sure we're in a safe place, before removing our clothes." "Of course," she sighed.

"Des, Do you see this black nut?" She held it up to his eyes. "When I was about eight, Josephine's aunt from Pennsylvania came to visit. On her last day, she called me into her room. She gave me this nut. She declared she hated slavery. Her family did not believe in cruelty. She said Josephine's mother died of a broken heart from witnessing cruelty and was helpless to do anything about it. Her aunt told me if I ever got away, to go to Cincinnati, Ohio to look for a Quaker family. They would help me to get to freedom. She said it was called the Underground Railroad. Have you ever heard of it, Des?" "No!" he replied, but I do believe the Lord made us to be free, so let's head to freedom." They both climbed out of the boat. Standing in the shallow water, they washed the dirt and sweat off their bodies. The sun would be coming up soon. It would be time to discuss what their next move would be. Always thinking of freedom.

*For this present moment
is shared by all living creatures,
but the time that has pasted is gone forever,
No one can lose the past or the future.
For if they don't belong to you,
How can they be taken from you?
Marcus Aurelius Meditations*

St. Nicholas Hotel. Second Day of Honeymoon

New York City, New York

For that moment, Chad is totally at a loss for words. Maud has surprised him by her shy but enthusiastic receptivity to learn about their physical bodies. He reaches for the hand mirror on the chest by the bed. He asked, "Maud, would you please look into the mirror and tell me what you see." "My neck, chin, and nose," she answered with a puzzled face. He then took hold of her hand and placed it on her neck, then he guided her fingers to touch her neck, then said. "Pretend your fingers are feathers lightly touching your neck, your throat, now tell me what you are feeling." "Hmmm, I feel softness, a tingling in my insides, almost like the strings of a violin as it approaches a crescendo, then rests."

"That's wonderful!" He then guided her fingers across her breasts, all the time encouraging her to gently massage, squeeze, and gently pinch and pull her nipples, while all the time viewing that part of her body in the mirror. "Notice, my love, the changes in the way your breast look and feel with every touch. Share with me, if you will, what you are thinking and feeling?" She is silent for just a bit. "I'm thinking, I'm feeling a little embarrassed about," "Sweetheart, it's your body and you have never known it, nor have you ever enjoyed it." "Chad, I honestly enjoy how this makes me feel." "And that is how you should feel. If I may, allow me to guide your hand across your beautiful tummy. Notice how it looks, feel it's elasticity. Your tummy has the ability to expand and nest a baby as it grows for nine months; truly a miracle of God." Her eyes become dilated, breath quickens as he lays her hand on her pubic bone. He turns loose, as she began to explore, when suddenly! She is startled by what she is seeing! He then encourages her to view that part of her body that has been hidden from her, all of her life.

"Sweetheart, what we don't know, makes us prime to be hurt, but what we know about ourselves, becomes a strength and a choice. You and I are a married couple, blessed by our Divine Mother/Father God with the divine potential to fully engage with each other, mentally, physically, and spiritually. However, this joyful spiritual oneness can only happen if we are willing to share and be open with each other. It takes trust and faith, both in each other and ourselves to move forward. Maud, am I being understood?" "Maud pulls him forward, kissing him on his cheek, neck, and mouth, then whispers, "Chad my love, I am beginning to realize how much I truly love, trust, and adore you. Please may I have the honor to inspect your body?" With a sweet kiss on her tummy, he stood up by the side of the bed, salutes her saying, "Mistress Somerset, I am now ready for inspection. Where do you want to begin? "

Dropping her head down, giggling, but still rather nervous, she responded rather strongly, "Chad, please sit down on the bed! You are so large of a man, you kinda frighten me." Grabbing his robe, he calmly sat next to her, then gently spoke, "But of course, my love, I'm six foot, two inches tall; if your lying down and I'm standing, I must appear a giant exposing himself inappropriately. I'm so sorry, please forgive me." "There's nothing to forgive. I was just a little overcome by you showing me things I've never seen. I love the way you tease, the gentleness of your heart and how patient you are inviting me to explore new things I've known very little about. "

Reaching out to hold her close to his chest, he felt her fingers slowly massaging his back, then she raised one of his arms up and said, "My you're hairy. My father does not have much hair on his chest I've seen him at the dock, sometimes shirtless."

"We Somerset's have a great amount of hair on our bodies. Sorry to say, even in our ears and nose. I have to cut them regularly. It's part of my regular shaving ritual." She continued to explore his chest to discover his nipples also harden. "Does my touching your nipples make you feel kinda excited?" "It sure does! Do you get excited when touching them?" "Yes, my stomach does flip flops just looking, smelling, or touching you." As she continued to explore his stomach, she is fascinated at how the hair from his navel goes directly down to his male part. She asked, "Does this also excite you? Because I'm feeling goose bumps all over my body, excited to touch your penis, may I?" "Oh, please do, it is pure pleasure, not pain." Curiosity was getting the best of Maud as she held his penis, noticing it got larger in her hand, "Does it hurt when it grows? I've seen rams at breeding time, and I've wondered will it hurt me when we mate?" "It could, possibly the first time. It is my job to prepare you, to take my time, and if at anytime you want me to stop, I promise to do so." Maud grabbed his neck, pulled him close to her body, beginning to kiss his face, lips, neck; accepting an invitation to begin foreplay. Fondling her breasts, navel, pubic bone, vagina; an hour later, Maud was purring like a kitten laying in the arms of her beloved. Smiling with gratitude, Chad thought. "Thank you, Holy Mother for all your blessings."

Chad awakened before Maud. His eyes once again, charmed by her beautiful body laying snug under the feather coverlet. He thought about his many blessings. His father's insistence he listen and learn the nature of what a true marriage can be. He was grateful for his devoted mother who always impressed on him to follow his heart in making major decisions in his life. And how blessed to learn from top quality medical and surgical instructors at Harvard, who always insisted on cleanliness before medical examinations and surgical procedures, and the need to continue to study, observe and be open to new ideas and procedures in the field of physical and mental healing. He knew the physicians sacred oath by heart. Chad was dedicated to heal while trying not to harm the patient and to always treat humanity with dignity and respect. Lastly, to be willing to share a part of his abundance with those in need.

"Mrs Somerset," kissing her, "This is the real thing. Time to get dressed to see what the City has to show us. We can return to more of what we enjoyed, when we return."

And so began a week long honeymoon of museums, theatre, gourmet restaurants, meeting people of every color and nationality, and a lovely park groomed with beautiful flowers and trees. Everything excited Maud with genuine interest. As they were walking down a fashionable street, they were shocked to see a gentleman step behind a tree to relieve himself. They noticed a trough that ran along the street filled with human and horse waste. Maud surprised, "Why doesn't the city build a system to take care of human waste like St. Nicholas Hotel?" Chad responded with great anger and passion in his voice, "Because the citizens must be willing to put up money to build such a system. Unfortunately, most people, especially the politicians and wealthy care more about feeding their own pocketbooks than making a safe environment for their citizens. It was in that moment that Maud was introduced to a part of Chad she'd never experienced. A part she loved and respected. His deep passion for doing the right thing.

Chad raised his arm to hail a cab to take them back to the hotel. He asked, "Tomorrow is our last day in New York. What would you like to do before we leave this city of innovation and prosperity?" She smiled and without hesitation, "I think, if no one is playing the piano on the second floor, I'd love to try playing it. I've only played a piano a few times; always a harpsichord. What do you think? \" "Why not? We're paying guests. I think it would be great fun! Do you need \any music? "No, I'll play what I know by heart. Oh, Chad, this will be certainly another dream to come true! To play a fine grand piano, can you image?"

The taxi arrived right in front of the main entrance. The sun was shining brightly as the couple exited to enter the lobby. Chad went right to the main office. He asked to see the manager. He was escorted to an office behind the main desk. The manger stood up to welcome him, then asked, "Sir, is your stay here satisfactory?" "Oh yes! Very satisfactory. My wife and I were wondering if there is a possibility that she might be able to play the piano on the second floor? She is an accomplished pianist and would enjoy playing a few classical pieces, if it is not being used?" "Of course, Dr. Somerset, I believe this can be arranged. Let me check the schedule. I'll get back with you before dinner. Now if you'll excuse me, I must get to this right away." He rises to shake hands, then escorts Chad to the door. Chad checked his pocket watch for the time. It once belonged to his grandfather, who passed it on to his father when he graduated from Oxford, and then when Chad graduated from Harvard, he received the precious gift.

On his way to find his wife, he wondered if the manager was seriously trying to find a spot for Maud to play the piano? He found her in the gift shop purchasing gifts for her family. He was surprised to see the manager speaking to her with great enthusiasm. As he approached, she turned to him, excited to share that she was scheduled to play the piano at four p.m. Chad nodded to the manager, in obvious appreciation.

"Chad, can you believe it? I can play for half an hour. We must go to our room so that I can plan the music I'd like to play from memory." She took his arm to hurry him on, forgetting the packages being wrapped. Breathlessly she suddenly stopped, then pulled him back to the main arcade. "I almost forgot, the gifts that are being wrapped. We must return to pick them up." "Of course, while we're there, I must make dinner reservations for our last night in the main dining room."

Refreshed, dressed in formal attire, Chad and Maud arrived promptly at 3:45 on the second floor where the hotel's ornately carved rosewood Acolion piano with pearl keys, stood majestically. Maud was shivering with both fear and excitement. As the manager approached, they noticed he was having about fifteen chairs set in a semi-circle around the piano. Stunned, she whispered to Chad, "Do you think they are expecting a concert? Oh my God, Chad! I'm not a concert pianist." "Well my darling, you are now. You will do great!" "Play as if they are your siblings, and make your final number an Irish Jig. That will wilt the starch out of their stiff shirts."

After the manager introduced Maud as a guest on her honeymoon, he invited the audience to listen attentively to the beautiful Mrs. Maud Somerset, the wife of Dr. Chadwick Nicholas Somerset III as she plays for your entertainment and enjoyment before dinner."

Smiling shyly, dressed in her beautiful purple velvet gown trimmed in Austrian lace, wearing her mother-in-law's pearl necklace and earrings, she was gracefuly escorted to the piano by Chad, then nervously said:

"Thank you for your patience as I attempt to play this magnificent piano. My full name is Mary Maud Murphy-Somerset. I am indeed the wife of Dr. Chadwick Nicholas Somerset III. I did not expect an audience, but I am pleased you are here to support me. I've not played for some months; however, I will do my best not to embarrass my husband or myself by butchering Mozart's Piano Concerto No. 26 in D major, the "Coronation Concerto:" composed for the coronation of Leopold II in Frankfort in 1790. I will also play just a few movements of Beethoven's

Fourth Movement, from the Ninth Symphony, "Ode to Joy" and finish with an Irish love song I often play for my siblings."

Chad assisted her to be seated as she arranged her gown, then to find the pedals of the great instrument. Taking a deep breath, she rubbed her hands together, closed her eyes, placed her fingers on the ivory keys, then began to play.

Mary Maud, as if transported to another world, is totally mesmerized by her artist's intended expression of royal pomp and circumstance. She allowed her fingers to interpret the beauty of Mozarts sacred music. When finished, she paused to allow her body and spirit to enter into Beethoven's "Ode to Joy," embracing with every cell in her body, the beauty and majesty of his masterpiece. She came alive with the soul of the music, her very essence intense with the crescendo of joy! When finished, her hands still on the keyboard, tears streaming down her cheeks, aware of the beautiful music she has just orchestrated. In that moment, Maud felt the pure solitude and connection of being present to The Presence. After a long pause of total silence, the room burst with great applause, then with shouts of "Bravo! Bravo!," the audience was brought to their feet, with great appreciation. But instead of taking a bow, she began to play her favorite Irish Love Song by poet Robert Moore, "The Last Rose of Summer." When finished, she graciously stood to take a long and deserving bow.

Chad proudly escorted his lovely bride through the admiring crowd's congratulations, then through the long hall to the elegant dining room After being seated at their table by the window, Chad took his lovely wife's hand and said, "Maud, I'm so proud for you. I say proud for you, because you did this performance for your own enjoyment and soul's well being. Not for anything or for anyone. I know how that feels. The day I did my first surgery, I knew I had made the right choice for my future vocation. And the day I married you, I knew we were meant to be together. Today, I witnessed your soul expressing Mary Maud's uniqueness. I promise you, I will always support how, what, where, and when you choose to share your gift and will be honored to do so."

They both looked up just as the waiter brought a bouquet of roses for Mary Maud, compliments of the St. Nicholas Hotel in appreciation for her generous sharing of her beautiful music.

The waiter approached their table, "May I leave you this menu? I'll be back in a few minutes to take your order." After seeing they had corned beef and cabbage on the menu, Chad ordered, "My wife and I, both would like to order your Corned Beef and Cabbage, It's so hard to find it back home." Chad looked at Maud as they both burst out in a fit of laughter. The waiter left not understanding what was so funny.

The next morning, the couple were packed and ready to leave when their taxi arrived to take them to the train station. They enjoyed their last breakfast which was both beautifully presented and nourishing. An egg dish, made with potatoes, sausage, and onions with blueberry toast, orange juice and coffee with sweet cream. Chad left a nice tip for the maids and bellboys. "Tonight, we will be home in Philadelphia. The train ride should be enjoyable, no rain in sight." "Well, Mrs. Somerset, are you ready for our next adventure?" "Yes, Dr. Somerset, as long as I'm with you."

Love gives naught but itself and takes naught but from itself,
Love possess not nor would it be possessed;
For love is sufficient unto love.
When you love you should not say,
"God is in my heart," but rather, "I am
in the heart of God."
And think not you can direct the course
of love, for love, if it finds you worthy,
directs your course.

To rest at the noon hour and meditate
love's ecstasy;
To return home at eventide with
gratitude;
And then to sleep with a prayer for the
beloved in your heart and a song of praise
upon your lips.
Love, from "The Prophet," by Kahil Gibran, pages 13 & 14

Three Days by Row Boat

Mississippi River

The struggle for freedom kept Desmond and Jade awake for fear of being captured, eaten by wild animals, or starving to death. They lost track of how many days they rowed, bailed water, and rationed out the food stuffs they carried.

Weary, exhausted and hungry as dark clouds of rain began to gather, Desmond told Jade they needed to find shelter before the cloud burst and flooded them. The boat was already damaged by a strong wind that pushed them into a floating tree trunk. Their only mode of transportation could possibly sink any minute in heavy rains. With darkness just a few hours away, they desperately needed to find an inland cove for shelter.

Alerted by a sound, they stopped rowing, became very still. Suddenly a covey of wild geese took to flight. Relieved they floated into a cove of tall reeds. Holding his finger to his lips, in warning, Des knew that duck hunters could be close by.

Just then, voices from about 30 feet away, "Butch, that thar is a coon scarin them birds. They be back tonight to watch nests, we'd best git along, best get up four in mornin to kill them birds, Dogs ken shoo them up and git 'em when ded."

Listening to the hunters making their way back to their truck, hearing the vehicle's engine start, Des felt certain the hunters had left. Desmond and Jade waded to shore to find shelter. The rain began to trickle down making it very difficult to unload the boat. Jade's trunk was heavy and became heavier as it rained. Inside the forest, they found a thick clump of trees, growing very close together with several tree stumps and broken limbs. The spot was far enough away from the shore that they believed the hunters would not see them.

Stacking the boat upside down on tree trunks and rocks, they began to store their precious items. Their clothes were filthy. Des had only two sets of clothes, his and Phillipi's, Jade had many dresses, hats, shoes, jackets, jewelry; but nothing suited for hiking and camping in the woods. There was no food left. Jade tucked the letter to the Bishop and money her father meant to go to him deep inside her under-garment. All of this, if caught, would be cause enough for them to be hung. It took hours to build a type of fort, hidden behind trees, raspberry vines and brush. Totally exhausted, soaking wet, and starved, they crawled into the shelter, huddled together and tried to get warm.

Desmond whispered softly to Jade, "We've got to get out of these clothes before we get sick. Do you have anything dry in your trunk 'cause the only thing I've got is Phillipi's vest. If you do, I'll do my best to protect your modesty." Shivering so hard her teeth chattered, Jade responded realistically, "Desmond, I don't see how we are going to get through this escape without sometime seeing one another without clothing. I'm just being practical, our bodies are cold, so let's get with it. We trust each other to look the other way." She found a cotton dress that was not wet and a vest. Taking turns stripping. Des, still feeling modest, left his trousers on. She told him to take them off, he could use the tail of a dress to wrap around him. Cuddled together, they soon stopped shaking. Jade said, "Maybe if we talk, we won't think about being hungry."

Des thought to himself, "It's not my belly that is hungry, please help me to not do anything I might regret." Jade interrupted the silence by asking,

"Des, what do you know about your mother?" Clearing his throat, in an attempt to clean up his thoughts, he gasps, "Unlike most slaves, I was permitted to have a relationship with Rochelle. She was very tall with a long elegant neck and jet black hair. She was dearly loved by Master Jean Michel. He called her his Ebony Queen and even built her a cabin at the edge of the woods. Phillipi and me were allowed to visit with her to listen to her stories and learn her chants. He furnished her little home with tapestries, elegant fabrics, and beeswax candles. Often, he chose to stay with her instead of in the big mansion. When his wife began to show signs of being insane, threatening to shoot his prize horses and servants, he hired a white nurse to stay with Marion at all times. She died about six months ago of lung disease. My mother said she had herbs that would help calm her, but the doctor told Jean Michel that Voodoo stuff was nonsense. The doctor continued to let blood from her. Rochelle told Jean Michel that blood letting was what killed her, that white folk know nothing about healing." "On the evening of his mother's death, Phillipi surprised me by wanting to play chess, instead of going upstairs to say goodbye as she was on her way to heaven. That evening when I had a few moments with Master Jean, I offered my condolences. He looked into my eyes. laid his hand on my shoulder, paused for a few moments, then surprised me by saying, "Son, she was a troubled woman, she is out of her misery." "Jade, when he called me Son, I believed in my heart, he really meant it!" "I can't help wondering if he really believed Phillipi's cock and bull story about us?" "I've been wondering to myself, if mine and your father be so dumb, or ignorant to not see Phillipi's evil, or do they just not care? Anyway, I'm not going back to Mississippi, I'd rather die first." "So, what do you remember about your slave mother?"

"My mother was a kitchen slave. named Missy. She was only about fifteen when she had me and my twin baby brother, that died. I rarely got to see her, because Miss Josephine, adopted me to be her very own "baby doll." She made my clothes, hauled me around in her doll buggy and dared anyone to stop her. The Master began to notice me when I was about four. Along with Josephine, he became my great champion. He allowed me to go to chapel, study with her from the professor, learn to play piano and the fine art of painting. Josephine, insisted that I occupy her bedroom. We had twin beds. Although much older than me, she treated me like a peer, allowing me to pretend along with her, a future I could never believe possible. When she married, she made Master promise to protect me from harm and to free me when I turned eighteen. I knew he was my father. Although I have green eyes and he has hazel, we both have a "v" in the middle or our forehead, and a birthmark on the back of our neck shaped like a star. I saw his birthmark after fencing practice wearing no shirt. My tall stature also came from him. Like your father, his brother, they are both over six foot tall." "I can tell you this Desmond, Phillipi is in for a heap of trouble if the Master ever finds out he tried to rape me."

"Except" said Des, "Phillipi will make up a story that will have me, the devil trying to steal and rape you and that I overcame him, left him humiliated in only his drawers. No, I'm sorry Jade, but your father will never know the truth!" She gasped changing the subject, she asked, "Des, did your mother ever call you by another name?"

"Yes, she called me, "Jeb" she said came from some African King, I can't remember his name. I think I'd like for you to call me Jeb from now on. Do you remember being called by any other name?" "That's just perfect! No, I was just a week old when I left her arms to be Josephine's baby doll. I always felt loved. I was about six when an old slave told me that my mother was named Missy, and that she died a few years earlier. Since we're beginning a new life, I'd like for you to call me Bess. Josephine's aunt that gave me the black nut was named Bess. She said her real name was Betsy, but was always called Bess.. What do you think?" "I like it! From now on we're Jeb and Bess, but what's gonna be our last name? Certainly not Beaumont!"

"I guess we've got to think on it, but right now I"m too tired to think? Goodnight Bess."

The next morning, they awakened to birds chirping, dogs barking, and voices eager to shoot some ducks. They laid perfectly still, praying that the rain washed away any of their scent. It wasn't long before they could hear no more chatter. Carefully, they crept out of the shelter to take care of their morning business in the deep forest so that their personal scent could not be detected by the hunting dogs. About two hours later, they heard the hunters leave the reeds carrying several ducks as their hounds barked excitedly over recovering the birds. One hunter remarked that after he had a big breakfast of ham and eggs, he needed to go into Memphis and do some trading for salt and flour. Jeb and Bess smiled to learn they were close to Memphis, Tennessee, a town they heard about. They believed they could mingle with the towns people, in order to get provisions. It was in that moment, Bess surprised Desmond by asking him, "Des, are you attracted to me?" "Well, of course any man would be, your beautiful!" She interrupted him, "I asked are you attracted to me?" He turned his head and looked at her, "Yes, I am, completely enamored by your sweetness, are you attracted to me?" She kept eyes on him, glowing and radiating like dancing jewels. "I'm surprised and grateful for your kindness in protecting me and for never trying to molest me. I've observed your compassion in everything you say and do. I love that you are a religious person who believes in the Sacraments as taught by Our Lord Jesus Christ. I've decided, if it's something you'd want, I'd like to marry you. We can find a priest. I heard Memphis is a Catholic Town, and it would be risky, but I don't believe a priest would sell us to slave traders. What do you think?"

"My God, Bess, I don't know, I couldn't bear seeing you in chains if we were found out, I have been dreaming about freedom. Being a free man, married, living on a small farm, maybe teaching school," interrupting Desmond, "That is a dream I believe can come true. We can pass for white until we get up north, we both are very fair, speak perfect English."

"Listen to me Jeb, I'm sure I want to marry you, be your wife, and if we get captured, strung up to a tree, then nothing or no one can ever take away from us, the freedom, being married, feeling that love, if only it is for a short time. I've been starved for love, and I believe you have too." Taking Bess into his arms, holding her tightly, as if they were molded together,"I love you Bess, now and forever." "That's all I need to know," She kissed him with such loving passion that made Jeb pull away. "Whoooo, you're not my wife, so I need to be careful Mistress Bess, but when you are, Lordy have mercy"

I dreamed of freedom
not looking behind my back
Expressing, neither fear nor lack.
-Jeb, aka Desmond Lafayette-

Home of Uncle Ben Sterling

Hopkinsville, Kentucky

Saturday morning, day of the Hopkinsville Presbyterian church social and market. The Sterling girls, Jenny and Beth are up, dressed, packing their individual baskets to be auctioned at the church gathering. Their lunch baskets are identical, except Jenny's cookies are sugar cookies and Beth had made some apricot jam bars. Jenny's basket has a big blue ribbon tied around the top and Beth's a yellow ribbon encircling a few wild Daisy's. They spent the whole Friday in the kitchen frying chicken, baking biscuits, cutting onions and boiling hard boiled eggs for potato salad. In the cool root cellar, they found canned mustard pickles, cucumber pickles, and pickled okra to serve as condiments along with a crock full of apple cider to share

Giddy, whispering with excitement, both girls hope the boy who buys their baskets will be handsome, perfect gentlemen, and can converse about anything other their cow's milking time, and when they needed to bring in the hay. Uncle Ben asked Aunt Lizzie if she packed them a lunch? Hands on her hip, "Why Ben, I can't believe you'd think I'd forget to fix some vittles for my favorite preacher!" Winking at the girls, then asking BJ if he had money to bid for a basket for his lunch? Blushing, he reached into his pocket and pulled out a pouch full of money. "I've saved for month's so I could out bid anyone trying to buy Miss Kathaleen's basket." Red as a glowing fire, he ran out to hitch up the buggy.

Arriving at the church grounds, they saw booths with women selling quilts, canned goods, pumpkins, squash, popcorn, knitted scarves, caps, baby blankets, etc. Everyone was in a festive mood, certainly enjoying themselves. There was a dart board with a long line of men and boys eager to win some prizes. It was while standing in this line, that Jack Tom Jones noticed Miss Jenny Sterling. Disappointed that she was already walking with a girl that appeared to be a younger sister tat who he knew to be the daughter of the preacher of the church. Darn bad luck for a man who doesn't attend church, can't stand prissy gentlemen like behavior. He loves to gamble and drink hard liquor. They had none at this event, except the small flask he had hid in his shirt pocket under his black vest. Smiling and making sure Miss Jenny saw that he was admiring her, he stopped at booth selling flowers, and purchased Miss Jenny a bouquet of flowers. He strolled over to her, bowed, smiling and said, "May I present to a beautiful and charming young lady, a token of my respect and esteem?" as he handed her the flowers, he asked, "Are you auctioning off a basket today?" She nods smiling. "Then my lady, I shall out bid any man here today." and again, he bows, smiling confident and walked away.

Beth hugs Jenny who is afire with embarrassment, frozen, not knowing quite what to say or what to do. Finally she said quietly, "Come, I must use the privy before the auction begins."

Meanwhile, Uncle Ben had observed all that has just happened. As a father, he decided to speak with the sheriff as to what he knew about this gentleman. A mystery to be solved. Necessary due to Jenny visiting for another week before returning home to Cincinnati.

BJ ran into his sister on their way back from the privy. He asked who that guy they were talking to? "We weren't talking to him, he was talking to Jenny. He said he was going to buy her basket lunch. I guess we'll learn soon, if he does." "I sure don"t want him bidding on Miss Kathaleen's basket. I'm not sure I have enough money to out bid him."

Jenny walked towards the balcony of the church where the baskets were stored. The auctioneer was about to start the bidding. Rev. Sterling laid two blankets on the ground for his family. The ladies gathered beside Aunt Lizzie and the men were seated beside them on the other blanket.

The bidding began. The first basket belonged to Beth's school friend, Rachel Smith. The bid started with fifty cents, got up to a dollar and ten cents. A boy of about sixteen won the basket. He paid his money, then grinning like a possum at dinner time, he joined Sarah on her quilt. Finally BJ's excitement was satisfied when Miss Kathaleen's basket was held up. The auctioneer started the bid at fifty cents, then asked for sixty cents, when BJ stood up and bid three dollars. The auctioneer asked, "I have three dollars, who will bid three dollars and fifty cents?, going once, twice, sold to BJ Sterling for three dollars." BJ handed the three dollars to the auctioneer, then strutted like a cock rooster heading towards the hen house to take his prize. He joined Miss Kathaleen, who was smiling and rather relieved. He sat beside her on the quilt next to her parents.

The auctioneer picked up Beth's basket. Looking at her he smiled as he raised her basket high above his head. He began the bid at fifty cents, then when it got to three dollars he said, "Now gentlemen, I know from experience, Miss Beth Sterling can make a plate of fried chicken that would please a king. Now I have three dollars," before he could get out another word, Joseph Miller, nineteen year old son of the largest dairy farmer in the county bid four dollars. Men and boys were checking their pockets to see if they could out bid Joe. Then the auctioneer continued. "I've four dollars, once, twice, sold to Joseph Miller." Joe proudly paraded over to the Sterling blankets, handed the money to the auctioneer and then politely sat down beside blushing Beth.

Finally, the auctioneer picked up Miss Jenny Sterlings's basket. Holding it high above his head, he introduced Miss Jenny to the anxious bidders. "This here basket was made by Miss Jenny Sterling from Cincinnati, Ohio. She is visiting Rev. Sterling's family for another week. I will start the bid at," Interrupted by a gentleman standing to the back of the crowd raising his hand with a bag of coins. '"I bid five dollars!" Jack shouted with confidence.

The crowd was silent, then began to chatter with one another. The auctioneer said, "I have five dollars, do I have a bid for five dollars and twenty-five cents?" Again, no one raised the bid. He then said, "Five dollars once, twice, sold to the gentleman in the back."

Jack's cockiness irritated the crowd. He gallantly strolled to the Sterling blankets. Miss Jenny never spoke a word as she moved closer to Beth so that he could sit next to her.

Jack very politely introduced himself. He said he owned a little farm about forty-five miles across into Tennessee. He was a blacksmith by trade and enjoyed buying and selling horses. When asked what brought him to Hopkinsville? He stated he was buying supplies and saw the church social advertised in the hardware store. Decided it would be an opportunity to meet some good Christian neighbors. He complemented Miss Jenny on her fried chicken. "Your potato salad is just like my mothers. And these sugar cookies, hmmm are the best I've ever tasted."

At the closing of the church social, Jacked asked Miss Jenny if he might be able to come courting? She explained as a guest of her Uncle Ben, courting would have to be done in his presence. He bowed to her and agreed that would be the proper arrangement.

Jack made arrangements to stay in Hopkinsville for Jenny's last week before returning to Cincinnati. Each day he showed up at Rev. Sterlings's home, always with a little gift for Miss Jenny and one for Aunt Lizzie.

He also attended Sunday church service and Wednesday evening prayer meeting. Jenny was so impressed with how pious he appeared and how he listened to every word Uncle Ben preached, then commented to both she and her Uncle how fitting his sermons were during this uneasy time in our Nation. On her last day, while sitting on the back porch swing, Jack asked Jenny to be his wife. Holding her hands, he said, "Miss Jenny, In these past days, I've come to honor you and believe I've fallen in love with you. I'd be so honored to have you be my wife, to love and cherish all the days of my life?" "Jack, you honor me with your proposal. But my father must decide when I marry and with whom. If you're serious, you will need to come to Cincinnati to ask my father for my hand in marriage. "But Jenny, are you not of age to decide for yourself?" "Of course, but after my mother died, my father and I consult each other about everything. He's a minister of a big church, in Cincinnati, I'm his hostess for all services and meetings. I would never marry without first consulting my father and getting his opinion. I'm sorry Jack, but that's the way we do things. If you choose to come to Cincinnati, please write me in care of Rev. Henderson Sterling, at the Presbyterian Church. He will give me your letter and then we can arrange a time for you to visit," pausing for a moment, "I know this may appear archaic to your way of thinking, but it's very Presbyterian." "It's late, I'm sorry, I must say good night, as my Uncle is escorting me early tomorrow to my home." They both stood up, as she used her key to open the door, Jack reached to hug and caress her. She turned her cheek to only allow a hug, As the door opened, she quickly closed it with a prayer, that the two slaves in the root cellar would not make a sound until they received the signal from Uncle Ben that it's time for them to move on."

*Sometimes, I feel lost, not here on land
but in my head, a paralysis created by fear,
a hopeless sensation of perceptive death.*
-Jenny Sterling-

SECTION II

A Call to Serve

The mind and the heart are in constant battle until
the heart recognizes that love is stronger than ego.

Somerset Medical Clinic

Dayton, Ohio

After their five day honeymoon trip in New York City, the couple arrive in Philadelphia to loving and supportive friends. Franklin Mitchell, Dr. Chad's handyman in Dayton, drove a big moving wagon, pulled by two huge draft horses, to haul Dr. Chad and Maud's possessions to their newly purchased home in the Lake Side Area of Dayton, Ohio. Frank had coordinated the medical clinic's remodel and final touches. He was proud to report everything was ready to go forward. All they needed was a doctor eager to serve the sick. They estimated the trip from Philadelphia to Dayton would take at least two weeks, more if bad weather set in. Dr. Chad and bride had reserved seats to travel by an overland coach and railroad, with an expected time to arrive in about eight days.

The couple were supported with goodwill wishes by receiving more gifts and acts of kindness. Maud's father built the couple a beautifully hand carved full size bed, extra length because of Chad's six foot two height. It was made from a hundred year old huge oak tree on his property. Her mother and sister, Patty made a feather tick bedding and a coverlet from the purple silk she purchased from a supplier in Paris, France many years ago.

Chad's father, commissioned Mr. Murphy to pack for moving, Chad's grandmother's piano, grandfather's violin, and his mother's tea cart she brought from London, as well as the rest of the household furnishings they intended to move with them. After everything was loaded into the moving wagon, the family gathered around Frank and Junior to wish them God Speed. Frank could be seen wiping his eyes as this type of emotion was foreign to him since he lost his wife.

Two days later, Dr. Chad and Maud caught a train to begin half of their journey. The final part of the trip would be by coach, driven by an Overland driver with a well trained team of horses.

Eight days later, the couple arrived at their new home with only the bags and trunks they carried with them. They immediately contacted Mother Superior to recommend a hotel. She insisted they stay at the convent until their furniture arrived. While at the convent, Dr. Chad could walk to the new Soldier's Home, A federal facility treating the sick and injured men of the Civil War. They were very pleased to make his acquaintance; especially since his services would be for gratis. He was happy to serve the facility by performing surgeries. Dr. Chad was impressed by Soldier's Home commitment to serve, but felt their sanitation procedures needed a big boost. As a Harvard graduate, a physician and teacher of medical practices, he felt a responsibility to share what he had learned as part of his sacred oath. Some doctors were very receptive, others not so much. But Dr. Chad being who he is, moved forward with gratitude and patience. Two weeks went by fast! Maud was so excited to begin the process of moving in to her new home. However, she insisted that Frank and Junior take a day off to rest and eat some home cooked food. Frank had purchased a little home in the neighborhood of the clinic. He awakened the next day with Mrs. Somerset standing at the door with baskets of home cooked food. He asked her in, but she thought they both needed a day to just relax and enjoy being at home.

Maud walked to the clinic to assist her husband in setting up his clinic with medicines, bandages, hanging herbs, and clean linens. But first, every piece of furniture must be cleaned with hot vinegar water before anything could be set inside of it or sat on it. Chad could hear how much she enjoyed being of service by the way she sang with all her heart, the Irish songs she loved and enjoyed.

Dr. Chad was setting up his accounting system. The book he was using had blank pages. He used his ruler to draw lines across the pages. At the top of the page he wrote.

Name   Address   Ailment   cash__gift__

Knowing that Mary Maud was excellent in organization and account-ing, he offered his book for her opinion and suggestions. "I think this is perfect for the time being. However, in the future, we may want to have a line for referrals. That could become very important." "You're right! That is an important factor. I'll hire the printer to make us a ledger for your accounting. Thank you, Sweetheart. " Kissing her on her head as he located the piece of wood he found in the backyard. With a small paint brush and black paint; Dr. Chad painted in Old English Lettering: **OPEN and TAKING NEW PATIENTS**

Pleased by all they had accomplished, he invited Maud to go with him to visit a patient Mother Superior heard about on the lower east side. "I'd like for you go with me to visit an ill child, then we could go to the hotel dining room for their Wednesday evening Prime Rib and Mashed potatoes, How does that sound?" "Wonderful! I'm starved, but I need to change into something clean first." "I could use a clean shirt while we are at it, but we do need to hurry."

Looking and feeling a little more clean, Dr. and Mrs Somerset arrived at the address Mother Superior had given them. Knocking on the door, a frail lady of about forty opened the door. Stunned, she said, "Sir, Iz dunt ave the rnt mune, my babee sik knt wrk." "Madam, I'm sorry you're not able to work, but I'm Dr. Somerset, Mother Superior told me about your sick child. If I may, I think I can help" "Doctor, I ant got munee to pay." "It's okay. I help folks that are sick, that's how I serve the Lord." She opened the door to the smell of beans cooking and a young girl of about twelve lying on the floor.

Dr. Chad bent down to touch her forehead to find she was burning up with fever. "How long has she been like this?" What's her name? How old is she?" "Ten das, she km frm feld sk az dg. I dnt no wht to do. Nazzii 12." Dr. Chad asked the woman to boil some fresh clean water. He directed Maud to get his box of herbs, some vinegar, and quinine out of the buggy. He felt if his suspicious held true, the young girl was suffering from Malaria, a tropical disease.

As Dr. Chad sponged the young body, he could see how thin and needed to be fed some wholesome food. He looked at her mother and asked where they came from? He detected fear in sharing, because of her heritage. "New Orleans, is that what you said?" She nodded, "Okay," he continued, "I have a medical clinic a few blocks from here. I want to take your daughter there so that my wife and I can help get her well." The woman started whaling. "Ma'am "If you like, you may come with us to help with your child." To that statement, she started smiling and gathering her stuff. Dr. Chad told her she could not use snuff, smoke anything, or drink liquor. Only water and tea that he would provide. We"ll need for you to get washed up so that you can help with Nazzii. Get a change of clothing for both of you." She frowned, "Aint got nun." "Alright, we'll find you something to wear. Help us to get Nazzi in the buggy." As soon as they were in the buggy, he gave the horses the signal to go. Hoping in his heart Nazzii did not have anything else that was contagious.

When they arrived at the clinic, Maud went into "medical nurse" mode. She put fresh sheets on the bed, hot water in the big galvanized tub with soaps, towels, and blankets ready to assist in the bathing. She was so grateful Frank had seen to every detail when given the job to "fix up" the place for a proper medical clinic.

Nazzii's hair was a matted mess! It took a lot of soap and vinegar to work all the tangles out. After Maud was finished, Dr. Chad gave Nazzii a cup of tea to help her relax and go to sleep. He added a little aloe and peppermint plus quinine to get rid of the malaria symptoms.

She drank the tea and ate saltine biscuits that Dr. Chad had shown Maud how to make a few days ago . They were good for stomach cramps. He explained that they digest easily and will add natural minerals to her diet.

When Nazzii was finished, she cuddled up to a pillow and fell asleep. Paula, her mother, started to undress to get into the tub. Maud instructed her that they needed to refill and clean the tub. After Dr. Chad carried out the water, one bucket at a time, Maud scrubbed the tub with more vinegar. They added more hot water. Anxious, Paula tried to get in before Mary Maud could check her hair and body for lice. "Poor soul probably has never had a hot bath." Maud scrubbed her back, hair; watching for lice eggs. She pointed to Dr. Chad, who grabbed more vinegar and lye soap. Maud went to work on her head, under her arms, pointed for her to use soap on her private area.

After her bath, Maud gave her a towel to dry with, then another to wrap her body in. .Dr. Chad took their clothing out to the burn barrel. Paula just stared, asking no questions. Maud directed her to the table to eat a bowl of vegetable soup, soda crackers and a cup of the same tea given to her daughter. She ate and drank every drop. She started to climb into bed with her daughter, but Dr Chad explained it was better for her to sleep on the cot, because her daughter was very ill and needed plenty of rest to heal. She laid down on the cot with a sheet and blanket and fell fast asleep.

The medical team quietly but quickly cleaned up their mess. Putting everything back into its place, they sat down to have a cup of coffee.

"Chad, I'm so happy to be here with you. You make me proud by the way you treat these poor suffering souls who have arrived on the Underground Railroad." Dr Chad shook his head, "With little Nazzii too sick to go on, her mother had to go into hiding That's why Mother Superior is involved. Malaria returns when the patient is run down. Poor nourishment and living in a hot and humid climate keeps it active. Maybe, if they make it to Canada, the symptoms will go away. We'll pray this is so. I appreciate you sweetheart, for your help, and always being by my side."

It was three days later when Mother Superior showed up at the clinic. Dr. Chad and Maud took turns sleeping while caring for Nazzii, and her mother. Mother Superior did not recognize the medical team she met about a week before. Instead of dreaming about their medical clinic's possibilities, they were living it with hard work, confidence and joy.

"Dr. Chad, how is the girl doing?" Her mother stood close to hear what was being said. "I think she is going to be alright. She's eating well and the symptoms have disappeared. We caught it just in time. Paula has improved by resting with good food. What have you in mind?" "Thursday at around midnight, the two can meet with a conductor to head north. I'd like to see that happen, they've been through so much, and deserve a chance to freedom." "I certainly agree. Prejudice is our country's worst disease."

Dressed layered in clean clothes and carrying two muslin bags, Paula and Nazzii, left with Mother Superior to meet a conductor going north on the Underground Railroad. The two hugged Dr. Chad and Maud who knew it was perceived unprofessional to hug clients, and especially those on the underground railroad. Both felt it was a needed bit of kindness and compassion to wish them well on their journey north. They delighted in serving and were grateful to do so.

My Soul Called, I asked "Why Me?"
It answered, "Because you can."
-Dr Chadwick Somerset-

St. Agnus Convent and School

Outside of Memphis, Tennessee

Bess carried her parasol with Jeb beside her as they left the forest. She greeted folks smiling as Jeb tipped his hat with a nod. Everything was going very smoothly until two women wearing an unfamiliar costume, a long black robe with a big white and black head dress. They were covered from top to toe, nothing showed but their faces and hands. A large crucifix hung on a chain from their waist. People walking by addressed them as "Sister." Bess surprised Jeb by approaching them asking, "Sister, excuse me, but do you know where we can find a priest?" Puzzled, the sisters looked at each other, and then to the couple. Sister Louisa asked, "Child, why do you ask?" "We'd like to be married. If you know of a priest, we'd be very grateful." "I certainly admire your use of the English language. Where did you learn to speak it so perfectly?" Before the couple could come up with an answer, "Please follow us. We must take you to the convent to meet with Mother Superior. By the surprised look on both of your faces, I believe you have never seen a Catholic Nun before, and you both are Catholic, am I correct?" The couple shook their heads affirmatively. Confused, wanting to run, but also, wanting to stay.

"We are teachers at St. Agnes Convent and School. If my hunch is correct, we need to protect you from the citizen on the streets of Memphis, who might try to harm you. Please trust us, we are all children of God."

Half paralyzed by both fear and relief, Jeb and Bess followed the nuns as they unlocked the gate entrance to their convent. They entered into a lovely garden surrounded by young fruit trees. Sister Louisa asked them to take a seat by the door to the convent, until she returned with Mother Superior.

While waiting, Jeb felt very anxious, "Bessie, I feel the need to pray, would you join me?" They both kneeled, head bowed, as they began to pray by offering the sign of the cross, chanting the rosary, in quiet solitude, they felt the hand of Mother Superior as she said, "Amen." "Now my children, please follow me. I believe a cup of hot tea and a plate of bread and cheese sounds pretty good, what do you think?"

They followed her into a parlor, sparsely furnished with a divan, table, lamp, and chair. Mother Superior sat dowb in her chair and invited the couple to sit on the divan. Sister Louisa brought in a tray with cups, pot of tea, and some short bread and cheese. She served first Mother Superior, then Jeb and Bess. Sister Louisa was then dismissed. Mother Superior went right to the point. She asked if it was correct they wanted to be married? Both nodding. She asked, "Where did you receive your baptism?" Bess stated she was baptized at a mission in Merci, Mississippi. She handed her a certificate verifying her baptism. Mother noticed immediately that the name on the certificate was Jade Nicole Beaumont. "But you call yourself Bess, which is correct?"

Bess started to weep, fell to her knees in front of Mother Superior, telling her story. Jeb reached to comfort her, but Mother Superior asked him to please let her share her story, when finish, he could tell his. He sat back down as Bess shared everything; how Phillipi tried to rape her, Jeb saved her. She told how they ran away and was rowing for days on the Mississippi until the little boat started to leak. Then came ashore to find shelter, building a little camp in the woods, so that they wouldn't be spotted. Suddenly she exclaimed enthusiastically! "Mother, during the whole trip Jeb was a perfect gentleman. When I realized I loved him, it was me who initiated the possibility of getting married. She explained that they decided to risk everything to be married properly. They had heard Memphis had a Catholic Church, and wanted to be married in a church by a priest? Bess paused, wiped a tear from her eye then said, "Mother, We know the risk of being caught, but we'd rather be married for a day, then die never to have been married in the eyes of God."

"I see," then prioress asked Jeb to tell his story. He shared that he was the half brother of the Master's son, Phillipi, just months apart. "I grew up as his personal property, permitted, to dress as he did, learn to ride, hunt, shoot, and was educated by the same professor that Bess and Josephine learned from. I loved classes taught by the priest who came to the plantation. Phillipi made fun of me because I liked to read the Bible, hear stories about Paul, Daniel, and Jesus. It was when Phillipi showed disrespect to Bess, I knew something bad was going to happen. I asked God to help me protect Bess and God answered my prayer It has been on our run away trip that I came to love and respect Bess. She shows kindness to everyone, her deep religious beliefs, and because we understand each other." He exclaimed, "Rev. Mother, It's also my dream to marry Bess and head north by the Underground Railroad . I know if we are ever found and sold back to the Beaumont's, we will be strung up as animals. Phillipi has an evil heart. Also, both Bess and me speak and write two languages, do you think that is a blessing or a curse?"

Astounded by their confessions, Mother Superior took a deep breath "My children, you both are very courageous. This is the deep South, and yes, many will string you up in a heart beat. St. Agnus Convent, Congregation of Dominican Sisters all have taken an oath to dedicate our lives to our Lord. Remembering this, we all take great risks, knowing that the

Lord will help us solve our challenges. It is our responsibility, as a teaching society, to prepare you two to be proper Catholics. In doing so, we will need to locate a priest to perform the Sacrament of Holy Matrimony." Pondering for a moment, "And of course, we will need to assist you in finding your way to freedom."

"Do you know where your possession are hid?" Bess responded, "Yes, Mother Superior, I know exactly where they are hidden." "Jeb, I'm afraid it is too risky to take you with us. A gentleman alone with nuns

could cause some questions. I will disguise Bess as a novitiate, in order to help find your personal items. The two of you will be required to stay a full year here in order to meet the qualifications to receive the Holy Sacraments. Is this agreeable with you?" Both nodded affirmatively their desire to follow the nun's sacred plan.

"Fine, Bess you will be assigned to the kitchen with a space in the corner to sleep and study. Jeb you will sleep in the barn where your job is to tend to a team of horses, cultivate the garden, plus barn work as directed." "Your daily lessons will be taught by Sister Louisa in the kitchen after your chores are done. You must understand this rule: AT NO TIME CAN YOU LEAVE the convent for any reason. It is far too dangerous. Not all Catholics in Memphis accept Negro blood belonging in society as our great Constitution requires. Do you agree to these terms?" "Yes, I do," said Jeb, "So do I," replied Bess. "Mother, What's a Constitution?" "That will be a lesson for another time." As students of St. Agnes Convent and School you are about to receive an education more diverse than you learned cloistered in the walls of a Southern Plantation. It's almost time for vespers. All sisters join together for prayers Their singing is very contemplative and worthwhile to enhance our daily life. Sister Louisa will show you where to wash up, use the outhouse, and to prepare for dinner. I must advise you, the rules of the convent begin this very moment. God Bless You and

Welcome My Children to St. Agnes." The Prioress left the room with head held high, a quick step, and a prayer on her lips.

We sought, We found
With deepest gratitude,, Holy Mother
-Bess, aka Jade Nichole-
A Course In Miracles
Lesson 264
Father,
You stand before me and behind, beside me,
in the place I see myself,
and everywhere I go.
You are in all the things I look upon,
the sounds I hear,
and every hand
that reaches for my own.
In You time disappears,
and place becomes a
meaningless belief,
For what surrounds Your Son
and keeps him safe is Love itself.

Presbyterian Church. Jenny returns to Cincinnati

Cincinnati, Ohio

Uncle Ben loaded his wagon with Jenny's baggage and a lunch for the trip to her home in Cincinnati. The sun was hidden behind dark clouds promising to rain before the day was over. Uncle Ben broke the silence by asking, "I was awake when you and Jack arrived home. Is everything alright?" "Oh yes, Uncle Ben, he asked me to marry him. I told him it was late, we were leaving the next day, and that he would need to come to Cincinnati to ask for my hand in marriage. I'm so excited!"

"You've known him for such a short time, I hope things workout for you." A loud thunder clap interrupted their conversation as they sought shelter by their heavy coats and large hats. It began as a slow drizzle, then in about an hour rain poured down in buckets, drenching both, making them miserable.

Jenny began to weep as she thought about the poor slaves that left that morning. "They must be drenched and starving,". Uncle Ben reached to touch her shoulder, "Now Jenny, things are going to be alright." "But Uncle Ben, I fear for those poor souls, no family, no love, always running away from being lynched, I can't bear it, my heart hurts." It was then he realized, she was upset about the slaves that left that morning and not the possibility of being married. He thought to himself, "She's so trusting! I just don't feel good about that man! God help her!"

Up ahead, Jenny spotted a tumble down shack just off the side of the road. Uncle Ben pulled the wagon over to the side. He helped her down. Both looking for a place to relieve themselves, eat, and feed the horses. She grabbed the lunch basket, unpacked fried chicken and apple pie. The horses ne "How far to the river?" Trying desperately to start a little fire. "About another two hours if the rain don't let up. Less, if it does."

Jenny was confident her father would be at the dock to pick them up. She just could hardly wait to tell him her good news! Her mind wondered to her cedar chest filled with her mother's dishes, silver, and linens. Also, her mother's beautiful lace wedding gown. How she wished her mother could be here to give her womanly advise. After delivering Jennifer Pricilla Sterling, her mother died two days later.

Drenched, hands and feet freezing, Uncle Ben and Jenny were happy to see Rev. Sterling standing on the dock standing under an umbrella. Jenny yelled, "Father, it's so good to see you! I can't wait to hug you. You look as wet as we are!"

The barge hauling the horses and wagon pulled up very close to the dock. Rev. Sterling pitched a rope ladder for them to climb up. Yelling, "Be careful, don't move until you get your balance." Following Jenny was Uncle Ben. When they reached the top, Rev. Stirling handed each a blanket, and directed them to take refuge in the buggy while waiting.

The dock workers tied the wagon, securing it to be lifted up to the dock. Everything was soaking wet, but safe and shouls dry out. Rev. Sterling and Jenny would ride in the buggy while Uncle Ben would drive the wagon filled with their luggage.

The rain stopped as they drove through the streets to the church. Rev. Sterling had a nice fire burning, some hot soup on the stove, a warm bath and feather beds to sleep in tonight. After arriving, Rev. Sterling unhitched the horses while Uncle Ben unloaded the baggage. Jenny was already upstairs tending to her bath. When finished, she came down singing a little ditty she learned as a child. Jenny was wearing an old cotton night gown and slippers she found in her dresser drawer.

"Uncle Ben, it's your turn now. I laid out some fresh towels for you in the bathroom. I'll help father with setting the table and dipping that wonderful soup. Oh my goodness, someone made an apple pie! I'll bet I know who! Mrs Vickers, right Father?" "You guessed correctly, my sweet girl," As he hugged her tightly. "I sure missed my morning sunshine, did you miss me?" "Yes! yes! but Uncle Ben is a wonderful substitute! Beth and I had a great time together." She is such fun!"

Uncle Ben came down the stairs declaring, "That soup smells mighty good and I'm as hungry as a bear caught in a trap." Everyone took a seat at the breakfast table, said a prayer of thanksgiving, and began to devour the feast. Rev. Sterling had popped the pie in the oven to warm, making it a treat from heaven.

After Jenny cleared the table, did the dishes and put things away, she announced she was going to her room to write in her journaland crawl into that warm inviting bed. Both men wished her a good night sleep. She declared, "Tomorrow is another glorious day."

The Sterling brothers, gathered their cup of coffee and adjourned to the parlor. After some small talk about their trip, Ben said to his brother, "I'm sorry to be telling you before Jenny is able to, but Jenny believes she is in love." "Oh, with whom?" "That fella that bought her basket at the Church Social. He has asked her to marry him. She's invited him to come to Cincinnati to ask you for her hand in marriage. And, Henderson, I'm sorry to say this, but I don't feel good about him. Something just isn't right."

"Maybe being here and he there, the attraction will wear off for both. She's terribly young to be living down in the Tennessee woods, especially with this war hanging on. Would you join me in praying for guidance and acceptance of God's will. This is not how I imagined my sweet Jenny being married and living so far away." The two brothers, closed their eyes, sat quietly in contemplation, Rev. Sterling began: "Eternal Father, our Lord Jesus Christ, who knows before asking the fear I feel for my precious Jenny. I've tried to rear her to be a confident, loving, and compassionate young woman. As you know, she radiates all those qualities, grant me strength and patience to say and do your will, to trust Jenny in making wise decisions as she goes forward in her life. Help my brother and I, as we do your will in stopping slavery, saving those we can, and to protect our children as best we can. With deep gratitude, I humbly pray in the name of Jesus, our Lord and Savior, Amen."

"Henderson, we've asked believing, now let us allow God to do His Good Works, Goodnight Brother, I love you and Jenny very much. See you in the morning. I must leave for home right after breakfast." He turned and walked up the stairs. Rev. Sterling gathered the cups and put them on the cabinet. Checked on the dog laying on the porch stoop, then climbed the stairs for a goodnight's sleep.

Jenny came down stairs before the men. Looking at the clock she couldn't believe it was only 5:30. She smiled to herself, "If I'm going to be a married woman, I will need to get used to being up early to feed my hungry, working husband." She took the biscuits out of the oven, turned the sizzling bacon, and pulled the coffee pot to the side of the burner so that it could perk more slowly making a good pot of coffee.

Uncle Ben arrived first, then her father. They devoured their breakfast with graditude. Uncle Ben gathered his things. Jenny and her father walked him to his wagon. Jenny hugged him. "Uncle Ben, thank you for a wonderful time and for bringing me home." Her father hugged his brother, then shook his hand, and wished him God Speed. "Jenny, turned to her father and said, I can't wait to tell you my good news!"

Once in the house, she gave her father another cup of coffee and asked him to sit down so she could share. "Father, I'm in love. You met Jack at the Church Social. He's asked me to marry him and I told him he'd have to come to Cincinnati to ask you for my hand in marriage." "Slow down, please, isn't this a little premature since you've only known him less than a month?" Jenny is shocked that her father couldn't see immediately how much she loved him and how perfect he was for her.

"Tell me Jenny, what do you know of this Jack?" "First of all his full name is Jack Tom Jones, he owns a little farm in Tennessee, just on the other side of the Kentucky Line. He has two brothers, his mother died when he was ten. He is a blacksmith by trade, buys and sells horses and livestock, is a Christian, and completed school in Somerset, Kentucky. His dream is to marry an honorable woman who will be a great parent to his children. He feels strongly that I am that woman, and I believe I am."

"I see. When does he plan to make that trip to Cincinnati?" "In about a month to six weeks as he's got some harvesting to get done first. He said he'd write me as soon as he knew when he was coming."

"Do you know his age and if he's for Lincoln and against slavery?" "Yes, that's the first question I asked him. He said he's 24, admires President Lincoln, and thinks slavery is the most evil thing he's ever seen. And Father, I have never, nor will I ever tell him or anyone about our dedication as abolitionists, working on the Underground Railroad. It's a sacred trust never to be shared." "Thank you Jenny. Just one slip of the tongue could cause the deaths of hundreds of dedicated souls to the true teachings of our Lord Jesus Christ." Holding her hand over her heart, taking a deep breath, Jenny asked, "Father, what are your plans for the day?" "I have some work to finish at the church, and I thought I go into town to buy some stamps. I've been writing to a gentleman in Scotland, an elder in the Church of Scotland (Presbyterian) who desires to immigrate to America and dedicate his service to a church in need of his service. I'm not getting any younger, so I thought he might be a good person to have on board."

"Could I come along? I feel I will need to make some alterations to Mother's wedding gown. I'd love to be married in it! It's a way to feel her presence on my very special day. Maybe later today, you can tell me about how you met, fell in love, married, where you lived; those intimate things you've never shared with me growing up. Okay?" "Yes, I believe now is the time to share our great love story with our only child."

Father and daughter visited every store in Cincinnati. Jenny purchased two rolls of fabric. One was red checked and the other was an off white muslin cotton. She also purchased some white lace, ribbon, and satin covered tiny buttons to be used on her mother's wedding dress. She wanted to keep her mother's design, but she also wanted it to have some of her own personal and unique style..

For the next three weeks, Jenny was busy sewing, redoing her hats, polishing her shoes, and embroidering tea towels, pillow cases, and table cloths. She labored at washing them after years of not being used. She washed them in boiling soda water, starch and ironed them with a hot iron to absolute perfection. Everything was folded neatly, put into the cedar chest for her new home with her husband. Each day she went to the church to see if any mail had arrived. Nothing, she tried not to worry, but still she felt maybe Jack had changed his mind. She feared being jilted and becoming an old maid at nineteen.

On the fourth week, she received a letter from Jack which read.

Dear Miss Jenny,

I will arrive on Nov. 21 or earlier. I will be driving a wagon, I can find the church. Have everything ready as we leave right after wedding love, Jack

Jenny was so elated, she ran to tell her father Jack's plans. She asked him what all she needed to do to prepare for the wedding? "The church ladies will prepare a bridal shower for you. We will need to

plan the food to be served, the cake and ask the Ladies Society to help prepare the event. How I wish your mother was here. but of course, she is." Lowering his head, feeling terribly lost with the thought of his daughter leaving." Jack has not shown the courtesy to ask for her hand, and is still taking charge to have it his way. I'm so afraid Ben is right, what am I to do?"

Jack arrived on the afternoon of the November 21st, dirty and smelling of alcohol and sweat. Jack tried to cover it up with a cheap cologne. Jenny was caught off guard! Trying to convince herself that he was just worn out and hungry, she showed him where he could take a bath and a nap. She wanted him to be fresh and clean when her Father arrived home. She asked him. to put his clothes on the outside of the bathroom so she could get them washed and dried.

As her father stepped into the kitchen, he asked if that team of mules belonged to Jack? She responded, "Yes, he took a bath and is now napping before dinner, why?" "That team needs to be unharnessed, fed, and brushed, that's why? Does he think we have a livery?" Surprised by her father's anger, Jenny said nothing in reply. At that moment, Jack arrived into the kitchen, greeting she and her father, then remarked, "I'm so sorry, I must get the team unharnessed, watered, and fed. Forgive me, but I was so tired." As he hurried out the door to the team.

Rev. Sterling left the kitchen to go upstairs to find a book he had misplaced. He walked into the bathing room to find it cluttered with wet towels, wash cloths, and a bar of soap on the floor. He called Jenny up stairs. "Jenny, I'd like for you to look into the bathroom!" With a face filled with both sadness and fear, he left her to ponder a life with Jack Jones.

The wedding was held on November 23rd, just before the Community Harvest Festival. Jenny wanted to stay to attend it, since this might be her last chance to enjoy their beloved community. However, Jack stated they had to get back to Tennessee before snow began to fall. He said they'd already had two blizzards this fall. After the reception, they loaded up with the left over food, said goodbyes to the congregation. As she was hugging her father, he whispered, "I gave you stamps to write weekly, and if you ever need anything, please let me know." He wiped the tears from his cheek, kissed her on her cheek, while noting Jack never once asked for Jenny's hand. He knew it didn't matter, she was determined to marry Jack. He waved goodby to the couple, then turned to return to their home; to be alone with his fear and emotions.

After crossing the Ohio River, the couple started towards their destination. But as soon as they left the river, Jack announced that they needed to find a place to stay the night He finally came to a log saloon. He jumped down to go inside leaving Jenny alone in the wagon. He returned to say that he rented a place in the back for the night. When he pulled around back, she was aghast to to see a shack with no windows, just a door. She exclaimed, "Jack this is no place for our honeymoon night!" Angry, he yelled, "Get out, this is where we stay the night and don't give me any guff!" Weeping as she stepped down, carrying her own bag, and praying in silence, "Oh God, Oh God, what have I done? Jack is a different person, Oh God, Oh God, please help me."

Once in side, he pulled out the bottle of liquor he bought in the Saloon. He drank right from the bottle and handed it to her. "You might need this, since it's your first time." As he began taking off his shirt, boots, and pants."

"Little girl you had better get busy, or I'll rip everything you have off. Now's the time, so get at it." Tears streaming down her eyes, so afraid to say anything, but feeling she must, sobbing and hiccuping as she pleaded, "Please Jack, you promised to be easy, loving and caring." He drew her head back and slaps her face causing her nose to bleed. "How's that for being loving and caring? From now on, Little Miss Prissy, remember this, I'm the boss, you'll do what I tell you to do, and give me it when I want regardless of how you feel." At that point he ripped off her under garments, pushed her in bed, took another swig of the whiskey, then spread her legs apart, put one hand over her mouth, and shoved his penis in to take her maiden head. Then he spit on the floor, laughed out loud, and like the devil he is, said, "Don't know what so special about being a virgin. I prefer a woman that knows what to do. Here, take a drink, it'll make it easier. Now take a swig, and git ready," Jenny swallowed hard, started to scream as he covered her mouth and pounded again on her battered and sore private area. She had no idea how many times he took her. She was covered in seamen, blood, and sweat but dared not move. Finally he awakened, told her to get dressed and pee before they got started. She found no chamber pot, went outside and all most screamed because it hurt so much. When she came back into the room, Jack stood relieving himself on the wall. She thought, "how disgusting!" as she prayed in her mind, afraid so speak. "Dear God forgive me, help me, to get away from this devil,"

Traveling over muddy and bumpy roads was miserable. She hurt so badly that she thought she'd die. All the while, Jack was drinking, talking to himself, and laughing like an insane person. They made a few more stops, each time he got out, he threatened her, "Miss Prissy Do gooder, if you try to leave, I swear I'll kill you, hang you in a tree like the niggers your Pappy loves so much." Jenny looked ahead, thinking, "Does he know, or is he guessing because we admit to be abolitionists."

Jack returned yelling, "Give me your wedding ring ,and those ear bobs. Now! before I cut it off your finger and tear it off your ear." She handed them to him wondering why he wanted them. Soon enough she would know. This saloon bought and sold jewelry. He'd just sold her wedding ring and her mother's pearl earrings. She tried not to cry, but tears just wouldn't stop.

The farm was about 10 miles down a dark and muddy road. No wonder he used mules. Horses would have a difficult time pulling a wagon in rain and snow on this muddy path. When she looked up, she saw a big tobacco barn, two sheds, and a house that was about to fall down. She thought, "So this is the little farm house he was fixing up for her. Jenny, you are such a fool!" "Well, he's not going to break me, my first letter out will be to tell my father to come and get me."

She started unloading her things. Her traveling bag, the box of her mother's china tea set, the china dishes, pots and pans, iron skillet, dutch oven, the bolts of fabric to make curtains and quilts for their kitchen and bedroom. Her leather journal given to her by her father on her 16th birth-day. Her stamps, a portrait of her Mother and Father on their wedding day, and one of her when she was baptized at Easter when she was twelve. She asked politely if he would bring in her chest as they could use it as a table next to the bed. He grinned, then picked it up and yelled, "What in the hell is in here?" "Sheets, pillow cases, linens, table cloths, items that I've been working on to make our home beautiful and comfortable."

"Don't expect me to be around much. Tomorrow, I take a load of moonshine to the Rebel Army down South. And little girl, "yes, I am a bootlegger, and just remember what I'll do to you if you try to run away."

Jenny started in the kitchen. Pumping water to heat for washing dishes, and the filthy table and chairs. She removed the linens from the bed (rags really) then put on some clean sheets and quilts. She found her two feather pillows that she had embroidered while visiting with her cousin, Beth. She did not get out her china or silver, hoping to find a place to hide them. She had a half of chicken left over from their reception, fried some potatoes she found by the door, and made a pot of coffee with the coffee she brought with her. She hoped to find some flour and lard, or she'd starve while he was gone.

She called him to come for dinner. He walked in without washing off his manured covered shoes. He reached into the skillet and took the whole side of the chicken, most of the potatoes, leaving her a wing, and about three sliced potatoes. Realizing she was in hell with the devil and no way to get out of the fire.

After he gobbled down his food, he said for her to get undressed, he wanted some before he had to leave early the next morning. She did what she was told, The next morning, her beautiful bed linens smelled of his filthy body, manure, and moonshine. Jenny prepared him a lunch of left over wedding cake and the back pieces of the last bit of chicken. He left without a word, just a stare, that said, "Don't forget what I'll do to you, if you try to runaway." Finally he was gone! Leaving her time to talk to God. She began by getting on her knees, "Why God? Why did I believe his lies? What am I to do? Tell me God, what I need to do to get away from this devil?"

She check again to see if he was truly gone. Yes, she was alone. No flour, oil or food, just a kitchen knife to protect herself, no one to help." Just then she heard a sound by the door. She looked out the window, seeing a skinny half starved hound dog panting, teats hanging low. She opened the door, speaking softly, holding a pan of water, as she coached the starving critter into the kitchen. Speaking softly, she gained her trust. Naming her Toby, "Well girl, I guess it's just you and me to deal with this devil of a man. I'll find those chicken bones, but please be careful and don't get choked."

Jenny worked very hard to clean up the place. She found a partial bag of flour, crock of grease, two chickens in the back running around looking for stuff to eat. She was thrilled to find two eggs in a bush behind the garden, some sweet potatoes that had not been dug up, and an almost dead blackberry vine, a hoe and spade in the shed along with a black snake. She told the snake that there are plenty of mice, "so please get your belly full."

While in the barn, she located Jack's still. She found the mash stored in the hay loft. She decided to leave that area alone. Besides, she already had lots do in the garden and the house. She made curtains for the kitchen, and also a red checked table cloth to match. She used the old burlap hanging on the windows as good tough cleaning rags. She looked over his clothes and decided to wash them with lye soap, patch his shirts and pants, and hung his dress coat on the line after giving it a good brushing and spot cleaning. She gathered wild flowers to put in the middle of the table. Baked two sweet potatoes, two eggs and harvested the dying tomato vine that produced 6 ripe tomatoes. Feeling very proud of herself, she searched for something to make as a tea. She remembered that Aunt Lizzie made blackberry tea from leaves on her vines. But her greatest find, was a jug of molasses high up on top of the cupboard. A couple of bees were feasting hard on the dried syrup on the cork. She begged the bees to allow her to get the jug down to clean, and she would pour a little syrup on the chopping block. They obeyed by leaving as she opened the door. Gathering the crock, she poured about two spoons full, on the chopping block. Instantaneously, the bees flew to the block to feast. She cleaned the jug on the outside, washed the cork real good, and placed it by the pots and pans on the cupboard. Just as she was getting ready to bring his coat in from hanging outside, Jack came into the yard. He tied the team to the make-do-hitching post and walked towards Jenny.

"What are you doing to my clothes?" "I washed them real good, repaired them and shined your other pair of boots. I have them all ironed, folded, and your trousers are now hanging on the pegs in the bedroom."

He stood there, trying to think of something sarcastic to say, but instead, turned around and went into the house. She followed wanting to see his face when he saw how pretty everything looked.

"Where in the hell did you get these prissy curtains? Where's my burlap sacks?" "I made the curtains from the cotton I brought. The burlap sacks made good cleaning rags.that I've been using to scrub things clean."

Still he did not say a kind word of appreciation. He smelled of moonshine, filth, and sweat. "Jack, I found two hens back of the garden, they laid a couple of eggs, and I dug up the sweet potatoes and baked them for us to eat. Would you like to eat now?" "No! What I want is for you to find me some branches to start a fire so I can do my job, Rebels want as much moonshine as I can make for them as soon as possible. Do you hear me? Now get to work, find small dried branches so that I can start a fire under these bigger ones." "Please, I need to eat something, I've not eaten anything today and," "DO IT NOW! You eat when the work is done." He unhitched the mules, took them to the trough to drink water. Fed them some oats he had in his wagon, then picked up the horse whip laying on the seat of the wagon. He tried to kill a bee buzzing around the wood block. He missed, then whipped it around a small birch tree when suddenly he saw Toby, the blue tic hound dog. The dog saw him and ran away to the woods as fast as he could. Jack came back panting, "Don't you ever feed that hound. I've run her off before, she's good for nothing." She asked, "Is this enough to get started, or do I need more?" "About three times that much, than dinner time."

It was about 7:30 when they finished chopping wood when Jack finally said they could stop. Jenny's clean work dressed was dirty, torn, and her boots were muddy. She removed her boots and left them by the door, pumped some water to wash her hands and face, and dried them on a new towel she had just made. Jack grabbed the towel, wiped his face and hands, and never bothered to use the pan of water. She put on her apron, took the sweet potatoes out of the oven, and peeled the eggs. He rudely grabbed both eggs right out of her hands. He said grinning, "I like boiled eggs, they make me fart real good." as he bent over laughing.

All the time Jack was there, he complained about everything. She tried everything to please him, but it seemed to make him meaner and meaner. When she started to light the lantern only to find they had no more kerosene, Jack just grinned and shrugged his shoulders as if it was her problem, not his. She washed dishes in the dark, put on her night gown, and went to bed. A couple of hours later, he came in from the barn tending to his moonshine, drunk and yelled for her to wake up, "Get up, you prissy preacher's daughter. Miss Innocent, it's time for you to earn your keep," as he pulled down his overalls and told her to bend over. Pushing her body against the kitchen table, jerked up her gown and started pushing and shoving until she was screaming so loud she woke the two hens. He told her he just loved it when she yelled and screamed!

"I can't get turned on, Prissy Preacher's Pet, until I know you're in pain." Finally, when he was wore out and drunk, he found his way to the clean bed, flopped down, snoring and farting so badly she had to go outside for some fresh air and physical relief. Finding some peace in the night air, as the crickets sang, she kneeled to pray, "Dear Lord Jesus, I don't know how much more I can take, I know I'm losing weight, I'm working so hard, not enough to eat or sleep, and I'm afraid I'm going to have a baby. Lord I don't want to have Jack's children. He is so evil and would treat them as slaves along with me. You know I've written Father that I want to go home, but I've heard nothing and I'm afraid he has given up on me. He tried to warn me, but I'm so stubborn that I thought I knew better. Jesus, I can't get to church, I'm a white slave to a cruel and evil devil, please help me, give me a sign as to what I must do. Thank you Jesus, and forgive me for not paying attention to the signs you gave me, and I ignored. I intend to do better, I love you, Jesus." Jack left early the next morning heading south to find the Rebel Colonel that wanted the moonshine to help keep his troops fighting. "Jenny, you know what will happen if you try to leave! Stop writing letters to your Pappy, he ain't getting them, he's not coming to get you"

As he drove away, and was completely out of sight, Toby the hound came to the door. Jenny bent down and rubbed her neck.

"Big Mama, I can see you've had a bunch of pups. Did your hubby dump you to starve to death just like me? Believe me, we-will-overcome-this evil that men have caused on women. You'er the answer to my prayers. God is telling me, we need to help each other. Evil is overcome by Love, responsibility, and accountability. Let's us go find some food. Cause we've got work to do."

Jenny's revelation that God answered her prayer, that she must have faith and trust by working with Toby in order to escape Jack's evil. Devil's Workshop! Toby understood everything Jenny shared with her. Jenny's first instruction to Toby was that she much keep alert to any sign that Jack was returning. The second was if Toby feels him returning, to high tail it to woods for cover, and third since God gave hound dogs highly sensitive sense of smell, hearing and seeing, Jenny will depend on her to find things they very badly need to survive, and fourth, Toby must trust her. Toby wagged her tail, jumped up and down to show Jenny she understood and agreed.

Food is a necessity! Toby's nose found a few envelopes of seeds. One bag was easily recognized as a mixture of bean and tomato seeds, another bag had very tiny black seeds; guessing she hoped they were onion seed. When and where to plant the seeds, was a mystery as this was still winter and they may not sprout. Thank God for Miss Toby's nose!

One late afternoon, just before a down pour of rain, Toby came running for Jenny! Jenny was so delighted with her find; roots of white potatoes that were not dug up last fall. As Jenny dug, Miss Toby kept sniffing. Jenny gathered the potatoes: 36 large and 17 small, the size of a silver dollar. That should feed them for a while.

"Thank you God, and thank you sweet Miss Toby, my friend! That night, after the two filled their tummies of wild greens and boiled potatoes, Jenny cleaned up the kitchen, filled Toby's water gourd located in back of the outhouse; and they both crawled into bed. Jenny was snoring soundly, when Toby suddenly raised her ears, got off the bed, then woke up Jenny wanting go outside. Toby was whining an alert that told Jenny Jack or someone was coming. Jenny opened the door, Toby ran behind the cabin, and it was then, that Jenny heard a cowbell. Slamming the door closed, she bolted it from the inside, then waited. Finally she heard someone walking, then trying to open the door, "Jenny, wake up, open the door, I've got a present for you." She opened the door to find Jack, holding a rope tied around a cow's neck chewing her cud. She smiled with delight, knowing that now they can have milk and butter to make a pan of biscuit's. "Praise The Lord!"

So lonely and terribly afraid,
God sent Toby, a canine with a nose, ears, and eyes to save us
from the Devils fire and pain.
-Jenny-

St. Agnes Convent and School

Memphis, Tennessee

The first week at the covent was very difficult for both Jeb and Bess. They had not been separated for a moment since running from their slave owners. They were very diligent in doing their assigned jobs as throughly as they knew how. As privileged house slaves, they had few jobs to do; the biggest was to be available for the Master's beck and call. Jeb, to serve Phillipi and Bess, since Miss Josephine got married was to be a model child, study the piano, be an excellent student in all her studies, and dress and act like a cultured young lady.

Bess was assigned to the convent kitchen to assist in any manner needed in preparing food and cleaning. Jeb was assigned to work with the animals, cultivate, plant, and harvest food from the garden. In Bess's attempts to peel potatoes, it took a week for her to finally get the hang of how to hold the tiny peeling knife to do a better job. Jeb was right at home with the team of horses, but milking the cow was foreign to him. He feared hurting the cow when directed to squeeze harder. He soon learned it hurt the cow more when she wasn't milked sufficiently than when her utter was completely empty. Mother Superior asked Sister Louisa how the new student's were doing?

"Mother, I'm very happy with the couple, they work very hard to learn their duties, are willing to ask questions so that they understand perfectly what is expected of them and are always polite, kind, and compassionate regardless of the circumstances. In their studies they are always on time, prepared and eager to become confirmed and approved for the Holy Sacrament of Marriage after Easter."

When the time approached for their first communion and Easter Celebration, there seemed to be a constant hum among the nuns as they prepared for the Holy Event. The kitchen staff were busy making short bread cookies, seamstresses were repairing old and making new lace for the altar and vestments, The churches candle sticks were cleaned and all candles wick's were trimmed, The floors and all the furniture were scrubbed and waxed. The garden's around the facility were weeded, cleaned, pruned, and hoed where needed. Bouquets of fresh flowers filled every vase in the church. The facility looked and smelled wonderful Bess was in awe!

On the evening before the priest was to arrive, Mother Superior called for Jeb and Bess to please come to her office. Nervous and wondering if they were not performing satisfactorily, the couple rapped gently on her door. Mother Superior asked them to come in. Gathered around her, were four nuns, of which one was Sister Louisa. Mother Superior began. "My Beloved Children, It has been a joy to have you here at St. Agnes Convent. You are both hard workers, great student's and wonderful human beings. You have followed our agreement with diligence and have never complained to me or any of the Sisters. I admire both of you greatly. I believe if you ever choose a life of service to Our Lord Jesus, your service would be well received."

"I've asked you here this evening to offer my gratitude for your beautiful service to St. Agnes Convent. Sister Louisa would like to say a few words.

"Bess, I have enjoyed your determination and love for your religious studies. You are exceptional in every area of your Christian Life. To make your first communion so quickly, as you have, is remarkable. Congratulations. Your certificate must read as your baptismal certificate, I hope that meets your approval. Now, Sister Clare has something she would like to share." "Bess, the seamstresses wanted you to have a special first communion dress and veil. So we borrowed one of your dresses, redid it, crocheted a veil to go with it." She held the dress and veil up to be seen. We hope you like it as we feel you'll look beautiful wearing it." "Oh my goodness," Smiling while tears stream down her cheeks. "Beloved Sister's, The dress is so beautiful, I just love it!" As she caresses it, "Rev. Mother, would it be proper to be married in it as well?" "Of course, my child. You will be beautiful for both occasions. Now please have a seat."

"Sister Louisa has a few words she would like to share.with Jeb." "Jeb, you are the first young man I have ever had the good fortune to teach. Every day you amazed me with your preparation, your intense desire to learn all that was presented to you, and most importantly your loving willingness to practice the teachings of Our Lour Jesus Christ. I admire your gentle spirit and forgiving nature. You embody the spirit of the Dominican Life and Teaching. It is imperative that you decide the name you will carry forth in your life. Your baptismal name states; your first, middle, and last name , and how exactly do you want it to read?" With a strong conviction, Desmond stated, "If it would be allowed, I would like my last name to be DOMINICAN, Desmond Lafayette Dominican, aka Jeb. What do you think, Sister?" "Why, I believe that to be a beautiful and sacred name. Congratulations!"

Rev. Mother called Sister Clare forward to say a few words. "Jeb, we had to borrow your shirt for a few hours from the laundry to be sure we could fit you. Everyone donated in the making of your communion, confirmations shirt. The sleeves came from a treasured tablecloth, the front from a white velvet drapery that needed some repair, and the back from a feed sack we found in the barn. Long hours of embroidery and stitching were donated by many Sisters to complete your shirt. We think it is beautiful.

We hope you like it." Jeb stood frozen, unable to speak with tears flowing, he took a long breath, looked at each nun present and said. "Sister's, as a privilege slave, I had many beautiful shirts. I wore what I was told to wear. But, this shirt, is not only beautiful and well stitched, it was made by loving hands, all with loving hearts. It is the best gift I've ever received. I will be honored to wear this work of art for my Holy Communion and the Sacrament of Holy Marriage. Thank you most sincerely, I love you all," Rev. Mother interrupted the moment by addressing Jeb by his baptismal name. "Desmond Lafayette Dominican, aka Jeb, please rise and share with us your beautiful gift." Bess was the first to touch his beautiful shirt, then added, "Jeb, your true character, will bring more honor and beauty to this work of art when you are wearing it."

On Holy Thursday before Easter, the visiting priest baptized Jeb and Bess then offered the Sacrament of Holy Communion. Both Mother Superior and Sister Louisa glowed as the priest congratulated the couple for their knowledge and desire to be life long Catholics. Before Mother Superior could say anything Bess respectfully asked the priest, could he please perform the Sacrament of Holy Matrimony for Jeb and she before he left the Convent?"

He excused himself from answering the question, by requesting Mother Superior if he could speak privately with her. They spoke silently so that their words could not be heard. Afterwards, Father Daniel called both Jeb and Bess to be seated beside him facing Mother Superior. Mother Superior spoke first. "Jeb and Bess, we understand your desire to be married and to participate in the Sacrament of Holy Matrimony. Father Daniel will be here only one more day. Are you willing to spend the entire day with Father Daniel in preparation for your wedding tomorrow evening?" "Oh, yes Rev. Mother, Yes, we will." both holding hands smiling. Jeb bowed his head making the sign of the cross and with humble gratitude said, "Thank you Father, you are most gracious to us, your humble servants." Father Daniel, responded, "Then, my children, I will expect you here tomorrow morning at eight to begin your class on the Sacrament of Holy Matrimony." Good Evening Reverend Mother, Jeb, and Bess, I must be excused."

As they all began to leave the room, Jeb and Bessie reflected on how the room felt like it was glowing with the light of pure love and joyfulness. The Prioress raised her hand, a signal to Jeb and Bess it was now time to finish their night time chores and say goodnight. Bess turned to the area of the kitchen, to the screen behind which she would undress and hang her beautiful dress. Before crawling in bed, she knelt by the hand craved crucifix Jeb made for the kitchen staff. It was beautifully detailed so that every part of Jesus' body seemed to glow with perfection as it hung above the small altar. Bess closed her eyes to pray. Meanwhile, Jeb, in the barn, knelt down in Old Boss's manger to pray in gratitude for their many blessings. He asked forgiveness for any ill thoughts or actions he had committed. He asked for a blessing as he and Bess enter into the Sacrament of Holy Matrimony and when they leave the convent to be guided on their journey to freedom aided by the underground railroad going north to Ohio. Hanging his shirt, to protect its beauty, he smiled thinking, "This is my last night as a single man. Tomorrow I marry my lovely Bess." Before climbing into bed, he checked to see if the gift he made for Bess was still in his personal cubby. Making the sign of the cross, he pulled up the covers and fell fast asleep.

Fully dressed in their wedding attire, Jeb and Bessie met at the door of Reverend Mother's office at five minutes until eight. Father Daniel arrived soon after, opened the door, asked the couple to find a comfortable seat. "We will be having tea in about an hour, but will not leave the room until lunch time, at when you will be excused to eat and use the outhouse." Father Daniel started the lessons with prayer. When they finished their lessons at four in the afternoon, he announced that they would adjourn and meet at seven in the Chapel for the wedding ceremony. He blessed them as they left smiling and mumbling to themselves.

At six-forty-five in the evening, refreshed by a lovely dinner of chicken stew, the couple stood by the double doors to the Convent's Chapel, cleaned and sparkling. At seven, the bells began to chime. Reverend Mother arrived followed by the Nuns of the Convent. Sister Clare began playing a classical piece on her violin. Reverend Mother, on Bess' left, and Sister Louisa on Jeb's right escorted the Bride and Groom down the aisle to the altar. Father Daniel stood smiling in front of a six foot hanging crucifix of Jesus as a constant reminder of His Sacred teachings of the Gospels, in the Holy Bible's New Testament.

The total ceremony lasted one hour, after which the kitchen staff brought in a white wedding cake and punch. Everyone enjoyed all aspects of Jeb and Bess' wedding. At promptly nine, the bells began to ring announcing evening Vespers.

Jeb and Bess felt Vespers was a perfect closing for their Wedding Day. The Nun's voices were angelic and pierced their hearts with unconditional Love. As they were leaving the Chapel, Father Daniel called them aside. He handed them their certificate of marriage and a certificate of ownership of a nine year old mare donated to him to do as he pleased. He had it officially certified at the bank as he, the seller, to Mr. and Mrs. Desmond Dominican for $25.00. He placed his index finger to his mouth, a sign to the couple to silently accept the gift, then excused himself. Jeb and Bess were advised they could prepare to the leave the Convent the night of Easter Sunday. And that they could reside in the barn's loft until then. "How symbolic, Jeb thought, to be leaving a life of slavery on Easter, the day Jesus resurrected to demonstrate there is no death, only change, life eternal in God's Love."

Now they could enjoy their wedding night in gratitude and celebration.
As the couple prepared to step up on the loft's ladder, over Old Boss'
manger, Jeb paused to give Bess his gift. "Bess, I don't have a ring, but
I made you this crucifix," as he placed the thin leather strap, holding the
wood crucifix over her head. Bess gently caressed Jeb and lightly kissed his
lips. They climbed the ladder, then Jeb folded the blanket into a pallet, to
consummate their marriage, Jeb said, "My precious and beautiful wife, I
will love you throughout all eternity." Bess began to undress, he removed
his trousers and shirt, they kiss as a Brilliant Light of New and Great
Possibilities glowed.

This is the Day that the Lord Hath Made,
Let us be Glad, and Rejoice in it. Amen

To learn is to live,
To study is to grow,
and growth is the measurement of life.
The mind must to taught to think,
The heart to feel and
the hands to labor.
When these have been educated to the highest point,
then is the time to offer them
to the senses of man, and not before.
Found on the desk of Manly P. Hall in his own written hand.

Home of Dr. Chad and Mrs. Somerset III

Dayton, Ohio

Mary Maud chose to stay home from helping at the Medical Clinic. Dr. Chad convinced her that he would not need her, as he was going to visit patients and be home for an early dinner.

Mary Maud spent the morning emptying boxes that were stored in the spare bedroom, someday to be the Somerset Nursery, and never unpacked the two years they have lived there. She wondered, "Where did the time go?"

Having put a roasting hen in the oven earlier, she decided to peel potatoes, carrots, and onions to add to the chicken pot already baking in the oven. Going out the door to the garden, she spotted an animal stalking in the woods behind their home. She told herself that she must remember to tell Chad so that he can investigate if it is wild or a lost dog. She gathered several kinds of greens that grew abundantly in the garden, some she had no clue as to what they were, but Chad informed her they were valuable for a balanced nutritional diet.

After cleaning the greens and chopping some onions in a bowl, she decided to toss them with a vinegar and oil dressing like her mother used to do. Her mind wondered to her mother, who passed suddenly last year from what sounded like "dropsy" according to Chad. The funeral was over before they had received word of her passing. Sadly,, they did not make the long trip back to Philadelphia.

Looking into the cupboard for a hint as to what to fix for dessert, her eyes caught sight of her last jar of canned peaches. "Yes, peach cobbler, one of Chad's and my favorites!"

She had just finished layering the pie dough on the peaches, when Chad opened the back door. "Is my beautiful wife at home? Hmmmmmm I can smell something wonderful coming from the kitchen!" Maud met him with kiss and a peach slice to sample for his starving taste buds. "How was your day, my husband? Did you make it to Soldier's Home?" "Yes, they definitely needed my services. A veteran who suffered a broken leg in battle, that was poorly set by an Army surgeon, had to endure me re-braking it while performing surgery to reset it. He said he was under U.S. Grant at the battle of Ft. Donelson in 1862. Poor soul has suffered a long time with that crooked leg. He said he was most grateful that I took time to help an old man like himself. I shook his hand, and told him. "it was honor and pleasure to be able to do what I can for someone who fought to stop the evils of slavery." "Oh my goodness, I think I could be accused of being a bigamist! Because, I love both my beautiful wife and this luscious peach pie! Is it almost time to eat?"

They sat down at the kitchen table overlooking the forest behind their home. Chad offered a prayer of thanksgiving. She shared, "Chad I saw an animal lurking in the woods. Have you heard of a lost or a wild coyote killing chickens?" "No Sweetheart, but I'll check it out after dinner. And I almost forgot, I will need to check on my patient tomorrow, do you want to come along?" "You know Chad, I believe I would, thank. you for asking me, I've not seen the new wing at the facility."

Chad grabbed his sweater and rifle as he left to check on the animal in the woods. Mary Maud finished the dishes, put away the left over chicken, vegetables and peach cobbler in the ice box Removing her apron after sweeping the kitchen floor, she reached for the cookbook her mother sent her a few months before she died. She wondered, "Do people have "a feeling" before they pass? So much to ponder and wonder about life, death, and divine intervention."

*I'm wondering Why", if the law reads, Freedom for All
Why do I see so many locked in chains of prejudice?
Mary Maud Murphy-Somerset*

Jack Jones' Desolate Farm

Tennessee Border

Jack was spending more and more time away from his home place. Jenny figured he probably had another woman somewhere. She thought if that was true, he'd probably leave her alone when he returned.

Jenny and Toby were working diligently to find a way to escape. Thus far, they were able to stockpile provisions, but not a way to get away. Each day they wandered farther down the dirt road to estimate the distance they would have to go in order to hide from Jack. But so far, no method seemed safe.

On the afternoon of his 28th day away, Jenny and Toby were in the garden hoeing, when Toby raised her ears and started an alert whine that told Jenny Jack would be arriving shortly. Toby ran into the woods while Jenny kept hoeing. Looking up as if she were surprised, she went to meet Jack as he entered the barnyard. She waved, smiled, and followed him to the horse watering trough. He told her to get him some food fixed, clean clothes, and make him a new bedroll. She asked him where he was going? He looked like a devil caught trying to leave hell, and said, "I've found two niggers hiding about 10 miles from here. I want to surprise them, because they'd bring a heap amount of money 'cause their educated house slaves as white as me and they speak another language. I heard them whispering to each other. I'll bring them here until I can locate their owners or sell them to slave sellers that will give top dollar for the likes of them. Git going! I want a bath some moonshine and food!" As he rubbed down his horse, he was muttering to himself about how smart he is and rich he will be when he grabs those slaves and gits the money.

Jenny high tails to the kitchen, pumped some water for his bath and dishes. Made him a dish of rabbit stew with potatoes and carrots. Put a left over biscuit beside his plate with some butter from the buttermilk she churned that morning. She rolled a blanket and tied it with a rope she made from string and burlap bags. She laid out a clean pair of trousers, a blue cotton shirt, underpants that had seen better days, a pair of knitted socks she repaired, and his other pair of boots. She opened the door to tell him everything was ready, "Jack, I've got everything you wanted, but I don't have anything to drink but some buttermilk. Do you want to bathe before you eat?" "I'll eat first, then take a bath, then be on my way. That nigger bitch will give me some before I leave to come back. Her nigger buck will get a kick out of watching me tie her and fuck her brains out." Laughing like a drunk goon.

Jack ate everything, burped real long and farted out loud as he scratched his privates and neck until it was red. He climbed into the tub, yelled for Jenny to git at it, to scrub his body and to massage his cock. Bragging he said, "This here cock is precious gold, it's planted seeds all over these here hills, laughing and snorting, so you best handle it with care. What time is it?" "Jenny responded by looking up at the old clock on the wall. "Fifteen minutes until nine." as she handed him the towel. He emerged from the tub like an old dog shaking water everywhere, dried himself, dressed, then headed to saddle his horse, He yelled again, "Git my food ready, I've got to git there while they are still asleep. They've got two decent horses, worth something. He jumped on his horse as she handed him the food. "I'm gonna feed those slaves, 'cause I know they haven't eat, got to give them energy for the long walk back. That'll show 'em whose boss." Then he took off like lightening.

Toby slowly came out from behind the house. Jenny petted her then sighed, "Thank God he's gone, but he's coming back with some slaves to sell, bragging about how he was going to rape the woman in front of her man. Oh God, what an evil devil! We'd better get some sleep, no telling when he will come back."

It was about two in the afternoon that Jack arrived, he on one horse, the two slaves walking barefoot and chained behind the other horses. Jack grinned from ear to ear announcing loudly, "This here is the honorable Jeb and Bess who think they are better than me. Jeb thinks he's stronger and smarter, but I'm the one who has the gun, his wife has been spoiled with my seed; but the big ugly son-of-a-bitch cried like a baby because I made him watch." Miss Prissy, Preacher's daughter, don't you dare feel sorry for them, because if you do, you'll never forget how I will punish you if you do . I'm dogged tired and need to chain these two in the barn."

Good to his threats, he took his whip to Jeb and Bess and his promise ringing in Jenny's ears. "Miss Prissy wife, daughter to a preacher boy, look what will happen to you" as he beats both Jeb and Bess with the horse whip.

After all the work was done in the barn, of which Jeb unharnessed, fed, water, and brushed down the horses, while Jack sat and watched with his pistol aimed at his head. To add insult to his evil ways, Jack pointed to a small trough for Bess to add oats and ground corn, then said proudly, "Come eat at your formal dining table and drink from the barrel with the first cup invented, your hands" Laughing like the devil he is, left them chained by one ankle to his blacksmith's anvil. He left the barn whistling, stopped long enough at the shed to relieve himself, then proceeded to the kitchen door. Again, yelling for Jenny, when he stood just two feet from her.

"Tell me, Prissy Wife, what have you invented for my dinner tonight?" Jenny responded quickly, but never looked at him once. "I made a pan of biscuits with the last of the flour I found in the top cabinet and with a bony piece of rabbit, I made some good milk gravy. Also a pan of wilted greens and blackberry tea. Are you ready to eat?" "You betcha, I am. No bath tonight, I'm worn out, too tired to git it up. But tomorrow, anytime, any place."

They ate in silence. Jenny only drank the blackberry tea and ate some greens. Her stomach finally settled from being sick all morning. She was determined to not let Jack know what she believed to be true. Besides, he never once shared a bit of the food she prepared. He was bent on breaking her spirits. Now that she had God's answer to her prayer, she knew sweet Toby Girl would help her through this hell until the path was clear to go.

Jack shoved her out of bed to get him the chamber pot, of which he called the slop jar. She brought it from the corner while he still laid in bed. She pumped some water to put on to boil and then went to the out-house, checking to see if Blackie, the snake was anywhere around the perimeter. She had scrubbed the inside of the out-house two days ago, but since Jack's arrival, there was filth on the wooden surface, "Oh God," she thought, "The man is so gross and seems to love showing off his filthy ways."

After she left the out-house, she heard Jack in the barn cracking his whip., "I'll find some way to help them," she promised herself, "God will show me how."

Arriving back to the kitchen, Jack demanded, "What took you so long? Are you on your monthly?" She lied, "Yes, I just started." "Damn, I guess my slave bitch will satisfy me until you're over it."

Jenny's stomach flipped over with guilt knowing she was causing Bess more pain. As the sun was at midday, Jack came in to the house to tell Jenny that he had to go hide in the woods, he heard horses and figuring they were Rebels wanting his horses and to draft him into the rebel army. He warned her to tell them he was already gone to sign up. That he left her with the two slaves and two mules to help garden and take care her. She'd have to make up a story they'd believe or they would steal the mules and whatever else they wanted.

Having his horses saddled, and with some food and water, he took off in the direction of the woods leading north, covering his tracks as he did so. Jenny immediately went to the barn, explained what was happening, she told them that she was going to unlock their chains and trust them to not run away. She promised them that she would do what she could to set them free, but they had to understand that she was also a slave to the devil that was her husband. Jeb and Bess looked at each other in agreement. Bess was already showing signs of being pregnant with Jack's rape child, and Jenny confessed to believe she was too. She shared that she was not telling him and pretending to being on her monthly, but because he would probably use Bess, she would stop that lie. She did not want him to know she was pregnant with his child, secretly praying she would lose it. "God forgive my soul," she cried.

"I will come to the barn every chance I get to make a plan for our escape. I know you are very educated, I recognized you speak French, Jack is so stupid, he doesn't know what you speak. Please try to talk like field slaves so that the rebels do not recognize you to be anything but my slaves. Also, God sent me a hound dog that Jack forbid me to have. She is so smart! She knows when he is coming and has helped me to keep from starving. She will help you as well. We can help each other. I am not prejudice, I came from a Christian family, we do not believe in slavery of any kind. You're wondering why I'm married to Jack, I don't have time to tell you that long story, but believe me, I'm ashamed and feel guilty every time he touches me. I feel he is the Devil and wants to take me into his private hell. I must go, but as soon as the Rebels go, we'll begin our escape plan."

As she was leaving the barn, a group of four men, with a lieutenant in command, rode in. She saw them as they arrived and went immediately to ask what they wanted.

"Good afternoon, ma'am, are you alone here?" "No" she responded shaking her head. My husband left to go volunteer proudly to serve the rebel army. He left me with two slaves to help me survive." Touching the quilt she placed under her dress to look pregnant in the last month, she continued with her tale. "He doesn't want his child to live where he can't have slaves. Ours have been with us since we married, a gift from his parents. They work hard and know their place. Do you want to meet them? Bess knows how to deliver a baby, since we're so far out, I'm happy for that."

The Lieutenant appeared nervous with the possibility she might have that baby anytime, insisted they needed to go, but wanted her to be on the lookout for any run-away slaves or Yankee's. Tipped his hat and was gone like a flash. Jenny, thinking that lying was getting pretty easy prayed,, "Forgive me Jesus, I don't know anything else to do with these evil men all around us."

Jack returned the next day with orders from Confederate General Polk's first lieutenant to get two barrels of whiskey to his army right away. They needed the liquor to help keep the men motivated to fight at all costs. Jack unchained Jeb and Bess to help him. Bess was still feeling sick from early pregnancy, but would not let Jack have any pleasure in knowing he caused her pain and suffering.

The still was going night and day after Jack returned. He told Jeb he needed to depend on him and Bess to make as much moonshine as possible. The rebels were desperate and Jack wasn't sure what they were up to. He needed them to load two barrels on the wagon hitched with the mules, so that he could get to their camp by the border before another snowfall. He told Jeb he'd like to take him but that rebels are taking slaves to fight and do labor. I don't know how Jenny sweet talked them rebels that came here, but they'll be back. Jenny heard their conversation as goose bumps stood up on her neck and back. The good news is, he's too busy to mess with either she or Bess.

Loaded with two barrels of whiskey, a lunch basket, and a blanket, Jack looked up to the early morning sky and remarked, "It's going to snow hard. Jeb keep those boilers going, and the horses hid in case more rebels come. Jenny, you keep Jeb and Bess busy with that whip and don't be afraid to use it. I don't know how long I'll be gone." Off he went into the wind and snow. Jenny couldn't believe the luck that evil man had. He'd survived by himself with all kinds of challenges, snow, rain, and humid heat. "I guess the devil can be tough, but the Lord is tougher," she said out loud. When completely out of sight, Toby came to the barn where Jenny stood trying to unchain Jeb and Bess with the big metal key that hung in the kitchen. Finally, she handed the key to Jeb. With his big hands and strength, he easily opened the lock. Jack was a pretty good blacksmith, but greed got in the way of sensibility.

They made their plan. After the babies were born and hardy enough to travel, they would head towards Uncle Ben's to get help for Jeb, Bessie, and baby on the Underground Railroad, and to get Jenny and child back home to her father's in Cincinnati. As Jenny began to feel the baby's fluttering, she asked God to please forgive her for wanting to miscarry. It's not the baby's fault its father is evil. Jenny knew her love for the child would keep it safe from being like its father.

Bess and Jeb had long talks about her pregnancy. He told her he'd love the child because it was a part of her. She prayed that they and baby could go to Ohio to find some Quakers so that the child could be truly free, not slaves forever.

Time seemed to fly, somedays faster than others, which just crept by. Jack would come and go, selling his services and liquor to who ever was buying. The bigger Jenny's body got with child, the more he was turned off. Bess, the same. She was tall, almost six foot, he liked little women like Jenny, scared, week, and quiet. But that damn belly stuck out like an over-grown watermelon, disgusted him so, he couldn't get it up! But whores, he thought, "I just love whores, their smart, not picky, and know how to satisfy a man!"

On a Fall September morning, Jenny began to have a back ache. Jack didn't want to be bothered with her aches and pains. "Git Big Bess! Don't brother me, I've got a load to deliver."

Bess came to Jenny's bedroom. She was in great pain, saying that it felt like her back was breaking. Bess asked permission to look at her privates? Rubbing her back, she said sympathetically, "Miss Jenny, I'm afraid you've got a ways to go. I'll get my herbs for tea, some hot packs for your back, clean sheets, and boiling water. Do you have a sharp knife to cut the cord?"

Jenny began blurting out where things were located in the kitchen. Bess instructed her to walk as much as possible. As they supported one another, a deep bond emerged. Two women, lacking experience in

having and delivering babies, bonded together as glue adheres two things together for a lifetime.

Miss Jenny, please take deep long breaths, now visualize a strong and happy baby suckling at your breasts, I see its head, now push, push hard, okay, okay, one more time, push, push!" "The baby's head is coming, its shoulders, arms, body, legs and feet are sliding out." Bess spoke softly but enthusiastically, "Jenny, you have a beautiful baby boy!" Jenny began to cry as she tried to see her son that was being cleaned up by Bess. When she was finished, she handed the baby to Jenny instructing her to place her fingers in his mouth, teach him to suck, then give him the real thing. As mother and baby lay quietly, Bess advised Jenny that she needed to deliver the after birth. In awe and with some fear, she asked, "Bess will this hurt? I'm a little scared?" "Don't be, now push! It's okay, it's all here. You now need to rest, drink plenty of water, and allow your son to nurse to that your insides can shrink back to normal."

Two hours later, Jack came in, looked towards Jenny nursing, then snarling and said, "A boy? name him Gunnar, it's a strong German name!" Then turned around and left as quickly as he came in. Jenny was relieved as she took a drink of water, then turned lovingly to her son, "Gunnar, you'll be strong enough to overcome your father's evil ways, I'm your Mama and I'll see to it you are loved and cared for, I promise.."

Three weeks later, Bess delivered a big strong boy with only Jeb to attend to her. Jenny did not know Bess was in labor, until she heard the baby cry. She had no one except Jeb whose very nature is loving and supportive. Jack was gone on one of his trips, so Jenny felt free to take Bess clean rags for diapering, hot water and tea and biscuits. But for Bess, the most important jester was Jenny's gift of kindness and compassion. Hugging, Bess and Jenny both felt a boost to face what ever came next. Bess told Jenny that they named the baby Willie, who was already at least a pound heavier than Gunnar. Jenny said, "The boys will be like brothers, playing and working together." Bess said nothing while enjoying her time with Willie at her breast.

The boys grew like weeds. Two year old toddlers getting into everything. Jenny was great with another child when Jack came home to announced that he had a buy for Jeb and Bessie. She asked him, "What about the baby?" He laughed, "They're not interested in a squalling brat. We'll dispose of him."

Jenny said not another word as she could tell Jack was drunk and it would get worse. She fixed dinner, was about to go get Gunnar from playing with Willie in the barn, when Jack grabbed her. "No you don't miss prissy preachers girl, you're not warning them," as he shoved her down on the floor, kicked her on her back, then bent down to slap her face when little Gunnar came in crying. "No, no Mommy, Mommy, don't hit Mommy." to which Jack ripped off his big leather belt, and started to beat the poor child. As he did, Jenny struggled to get up, but instead laid her body on Gunnar, taking the belt's lashes and pain. Jack satisfied that they both learned who was boss. sat down at the table to eat and guzzle the rest of the moonshine. When finished, he flopped down on the bed in a drunken stupor, snoring and farting as he dreamed of conquests and more torcher. Jenny whispered into Gunnar's ear, "Go quickly my sweet boy, to the barn and wait for Mama." The toddler, whose little body was striped with belt marks; sniffling, took off as fast as he could walk. Jenny got up, grabbed hold of the kitchen table for support, quietly moved toward the corner behind the door that stood Jack's shot gun. Picking it up, she quickly walked to the bedroom, took aim and shot Jack Tom Jones right in the face. Frightened, but with relief, she stood and watched Jack jerk until she knew he was dead. "Father forgive me, but this devil will never again hurt my baby, nor lay his hands on me, Bess, Jeb, or Toby again." Feeling Toby's presence beside her, she turned to the door, to see Bess, Jeb and the two boys in total shock. In a daze, but in control, Jenny said, "Boys, go to the yard and pick some wild flowers, and pretty rocks, while we clean this mess and bury Jack. He's never going to hurt you again."

Jenny told Jeb to move the outhouse so they could bury Jack there. Bess, Jenny, and Jeb carried Jack out in the sheet he died on. They dumped him in the hole, Jenny threw her silver coated wedding ring onto his chest. She paused for a moment, then took a deep breath, "Lord, Jack was an evil man. He beat me, my precious baby and these good people. I just couldn't let this happen again. I'm not sorry I did it, .if I am to rot in hell, let me live long enough to raise my children to be good Christians. The Lord giveth, and the Lord taketh. I guess I just helped the Lord. Amen" There was a moment of stunned silence, No one believing what they just saw.

"Come Bess, we have quilts to boil, and you boys need to get some sleep." Little Gunnar asked if he could sleep in the barn with Willie. She nodded her head, understanding how scared they were. Bess, Jeb and the boys all left to their beds in the barn.

About an hour later, Miss Jenny showed up at the barn saying that her water had broken. Bess grabbed her herbs in one hand while helping Miss Jenny to get back to the house. "I'm only 8 months, I don't think the baby lived through Jack's beating." "Miss Jenny, please try to picture life the way you'd like live it. Where are your rags, baby cloths, and boiling pan?" "Bess, please from now on, do not call me Miss Jenny. That's slave talk and you're my best friend, and if I die having this baby, please take Gunnar and go to my Uncle Ben's. He's a conductor and will help you get on the railroad, Oh My, God, I'm going to pass out."

Bess grabbed her, put her head as close to her feet as possible, asked her to sip an herb drink she had in a cup. After laying her on the bed, she looked at her private parts and said, "it won't be long." About twenty minutes later, Jenny sat up, grabbed Bess' arm, screamed a blood curdling scream that lasted for an eternity, finally Bess said, "Jenny he's dead, a boy child, very small, do you want to see him?"

Jenny took him in her arms, tears streaming down her cheeks, then exclaimed, "Jack killed him, Jack killed my little precious Maxwell. Oh! God, I can't help it," "I HATE JACK, I HOPE HE ROTS IN HELL" Still sobbing, she said, "Please Bess, find my wedding dress to bury him in. He's so innocent. Oh God, please forgive me."

Bess found her wedding dress in the trunk. After washing baby Maxwell she wrapped him in the satin skirt of the dress. He looked like an angel. She asked Jenny if it was alright to call Jeb and the boys in to see the baby before they buried him. She nodded, never raising her head, still in shock and disbelief. Jeb had busied himself digging a hole behind the garden. He found a box in the shed, lined it with the rest of the dress. He laid baby Maxwell in the box, the boys each put a wild flower and a pretty small rock on his tummy. Little Gunnar bent over to kiss his baby brother on the forehead. Jenny asked Bess for help to stand up and get to the burial site. As Jeb carried the baby's make do casket, Bess began to sing a negro lullaby. Jeb laid the casket by the hole, waiting for Jenny to say something. Finally after moments of wiping tears, Jenny spoke softly, "My sweet baby, Mama never got to sing you a lullaby, but I will love you always, I'm sorry you lived such a short time, but I know the angels are anxiously waiting for you to join their heavenly choir. Tell my mother I love her, even though I was too young to remember her. Go my sweet angel, I'll be seeing you when the moon glows brightly, and the wind whispers your name. I love you," She laid a tiny little white Bible she received at her own baptism on his chest, "Until we meet again, my baby boy, rest in peace."

Turning around from the grave site, sobbing she held tightly to Bess as they walked slowly back to the house. While Jeb completed burial details, he could hear the boys asking each other how Maxwell will get to Heaven.

Jeb answered softly, "God brings all his children back by rays of light. Little Maxwell will follow the light to join God's heavenly choir." Nothing more was said.

When all were gathered back at the house, Jenny announced that Jeb and Bess would no longer sleep in the barn. They were all one family. Tomorrow we will begin to make plans to escape to Cincinnati, Ohio. Now let's get some quilts for you all to sleep on. This has been a long day, let us be through with it. Amen

As Jenny lay in her bed with both boys snuggled close to her and Toby at the foot of the bed, she listened to the silence of the moment, the soft hum of all their breathing, Toby's snorts as she slept, and the full moonlight shining through the window. Her eyes fixed on the moon's silver glowing rays, she offered a prayer of gratitude for these four beautiful souls, then she saw a flickering light in the center of a ray gliding up, up, and away. Little Maxwell was sending her his love farewell. "Thank you, Jesus for all my many blessings." She closed her eyes to a deep and grateful sleep.

Jenny and the boys awakened to the wonderful smell of homemade biscuits, gravy, scrambled eggs, and hot chicory. Toby had already been dismissed to do her morning business. Jeb was at the barn doing chores, while Bess had a wonderful breakfast under control. The table was set with Jenny's mother's china, and some dried plants placed in the center to complete its beauty. Jenny was thrilled. Bess smiled as she came to hug her friend, then speaking with a loving lilt, "Jenny, today we baptize this house and farm with God's love. Everything here will be changed, because love changes everything." Jeb came in with a wooden cross for Maxwell's grave. He had painted,

Baby Maxwell
born and died
9-23-1861

Jenny put her arms around Jeb, looked into his eyes that were weeping, then said, "Jeb, I thank you from the bottom of my heart. You are the kindest, and most loving man, along with my Father, I've ever known. Your generosity is in my heart forever." Bess cleared her throat as the boys came in from the outhouse, asking,"Is it time to eat? We're hungry, those biscuits look good." Jenny asked Jeb if he'd say the blessing before they ate. "Lord Jesus, Mary Mother of God, we are gathered together at the table filled with food that will nurture our stomachs, while your loving heart blesses our souls. Guide us always to serve you, show us the way to freedom, forgive our sins as we let go of pain and suffering. Thank you for the blessing of little Maxwell who has gone on to heaven to be a guiding light for others. Hail Mary full of Grace," They all responded joyfully, Amen" "Let's eat! As Toby barked in affirmation." Jeb advised that they needed to get busy harvesting the garden. Making cheese and butter, from Old Boss' milk and dry the herbs Bess needed to heal. They gathered pumpkin, squash, cucumbers, tomatoes to dry, corn to grind, and chicken's to prepare for travel. The family rested and were drinking water when Toby raised her ears, and took off to scan the woods. Jenny said,"Toby hears something that's not okay. She's never wrong. We need to prepare to play our little acts."

Jeb and Bess went to the barn, Willie put on the dress and bonnet he was to wear to pretend he was a girl that couldn't talk or hear. Jenny and Gunnar were to pretend that Jack had joined up with the rebels, leaving them to survive by themselves without their slaves that ran away a week ago. Toby returned wanting Jeb to follow her. He followed her deep into the woods until they saw rebels camped with some slaves tied to a tree. They returned quietly to the farm to notify Jenny. Jenny immediately, new that they all needed to leave. Jenny would take the boys in the wagon pulled by the mules, loaded with their harvest, Bess and Jeb would each ride a horse to Uncle Ben's to be led to the Underground Railroad. Jenny would follow, but would arrive later due to the slowness of the mules. She told Bess that they would meet in Cincinnati where her father was minister to a big Presbyterian church. Her story, if she should get stopped by rebels was that she got word that her husband got killed in Hopkinsville. She had to leave to go to her father in Cincinnati so that she could be protected and get help to heal her daughter that was very ill. Until she got there, Toby would be their eyes and ears for protection.

Bess and Jeb could see the logic in the plan, but she hated leaving her son. She knew Jenny would protect the boys with her life. Finally, she agreed to the plan. She got out her nap sack. She called Willie to her lap, showed him a large black nut, then with tears in her eyes, she said, "Willie, Mam and Pap have to leave you with Jenny. The bad slavers are close by and will try to catch us. Jenny feels it is safer for you to pretend to be her little girl, so the slavers don't steal you. I want you to take this black nut. It was given to me as my luck charm to find a Quaker who will help us to freedom. Hide it, be a good boy for Jenny, and remember Willie, I love you for ever. I promise, we'll do everything we can to find you. Bess and Jeb hugged Willie. Jeb said, "Be brave and God will take care and protect you."

They loaded the wagon, packed food for Jeb and Bessie, and left Old Boss to roam free close to the well for water and grazing. They hoped the rebels would milk her as her utter would be getting large and sore. They left the farm without looking back. Jeb and Bess went forward to lead, but was soon out of sight. Jenny followed with Toby up front beside her, the boys laying down on all the produce, two chicken's tied, with some straw for them to nest. Underneath all of this, was the shot gun and ammunition. Jenny carried Jack's pistol in the folds of her skirt hidden by her jacket. The clouds up ahead promised snow, Jenny prayed it would wait until they got to Uncle Ben's before coming down.

They made it to Uncle Ben's just as the sun was setting. He was surprised when he saw them out of his kitchen window. He shared that his son, BJ was married and joined the Union Army. His daughter was teaching school in Pennsylvania, promised to the Headmaster of the University in Philadelphia. He sent his wife to stay with her sister in Indiana by the Ohio River. He hoped that all would be reunited after this "un-godly war" was over.

He was sorry, but he had not seen Jeb and Bessie. He figured they found their own way to the next station if they were riding horses. He told them all to fill up on some soup and bread that one of church's ladies made for him. Jenny said they could share, as they had plenty of cheese, cucumbers, and tomatoes. Jenny figured to leave most of their produce and the chicken's at Uncle Ben's. Tomorrow at first light, if all went well, they would only spend one night on the road before getting to the river crossing. They all bedded down, one eye on alert, and the other sound to sleep.

After eating hard boiled eggs, bread and butter, and hot coffee they all climbed into the wagon with Uncle Ben driving and Jenny beside him. Toby was in the back between the boys, who were fast asleep under their pile of quilts. Uncle Ben refused for Jenny to head out alone. He said, "Henderson would do the same for me, if it were in reverse."

Uncle Ben began by asking the questions he did not want to ask in front of the boys? "Jenny, what happened to Jack?" "He's dead, pausing to take a breath, I killed him because he was an evil devil. He beat my Gunnar and me with a razor strap, so hard it caused me me to lose my second son. Gunnar and Willie are the products of Jack raping me, and Bess. Jeb is a saint, he loves Bess and Willie. He will be a great father once we get them to freedom. I asked God to forgive me; but if I'm not forgiven, then I'll go to hell, but Jack won't hurt anyone ever again."

"Wow! My sweet niece. I never felt good about him and neither did your father." "I know, Father tried to warn me, but I was so bent on getting my way, I never saw the signs. I pray Father will forgive me and allow me to come home with the boys." "Jenny, you never have to fear that your father won't allow his daughter to come home. Love is the strongest emotion, you're always welcome in his heart and home." He looked over to see that she had fallen asleep on his shoulder. Alone with his thoughts, he pondered, "Wonder what happened to cause her to do such an act? There by the Grace of God, go I."

Arriving at the Ohio River crossing at dusk, Uncle Ben thought it prudent that they wait until daylight the next day to attempt crossing with frozen ice floating on the river. They all laid close to each other, covered with the many quilts to get a good night's sleep. Uncle Ben stayed awake to watch for rebels in search of slaves and goods to rob. Uncle Ben left the wagon at daybreak to hire a barge to take them to the dock on the Cincinnati side. He found a little man, about five feet two named Jimmy who claimed to make several trips daily with no complaints by his clients.

After eating a little breakfast, they gathered their baggage and climbed aboard Jimmy's raft. He asked the women and children to sit in the middle on their luggage and for Uncle Ben to be on "look-out" at the stern. Jimmy remarked, "As you've probably noticed, I'm short. Can't see over your heads for chunks of ice, I need a little help and you are nice and tall. Thank you."

Before boarding the raft, Uncle Ben wrote a contract between he and Jimmy to protect the wagon loaded with produce until he returned the next day from visiting with his family in Cincinnati. He told Jimmy he'd earn another gold coin for his services if nothing was lost. He handed the contract to Jimmy to sign, they shook hands. Jimmy felt like a wealthy man. He'd never earned that much in two days time on the river. The family could see Rev. Sterling standing on the dock waving to them. He had received their letter saying they would arrive this week. He had been to the dock every day anticipating their arrival. As the family left the raft, they each thanked Jimmy for their safe ride across the river. He smiled, bowing like an aristocratic gentleman in deep gratitude.

Rev. Sterling was smiling in appreciation as he hugged his daughter and each boy. He was in the dark as to why one child was pretending to be a little girl, but he knew there must be a good reason, "Jenny, Jenny, my beautiful daughter, Father is so happy to see you!!! And my grandchildren, please give Grandfather a big hug. Now let's get into my buggy, you must be starved? Ben could you help me with their baggage?"

As Ben and Rev. Sterling loaded the baggage, Ben alerted him that the one boy was a slave pretending to be Jenny's daughter. After everything was loaded, Jenny and the boys crawled into the back, as Rev. Sterling and Uncle Ben climbed up front to drive to the Sterling home. Upon arriving and unloading, Rev. Sterling invited them into the kitchen where they found a stranger cooking. Jenny urged the children to follow her up the stairs to bathe before eating.

As Jenny and boys bathed, Uncle Ben was introduced to Elder Brock Burns, a new elder in the church, who had just immigrated to Cincinnati from Scotland. Uncle Ben explained the masquerade of the young slave boy, named Willie. Just in that moment, Jenny entered the kitchen. She apologized for her interruption, but she needed a favor. "The boys are finished bathing, but have no clean clothes, Is it possible that I might borrow two shirts until I can get their clothing washed and purchase some new clothing?"

Elder Brock said that he believed he had some things the boys could use. Excused himself to go to the church to gather them up. After he left, Rev. Sterling asked about Jack. "Jenny, did Jack join up to fight in this terrible war? Or did he send you home for safety reasons?" "Father, when we have some time alone, I will tell you all the gory details. I hope that's okay with you?" "Of course, Jenny, I understand. Changing the subject, "Elder Brock has prepared us a wonderful meal, "Let us all be glad and rejoice in it."

As Elder Brock entered the kitchen, he handed Jenny the clothing he had gathered for the boys, blushing he said, "I apologize for their condition, but feel they will do until we can get to the mercantile to purchase some new things." "Thank you Elder Burns, I'm most grateful," accepting, she headed up to help the boys finish their bath's and get dressed. In about twenty minutes later, all three entered the kitchen. The boys each wearing a man's long sleeved shirt, and heavy woolen socks. Their hair was combed back, finger nails scrubbed clean, and their teeth brushed. Neither boy knew the art of brushing teeth, but soon to learn with laughter and delight.

Rev. Sterling greeted them smiling, "Well here are my grandson's, clean as a whistle, and my daughter, beautiful as ever, and with deep appreciation and welcome to Elder Burn's wonderful meal. Let us honor his generosity by offering a blessing." They all gathered around the big oak round table, Rev. Sterling at one end, Uncle Ben at the other, Jenny and Elder Burns were seated across from the two boys. The table was set with a blue checked table cloth with matching napkins, white plates, and silverware. Everything looked beautiful Elder Burns had even placed a vase with a couple of geraniums in the center of the table. Rev. Sterling offered the blessing. "Heavenly Father, we are grateful for your many blessings, for Elder Burns' wonderful gift of our daily bread, for my Brother Ben's dedication to service to those less fortunate and for bringing my daughter and her family safely home after all their trials and tribulations, and Father, I will open this prayer for each present to share their unique appreciation for your blessings,

Gunnar opened his heart in prayer, "Jesus, I am happy to eat and sleep in a clean house, and know I have a Grandfather, please tell me what to call him, and thank you for this food that smells so good." Willie was next as they continued clock-wise around the table. "Jesus, I've always loved you, Mam told me about you when I would crawl upon her lap. She'd sing as she rocked me to sleep. I could feel you smiling 'cause she had such a pretty voice. Thank you for bringing Mam and Pap to Miss Jenny. even though Jack was a mean man who hurt Mam and Pap, Miss Jenny, Gunnar, me, and sweet baby Maxwell. Miss Jenny wanted to help us to go to a Quaker so that we can find freedom. Mam gave me her black nut , I'm dog tired, Amen."

Elder Burns continued with the blessing by sharing, "Father, I am grateful to be here in American, to be a part of Your Holy Service to the Cincinnati Presbyterian Church, the poor and slaves needing your love and humane service. Thank you for blessing this family to be home safe. Amen?" Then Rev. Ben finished the blessing, "Heavenly Father, Thank you for a safe haven here in Cincinnati, for good health and our love in service to you. Let us begin this meal, knowing all are a blessing to each other and to God, Amen"

Because of their late arrival, Jenny and Boys were exhausted after their long trip and filling up on such a wonderful meal. They said their good-night's, climbed the stairs to begin a new routine of washing up, brushing teeth, and saying nightly prayers.

Jenny and the boys entered the bedroom with twin beds and blue quilts her mother had made before Jenny was born. She said tomorrow she would take the boys to get new clothing, shoes, tooth brushes, and writing paper and pencils.. She shared, "I have some gold coins I found that Jack had hidden and never wanted any one to find. I divided the coins with Bess and Jeb so they could help those who were risking their lives to get them to freedom. I plan to give what is left to my father to help with our needs while living with him. You boys will soon be four years old. You are very smart, I plan to start teaching you both the alphabet and numbers. You've seen some ugly and evil things at Jack's. I am sorry that I had to put you precious boys through so much. However, I know God forgives us when we're doing the best we can. I promise you Willie, I will honor your Mam's wishes and find you the right Quaker family. But, until that time, I will protect you. You are Gunnar's brother and part of the family. Goodnight, my sweet boys, Mom loves you. And Willie, please, I'd love it if you could call me Mommy like Gunnar does. I'll never take your Mam's place, but I'll do my best,"

She hugged and kissed both boys as they all knelt to say their nightly prayers. After they were finished, she blew out the candle, and as she left the room, she saw that both boys were fast asleep..Entering the room she slept in from the time she was born, she could feel its sacred energy, like the temple in Jerusalem, because of all the love radiating within its walls.. On her desk were pictures of her father and mother on their wedding day, and a picture taken when she was just two days old in bed with her mother who died just a few hours after the picture was taken. She was so grateful, she did not take those pictures with her when she married Jack. Everything she took with her, Jack destroyed or sold for profit. She felt the anger in her heart well up, then she knelt to pray, "Dear God, My heart is heavy for the sins I've done. Please forgive me, I know it is wrong to feel such hatred, because even Jack is your son, but his acts were of the devil. Of course, you know all our actions; guide me to be a good mother, a daughter with a loving and grateful heart, and to know the best way I can serve Jeb and Bess in taking care of our precious Willie. I know Little Maxwell is with you as is my Mother, I feel their light shining all around me. Lord Jesus, help them rest in peace,. Amen"

As Gunnar snored peacefully, Willie lay looking out the window at the moon lit night and sparkling stars. He lay very still, thinking about his Mam and Pap. Addressing them, "Mam and Pap, he whispered, I'll be a good boy, I promise. I'll take care of myself, help Miss Jenny and Rev. Sterling at whatever they want. I'll always pray to Jesus , and keep my black nut safe from getting lost. I hope Mam and Pap are safe." as he dreamed of his Mam and Pap, and the road to freedom.

Meister Eckhart (1260-c to 1329)
For Remember this
The shell must be cracked open
If what is inside is to come out.
If you want the kernel, You must break the shell,
We must learn to break through things
If we are to grasp God in them.

JEB AND BESS MEET TWO FREE NEGROS HEADING TO FIGHT WITH U.S. GRANT

Hidden behind forest brush and evergreens, Jeb and Bess try to get warm after getting lost trying to find the Underground Railroad. Winter, with a heavy snow falling, Jeb raised his finger to his limps to alert Bess, he could hear a noise. They immediately put out their small warming fire, as footsteps were approaching. Are they friend or foe?

"Mos, Is freezin, we got to fix fire." "Shh, Is smel a fir, hol stil," Jeb recognizing the voices were of fellow Negro's. He called out compassionately, "Fellow's, over here, my wife and me are hidden well behind bushes. We have food and horses, we've been trying to follow the Underground Railroad."

Neither of the men moved, afraid it was a trick as the man's voice was too perfect English with a Southern accent. .Suspecting their fears, Jeb instructed Bess to start a fire in order to heat snow water for coffee. They began to hear movement, then suddenly, one of the men stepped right in front of them with his rifle pointed at Jeb's head.,

"Whoz yu? Yu no nigra slav?" Moses asked with fear in his voice. "We're run-a-way educated house slaves from Mississippi that have been on the railroad for weeks, but now we're lost." answered Bess. Moses fear increased due to the fact they had no more ammunition. They just fought in the all Negro army at Paducah, Kentucky on the Mississippi river and were defeated miserably. They figured Grant could use them in his Army.

Jeb, interested in the latest on the war, stated, "Fella's, put down your guns, we have one gun between us. Tell me more of what you know about the war, while you join us in a cup of coffee. Do you have your own cups, we only have the two?" Moses looked at Percy and decided to risk the invitation as being friendly and on their side. They shared that Percy was from Indiana and Moses Ohio. Both joined up to help the Union fight for freedom and found a Negro Unit organizing around Cincinnati. Some folks donated money, Abolitionists is what they're called, to outfit them with guns and ammunition. Winter was a hell of a time to get Negro's from the South to fight a war. They lost at Paducah because of lack of experience, number of troops, and canons.

"Weez lost lots of Nigra's n that batle." exclaimed Moses painfully. "So does Grant plan to take Ft. Donelson from the Rebels?" Jeb asked. Both nodded sipping their hot coffee as Bess shared dried strips of

chicken and apples. Jeb suggested, "Fella's, if we sleep close, covered with our bedroll's, we might be able to get some rest. Tomorrow is going to be a rough day." Tired and exhausted from their two day journey without a rest, Jeb and Bess snuggled together. Jeb pondered a decision he must make. Knowing he could be a big help to Grant's Army as a medic, he also knew how much he loved Bess and wanted to live free with her, to accomplish their dreams, find Willie and build a life in free Canada. As he moved to snuggle closer, Bess whispered, "Jeb, you're thinking of joining up with Grant!" Spoken as an exclamation not as a question with her eyes already filled with tears, she felt his eyes tearing and streaming down his face as he squeezed her tightly. "You always know what's in my heart. Bess, I can help our wounded soldiers who are giving their lives for us slaves, I refuse to carry a gun. I don't want to be tempted to use it against an enemy. You'll need it to protect yourself from being robbed and raped."

She kissed him gently, then responded in a soft and gentle manner, "Jeb, you are my beloved forever husband, You are loving, caring, and compassionate to all, even your enemies. Of course, I know your heart. We've been through so much together and all the while, we shared our hopes and dreams. I'll be waiting for you in Ohio so we can fulfill them." Quietly laying her head on his broad chest, she finally fell asleep with a prayer in her heart.

Next morning, Jeb announced to their guests his plan to also join up with Grant's Army. They would take one horse and give the other to Bessie to make it to the river crossing at Cincinnati. The men were shocked but certainly relieved to have Jeb willing to join up. After breaking camp, leaving it as if no one was ever there, the men took turns riding the horse carrying their gear, and walking along side, always alert to enemy signs and sounds.

As Bess loaded her gear, Jeb gave her half of the herbs she and Jeb carried from Jenny's, leaving him the rest to use in his role as a medic for wounded and dying soldiers. She knew in her heart that Jeb would treat all soldiers, regardless if Union or Rebel. He hid the pistol in her bed roll along with the pouch of gold coins Jenny shared that Jack had hidden. Jeb took her into his arms, looked into her eyes, sharing his last moment of undying love, he kissed her, then helped her upon the black mare. She pulled her felt hat down over her eyes, took hold of the reins and headed north, never once looking back.

Jeb suggested that old Percy ride first as his shoes were the most worn. Jeb and Moses walked on each side, always looking for Rebels. At sundown, they reached the fires of Grant's Army. The sentry caught sight of their horse and was ready when they arrived. With his gun pointed at the men, he asked, "Whose there?" Seeing they were slaves," are you being followed?" Jeb took the liberty to answer for them believing he could best explain their situation. "Sir, my name is Jeb, a run-a-way educated house slave from Mississippi. These gentlemen are free Negro's that fought at Paducah with an all Negro Army. We want to join up with General Ulysses S. Grant's Army."

The sentry looked at the other sentry; then asked him to stand guard while he took the gentlemen to General Grant's tent. The snow was falling down with flakes as big as silver dollars. The men were shivering from lack of water, warm clothing, and worn out shoes. Jeb walked the horse as they followed the sentry. When they reached his tent, that was on a wooden platform, the sentry cleared his throat. "Private Wheeler, requests permission to speak with General Grant." The flap immediately opened with General Grant's aide stepping outside, "What do you have here, Private Wheeler?" "These three men want to sign on to fight with General Grant, Sir." Just then a big man in a torn and dirty Union Army uniform came through the flap. He had a wood pipe in his mouth, not lit, but chewing on it. Looking over the three and Jeb's horse, he asked gruffly, "Where did you steal that horse? And just where did you come from?" Jeb stepped forward saying, "Sir, my name is Jeb, a run-a-way educated house slave from the Beaumont Plantation Merci, Mississippi. These gentlemen are free Negro's who fought with the all Negro troops in Paducah. They want to join up to fight. I want to join to be a medic as I know I can help save lives."

General Grant stood silent, chomping his pipe, looking over the horse, he asked, "So where did you get that horse? Pretty fine specimen of horse flesh." "She's mine , sir. My wife and I were smuggled into a convent in Memphis, and when the nuns sent us north, they gave us the mare that was given to them."

"And where's your wife?" Jeb answered with tears in his eyes, "She's on her way to Cincinnati, hoping to get to the river by sundown." "Gentlemen, you all have an interesting tale. We can issue some extra blankets and two rifles. Welcome, if you can take orders, shoot straight, and fire when ordered. Get some rest, we attack tomorrow!" He started to leave when Jeb stopped him to hand a pouch that was for his eyes only. General Grant returned to his tent, opened the pouch to find Jeb's, baptismal certificate, his wife's name and destination plus two gold coins. Stunned, he motioned for his aide to put this with all of the other official documents. Drinking his hot tea, he contemplated their attack. He knew this was a huge gamble, all that was at risk if they lost. As he pondered this war, he remembered former West Point friends, who now, some were foe. "War is Hell," as he took a sip of tea.

Bess was drenched to the bone, hungry, and so tired that she laid her head on the gelding's mane. He was beautiful and gentle. He too, could use some water, food, and a nice warm dry rub down. She heard horses long before she saw them. Guiding Raven into the forest out of sight, she watched as they approached. Relieved, they were Union Soldiers. She moved out of the thicket, and made herself known. The lieutenant halted his regiment, to find out her name and her mission? "Ma 'am, what is your purpose alone in the forest unprotected and vulnerable?" "Sir, my name is Bess, I'm a run-a-way educated house slave from the Beaumont Plantation in Merci, Mississippi. This horse was given to me by the nuns who sheltered my husband, Jeb and me while on the Underground Railroad." She hands him the Bill of Sale verifying that she is the owner. As he is reading the document, he asked, "Where is your husband now?" "Sir, he left to be a medic with General Grant. He's very good in healing the sick and wounded. I'm trying to find my way to the Ohio river where I am to meet some Quaker's that will help me to freedom. When the war is over, Jeb will find me, so that we can live free."

"Bess, you are on the right path, follow our tracks, we just crossed the river at Cincinnati. Part of it is frozen, but there are boatmen who know how to navigate it. Good luck to you, we'll be sure to inform your husband, we met up with you, and you're almost to the river, Ma'am. My name is Lieutenant Gerald Stuart. May God Bless You, stay safe."

When Lt. Stuart arrived at General Grant's Army, he went straight to General Grants headquarters to report in. He told the General about meeting up with Bess and the tale she told them. General Grant confirmed the story. The men were already at their posts and ready to engage in battle. "Lieutenant, I have found that war brings with it some of the most heart rendering stories; my journal is full of them. You're excused to bed down and prepare. Tomorrow promises to be a most interesting day."

Bess arrived at the river dock without incident. Her biggest challenge was in finding a boatman willing to haul she and her horse across the river to the Ohio side. Finally, a flat boat appeared, it's lantern's burning. At the helm was a little man, she thought at first to be a young boy. But in examining closer, she saw that he was a midget of about 25 years old. He motioned for her to come close to the edge so that she could hear his offer. "I can haul you and your steed across this icy river for gold. No gold plated, only two gold coins. Do you suppose you can produce that sort of payment?"

"Yes, I can. I know you think that I'm a whore to have that kind of coin, but believe me, I've earned it honestly teaching French. My name is Jade Nicole, what's yours?" "Well, I'll be dogged! I ain't ever met a real French Lady. Why are you going to Cincinnati?" "I have been appointed to teach French and English to the school run by nuns. Are you familiar with the convent?"

Yes Ma'am, my name is Jimmy Black. I can take you there for, "I know, for an extra coin." Red faced, he nodded and started to dock his raft. After everything was tied down, he led Raven to the post for hitching livestock. He helped Bess on board as he carefully navigated the river past the ice chunks to the Cincinnati Dock. After tying down his raft, and helping both Bess and Raven up the gravel path to the dock, he laid his hand out to be paid. Bess smiled, gave him two coins, then shook his hand, "Jimmy Black, you're a very talented and intelligent man. Should you ever want to improved your life, I'm sure the nuns will give you good counsel. Merci, Merci Black Au revoir."

Bess climbed up on Raven to find her own way to the convent. After stopping to ask directions to the nearest convent, she found she was just about one quarter of a mile there. She rang the bell on the outside of the tall metal gate. Counting, she was at 127 when an elderly nun approached the gate. Bess, smiled, "Sister, may I please see Mother Superior? It's an important matter." The sister told her to please wait until she asked Mother Superior if she may be admitted.

Again, Bess counted. This time to only 97 until the nun arrived with a large iron key, opened the door as Bess and Raven were admitted to the stables behind the convent. Dismounting, she found the hitching post, then tied Raven and followed the nun into a large hallway. The place smelled of burning herbs and candle wax. At the end of the hall on the right, the nun rapped gently on a tall hand carved wooden door. "Come in, Sister Margaret, Who is this person that you have brought to me?" Embarrassed she had forgotten to ask the guest's name, Bess rescued her by introducing herself. "Forgive my late arrival, but I am Jade Nicole Dominican, an educated house slave from the Beaumont Plantation in Merci, Mississippi. I've arrived here by my own wits, and the help of conductor's on the Underground Railroad. I call myself Bess to keep my true identity unknown. I was told you could also assist in protecting me from slave buyers and sellers."

"Wow! Your soliloquy was quite a mouthful, I'm quite impressed. Please have a seat while I catch my breath." Bess took a seat, nervous too, she needed to take a long deep breath.

"Now my dear, please start from the beginning. Tell me about your long journey and how you found your way to my convent." Bess told her whole life story. Beginning at her birth, her escape, and how she

and Jeb were baptized and married at the Sister's of Charity in Memphis. Their capture by Jack Tom Jones, her rape by Jack, bearing her beautiful rape child, Jenny's killing of Jack, and the dead child Jenny birthed. Their escape from rebel soldiers, Jeb joining up with General Grant, and her meeting Jimmy Black, who rowed she and Raven across the Ohio River dodging ice chunks, to finally finding her way to Mother's Superior's Convent. Mother Superior listened intently as Bess emotionally told her story. Exhausted, Bess laid down her head and wept.

"My dear, forgive my long questioning without first feeding you and allowing you to rest and recover from your terrible nightmare." "Sister Margaret, will you please escort Bess to the empty cell by the kitchen to bathe. Bring her a clean nightgown and slippers, and then take her to the kitchen to feast on the cabbage stew, bread and hot tea left from dinner." "Please Bess go with Sister Margaret, I will see you in the morning. Goodnight, my child."

The hot water felt good to Bess tired and sore body. Her hair hadn't been washed since leaving Jenny's. The lye soap was strong, but after rinsing it three times with vinegar, the red high-lights shown brightly on her dark brown hair. Her mother, Missy had auburn red hair and her father, the master, had hazel eyes. She loved looking into his eyes when they talked at dinner time. He was always so uncomfortable in her presence. She now understood this to mean he was timid with himself, for feeling fatherly emotions for Jade Nicole. How difficult it must be, to be limited by what society dictated as proper or just not done. She knew one thing, she could not allow any feelings she has for him, to permit her ever to return to the Magnolia Grove Plantation in Merci, Mississippi.

Mother Superior called for Bess to come to her office as soon as she had her breakfast. Bess arrived wearing her own clothing that the nun's laundered while she slept. She stood politely until Mother Superior asked her to have a seat. "My Child, did you have a restful sleep? I'm happy to see our laundry nuns washed and ironed your clothing. They almost look good as new." "Oh yes, Mother Superior, everything is just wonderful."

"I've spent most of my evening contemplating the best manner in which we can serve you, while also acknowledging your education and skills. We have a convent in Dayton, Ohio about 50 miles north of here that also protects souls from the railroad. My concern here is that you are a very valuable commodity to slave buyers. Being so close to the river, I'm afraid they would be brave enough to try to steal you from our premises, knowing we are unprotected and will bear no arms. I'm afraid, I judge Jimmy Black as a soul who might sell you for the right amount of gold. Your plantation probably has a large bounty for anyone bringing you back to Mississippi." Nodding Bess said, "I believe that it might be so." I am thinking, it might be safer for you, if I send you to our convent in Dayton as soon as possible. Their Mother Superior has greater means to protect you and further your journey to Canada. I've sent a courier this morning to Dayton. I expect a response by sundown if they can accept you. I have an escort who will drive my buggy with you and Raven tomorrow morning, which is our regular day to send communications between the two convents. As you know, everything must be done in secret, as to appear a normal busy day between convents." "Yes Mother Superior, I understand, I'll be ready when you call for me. May I attend Vesper's this evening? My soul is yearning for the chants, the silence, and the prayers." "Yes, my Child, they begin at 7, just after dinner. You may be excused."

Bess asked Sister Margaret if she might be able to walk in the Convent's Garden? Sister Margaret nodded, opened the door to the garden, then left to do her chores. Bess was in awe of its beauty. Even though was still February with snow on the ground, there were little buds beginning to appear on the peach, apricot, and apple trees. There was a Robin perched on a bird bath, noticing every movement she made, As Bess smelled apple blossoms, the Robin hopped down to follow her. She noticed herbs growing beside the garden shed. Bending over to smell each herb, she wondered if the gardener would mind if she dug up a sample? She must remember to ask Sister Margaret if this was a possibility. The dinner bell began to ring. She turned to address Mr. Robin, "Mr. Robin Red Breast, thank you for being my escort on my tour of your beautiful garden, you're a noble guardian."

When the bell for breakfast rang, Bess was dressed and ready to meet her escort to the Dayton convent. Bess was given specific instructions as to what to say if stopped by any suspicious encounter on the road. Sister Margaret escorted her to the courtyard to meet Father James Bellingham, her escort. Father Bellingham was about fifty years old, spoke with an English proper accent and full of questions. He shared he was employed by the Catholic Seminary where he taught English, Latin, and Poetry. He wanted to know her age and even asked how tall she was? She said she was 21 years old and five feet eleven inches tall. Both her father and mother were very tall. She wondered to herself if he knew that the Convent was involved with the Underground Railroad.

The weather turned out to be very nice, but cold. The wind was not blowing, so there were no drifts on the road. Father Bellingham told her the road went directly into the downtown part of the city. He said the city was founded by immigrants in the late 1700's. He loved the way the city was laid out with its beautiful European architecture. He shared, "Dayton is home of the first Soldier's Home and Hospital for Civil War vets." Bess enjoyed his rhetoric and ambling stories that made time fly. He slowed down, as to not miss his turn into the street the Convent was on. It was long passed dinner time. Both their stomach's growled announcing it was time to eat. Greeted by a novice, they were escorted to Mother Superior's office and then to the dining room for tea. Father Bellingham was not bashful in stating that he could use something with a little more nourishment, as they had driven quite a distance without a bite to eat. They were then served bowls of chicken soup with wide home made noodles and dark bread. The English and French Tea Cakes were also delicious, abundant and devoured with much appreciation. "All is well that end's well" exclaimed Father Bellingham patting his stomach.

Both guests were assigned rooms, given linens for bathing, the schedule for Vespers, and time for Morning Prayers. Father Bellingham left after Morning Prayers and Breakfast. Nothing was said, but there seemed to be a "sigh of relief" when he was gone. Convents like discipline, schedules, and do not want to be disturbed, if possible.

Bess was escorted to Mother Superior's office, thinking, "More questions, more explanations. However, the only question was, "Where did you get your beautiful horse?" Bess reached into her pouch to show the Bill of Sale, signed by owner to Jade Nicole of Memphis, Tennessee.

"Bess, Do you mind sharing what you are passionate about?" "Passionate about?" Squinting her eyebrows in complete surprise. "Yes, My Child, What do you love to do, enjoy, and dream about?" "Oh, of course, I love my husband, growing healing herbs, I love helping the sick to get well, and I dream of living with my husband and child somewhere free." "I don't have a magic wand, but I do think I can help with some things that you enjoy. I'll get back with you later today or tomorrow. But I must ask you to not leave the Convent Grounds. It is too dangerous." "You know Mother Superior, I recall another Mother Superior in Memphis saying those exact words. Believe me, I do know the dangers. I will not wander. Thank you and your nuns for all you are trying to do for me."

Cold, with snow still laying on the ground, Mother Superior sent word for Bess to please pack her things to be ready to leave for the north. Hearing this, Bess asked to speak with Mother Superior. She knew one thing for sure, she did not want to leave for Canada until she found out if Jeb survived Ft. Donelson's battle, and if Willie found a Quaker to help him. She tapped on Mother Superior's door. "Come in, my child. "Mother Superior, I must explain my situation and the reason I do not choose to move North. Hearing this, Mother Superior called, "Sister Margaret, please be quick, the conductor is waiting, tell him to go on," then turning to Bess, she said, "Bess, I'm sorry, please continue. "My husband left to serve as a medic with General Grant at the battle of Ft. Donelson. I need to be here in order to find out if he survived. And my baby, Willie was left with an abolitionist on the railroad to deliver him to a Quaker family for protection. Please, Mother, I appreciate you taking me in, but I know you will understand my heartfelt desires." "I see,"pausing, "I will need to leave for a short while. Please follow Sister Margaret's need for help in the Convent. When I get back, we will talk about how I might be of service to you. You now may be excused."

Mother Superior called for her horse and buggy and chose to drive it herself. She headed towards the Soldier's Home Area. Arriving at the home of Dr. Chad Somerset III, she tied her horse to the hitching post, then rapped on the door. Maud opened the door, astonished to see Mother Superior alone, she welcomed her in. "Mother Superior, what a surprise and joy to have you visit our home!" "I don't have much time, My Dear, is Dr. Somerset in?" Maud took her wrap, then left to inform Chad of his guest. He too, was surprised, but excited to welcome her. He asked, "Maud could you please bring a pot of tea and some blueberry biscuits that you made that morning?"

"Mother Superior! What do I owe this visit to at this time?" "Dr. Chad, I have a challenge, but one that I think will be a great addition to your medical clinic." As she sat down, Maud brought the tea pot and tea set with hot freshly made biscuits. She thanked Maud then spoke quietly and with purpose. "I've a young lady, she says she is 21, very light skin, claims her mother was half white and her father was the plantation's master. She speaks perfect English and French, loves growing herbs for medicinal use, and does not choose to go to Canada as her husband left her on the railroad to join General Grant as a medic. She has a male child somewhere on the railroad that was the result of a slave seller raping her. She too, wants to see if her child made it. So you see where I going with all of this?" "Yes, Mother Superior, I do. Maud has just discovered she is pregnant. Having someone to help would be a god-send." "Dr. Chad, she can easily pass for white, do we dare let your community to know about your new help?"

"Yes, we do! I shall pay her a salary plus room and board. The Somerset's do not have slaves or unpaid servants. All are treated as family. When do we get to meet her and to learn about her own thoughts and desires?" "Now! If it works with your schedule?" Dr. Chad turned to Mary Maud, "Sweetheart, could you go with Mother Superior? I'll come pick you ladies up after visiting my patient's in the hospital." Excited, Maud responded, "Oh, of course, let me get my heavy cape, I'll be ready as soon as I put the tea tray in the kitchen."

Mother Superior and Mary Maud left at 9:35 to return to the Convent. They arrived in less than a half hour to the silence of Nun's doing their morning chores and Bess enjoying being of help. After opening the door for Mother Superior, Sister Margaret was instructed to bring their guest in with a pot of tea. Bess, still wondering what Mother Superior was up to, smiled at the beautiful woman before her, then took a seat. Mother Superior immediately started the introductions. "Bess, thank you for your patience. I'd like to introduce you to Mrs. Maud Somerset, wife of Dr. Chadwick Somerset III. Mrs Somerset, Mrs. Jade Nicole Dominican, aka Bess, a recent arrival from the railroad. I believe the two of you might come to a mutual agreement that will satisfy both of your challenges.

Maud asked, "First of all, what name do you want to be called?" "I choose to be Bess, for fear of my former Master might have slave buyer's looking for me." Maud smiles and nods, "I'm so pleased to meet you Bess. I'm saddened by the circumstances that brought you here, but I'm pleased that we may be able to help. My husband and I are expecting our first child. He's a physician and I'm his assistant. After the baby is born, I'd like to be free to nurse my child and care for our home. We do not believe in slavery or having servants that are treated as lower in class. We will offer a salary, room and board in our home, and you will be part of our family, as a sister. Is that something you think you might enjoy? I hope so, I already feel a kindred spirit."

In just that moment, Dr. Somerset arrived and was escorted to Mother Superiors office. He stepped in, bowed to Mother Superior, and kissed his wife on the cheek. Mother Superior began the introduction. "Dr. Chad, this is the young woman I told you about, Jade Nicole Dominican, aka Bess, this is my good friend and physician, Dr. Chadwick Somerset."

"My dear Mrs. Jade Nichole, Bess if we can be on first name basis, I'm delighted to meet you and to welcome you to our home and medical clinic, if that be your desire." "Sir, It is, both my desire and my honor to be in your employment. Merci"

The happy couple stood up Maud hugged Bess, then said goodbye to Mother Superior and to all the smiling Nuns surrounding them. They climbed into the buggy and headed to the Somerset Home with their new employee, Mrs. Bess Dominican, housekeeper and medical assistant.

Taking in the beautiful scenery on the trip to the Somerset home, Bess was silently thinking about Jeb and if he survived the battle he so lovingly volunteered to serve. She thought about his gentleness for all life, his deep love for herself and her child. He left the handgun with her, knowing he'd never use it, but hoping she would if in danger. As the buggy arrived in front of her new home, her eyes lit up with anticipation, praying she could be of service to sweet Maud and anxious to work in Dr. Chad's Medical Clinic for the poor. What a wonderful new beginning!

Dr. Chad opened the door after tying the horses to the hitching post. He helped Bess with her things as Maud lit the candles in the front room and kitchen. Maud guided Bess to the door next to the kitchen, then escorted Bess into her new room. She opened the curtains so the light could announce to Bess the beauty of her new environment. It was decorated in shades of blue. The walls were light blue, the woodwork was a darker shade, the curtains were sheer with a gathered flounce made on a print of blue bells, violets, and iris flowers to compliment the window coverings. The trundle bed, had a white handmade lace covering, and a feather tic mattress. A rag rug covered about a half of the oak floor, a small desk and book shelf was in the corner next the window, and an old foot locker was at the foot of the bed. In the other corner was an upholstered dark blue chair with several small cushions of various colors. A globe light was on a small table next to the bed. Bess was speechless! Maud put an arm around Bess and asked, "I hope you like it! I just finished making the curtains, pillows, and bed covering. The furnishings were in my bedroom growing up in Philadelphia. The foot locker followed Chad through all of his college and internships." Bess began to cry, then sob, and fell into Maud's open arms. Bess, was about eight inches taller, but she felt so much love and tenderness, that she just let go and felt the release of all the pain and fear she had so long suffered, and kept within.

"I'm so grateful! Your kindness is overwhelming to my soul!" "Please Jade, have a seat, handing her a clean handkerchief, you must be exhausted." I'll get us some tea, we'll have a little chat, then you can take a hot bath. Tomorrow we'll buy you some new clothing, but in the meantime, we will find you some of both mine and Chad's clothing to make do."

She left to make the tea, gathered clothing from Chad's and her closet, and to heat the dinner.she prepared earlier. She'd made a pan of roasted root vegetables with garlic and onions, a roasted hen, biscuits, and a pumpkin pie. After putting the coffee on to boil, she went to invite Bess to see the rest of the house.

Bess was sitting on the blue chair in the corner of her room. She'd removed her shoes to be cleaned, and hung her coat in the closet. When Maud knocked, she answered with a very low sounding emotional voice, "Come in please."

"While Chad is tending to the horses, would you like a tour of the house?" I confess, we've only been in the house for a few a months waiting for it to be finished. We just received our furniture from Philadelphia. It is rather big for just two of us, but we are planning on having a big family. I come from a big Irish Catholic family and I loved it. Chad was an only child and did not like it at all."

"Yes, Mrs Somerset, I'd love a tour!" "Beginning right now, please call me Maud, I feel you're like a sister to me. I miss Patty, my sister next to me. She's engaged, I won't be able to have bridal showers for her, as she lowered her head and sniffled, "I'll miss the wedding because of my pregnancy. But she understands. They may come here as part of their honeymoon, eyes glistening brightly. That would be such fun! You and she will just love each other."

The tour with all its fine furnishings reminded Bess of her home on the plantation. Each room seemed to have a theme with memories of loved ones. The master bedroom was decorated with soft colors of brown and beige. The bed was made by her father and the bureau was a wedding gift. The quilt was made by her mother and sisters. Paintings of family members hung on the walls and small portraits of loved ones were scattered on the bureau, desk, and book shelves. The small rug at the side of the bed was wool with roses and leaves woven in its fabric. She shared the rug was purchased on their honeymoon in New York City. A small room next to the Master Bedroom is to become the Nursery. Dr. Chad painted it a very pale yellow.

"The other rooms are in process." Sighed Mary Maud. "I'm hoping you can give me some ideas and we will work together to finish them. I'm just about six weeks pregnant, so we still have plenty of time."

Descending the winding staircase, Maud remembered the coffee boiling on the stove. "Oh, I forgot the coffee!" "I'll remove it," said Bess, "you stay right there, I'll be right back." Relieved, she waited, Bess returned breathless, then asked, "I'm interested in who that lovely couple is on the wall at the very end of the staircase?" "That beautiful couple is Chad's grandparents, Chadwick Somerset I and Victoria Amelia Campbell dressed for their portrait in their formal wedding attire. Don't they make a handsome couple?"

Bess stood in awe as Maud shared that Chad's parent's portrait hung in his office next to the parlor. "His grandfather was a Barrister for the King, they lived in London, England As soon as we find a good portrait artist, we will have ours painted." The first room down the winding staircase was the formal parlor. It had several family heirlooms. A beautiful piano, a small English Tea Set, a brocade settee and a small French Velvet Boudoir chair. The kitchen had a big round oak table and chairs, modern wood cook stove, a stainless steel sink with hand water pump, and an oak ice box. The dining room was empty except for a walnut English glass china dish cabinet and an enormous red, gold, and blue Oriental Rug. The room was papered with velvet tiny roses embossed on wallpaper and walnut wood wainscot paneling. "Chad surprised me on our 2nd anniversary by ordering that beautiful rug. His next challenge was to get it delivered here. It just arrived a month ago. He saw me admiring Persian rugs while we were in New York. Chad's such a sweet, romantic and unselfish soul. I love him more everyday. So you see, we've got lot's to do and a whole lot of time to do it in. No hurry, as each baby comes, ideas will also come. "I'm ravished! I haven't been able to keep food down until the late afternoon and evening. Let's set the table."

Maud called for Chad as she began dipping the roasted vegetables into china bowls. She set white coffee mugs, a cream and sugar bowl, butter, salt, pepper and biscuits on the table. Bess offered to take the roasted chicken from the oven so that Dr. Somerset could carve it. She was wearing one of his shirts over a night gown of Maud's. She had cleaned her shoes of mud and dirt so as to not mess up the clean floors. Dr. Chad came through the side kitchen door, hung his coat on a peg, changed from his boots into bedroom slippers stored in a cabinet next the kitchen door. Kissing his wife, he nodded to Bess, then washed his hands in a wash stand by the door. They all sat down. Holding hands, Dr. Chad asked the blessing. "Father, thank you for this day, blessing us with a baby on its way and for Bess as she joins our family sharing her love, talent and medical assistance. In the name of The Father, Son, and Holy Ghost, Amen." With a big wide grin he lovingly said, "Everything smells great! Let's eat."

Epitaph, by Merrit Malloy

When I die, give what's left of me away to children

and old men that wait to die.

And if you need to cry, cry for your brother

walking the street beside you,

Put your arms around anyone and give them

What you need to give to me.

I want to leave you something,

Something better

than words

Or sounds.

Look for me

In the people I've known

Or loved,

And if you cannot give me away,

At least let me live on in your eyes

And not your mind.

You can love me most

By letting

Hands touch hands,

By letting bodies touch bodies,

And by letting go

Of children

That need to be free.

Love doesn't die,

People do,

So, when all that's left of me

Is love, Give me away.

L illian Rose Somerset, aka GrannyRose continues to share from her journal:

The grand children are very attentive, snacking on popcorn as Granny Rose's granddaughter, Lily Kai took notes and husband, Ardon Morning Star Joseph, made sketches on his artist's pad. GrannyRose introduces this segment starting at Ft. Donelson with Ulysses S. Grant in command.

Freezing cold, fog so thick one could barely see one foot in front of another; 24,500 Union troops fought hard to accomplish an unconditional surrender from the Confederate Army on February 16, 1862. Brigadier General Ulysses S. Grant, under his command, Brigadier General John McClernand surrounded the Confederate armies. During the battle, they fought in horrific conditions, freezing weather, lack of warm clothing, food and water. After several retreats, the Union soldiers were able to capture 12,000 Rebels. It was reported several thousand Rebel troops escaped, retreated, or surrendered before the battle got underway. The Yankee's tightened the noose around the Rebels, forcing Rebel General Gideon Pillow to retreat, as General Floyd and General Forrest abandoned their commands. Rebel General Simon B. Buckner was put in command. Buckner inherited chaos among his troops. With no way to get supplies, he decided to wave the white flags of truce in order to speak with General Grant personally. He asked what conditions he could get for a surrender? Grant replied, "None, it must be an unconditional surrender." It was estimated that Confederate casualties were approximately 14,000 wounded or killed, while the Union total casualties were around 2,700.

"The art of war is simple enough.
Find out where your enemy is.
Get at him as soon as you can.
Strike him as hard as you can, and keep moving on."
Lt. General Ulysses S Grant
Commander Union Army, Civil War 1851-1865
Ft. Donelson Battle 1862

By his own estimation, Jeb awakened at about 4 a.m. Their orders were to NOT shoot until you can know for sure, you are shooting a rebel and to keep your flank close and straight. As a medic, he carried only his medical bag with bandages, water, whiskey, a small saw, calming and sleeping herbs, and bee salve. He wore his own boots, jacket with a big white cross painted on its back, and the felt hat given to him by Miss Jenny and knitted socks made by Bess, his beloved wife. "Dear God, please see her safely to Cincinnati."

He dressed, ate some jerky, and drank hot chicory given to him by the mess squad. Hearing the bugle, he quickly tied his rolled blanket around his waist, and hung his leather medical pouch over his head. Lining up, he thought about this ungodly war being fought by young children, flag bearer's and drummers only about 12 to 14, Infantry age 15 to 40, all excited to fight to defeat the Rebels' thirst for slavery. He felt chilled to the bone, but knew to think loving and warm thoughts as the best remedy to stay warm. "Father, guide us to learn how to live in peace and harmony. Thank you for marching beside me, reminding me of our Savior's sacrifice for all of humanity, Amen."

The Yankee's knew the Rebel army lacked items necessary to keep fit and healthy troops, but they certainly did not lack enthusiasm to kill Yankees! Their Rebel yell was blood curdling and frightening, especially when you couldn't see anything and did not know from where they were coming. Also, in most cases, the Rebels lacked guns, so they fought hand to hand with or without bayonets. Jeb also knew that wearing his red cross on his arm did not necessarily mean a rebel would honor a medic as neutral. His orders were to to do what he could to save a life, communicate to the ambulance drivers how many were alive waiting to be hauled to the army hospital where "God's Angel Sister-Nurses" waited to save lives and give comfort. Both sides knew these angels did not choose sides or see color of a man's skin. Their resolve boosted him to serve God and his fellow man. Shooting began. He patiently marched through heavy snow, looking to see if anyone had fallen. It was difficult to recognize Union troops from Rebel. He slowly moved forward, in snow up to his knees, Suddenly he felt his boot hit something hard. Looking down into the heavy snow, he saw a man lying on his stomach. He knelt down, tapped him on his shoulder, saw blood running from his head, then whispering directly into his ear, "Son, I'm a medic, where are you hurt?" In that moment, he saw heavy blood flowing from a rag tied around his eye with only half his face. He gently turned him over. A rebel with part of his right eye and skull missing. Reaching into his medical pouch, he found a large cotton pad, tied it over the rag, then asked gently. "Can you hear me?" No response. "Son, please squeeze my hand if you can hear my words," a weak squeeze. "You are at Ft. Donelson battlefield. I'm a medic doing my best to help you." Through the loud sounds of battle, a low, faint, and desperate response could be heard. "I'm Capt. Phillipi Beaumont, from Merci, Mississippi. I'm dying, please tell my father, Jean Michel Beaumont, that I was brave and that I'm sorry." Surprised and shocked, Jeb gave him a sip of whiskey, rubbing his hands, said, "Phillipi, this is Desmond, your brother. Phillipi gasped, "I'm a medic in the Union Army, I promise to notify Father," as he embraced Phillipi, "I've always loved you, even when we disagreed. I forgive you Phillipi, I know God forgives you, Brother, go in peace."

In that moment, Desmond felt his brother pass on, Holding him in his arms, he covered him with his blanket, searched for personal items to be sent to Father, while all the time sobbing, grieving, broken hearted, as he spoke softly to his dead brother, "Phillipi, Jade and I married in a church. I know she forgives you, as well."

Placing his brother's body on a hard mound of snow, he thought, "I must remember this date so that when I write Father." So surprised to refer to himself as a son of Jean Michele and as Phillipi's brother. He did the sign of the cross then fought his way through the blinding storm to the unending job of serving the sick and dying. Yes, he was Phillipi's brother, but so were all these men on this field of hate and prejudice. He said out loud to the wind, while tears froze on his face, "In moments such as these, One can only speak, Absolute Truth."

The day seemed to go on forever. Listening to gun blasts, men yelling and crying, horses snorting, the beat of war drums; all of which saddened his soul. He had no idea how many men he patched up to be picked up by the Sister's of Holy Cross Ambulance team. He was doing what his heart told him to do, "give comfort to the sick and dying." Mother Angela had the best run Army Hospital. Sisters do not see color of shirts or skin, they treat all equal as Jesus did. His mind wandered to his growing-up years, his beautiful mother, Rochelle, he and Phillipi's education; their competitive desire to please Father, and then, that fatal day when he tried to rape Jade, their flight to freedom, confirmation and marriage, evil Jack Jones, sweet baby Willie and Miss Jenny; all contributors to this moment. "God's plan is freedom for all!" Pondering this infamous day of transition and transformation, Desmond Lafayette Dominican, aka Jeb wrote to his father and of his destiny.

They came, Thousands marching,

Deep snow, freezing, barefoot, starved

Few guns, no amo, Waving proudly Rebel Flags,

Yelling, "Yankee go home! We love our slaves!"

The sin of prejudice

Carved deeply into their souls.

Desmond aka Jeb, Medic-

That evening, he found his way to General Grant's war tent. He asked if he might be able to speak to the General. Opening the flap, General Grant greeted him chewing on his wooden pipe, the General asked? "What do you need, medic? As you can see we've got a war going on?" "Sir, I'm medic Desmond from Mississippi. I would beg of you to please mail this letter I've written for a soldier that died in my arms asking me to please let his family know of his death and that he fought bravely. I don't have money for the postage, because Sir I gave you all that I had when I joined up." Grant's mind immediately recalled the educated slave who so generously volunteered to serve as a medic and gave all of his possessions to General Grant for the Union's cause.

"Of course, Son, I'll see to that. By the way, could that mare you gave us pull an ambulance wagon?" "Yes Sir!" She wasn't bred to do that, but she could do it very nicely." "I'd like to give her to Mother Angela, compliments of our men. Stay safe tomorrow, we still have a war to win." Taking the letter, he closed the flap, then placed the letter on his battle log.

Rumor was the Yankee's had the Rebel's surrounded. The Union Army was alert and ready to attack. At sunrise, the battle began in full force. Desmond had only gone about 15 yards when he spotted a deep mound of snow. He carefully approached, then stood very still, as there was no movement. Looking over the mound he discover a body covered with snow. Checking to see if he was alive, he was shocked to find a young Union Drummer of about 15, unconscious, no apparent wounds of any kind. His drum lay by his side. Jeb tried to awaken him to give him some whiskey, but to no avail. Hearing yells of Rebel infantry attacking, he quickly laid down on top of the boy to protect him. As he lay, he could see the battle taking place all around him. Hand-to-hand contact; bayonets striking, causing deafening fearful sounds. Suddenly, total darkness! Silence!! A rebel had jammed the butt of his gun into Desmond's head, stomped on his back while yelling, "Go to hell, Nigra Lover."

Desmond Lafayette Dominican, aka Jeb, husband of Jade Nicole Dominican of Merci, Mississippi, passed on to his Father's Heavenly home at age 22 years, serving courageous as a Union Army medic on the battlefield of Ft. Donelson, February 16, 1862.

Ulysses
by Alfred Lord Tennyson 1833
Tho' much is taken, much abides; and tho'
We are not now that strength which in old days
Moved earth and heaven; that which we are;
One equal temper of heroic hearts,
Made weak by time and fate, but strong in willingness
To strive, to seek, to find, and not to yield.
Pages (65-70)

Rev. Sterling's Home

Cincinnati, Ohio

Entering the kitchen, Jenny found her father, Elder Brock, and the children having a chat. She noticed there was a large sheet of paper, and a ruler on the table. "Are the boys bothering you with nonsense questions, Father?" "Why, no Jenny. We're getting acquainted. Seems like these boys have been through a lot in order to make their way to old Grandad's house," chuckling. "Brock and I are measuring the boys for some new clothing and shoes. Figure their growing so fast, we need to add a little more to their boots and overalls."

"How can I help?" Putting an apron over her fresh morning dress. "We've got sausage cooked and the pancake mixed ready for the griddle. Maybe you could start making pancakes so that we can all eat and get out of here to head to Johnson's Mercantile on Main Street." "Right on it, Father!" she responded.

Jenny located the big iron skillet and bacon grease, added a glob of grease to the skillet, then measured the coffee grounds to the boiling water in the big enamel coffee pot. The men were having fun taking measurements, while tickling the boys in the process. After setting the table, Jenny called for everyone to come to the table. When everyone was seated, Rev. Sterling asked Jenny to say the blessing. Before she began, she asked, "Boys, I believe we would love to hear your prayer for your new beginning. Gunnar will you begin?" "Let Willie go first, I don't think my prayers are good enough." "Boys, no one expects you to sound like you're an adult. But it will give you practice, because gentlemen are always asked to give the blessing as a guest. Gunnar wiggles, shakes his foot, then looked his mother right in the eye and said, "Then I'll do it right now. "Jesus, I know you know I'm hungry, I'm only four, thank you for this sausage and pancakes, Amen" Elder Brock reached over to touch Gunnar's shoulder and declared! "Why, I believe that's the best breakfast blessing I've ever heard! Let's eat. 'cause we've got some shopping to do." Willie speaks up nervously, "I believe I should stay here, in case someone want's to sell me." Jenny responded, "I think Gunnar and I will stay home as well, we've got chores to do." Elder Brock volunteered, "I'm happy to go to Johnson's Mercantile to purchase the Church supplies and fit these boys with some decent clothing." Careful that he had written down the correct measurements, he wondered what the boys each weighed? He thought to himself, "We'll need to go the mill for that."

Rev. Sterling asked to be excused to go to the church to ready it for Sunday church services. Jenny kissed her father on the cheek and each boy hugged him as he left to go next door to the church.

"Okay, my sons. Go to the outhouse and do your morning duty, wash your hands in the basin at the back porch." "But if we're going to work, why do have to wash our hands." complained Gunnar. Jenny frowned, then she sat the boys down, "Boys, beginning today, we start your education. I see I've waited too long. Go do as I say, and always remember to wash your hands after using the outhouse. That includes when you stand by a tree to pee, you need to wash your hands after you finished. There will always be a basin filled with soap, and a bucket to get a drink when thirsty. Now git!"

The boys took off running a race to the outhouse. Afterwords they washed their hands and negotiated how to gather the eggs. The rooster,

Mr Big was very protective of his ladies and their nests. They found 4 eggs from the 5 ladies. Next they cleaned out the barn poop. Willie, being the biggest, used the shovel, Gunnar, the rake to pull the poop to the side of the barn yard. The two horses, one pig, and cow were in the pasture grazing. The cow, who stood chewing her cud was nameless. Gunnar thought maybe they should name her, "everyone needs a name." "Hey Willie, what name should we call this cow? I like Tilly?" "I don't. How about something pretty, like "Rosebud?" "Yeah, I like that and maybe call her Rosie for short?" "Where's Toby, I haven't seen her this morning?" Just then, Toby came around the corner of the barn chasing a rabbit. "I think she believes she still needs to help us find something to eat." "Hey Toby girl, come here, you don't need to chase rabbits, we've got you some food and water."

After about 2 to 3 hours of hard work, the boys finished then high tailed it to the well for a dipper full of cool water. The well had a little roof over it with a bucket hanging full of flowers. There was another bucket attached to a long rope. They dropped the bucket into the well, both held tightly to the rope to pull up the bucket. Gunnar screamed, "It's a miracle! "This will be my daily job!" Will responding jokingly, "You think it will fun to carry water every day? "Well, we'll see."

Hearing a bell ringing, they looked to the back door and saw Mom ringing the bell that hung on the side of the door. She informed the boys that she would ring the bell when she needed them. She led them to a pump by the back side of the house. Immediately Willie figured it out, that this well was closer to the church and the water they would be carrying would be coming from this pump. "Gunnar, you get to carry water from this pump. Want to try it out?" Gunnar, pulled down on the handle, which took all of his strength to do it. He said, "Willie you pump and I'll carry the bucket." Jenny watching the drama thought, "All is well that ends well." grinning happily. The boys washed their hands but their clothing smelled of barn poop. Jenny ran into the house for two big towels.

"Strip naked, wrap these around you and head upstairs, I have water running for your bath. It's going to be cold, pretend your swimming." Giggling the boys stripped, and ran upstairs as she picked up their soiled clothing to go into a big galvanized tub for washing.

When the boys finished their bath, they wrapped the towels around them to answer Grandad's call to come to the front parlor. They did as told. Grandad asked, "You fella's been working hard?" Standing tall and erect, they both said, "Yes Sir!" Like two little soldiers on parade. "At ease troops, Elder Brock has brought you some fine new work clothes."

They scurried to where Eder Brock sat with packages all around him. Elder Brock handed Gunnar and Willie each, two pair of drawers, they neither one had ever seen a pair before, two pair of socks, knitted by the ladies in the church, two pair of overalls, two plaid shirts, Gunnar's were blue and black, Willie's were brown and green, and each a pair of boots. Willie was stunned! He'd never had a pair of boots or anything to put on his feet. Big old tears came to his eyes as he tried to put them on. He mistakenly tried to put the left boot on the right foot. Jenny spotted his struggle while Granddad help Gunnar with his boots. After they were laced up, Jenny relieved their fears by saying, "Boys, this will be one of your first lessons, how to tie your boot laces? But for now, we'll tie them for you in order for us to know if they fit." After the boots were tied, each boy stood up to let Elder Brock measure if they had enough room to grow, everyone exclaimed THEY ARE PERFECT ! "Ooops," said Grandad, "We forgot the socks. Fella's please take your boots off, we need to start all over."

Luckily, the boots fit with the socks on with plenty of room to grow. Gunnar's boots were black and Willie's were brown. They declared they'd clean and polish them nightly. During all the fun of trying on clothes and shoes, Elder Brock had left the room. He returned carrying two boxes. He handed each boy a box. "Boys, this is your welcome home present. Hope you like it." Willie's heart was ticking so fast, he'd never had a wrapped present in his life. He opened the brown wrapping paper very slowly as if something would jump out and bite him. There it was! A beautiful straw hat. Everyone yelled, "Try them on!"

Jenny guided the boys to the mirror in the hall. Willie and Gunnar both starred at their reflection. "Why, gentlemen, you two are very handsome. I'm so happy they fit." "Oh, I do love it! I love everything! Elder Brock, whatever help you need you can count on me to pay you back!" "Willie, no money owed, but I can always use some good help now and then"

The presents continued, Jenny handed Gunnar and Willie each two handkerchiefs purchased from a lady at church. Gunnar had a blue and white one, and Willie had a green and white one. Jenny explained the white was for church and the colored one was for everyday work. She promised to show them how to properly use them in their daily classroom lessons. She stopped them on the way upstairs to give a box that she forgotten to give. "Boys, I'm sorry, I forgot to give you these. They are cigar boxes that cigars come in. They are perfect for your treasures. Inside there is a pencil and a little notebook for you to keep your thoughts and wishes in." She kissed each boy and told them to head up stairs to put their clothes away in the closet. Willie had a hard time believing the change in Gunnar since he put on his new clothes. "Gunnar, honestly, you look more grown up in your new work clothes. I never noticed your light brown curly hair before."

"Gee, thanks for the nice words. I think I need to act more grown up since I don't have a daddy and I have to learn how to be the man in the house." Willie became very quiet, wondering if Mam and Pap made it to the Quakers to freedom. "Gunnar, I was just wondering, do you think

Mam and Pap made it to freedom?" "Yep, because Jesus always takes care of children, and we're all children so you'll find your Mam and Pap and I'll find a real good new Daddy."

The boys were called to come downstairs and wash up. Willie headed to the outhouse. He opened the door, then closed it. Started to take down the straps of his overalls, but noticed the hole in front of the overalls. He stuck his finger in and discovered that he was to pull it out, which made it easier to pee. Feeling a little embarrassed, he push it back, then went to wash his hands. He said to himself "How wonderful my new overalls are!"

Life for Willie was very pleasant living with Rev. Sterling and family. He noticed that Elder Burns was kinda sweet on Miss Jenny. It was also about that time when she sat Gunnar and Willie down for a very important talk. She explained that Gunnar and Willie were real brothers, half brothers. She explained Jack Jones was their father, but they each had different mothers. Willie listened intently. He was a few months older than Gunnar, had always been bigger, but Gunnar had caught up, they stood nose to nose in height. Gunnar had blue eyes and light brown hair, Willie had dark brown hair and brown eyes. As they stood side by side, Willie noticed his hands were darker than Gunnars. Jenny went on to explain, "Willie, your mam was part white and part negro. That makes you three quarter white and one quarter negro. You will always have a nice sun tan, and Gunnar will match you in the summer time. You truly are brothers, and I love you both so very much." The boys looked at each other and hugged. Their hearts knew they were connected in more ways then blood.

"Are you boys happy here in Cincinnati? They both shouted with joy! How are you getting along with Grandad and Elder Brock? "Grandad is wonderful! I'm glad to be his grandson and Elder Brock is a good man, he likes to have fun." Willie continued, "Grandad is a great preacher and a loving man, Elder Brock is a patient and caring gentleman, and I think he is kinda sweet on you." Jenny blushed, putting her arms around both boys and said, "Brock J. Burns has asked me to marry him. He wants us all to be a family. We will all be living here together, the only change is that our last names will become Burns."

Willie was quite confused. He never had a last name. He never knew himself to be anything more than "Willie." As the days came closer to Brock and Jenny's wedding day, Willie seemed to be less talkative, finding more and more chores to keep him absent from around the house. He shared meals, but seemed to be obsessed with work. Jenny, in her new found happiness did not notice, but Gunnar did. Finding Willie in the wagon shed, oiling tools, he asked, "Willie why are you ignoring me? Don't you love us anymore? Willie looked up from the finely oiled tool he was oiling, tears flowing, he said, "Oh Gunnar, I love you, your mother, Grandad, and Elder Burns. I love everyone. I just feel that if I stay here, I won't be doing what Mam wanted me to do. I think it is time for me to find some Quaker people like Mam wished."

Gunnar listened intently, then turned slowly walking to the door, "You are my brother! Do you hear me? YOU ARE MY BROTHER! What will I do without you?" Sobbing he ran out the door, then out of the house.

After the wedding ceremony, Willie and Gunnar were in the corner drinking the delicious strawberry punch and sampling the various cookies, cakes, and pies that adored the buffet. Willie turned to Gunnar, addressing him with his thoughts, "I was just thinking. We've been together since we were born. We've shared, did some mischief, learned together from McGuffey and the Bible. That seems like a long time. In a few years, we'll be grow'd men. But Gunnar, don't you see? That you will always be free and I'll still be a slave? I just have to go find the Quakers, maybe they will find me freedom. But nothing can ever change that we are brothers for ever."

"But Willie, I'll never stop looking for you. I'll visit you, Okay Willie?"
Locking arms together, they left the room running into Grandad in the
rose garden. Walking over and taking a seat beside him, Willie asked, "Sir,
I mean Grandad, can I talk to you man to

man?" "Why yes, of course Willie, what have you got on your mind?"
Gunnar walked away with his head hung down, his faithful dog, Toby
following. "Grandad, I want you to know how much I love you, how
grateful I am for all you have done for me. You are such a good and honest
man. I love listening to your sermons and studying the Bible with you. You
make me feel like Jesus is with me and helping me as I struggle to fit in."
Pausing to pull up what all he wanted to share, he continued, "Mam gave
me this beautiful nut the last time I saw her. She told me to keep it safe,
and when I got to Ohio, I was to find a Quaker to help me to freedom. I
think it is time for me to move on and find freedom. Do you understand?
Gunnar doesn't, but I just have to move on." Wiping his eyes with his
Sunday handkerchief, then blowing his nose just like Miss Jenny taught
him to do, Willie waited for an answer.

"Willie, Grandad is very proud of you. I'm so happy that you have felt
safe enough to share with me your desire and decision. Yes, of course, I will
help you find a Quaker. But always remember, if you ever choose to come
home, you'll always to welcome and I am your Grandad forever. How
about we go celebrate with the family?"

They returned to the reception and the unwrapping of the Bride and
Groom's gifts. Joy was in the air! Willie reached inside his pocket for the
Buckeye nut he carried in his trouser pocket, tossed it up in the air, caught
it in the other hand thinking, "Now, I can dream my way to freedom!"

It took Rev. Stirling almost a year to find a Quaker family on the Underground Railroad that could be helpful to Willie. They lived West of
Wilmington, Ohio, in a town that was inhabited by Quaker families and

boasted a Quaker College. The conductors on the Underground Railroad owned a farm, were childless, and desperately wanted to meet Willie. Grandad sent a letter with the best time he could bring Willie to their farm. They replied immediately that they would be home and ready to meet the precious child.

It was Spring, all the trees were budding, flowers in the church yard were in bloom, ready to announce Easter, and the Risen Lord in a couple of weeks. Rev Sterling and Gunnar were in the carriage anxiously awaiting Willie, who was saying Goodbye to Jenny and Brock. Jenny trying desperately not to cry, hugged Willie so tightly he found it difficult to breathe.

She and Gunnar just couldn't understand why he felt he had to go, but it was Brock who finally made them aware of the danger Willie was in by living in Cincinnati. He told them there were slave sellers constantly roaming the streets in search for run-away slaves to sell for a profit, back in the South. It made no difference that the war was over, and their assassinated beloved president had emancipated the negro's; prejudice and hatred still kept them in bondage by the wealthy land holders willing to pay a big price for a Negro's body, heart and soul.

Excited and ready to begin his new life, Willie climbed into the carriage next to Gunnar in the back seat. Seated next to Rev. Sterling was Toby, Jenny's devoted dog who had saved all their lives from that evil man, Jack Tom Jones. Willie had the stationery and stamps Jenny had given him after getting a promise he'd write at least monthly to keep them informed of his new life. He placed them into his satchel and asked what all children ask while on a trip, "Grandad, how long will it take us to get there?" "About four, maybe five hours. We'll stop along the way to have the lunch your mother fixed for us."

The children were in awe of the scenery. All the trees were in bloom or filled out with their colorful leaves. They stopped to pick some wild flowers to give to Mrs. Bailey. At about 12 noon, they pulled to the side of the road, Toby hopped out to squat by several trees. The boys and Rev. Sterling found some privacy to take care of their body's needs. Rev. Stirling asked the boys to hold their hands out to be washed, then they laid on the blanket they brought for their picnic. Jenny had fixed fried chicken, some peeled boiled potatoes, tomatoes, homemade corn muffins, and apple cake. Gunnar said proudly, "I'll bet your Quaker mom can't fix friend chicken like my mom does." "Gunnar, I hear tell that Quakers are known for fixin' great food."

"They began to clean up their mess, careful not to leave anything behind, everything must be loaded back into the carriage. Both boys fell asleep after eating, but awaken with a jar when they saw two huge draft horses pulling a wagon, coming their way loaded with hay. The man was wearing a big Black hat, dark shirt and black pants. He stopped the horses, asked if he could help them. Rev. Stirling asked, "Do you know where the Bailey Farm is located?" "Thee are about there. as soon as I unload, I'll show thee where to go." The boys were mesmerized by the sight! The huge horses and the man's way of talking! Rev. Stirling reminded them to remember their manners. Willie called out to Mr. Bailey if he could be of help. "Well, that's mighty kind of thee, but thee have on your Sunday best. I appreciate thine offer, but please go ahead. Martha is awaiting thee." After Mr. Bailey turned the wagon, they followed closely as he led them to the entrance into the farm. A dog came running out barking. Toby recognized it to be a friendly greeting as they each sniffed each other to get to know one another.

A woman dressed in grey and black and a bonnet came out to greet them. Mr. Bailey was tending to his horses as they unloaded from the carriage. Rev. Stirling introduced himself and the boys. She invited them in and offered a cool drink of water. "Welcome, I welcome thee. I pray thee trip was without incident while enjoying the Lord's beautiful natural landscape." The boys followed her, careful to wipe their boots on the mat by the door. They were intrigued with the simplicity of the surroundings. The kitchen was very organized. Everything had its place. Herbs hanging from the ceiling, pots by the huge fireplace, a beautiful oak cabinet that held all the dishes, mugs, and wooden carved forks and spoons. Two wooden rockers draped with patch work quilts were by the fireplace and a round rag rug under the table, and a door cut in half to allow fresh air and sunshine when needed. In the corner stood a straw broom, a metal ax, and a small shovel. To the back of the huge room, pass the kitchen were stairs that led to a loft. Under the loft was a bedroom that had a bed, dresser, and rocking chair. Everything was immaculate, simple, and comfortable.

The most delicious aroma's were coming from a pot hanging in the fireplace. On the chopping block table, there was a dessert that smelled divine. Rev. Stirling noticed a loom and spinning wheel, a violin case and a basket of wound wool thread. He commented to Mrs. Bailey, "Your home is beautifully hand crafted and a most efficient work of art." "Thank Thee. We Quakers believe in simplicity, make it useful and to last."

Hearing the door open, they were pleased to see Mr. Bailey and sheep dog, Shep and Toby come through the door. He instructed Shep to bring the cows in for milking. He took off like a flash with Toby right behind. The boys ran to watch Shep herd the cows and the sheep to the barn. Each animal knew exactly where they belonged except a few lambs and a young calf. She worked them until they each went to be by their mothers. Toby was very attentive. Seemed she wanted to learn another skill, or just plain glad she didn't have to do much field work since moving to Cincinnati. She was up in age and had delivered God only knows how many litters of Blue Tic mixed with unknown's into the world. She deserve to retire.

Mr. Bailey washed his hands in the pan by the door, then took the water and sprinkled it on the flower garden next to the house, he announced, "Martha, your sweet peas are beginning to bloom." then called to the boys, "Dinner is almost ready, you boys need to climbed down from the tree, and wash up for dinner." "Yes Sir! They yelled excitedly. He informed the boys that they would hold off milking, feeding and bedding the animals until after eating dinner. He asked, "If thee feels ye'd like to help with chores, I'd suggest thee get your clothing changed right now." After the boys brought in their satchels and changed into work clothes." They quickly changed to report they were ready to do the next job. "Thee look wonderful!" Mrs. Bailey announced. "Table is set, thee may take thee place at the table." Every one took a place at the table with Mr Bailey and Rev. Sterling at the ends. Mrs. Bailey close to the kitchen, and the boys sat by each other across from Mrs. Bailey. Mr. Bailey had brought in the milking stood, wiped it off, added a folded quilt and sat down. Rev. Sterling offered his place, "No, thee are our guests." He announced that they would be in silence. Everyone followed the Bailey's, folding their hands, closing their eyes. Ten minutes seemed like an eternity with a smell of baked ham in the air. Mr. Bailey broke the silence, "Thank Thee Spirit for the safe journey of Rev. Sterling and boys. Thee's bountiful blessings fills our souls with gratitude. We thank thee. Let us break bread together in love and peace, Amen" He passed the platter abundant with slices of ham to Rev. Stirling, then to the boys, to his wife, and lastly he placed a large slice of ham on his own plate. Mrs. Bailey stood to place large dobs of sliced potatoes smothered in goat cheese, onion and butter. She then passed a big bowl of hot baked beans, and then a dish of hot greens with bacon and vinegar dressing, followed by hot crusty bread with gobs of butter. Everything tasted every bit as good as it smelled. There were two pitchers on the table; one buttermilk, and the other cool sweet milk brought in from the Spring House. White mustaches were evidence of how much they enjoyed the delicious treat.

After everyone had seconds, Mrs. Bailey announced that after the dishes were washed, milking and barn work completed, they would have hot berry cobbler with fresh crème. The boys jumped up to clear the table, but Mrs. Bailey said "Thee are excused from the table to assist Obadiah at the barn." The boys cheered, grabbed their coats and hats then followed Mr. Bailey to the barn. Rev. Sterling asked how he might be able to assist in the chores? "Thank Thee," handing him two buckets, "the one is for spring water and other is for well water." He responded by asking, "Ma'am, what's the difference?" "Oh my, not much. The spring water is more softer and the well harder. My lye soap works better in spring water."

Rev Sterling reflected how interesting all of this was to a man raised in a city most of his life. The city had no running water or toilets, but the water came from a large well shared by all residents. He recalled a neighbor woman that caught rain water in big tubs when it rain. Embarrassed at how little he knew about the "art of survival" as he carried the buckets into the house. Mr Bailey had already directed the boys to clean up before entering the house. This meant to use a wet rag to wipe off spots on their clothes and to scrub clean their boots. The boys were very proud of themselves and just couldn't stop giggling by having so much fun.

Cleaned up and smelling decent, they all entered the kitchen to the smell of a warm berry cobbler with slices of cheese and whip crème. Again, they paused for minutes of silence. It was after they were finished that both dogs began to beg for their dinner. Willie asked, "Do you suppose the dogs knew to be in prayer before asking for dinner?" "Boys, Mr Bailey responded, all living things, when shown honor and respect will do so as well." Gunnar eagerly responded, "Just like the "Golden Rule, right Grandad." "Yes, Gunnar. The Golden Rule can be found in all religious texts everywhere. Phrased a little different, but with the same spiritual meaning."

"Mr and Mrs Bailey, I feel this conversations is a good lead into our mission here today. With your permission, I'd like to share Willie's story and explain our purpose." The Bailey's nod affirmatively. "Willie was brought to Cincinnati with my daughter and Gunnar with instructions by his mother to help Willie find a Quaker family that could help him to freedom." Mr Bailey asked, "Willie, is that what thee wants?" Willie nodded his head and said, "Yes Sir, I want to do what my Mam wants for me to be free." No one said a word as Mrs. Bailey hung her apron on a peg by the fireplace, then joined the men at the table. Mr. Bailey spoke in a most serious tone to Willie. He explained that as a boy of his age, it was very dangerous to take a journey to Canada. He would not be old enough to find a job to support himself; and if he should succeed he would need a trade and an education. There is no guarantee that freedom would be granted him at such a young age, especially by himself with out a trade. Canada is a whole lot colder then Ohio or Tennessee." Willie sat very still, listening intently to all being said. With conviction and compassion, Mr Bailey said, "Son, we are willing for thee to live here and when thee is old enough, thee then could leave to find freedom."

It was in that moment Mrs Bailey, did something she would not normally do, she interrupted her husband to speak. He was startled, but nodded for her to say what was on her mind. With a light shining all around her, and with conviction and strength she spoke saying,

"The Lord has spoken to my Spirit. Willie, as a 28 year old woman who as yet to be blessed with a child, I feel God is blessing me with thee to love and care for. Obadiah is a good, good man. He needs help here on the farm, but not a slave. Slavery of any kind is not a Quaker belief. God created us all alike. If thee chooses to stay with us, thee will work side by side with Obadiah as any son would and thee will be taught to read, write, do arithmetic and how herbs heal; and anything else the Lord would guide us to teach. But, thee must know that thee cannot place fear in our hearts, that any day thee might run away, to head north, be caught by slave sellers and sent back into slavery. Thee must decide for thee self what thee wants. When a Quaker makes a commitment before God and mankind, nothing will dissuade that man from his promise. When thee turns eighteen, and thee still wants to leave us, we would treat you as any Quaker parent would treat their child. We will give thee our blessing and anything we can do to help thee on thee way." Suddenly realizing how much she had shared without first speaking with her husband, Martha sat down at the table, folded her hands in her lap and lowered her head in embarrassment. Obadiah acknowledged Martha for her courage to speak the words Spirit was giving to her. Looking directly into Willie's eyes he said, "Willie, thee are the son God sent to us. If thee wants us, we want thee." Willie jumped up, ran to Obadiah with open arms, then stopped and asked, "Do Quaker's hug?" Obadiah embraced the boy, then directed him to Martha. "Come My Son, We've waited so long."

Silence

Sitting in Silence,

Waiting for The Light,

Spirt shown brightly,

A promise of New Life,

-Martha Jane Bailey-

Somerset Medical Clinic

Dayton, Ohio

Everywhere Bess looked, trees were in full bloom, garden plots were being cultivated, and children felt free from the prison of winter ice and snow. The acreage around the clinic, was gradually growing into a community. Dr. Chad purchased 15 acres with a dream to build a community that lived cooperatively regardless of color, country of origin, and economic status. His decision to make the Medical Clinic central to his plan was quite unique. He believed that when people felt good about themselves, they were more apt to care about others. He purchased another house that was about to fall down with the intention of building a Community Center. He had Frank to renovate it. Frank not only rebuilt the inside of the house, he took care to prepare the land around it for both children and adult use. On the part of the land that was barren, with no vegetation, he laid out a baseball diamond and tennis court. He knew nothing about baseball, except it was becoming the nation's past-time. Even Cincinnati got into the swing by organizing the first baseball professional team, calling them, The Red Stockings. fter the war was over, it felt good to see new life with great possibilities.

Bess looked up to see a large buggy being pulled by two beautiful draft horses turn into the gravel driveway. She removed her wide brimmed gardening hat to greet the new patient. Dr. Chad was doing his rounds at the Soldier's Home, while she handled patients and restocked shelves.

Approaching the buggy, she noticed the back area of the buggy had a feather tic laid with many quilts on top. A young beautiful woman, definitely in pain, moaning was lying there. "Please, Jimmy, I need something NOW! Bess was startled to see that the driver with the Captain's cap was none other than Jimmy Black from the raft on the Ohio River. He began rattling off, "Ma'am, my wife is about four months pregnant, in terrible pain. Please help, the nuns said Dr. Chad would help us." "Let's get her inside to be checked out. "Seeing the sign on the door, Jimmy followed Bess into the clinic.

Chad Somerset M.D, Physician Surgeon
Bess Dominican, Medical Assistant.

"I thought you were teaching at the Convent?" "And I thought you were some ignorant southern boy with a raft. We both lied. Here, put this gown on your wife, while I get things ready for an examination. Dr. Chad should be arriving back anytime now." "Jimmu undressed his wife as she cried and moaned, definitely in pain. However, she was not holding her stomach, but kept pressing down on her forehead. Bess checked her body for any evidence of miscarrying, but nothing, not even a bruise that could indicate she was abused by her husband. She looked at Jimmy, then asked his wife, "Mrs Black, may I asked, what is your first name?" "Antonette Marie, but I'm called Annette. Oh please, my head hurts so much. I need my drops! It's the only thing that helps, Jimmy won't give them to me." Bess asked Jimmy to show her the drops. "Holy Mary, Mother of God! Laudanum comes from opium, it could harm your baby. Jimmy, I'm very proud of you! How'd you know the dangers?" "My father died from it. He drank and used laudanum. He was only 38 when he died, leaving my mother and me to survive. Please help Annette!"

"Annette, I believe you are suffering from an infection in your sinus canal. I have some water boiling. I'm going to make a poultice to place on your forehead, so please close your eyes. I have some Chamomile and Anise Tea that will help calm you, but will not harm either you or your baby." She smiled as she held the cup to her lips, "I know these herbs, but by another name. My mother was a kidnapped French child from Quebec, who was sold to another tribe. She had me, but was unable able to have anymore children. My father, son of the chief, took another wife, put me and my mother in a lodge by ourselves. After his wife bore him a son, his plan was to sell us, but I ran away when my mother died with a rash. I saw Jimmy's father's river boat ready to set sail, I jumped aboard and hid in a storage room filled with champaign that he sold on the Mississippi. Jimmy discovered me. We kinda grew up together. I was ten and Jimmy was twelve. His mother, Clare Bombazine, kinda adopted me. She and I spoke to each other in French. Jimmy was an eager student. Thank you Nurse Bess, I feel we can trust you."

The back door opened. There stood Dr. Chad and Frank Wallace sharing their day's activities. Dr. Chad greeted Jimmy in the waiting room then rapped on the door to the patient's treatment room. Bess welcomed him in. As he was washing his hands, she up-dated him on the patient's name, condition and her diagnoses.

"Welcome Mrs Black. You are in great hands. My assistant, Bess is an excellent addition to my clinic, very knowledgeable in women's health and medicinal plants, seeds, and nuts. My name is Dr. Chad, how many months pregnant are you?"

"I think I just began my fourth month. I've been having terrible headaches, and ear aches. Some quack wanted to pull all my teeth! Jimmy said he'd kill him if he touched my teeth or any part of my body. I'm so grateful!" "Sounds like you have a very wise husband. Your teeth look as though they are strong and well cleaned. What do you do to take such good care of them?" "My mother-in-law taught me to use a small branch from a walnut tree, peel back the outer layer until it takes the shape of a brush, then use it around the gums to massage them. She said they need to be massaged daily to keep the blood circulating. I am to drink plenty of boiled water to keep them rinsed.

"You have a very wise Mother-in-law. My patients at the Soldier's Home have rotten teeth due to chewing jerky, smoking or chewing tobacco, and sucking on hard tack sweets and rarely drinking good clean water, preferring instead, to get drunk on moonshine or beer. We've got a lot of educating to do to correct these grave mistakes. Want a job?" "I think you're joking, I'd love it. But we're gonna have a baby, so I'll have a big job to take care of her and Jimmy. I just know I'm having a girl!"

After she had the poultice on her forehead for an hour, Bessie placed a towel over her head, and had her lean over a steaming pot of boiling water. She instructed her to breathe slowly and deeply so that the steam can open your sinus cavities to drain. After Annette was finished with the treatments, she was given a bowl of thick chicken soup, with rice and dark garden greens and, a mug of ginger and lemon grass tea, with a big oatmeal/walnut cookie. Bess explained that she would have her do the same process the next day, but would add massaging her back, legs, arms, and head as part of her healing plan. She covered her with a clean sheet and a quilt donated by a former patient. She smiled and added, "Annette, your beloved husband is very anxious to see you before you fall asleep. You are a very fortunate young woman to be loved so deeply by your spouse. I too, have a loving and devoted husband who served as a medic at the Battle of Donelson. I've not heard if he lived through it. I pray he did and is trying to find me. Sweet dreams and God Bless You" "Jimmy, your beautiful wife awaits her goodnight kiss."

Dr. Chad was in the lab. He'd been showing Jimmy the importance of boiling water as they looked under the microscope for bacteria that could spread disease, and complimented Jimmy for his wise choices in protecting his young pregnant wife. Together Dr. Chad and Bess cleaned the clinic, made up a bed for Jimmy to be able to assist his wife during the night. They assured him that she would be fine, after a good rest, food, and tender loving care. When they entered the Somerset home, Maud and baby Lillian Rose greeted them with loving kisses and a hot meal. As Bess was washing her hands in the sink by the back door, she noticed a letter lying on the table by the entry way. After drying her hands, she picked it up. Surprised to see it addressed to:

Mrs Desmond (Jeb) Dominican

c/o Sister's of Charity Convent

Cincinnati, Ohio

with a return address from:

General Ulysses S Grant

Union Military Commander,

United States of America

"Oh My God!" she screamed as she crumbled to the floor. Envelope unopened, lying beside her, Dr. Chad rushed to her side calling for some whiskey and a blanket. When she came to, she begged for Dr. Chad to read the letter to her. He waited until she was beginning to have some color return to her face. "Bess, let me help you to your room." She nodded as both he and Maud help Bess into her night gown and bathrobe. As she lay in her bed, Dr. Chad slowly opened the letter. The letter was dated five years earlier. Impressed at the diligence of the US Mail to deliver mail during challenging times.

March 17, 1862,

Dear Mrs. Dominican,

During these times, I pray this letter is received in a timely manner. I sorely regret to inform you that your brave and courageous husband, Desmond aka Jeb Dominican was wounded and died saving the life of a 15 year old Union Drummer boy's life. He did this by laying his full body to cover the young boy during zero weather while the battle was in full force on February 16th, which resulted in an unconditional surrender by the Confederate Army.

Jeb impressed me immediately when he and two Negro's that survived the battle of Paducah chose to sign up with me to take Ft. Donelson. He gave me his horse, a pouch that contained some gold coins, his Baptismal Certificate and the name of his cherished wife.

His first day on the battlefield, he asked me to mail a letter he wrote to his father notifying him that his son, Phillipi Beaumont was killed in battle pleading forgiveness for past mistakes, and to let him know

he was brave while defending the Rebels. Jeb demonstrated a loving and forgiving nature while treating any hurt or dying soldier regardless of his color or whatever army he chose to defend.

The young drummer boy is from Maine. His name is Daniel Jacobs. When I sent the boy home, I attached the information Jeb gave to me as a way to notify you should anything happen to him.

Enclosed is his leather medicine bag with your husband's personal items.

I sincerely pray that you are well and united with your son.

General U.S. Grant

U.S.A. Army

Dr. Chad and Mary Maud wrapped their arms jointly around Bess. Wisely, they knew words could not express fully their soul's grief for her loss. They kissed her on her cheeks, pulled the spread over her limp body, and tip toed out of the room. After arriving into the kitchen, Maud announced that she would make Jimmy a plate with the food that Bess would have eaten. She asked Dr. Chad to please take it to Jimmy while she made Bess a hot toddy with a little whiskey, honey, chamomile, and anise leaves. She gently opened Bess door,

tip toed to place the mug on table next to her bed, and left the room. Afterwards, she knelt beside the large crucifix hanging in the dining room and prayed. "Mary, Mother of God, pray for us sinners now in this hour of grief and loss. Be with Bess as she goes through this great loss of her beloved husband. Guide her and give her strength to find peace and acceptance. In Jesus, Holy Name, Amen." Respectfully and in quiet, Dr. Chad affirmed, "I too, Holy Mother, affirm your grace and ask guidance to do and say what you and Our Father would have us say and *do*, Amen."

Oh God, I let go, In letting go
I lost Missy, Josephine, Master Louis, Jeb and Willie,
Oh, God, I feel emptied out,
All used up!
Bess, aka Jade Nichole

Obadiah and Martha's Farm

Wilmington, Ohio

Willie was not only given a new home, he was given a new name. No longer Willie, the Slave Boy, he became William Lincoln Bailey, son of Martha and Obadiah Bailey. When he became thirteen, he was formally adopted. His new parents told him that his first name came from William Penn, a Quaker and his middle name was for President Abraham Lincoln who signed the Emancipation Proclamation, and his last name, Bailey, an honorable Quaker name.

Will, as he became affectionately known was a very happy and content young man. He loved working with Papa on the farm and helping Mama around the garden and kitchen. He especially loved his daily lessons, studying about healing plants, and walking the perimeter of the farm with Papa in the evening after chores were done. Papa educated him about his own personal love for all animals and his deep love for being a simple Quaker, whose basic principle is to love and one another. He explained the growing season, holding back seed for the next year. He emphasized, sharing your bounty with others and to never waste nor destroy God's gift of natural resources.

Will's heart always beat extra hard when he observed Mama and Papa share and serve others in need, regardless of their color, religion, or how they talked. Will admired his parents as they never seem to be upset when children mocked their way of speaking. He hoped he could always have

that much love and patience. Mama informed him that he was now qualified to enter the higher grades. She remarked that he was very intelligent
and needed more formal education in order to be prepared for college.
"College?" he thought, "Mam would be very happy to know I found a
Quaker family and might be able to attend college. Oh, God, I pray she
and Pap are well and free."

First Saturday of every month was Wilmington's farmer's market. Oh
how Will loved helping his Mama and Papa sell items they brought to
town on the back of their wagon. Will was a shy young man. His favorite
past-time was observing everything around him. Life was so interesting.
They had quite a variety of items to sell. Mama made jelly and jam,
knitted baby clothes, homemade noodles and breads to sell. Papa brought
eggs, butter, ground corn, honey, and fresh produce from the garden.
Everything smelled so good. In the fall after butchering, they sold lye
soap, and smoked meat to those who drove out to make an order. The
Huffman Mercantile promised to buy all medicinal herbs Mama wanted to
sell. Farmer's Market was an active day. But Will had to admit, he enjoyed
going home at the end of the day, to feel serene and quiet moments with
Mother Nature in all her majesty. However, today at the market, a poor
gentleman with several children hanging on him, asked Mama if she could
come to his house? His wife was beginning to have labor pains. On their
trip home, they stopped so that Mama could check on the woman. Mama
knew their family's financial situation. Although she never criticized or
judged, she always prepared some extra food to give when they were in
town.

Mama found the woman about to have the baby and in need of some of
Mama's herbs. She told Will if he was a girl, she'd have him help her. He
was thrilled that she trusted him with such a responsibility as delivering a

human baby. He helped in lambing season, and helped Papa deliver a few calves, but only women delivered babies!

Papa had brought some wood to carve stirring spoons and Will had one of his books to read while waiting for the baby to be born. Papa warned, "Will, if the delivery is going to take very long, we'll leave Mama here so we can tend to the animals. She'll know when we will need to come back for her. How does that sound to you?" "Papa, I'm happy you asked. I will be happy to do the feeding and to ride back with you. It's not wise to drive a big wagon by yourself with out much light." "I thank thee, Will, it's always a comfort to be with thee."

It was about midnight when they made it back to pick up Mama. She came out of the house smiling. "It's a little girl. The mother said she was going to name her Grace, after my middle name. I'm going to make her a blanket, booties, and a cap." Climbing into the wagon's back seat, she said, "Thee were right on time, Thank thee." Will felt the tiredness in her being, and in a short time, heard her restful breathing in the back of the wagon.

Shep came out to greet them. All animals were bedded down, and the farm was very silent. Tomorrow would be Quaker Meeting. Will loved attending them; the silence, and speaking only when Spirit speaks to your soul. He had also enjoyed the Presbyterian service conducted by Grandpa Sterling. Will was excited, because next weekend, they planned to visit Gunnar and family for Will's fifteen birthday. He and Gunnar kept in touch monthly by writing long letters about everything they were doing and learning in high school. Gunnar wanted to become a writer for the Cincinnati Newspaper and travel the world as a journalist. Will thought he'd study science and astronomy. Maybe find a cure for a deadly disease.

Gunnar came to visit for the summer when he turned fourteen. He muscled up during his stay. His letters home were all about loving the farm and his brother Will, their walks into the town of Wilmington, eating maple sugar candy, ice cream and meeting new friends. He became kinda sweet on the daughter of the Presbyterian minister, but she was still too young to court. However, her father gave permission for them to correspond with each other after he returned home to Cincinnati.

Will and parents visited Gunnar and family for Will's fifteen birthday. They went shopping in the big city of Cincinnati for ice cream and to find Will a new pair of shoes. Will's last measurements were that he topped six foot with an eleven shoe size. Twice a year they purchased shoes from the local cobbler to keep from stunting Will's "foundational growth." Papa teased, "Why Will, if thee feet weren't so large, thee would be at least 6' 7" tall."

Will thought that he probably got his height from Mam, his birth mother who was at least 5 feet, 11 inches tall. Her daddy, the master at the plantation was over 6' tall. Gunnar complained, "You could at least pass a few inches this way, Brother Will." Gathering all their purchases, Papa announced it was time to head back home to the farm.

Will and parents returned to the farm that evening. Obadiah announced that they had an appointment at the Court House the next day. He shared, "Your Mama and I have some business to attend to. We'd like thee to go with us." As Will went to change into his work clothes, to tend to the animals, gather eggs, and milk the cows, he couldn't help wondering, but too polite to ask why? But still, he had a difficult time sleeping that night for thinking about it.

Early the next morning with the sun just peeking over the horizon, Will and his parents, climbed into the buggy; they were dressed in their best clothing, all washed and ironed, to head east towards Wilmington.

The trees along the road were bursting with new leaves and flowers. Song birds were producing a symphony of joy. Will said smiling, This is my

favorite time of the day. I love hearing and seeing happiness everywhere."
Mama agreed with will. "It appears after a long night of sleep, they're ready
to start the day." Papa added, "Birds know their jobs Each nest has a
least three baby bird mouth's wide open, waiting for their grub." "Why,
Obadiah, where did thee hear such a word for food?"' "Not quite sure,
just trying to improve thine vocabulary." Winking and smiling at Will.

He pulled the team up to the hitching posts in front of the courthouse.
Will spoke up, "Do thee wish me to stay with the horses?" "No Son,Thee
needs to come with us." The family walked together into the ornate
building. Opening the heavy door, Obadiah led the way. Will followed
behind Mama wondering what the big mystery was all about?. As they
entered into a large room, with a big desk and chairs lined in front of it,
A man in a uniform showed them where to be seated. Everything was
so quiet! Soon, a big man in a uniform, motioned for them to stand,
introduced a gentleman with a mustache as Judge Wilson Patterson. Judge
Patterson asked for Mr and Mrs Obadiah Bailey's family to please come
forth to his desk. The judge then addressed the Bailey's.

"I have before me a letter requesting Obadiah and Martha permission
to adopt a fifteen your old boy known as Willie. Is this correct?" "Yes,
Sir" they both answered together. "Is this the boy standing next to you
that young man?" "Yes, Sir." "I first must ask both you, Obadiah and
your wife, Martha, if you understand the full responsibility you both will
be accepting in adopting this young man?" They both looked at each
other, then Obadiah answered. "Sir, I know thee understands we are of the
Quaker faith. We see no differences in God's children. We know we love
Will, he loves us, and we can provide a good sound home and education
for him."

"And Mrs. Bailey, how do you see your role as Will's mother?" "Thee, I
mean Sir, A child is not always born of someone's blood. I know Will to

be my son. I love him, I enjoy teaching him his school lessons, and how to live a good Christian life. He's a good boy and a happy boy. He loves to sing, take care of animals, and share with others. I am and will always be a good and faithful mother to Will. He's been with us since he was seven and everyday is a joy. I am most grateful for the opportunity to make him a legal son to Obadiah and myself. She paused, "I thank thee, Sir" She bow's her head in prayerful gratitude.

"Well, Will, do you understand what it mans to be adopted by this couple?" "Not exactly, Sir. But I hope it means they will be my Mama and Papa for real. Only I don't how it can be more real? They love me, they teach me about the beauty of life, to be grateful and to share my many blessings. They feed me and make me clothes, why I grow so fast, they have to do it all the time and they never complain. I don't know what adopted parents do that they don't already do?"

"Will," the judge asked, "What do you remember about your life before living with the Bailey's?" "Sir, I don't like to think about my bad life in Tennessee. Mam and Pap getting stolen by mean evil Jack. He raped my Mam, then he beat Miss Jenny, his wife, then when he goes away, Miss Jenny tells Mam and Pap to run and find the Underground Railroad, Miss Jenny took me and Gunnar to run to Ohio. Miss Jenny is a wonderful woman, I love her, but Mam gave me, removing the nut from his pocket, this Buckeye nut. She said it was my lucky nut. It would help me find a good Quaker to help me to freedom. Mama and Papa are my parents now, Mam and Pap never made it!"

The judge reached into his coat pocket and wiped his nose and eyes, then said, "Well Will, Mr and Mrs Bailey, I am happy to sign these adoption papers," Taking his pen and signed the documents. "It is indeed my honor and privilege to be the first person to acknowledge Mr and Mrs Obadiah Bailey as parents, to you William Lincoln Bailey, to enjoy all the privileges as a parents and son, as a resident of Clinton County, the State of Ohio, and the United States of America. God Bless You. May you go in Peace." He shook Obadiah's hand, patted Mrs Bailey on her shoulder as she wiped the tears from her eyes. He then stood before Will, looked up to his face. "Will, you are tall in stature, but something tells me, you will be even more of an outstanding man with a character that is larger than life. Good luck, Son, I'm most happy to have had the honor to meet you and your parents." Turing around toward the door that led to his office, he pulled out his handkerchief, wiped his eyes and nose, never pausing to turn around. A new beginning for all.

On the trip back to the farm, Will kept reading the adoption papers, over and over. Overcome with emotion, he grabbed Mama's arm, and cried out, "Thank you Lord Jesus, I'll always be a good boy for my Mama and Papa. I'll study and work hard to make you proud of me." Obadiah stopped the team and pulled over to the side of the road, turned to Will, said smiling, "Will, you make yourself happy! Your Mama and Papa will always be happy and proud you are our son." Unashamed, with gratitude all three Bailey's let the tears flow.

President Abraham Lincoln, spoke at the Battleground of Gettys-
burg November 1863
Four Score and Seven Years Ago our fathers brought forth
on this continent, a new nation, conceived in Liberty ,
and dedicated to the proposition that all men are created equal,
Now we are engaged in a great civil war,
testing that nation or any nation so conceived and dedicated,
can long endure to the great task remaining before us
here highly resolve that this nation under God,
shall have a new birth of freedom---
and that government of the people, for the people,
Shall not perish from the earth.

Medical Clinic, Harmony Village Cooperative Dayton, Ohio

Dayton, Ohio

Joy was in the air. The Village had awakened to the news that Jimmy and Annette Black were in the birthing room at the clinic. Bess, the mid-wife, was in attendance. As she was scrubbing up, she instructed Jimmy to do the same if he wanted to be present during the birth. Wearing a gown, with scrubbed clean hands, and a scarf around his forehead to keep his hair from falling in his face, he asked for instructions?

"Your wife's comfort is most important. Ask her what she needs, here is a container of cool water and a sponge, keep her lips moist." Jimmy immediately knew what Annette would desire for comfort. He started rubbing up and down her spine, slowly and gently, and then he massaged her swollen feet. She moaned, trying to be calm and brave.

The Black's purchased a house in the neighborhood that was owned by the bank and rented by a widow of a Civil War Vet. She was not neighborly, wouldn't send her eleven year old to the school; choosing to educate him at home. She forbid him to play baseball at the community baseball field. Mr and Mrs Edison Allen were from Sidney, Ohio. She moved to Dayton when her husband was admitted into the Soldier's Home Hospital. His left arm was shattered by a close encounter with a Rebel bayonet, from which he was in great pain. The physicians prescribed laudanum to relieve pain. This caused him to have a complete reversal in his personality. He often beat his wife and shunned his son. He died about six months after entering the hospital, leaving nothing for his wife and son except heartache and distrust of Catholics. Her religion taught that the Pope was the devil.

The house was in terrible condition. Jimmy hired Frank Mitchell, the handyman to repair and add another room for a nursery next to their bedroom. It was almost completed when Annette's body announced, "It's Time!"

The day being Sunday, nothing was open. The Village Fellowship Hall was open for services every Sunday. Each religion represented in the community, alternated in conducting Sunday Services. They agreed on a reading from a religious text, an half hour of silence, and a Village Pot-Luck afterwards. The meeting room had displayed on the walls; a Cross, Star of David, and a painting of the Virgin Mary. There was a small table for an altar with candlesticks burning. Attendee's were very respectful. However, Mrs. Edison Allen called it, "The Devils Den." Secretly, most residents were glad to see her go; although they felt sorry for her situation.

Dr. Chad arrived at the birthing room around ten a.m. He was wearing his Sunday suit with LilyRose on his arm. He announced that Maud would be coming shortly to help if needed. At the moment, she was in silence at the Community Sunday Service.

"I brought my little sweet LilyRose, 'cause she was creating quite a fuss. She has a mind of her own, I just can't figure out where she got it, can you?" Enjoying his own joke. "Well, I see all is in order. Bess if you need me, I'll be at the Children's park. You look beautiful, Annette, Motherhood becomes you. Jimmy, old boy, stay on the job, birthing is a partnership you'll remember for life." As he left the clinic toting LilyRose on his shoulders.

Dr. Chad and Maud delivered Lillian Rose two years earlier. She came a few weeks early, but the delivery was normal. Dr. Chad was smitten with his little girl from the moment he heard her heart beat. At night, he'd lay his head on Maud's tummy, and whisper to the baby, "Enjoy being carried in mama's tummy, because after you get here, Papa will be rocking and carrying you as much as possible." He kept that promise. He never failed to sing her to sleep, or give her ice cream when Mama was not looking.

Fatherhood seemed to spur his creative gene to be of service in greater measure. He often daydreamed of Harmony Village being a model for living together peacefully, regardless of color, religion, and social economics. Frank Mitchell dived into the dream hook-line-and-sinker. His new wife, widow Mildred Grace Adkins offered to open a day care center for mother's to co-op. Her idea was that all mother's need some time for themselves to read, shop, or to just relax. Each mother would agree to be a child care nanny for every hour that they used the facility. Maud was so excited! She invited all mothers of small children to a tea at her home. The women eagerly agreed on a few basic rules and the means in keeping the records. Now it was up to Dr. Chad and Frank to provide the facility.

As luck would have it, or as Maud exclaimed, "Oh Chad, see how God works! When the need appears, the universe provides." "Yes my love; however, I think it was Ralph Waldo Emerson who made that principle so popular." "Well, who ever wrote it, God whispered it into his ears."

Another run down home owned by the bank, went up for sale. Dr. Chad enjoyed shaking the Bank President's hand as an affirmation that dreams do come true. "Hog Wash! Somerset, I can't believe a man of science to be superstitious!" As he left Dr. Chad and the teller to complete the transaction alone.

Bess asked Jimmy to ring the Village Bell to notify the villager's that the baby had arrived. He began vigorously ringing the bell as they left their feast at the Community Center. Weeping with joy, Jimmy exclaimed! "It's a girl! It's a girl! She's about a hand full, yelling and screaming like a new born pup looking for it's Mama's tit." "What's her name?" Someone asked? "She looks just like her beautiful mother," Jimmy cried, "But I'd don't think she's got a name yet." As he ran back to the clinic.

By the time Jimmy answered their questions and returned to the Clinic, Bess had delivered the afterbirth, washed the baby, and changed Annette's night gown. As he walked in, Mother and child were nursing beautifully. Jimmy just sat down and sobbed. He knew his beautiful mother would have loved to be here. She'd love having a granddaughter. She died too young. Just thirty-six with a fever undiagnosed. God rest her soul.

Jimmy washed his hands, then slowly approached Annette's bed. She was smiling with eyes glistening so brightly. "Jimmy she's so beautiful, Dr. Chad assured me that she's just perfect! Come closer, she's not going to break." "I'm such a blubbering idiot. How am I going to stand it when she starts to school, has a boyfriend, wants to marry? Honey, we've always been a team, we'll need each other even more raising a family." "Yes Jimmy, we're a team, with more courage and stick to it ness than ever before. Now, hold your baby girl!"

Holding his precious bundle, he asked "What do you want to name her?".."Oh, I just love Bess! She's my best friend. The name Bess comes from the proper name Elizabeth. What do you think about, "BethAnne?" "Beth for Bess, and Anne for me?" "I love it! My sweet girls, Annette and BethAnne. And, I think now, is the time for me to be known by my proper name, "James Conrad Black," "Oh, Honey, when we chose the rite of passage to be parents, it asked of us, to be more mature, full of love and devotion. Yes, we are from this time forward, to be known as The Black Family, James, Annette, and Beth Anne of Harmony Village."

That evening Dr. Chad shared with Bess that the Presbyterian minister had informed him that Rev. Henderson Stirling, of the Presbyterian Church in Cincinnati, had an adult daughter name Jenny Sterling-Burns.

"Bess, I feel certain this is the friend you're looking for. This is the church address, if you care to write her." "Dr. Chad, I'm sure this is she. But, I'm feeling a little scared to learn what has happened to Willie. I'll speak with Sister Terese for advice." Dr. Chad and Maud shared a glance of pure compassion for dear Bess.

No Soul that aspires
can ever fail to rise,
no heart that loves
can ever be abandoned,
Difficulties exist only
that in overcoming them
we may grow strong,
and they only who
have suffered
are able to save.

Annie Besent-Some difficulties of the Inner Life. Obadiah and Martha Bailey Farm

Wilmington, Ohio

Old Shep was there to greet them as they pulled up to the barn. Wagging his tail, grinning like dogs do, he kept jumping and circling around to get more of Will's attention. Both dog and boy were happy to see each other. Will jumped down to help unharness the team of draft horses, feed and water, and brush out their long mane's and tails. All the time he was doing his chores, he could be heard talking to every animal, calling them by name. Will named every flower and greeted them as well. Sometimes, Mama observed him making up songs to entertain them. Oh, how she loved that boy! She bowed her head in silent prayer. *"Thank you for William, whose spirit loves and accepts all living creatures, a true servant of God. Amen"*

On Obadiah's next visit to town, Will asked him to please post a letter to his brother, Gunnar. As Obadiah approached the post office window, the Post Master looked up and said, "Those boys sure do like to write letters. Here's another one from Mr. Gunnar Sterling for Mr. William Bailey. It arrived today." "Thank thee, Will will be happy to read it. I need to go to the general store for more writing paper and envelopes, I thank thee for ten more stamps." Receiving the stamps, he put his big black hat on and tipped his head, "Thank thee, I'm think this is a fine day."

After purchasing the writing paper and envelopes, Mr. Bailey decided to surprise Will and Martha with a treat. They loved peppermint sticks! He purchased three for a quarter. Tipped his hat to Mr. Huffman, untied the horse, and headed down the road to the farm. He missed lunch and was eager for some good home cooked food. As he Turned into the farm gravel drive, he saw that Will was there to greet him. "Aren't they beautiful Papa? I asked permission if I might pick a few for the table, and I believe they have granted me a blessing." "Son all things love to feel honor and respect. They understand their purpose and love to share. Be sure when thee is finished, to return the Mums and Daisy's to where thee found them. They will return to the soil to be born again. Your Mama will receive your gift with a blessing of joy, which will become another gift of pure love. Will believed his Papa to be very wise. How he loved him! Everyone and everything deserves to be loved and appreciated.

"Speaking of love, here's a letter from thine brother, Gunnar and some writing paper, envelopes, and stamps." "Thank thee Papa, thee thinks of everything." Mama announced supper would be ready in fifteen minutes. Papa and Will immediately headed for the wash bowl to cleanup for dinner.

Will was so excited to hear from Gunnar! He asked if he could open his letter before dinner? Both parents nodded their heads. Will opened the letter, and began to share. "Gunnar won a writing contest sponsored by the Cincinnati newspaper. They are publishing his essay and awarding him five dollars prize money." "Isn't that wonderful?" As he returned to his reading "Oh no! Miss Jenny is awful sick. She's been to the doctor twice. She has trouble breathing. Everyone is praying for her to get better. Please, let's us pray right now." They each folded their hands in front of themselves, Papa said, "Let us be still, as we allow our souls to listen to Spirit's guidance. God knows our heart, and will answer thee." During the period of about ten minutes of silence, not even their breath could be heard. Then Will said, "Yes, I know God is taking care of her. I feel Gunnar, Brock, and Grandad surrounding her with love," Then Mama added, "Miss Jenny's burdens are being lifted as she surrender's to God's Holy Breath. Yes, all is well." Feeling God's love supporting her as she heals, feeling grateful for God's blessing, they silently enjoyed their evening meal.

After the meal, Papa surprised Mama and Will with their peppermint treat. While sucking on their peppermint sticks, Mama joyfully exclaimed, "Thank thee! 'tis now time to tend to our evening chores".

After the chores were completed, Will chopped wood needed for banking the fire for the night. Before preparing for sleep, Mama read from the Bible, Matt:5, 3 "Blessed are the poor in Spirit: for theirs is the Kingdom of Heaven." and verse 4: "Blessed are they that mourn; for they shall be comforted." The pregnant eternal spirit permeated each of their being, preparing them for a night of restful peace.

Will knelt by the window in his sleeping loft. Staring at the night sky, the full moon, he prayed, "Jesus, thank Thee for your guiding stars, I feel them twinkling your love and protection. If Mam and Pap are still alive, I know you are guiding them to be your loving servants. I feel Miss Jenny's healing as she has asked forgiveness for her mistakes and is now serving more sick, weak, and poor souls. Thank you for guiding me to Mama and Papa, I love you Jesus, Amen" He crawled into bed, fell right asleep.

That morning, as he awakened, he felt God's healing love. The years of joy, safety, and learning at the Bailey Farm seemed to fly very fast. On the eve of Will's seventeenth birthday, he was given the gift to visit his brother in the big city of Cincinnati, Ohio.

The Stirling and Brock household's were over-joyed with Jenny's recovery and the homeless shelter they sponsored. The Burn's were thrilled to have an opportunity to share with the Bailey's their success in being of service to widows, orphan's, and returning veterans from the war. They sponsor a food kitchen, a shelter, and "for hire" job site to help those in need to find find employment. The Bailey's brought food from their garden, grain for the animals, and knitted scarves, mittens, and baby blankets from Martha and her Quaker lady friends for the shelter.

As their parents enjoyed viewing the shelter, church missionary programs, and the various stores, Will and Gunnar revisited their favorite spot in the hay loft. Their hearts were full of memories of good times as young boys learning to mow the yard, carry water for church functions, and dreaming about seeing the world. Today, as high school young men, their conversation was mostly about school, favorite classes, and how much they enjoyed attending classes with teachers, instead of just learning from their parents. They both enjoy the variety of courses. Gunnar, always the more talkative of the two, became rather serious as he asked Will, "Do you have a girlfriend?" Will, very shy but always direct answered, "No, I don't. I kinda like to look at them while in school or when we go to Farmer's Market. Why, do you?" "Yes, I....I...Oh gosh darn! Her name is Serena Sue, her daddy's a law officer. They attend our church." Lowering his voice, as he continued, "her family attend prayer meetings and singing on the ground. Mama is rather pleased to see me anxious to attend so many church functions without her having to remind me. If I told her how I felt about Serena Sue, she'd tell me I was too young for courting."

"Does Serena Sue know you are sweet on her? "I've been passing her notes during services. Haven't been caught yet." "Is she pretty? And what is it about her you like?"

"She has brown sparkling eyes, and smiles real pretty. I've written her some poems. Do you want to hear them?" "Yes, I'd love to hear you recite your poems." "Okay, but you're not gonna to laugh are you?" "Of course not, I love reading poetry. Mama reads me Shakespeare's Romeo and Juliet, even though she does not agree with them dying as they did."

Gunnar nervously cleared his throat, then took a deep breath before sharing. "I chose to use the letters of her name to describe my love for her." S, Serena is sweet, as her big brown E, Eyes twinkle with laughter, R, Radiating and E, Everlasting Joy, A, Always reflected in my heart."

"Be honest Will, what do you think?" Gunnar touched by emotion asked "Gunnar, do you? I mean, do you really believe you are in love? I feel your poem shows sentimental feelings, have you given it to her?" "No, not yet, but she smiles when she sees me. I thought I'd let you hear it before I gave it to her at prayer meeting Wednesday evening. I passed her a note on Sunday telling her I really like her. Maybe she will write one to me this week." Taking shallow breaths, he continued pleading, "Please don't tell anyone about my writing poetry. I have this journal that I call my "Ode to Poetry." I hope you will honor my feelings and keep them between you and me." "Of course Gunnar, you're not only my brother, you're my best friend. I feel that personal feelings should be honored and kept private. I love you for sharing. Do you have more poetry?" "Yes, this is my latest, I call it "Miss Serenity."

At night, as I lay watching sparkling lights

I feel deep with in, a joy I never knew

She comes smiling with open arms

We caress, I smell lilac permeating

her total essence,

A promise of eternal bliss.

"Oh Gunnar, that is so beautiful! You aren't finished are you?" "No, I thought I'd share it with her, just a few phrases at a time. But I feel I need to hear from her first. Thank you for listening. I hope when you get a true love, you will will share with me the poems you write." "I don't know Gunnar if I could ever write something as beautiful as your poetry. I don't know if it is possible for a part Negro to find love. But I sure am happy for you Bother Gunnar! Guess we better head back to the house; they'll be wondering where we are. They climbed down and brushed off the hay from each other's backs and legs. Arriving at the house, Jenny had made Will's favorite cherry cake with vanilla ice cream. Gunnar gave Will an album to keep his plant specimens and to note their descriptions. They embraced as Gunnar whispered in Will's ear, "I'll write more poems to share with you."

Then there must be a time of consolation,
before you accept this
as part of the process;
never become downhearted.
Eileen Caddy
"God Spoke to Me"

Jenny and Brock's home

Cincinnati, Ohio

The morning after the Bailey's left to return home, Jenny and Brock were reflecting on what a wonderful family the Bailey's were. Will had grown to be 6' 2", very handsome and polite young man. He demonstrated not only a great love for his adopted parents, but deep respect for their religion and way of life. He was ready to begin classes at the Quaker college in Wilmington for the fall. Gunnar was enrolled to begin classes at University of Cincinnati to study journalism.

Brock left to pick up the mail as Jenny cleared the dishes and to awaken Gunnar. Unlike Will, he loved to stay up late at night, and sleep late in the morning. Knocking on Gunnar's door, advising him of the time, she heard Brock come through the front door. "Sweetheart, there is a letter for you and a letter from University of Cincinnati for Gunnar. Hearing the news, both Jenny and Gunnar ran into each other in the hall. "Ma, do you think I got the scholarship?" "I'm sure you did. Not many high school students are hired by a newspaper to write opinions on world affairs. Don't worry, you'll still go to college!" Bouncing down the steps, Gunnar picked up his letter from Brock. Opened it immediately, then yelled! "I got it! Tuition and books, all paid for! Yippee!" Hugging his mother and shaking Brock's hand, he ran back upstairs to his room. Smiling Brock said, "I remember that feeling! I received a full scholarship from the Church of Scotland to the University of Edinburgh. I was one proud boy!"

Jenny put her arms around her tall and handsome husband, kissed his cheek, and reached out her hand for her mail. "Oh, my God, Brock it is from Bess, Will's biological mother."

She sat down to read the beautiful penned letter from Bess Dominican, Somerset Medical Clinic, Dayton, Ohio.

Dear Jenny,

I made it here by your help, underground railroad, and Sister's of Charity. I told Dr. Chad our story, yours and mine. He offered to do what he could to locate you. He found your father in Cincinnati and gave me the church address so that I might write you. I'm a little frightened as to what I might learn, but I know it will be the truth.

General Ulysses S. Grant notified me that Jeb, aka Desmond Lafayette Dominican, Medic for the Union Army died at the Battle of Ft. Donelson, protecting a 15 year old Union Army drummer from freezing to death. He died doing what he loved most, helping others. Jeb gave General Grant his leather medical pouch with his Baptismal Certificate, a wooden cross he made for me, and my name as his legal wife, being protected by the Underground Railroad and Sisters of St. Agnus Convent and School. Jeb and I parted on the Kentucky-Tennessee border. He told me to go on to freedom as he owed the Union his gratitude for trying to save Negroes.

I made it to a convent in Cincinnati, then to Dayton, Ohio. I chose not to go on to Canada, wanting to find out if Jeb and Willie made it to freedom. The nuns were pleased to find that I spoke fluent English and French. They found me employment with Dr. Chad as Dr. Chad and Maud's housekeeper and soon-to-be medical assistant. Mrs. Somerset is a wonderful woman and friend. She has asked me to teach and speak my beautiful English to their daughter. She hired a French nun, Sister Therese Ann to teach their daughter French and violin lessons. Sister is a beautiful soul, spent time in the Civil War as a volunteer SisterNurse, and has a very deep love for helping others.

She is both my friend, and counselor. She advised me to write to you so that I might find some closure. I attend Mass each morning and feel blessed by The Heavenly Father for all that you did for Jeb, Willie, and me.

Did Willie make it to freedom? I admit to being afraid of what you have to tell me, but I know it will be the truth. Jenny, I'll never forget your courage, and willingness to protect Jeb and me. I'm assuming since your last name has changed, that you are married. I'm am so pleased for you and your sweet son, Gunnar. He and Willie were so devoted to each other. I await your response.

I love you my beloved friend,

Bess, aka Jade Nichole Dominican

widow of Jeb aka Desmond Lafayette Dominican

and mother of Willie.

Jenny laid her head on the desk, sobbing as though her heart would break. Brock entered the bedroom, struck by her deep sadness as she prayed, "Oh, Heavenly Father, help me, help me. How can I uproot that precious young man from the family he loves and loves him. Heavenly Father, protect and guide me and all concerned to do the best for all affected by my decision. In Jesus name, Amen." Brock embraced his wife as she handed him the letter. After carefully reading the letter, he folded it, then replaced it back into it's envelope. "My sweet and loving wife, your faith has carried you through life's many challenges. You have been brave, demonstrated courage to protect those you loved and in need. Just try to remember the prayer you just gave. Trust God, in his Infinite love and wisdom. As you answer your friends questions, know that she too, is being guided. All is in God's Loving Hands, and all is well."

"Oh Brock, Will is a happy young man with the Bailey's. It will tear them apart for him to leave them and yet, Bess has a right to her son, what can I do?" "The Bailey's have a deep faith in God's guidance, so my darling, you keep listening and act upon what you are being told. Faith without trust has no power. I love you."

"Gunnar has left for school and I'm heading out to the church to pick up some more donations and volunteers. You stay at home, do what your heart calls for you do. I love you more each day in every way .See you at dinner, and remember," in his best Scottish brogue "Have a cup of tea and think of me," kissing her on her forehead, then leaving the room.

Jenny took a shower, put on her favorite everyday dress. Added a little lipstick, and combed her hair into a French twist. She was already feeling better. At about noon, she made herself a toasted cheese sandwich, ate an apple turnover, and drank a pot of tea. She was ready to write Bess' return letter. Picking up her pen, she began.

Dear Loving and Faithful friend, Bess,

Since we last saw each other, the children and I escaped to my Uncle Ben's home. He guided us by way of the underground railroad to Cincinnati where we met up with my father, Rev. Sterling. He welcomed us into his home with love and forgiveness. I confessed my great sin. He said God is love and that love heals all mistakes. After about a year, I married Elder Brock Burns, a wonderful man willing to adopt both Gunnar and Willie. But Willie wanted to do what his Mam wanted him to do," find a Quaker to help him to freedom. My father found a truly beautiful and loving Quaker couple who were not able to have their own child. They adopted him. He now lives happily on a farm and is ready to attend college this fall. His adopted parents were conductor's on the railroad, and understood the dangers of a young boy traveling alone to be free in Canada. After explaining the dangers to Willie and their desires to keep him until he was of age to travel alone, Willie agreed to stay and learn the trade of farming. He has since been adopted, his own choice, as he believed you and Jeb "just didn't make it." The adoption is legal, he is a citizen with all the rights and privileges entitled an American citizen.

They promised, when he turned 18 if he still wanted to go to Canada, they'll do everything they can to help him on his way. They are wonderful people who will honor and respect your decision concerning your son's future home. If, however you decide to take him back, I know they will be totally heart broken as any loving parents would be. If this is what you want to do, I will honor your decision by giving you their names and address. However, only if you decide to take him to Dayton, will I divulge this information. I know you to be a very spiritual and loving soul. I know God will guide you to the best decision for all.

My heart if filled with joy in knowing you have such a caring employer. They sound like loving and supportive couple. I know you are doing an excellent service at the Clinic. Your integrity and knowledge concerning the proper medicinal herbs to help healing is certainly an asset to their clinic. I also feel deep sadness to learn about Jeb's passing. He was the most beautiful and loving man I knew at the time; a compassionate and kind soul. We can be sure his soul is with our Heavenly Father, guiding us all. Your spiritual journey through all you've experience, remains constant. This fills me with joy. I don't know what I would have done without my connection with God to see me through all the chaos in my life.

Brock, is a wonderful life partner. Like you and Jeb, we share everything. I love you Bess, I honor your strength and commitment to be in service to humankind. I await your return letter,

Always and forever, your friend,

Jennifer Sterling-Burns aka Jenny

Cincinnati, Ohio.

She folded the letter, placed it into the envelope, addressed it, then sealed it. Gathering her heavy sweater, she walked to the mailbox at the end of the street. Her heart felt release, knowing all is in God's hands. As she returned home, she found Gunnar and Brock in deep conversation about being a college student. She smiled, allowing her mind to think, "Hard to believe, he's almost a grown man, soon to be on his own path. Life is truly an amazing journey!"

You will decide on a matter
and it will be established for you,
and light will shine on your ways.
JOB 22:28

SECTION III

Closets Running Over

Hatred grows fear. Bigotry, incest, rape, and abuse become a societal norm until the heart takes courage and risks change.

Dr. Chadwick Somerset Home

Dayton, Ohio

"Bess," Dr. Chad calling from the kitchen,, "There's a letter here from Mrs. Brock Burns in Cincinnati, Ohio." Bess came quickly from the kitchen, drying her hands on her apron. "Do you want some privacy or do you need for Maud or myself to stay with you as you read it?" Taking the letter, hands shaking, eyes

watering, lips and voice quivering, she whispered, "Please, please stay with me, I feel faint!" Dr. Chad grabbed some smelling salt and helped her to a dining room chair. Carefully she opened the envelope, fearing what she might learn. After, what seemed to be eternity, she whispered, "He's alive! But, but he's been adopted by a Quaker family, is very happy living on a farm, and getting ready to start college. Jenny wants to know what I want her to do? She will honor my wishes." Handing the letter to Dr. Chad as Maud entered the room. Bess quietly sobbed as her wonderful employers read the letter. Their daughter, Lillian Rose is in the back yard playing in her tree house, lovingly built for her by Frank, the handyman. Maud sighs, "Oh, Bess, this is so bitter sweet!" Hugging Bess, her very tall, statuesque friend, whose very nature is nurturing and supportive. and dear friend. "You know Bess, you are like my blood sister, I'd do anything for you that I could, but this is your decision to make. We'll support you in whatever way you choose for your precious son's future." Dr. Chad put his arms around both women, allowing the deep silence to penetrate the sacred presence as each in their own way prayed.

He then said with deep conviction. "Bess, Maud, you both are very strong women. You both have the faith and capacity to move mountains, ford deep streams, and love the unlovable. I know the best for all concerned has already been decided by the Divine Holy Spirit. Rest in God's Peace, you Loving Teachers of God's Divine Love."

Dr. Chad left the room, wiping his eyes from the handkerchief in his vest pocket. He paused just outside the door, then looking up, God's miracle appeared. "Why Hello Sister Therese, Bess and Maud await your presence." Closing the door behind her, he whispered to himself, "God's answer, quick as a wink of the eye!"

Sister Therese came to America to serve the less fortunate. Her father was a wealthy Duke, who wanted his only daughter to marry into a well established and wealthy family. Ever since her birth, he sought the right family with an heir that would be kind and generous to his beautiful Therese Anne. When she turned eighteen, and completed her formal education, well versed in three languages, mastered proper etiquette to be a perfect hostess, and played the classics on both piano and violin to the pleasure and surprise of family and friends, it was agreed that it was time to introduce her into society. Therese Anne pleaded a desire to enter the convent to become a nun. Her father was shocked and confused. He told her that if after six months of courtship, she still wanted to enter a convent, he would grant her permission. She was courted by men from France, Russia, Spain, and Austria, but none pleased her with the kind of love being "the bride of God" offered her soul. .She entered the convent on her nineteenth birthday. She kissed her parents, then closed the gate to be cloistered for ninety days. She declared those ninety days being cloistered in the arms of God, removed any doubt she might have had. She wanted to serve the poor, sick, and abused. After eight months, her prayers were answered, the convent in America needed nuns to teach the poor. She arrived in Cincinnati, Ohio ready to teach, but was sent to be a SisterNurse in Civil War field hospitals. She did an excellent job in healing the sick and giving comfort to the dying soldiers.

After serving on a long six month rotation, she was granted the opportunity to help set up a new convent in Dayton, Ohio. She, along with Mother Superior, and three sisters were housed in an old rundown warehouse on the westside. Upon arrival, they began to create miracles. Soon the place was spotless, with cells for several nuns, and a prayer chapel. It was where Bess went for solace and spiritual support that she met Sister Therese. Their common denominator was conversing in French. Sister Therese greeted Dr. Chad as he was leaving. He opened the door for her. "Sister, go on in, Bess and Maud will find comfort with your loving presence." She walked in, softly calling, "Mrs. Somerset, Bess. may I come in?" Maud arrived in seconds after hearing her voice. "Oh Sister, please come in, Bess needs you." They both found Bess, her head lying on the table, her right leg jerking up and down, silently pleading, "God please, I don't know what to do?" Sister Therese touched her shoulder, "Bess, I'm here, God will show the way." Bess stood up, embraced her friend, while Maud quietly left the room, knowing all is in God's hands.

Later that afternoon, Bess asked if she might be excused to go to the convent to pray? Maud hugged her affirmatively, then said, "We'll eat around seven, as Chad wants to check on a very sick patient. Do you plan to walk or ride your horse?" "I'll walk, the weather is beautiful!" as she grabbed a light jacket and waved goodbye.

Bess arrived home a little after six, grabbed her apron and asked, "How can I help with dinner?" "Everything is ready except setting the table. Let's eat in the kitchen? What do you think? "Yes, its more cozy and intimate."

Setting the table, Maud noticed Bess was more relaxed and peaceful. She did not feel it appropriate to ask her any questions, but felt Bess will share when she felt ready. Dr. Chad could be heard tending to his horse. He loved doing his own stable work, said it always helped him through any stress he was having.

Bess broke the silence, "Dr. Chad loves his horse. I understand how it feels to be connected with a horse and nature. As a child, I was not permitted in the stables, but would sneak in when no one was around."

"You've not spoken about your childhood? Was Josephine a loving play mate? "Oh, yes, she was kind and loved spoiling me. I missed her terribly when she married and moved to New Orleans." Door opened, Chad entered, "Something smells wonderful! Where's my little angel?" "Still taking her nap, she wanted to sleep on Bess' bed, go wake her, if she sleeps too long, she will not want to go to bed this evening."

"Daddy, Daddy, I slept on Aunt Bess' bed, It felt so good." Everyone was taking turns washing their hands at the hand pump. When finished they gathered around the kitchen table to say Grace. Little LilyRose, surprised everyone by asking to say the prayer. "Now I lay before my food, I pray dear Jesus to bless us all, especially my Aunt Bess, she's sad, help make her happy, and please give me a baby sister. Thank you Jesus, Amen" Everyone was stunned at how alert and sensitive she was to everything going on around her. She sat tall and said, "Let's eat, I'm starved!" Everyone laughed and cheered.

After the Baked Beans, Sliced Ham and Cheesy Corn pudding was served, Bess surprised everyone by opening the conversation. "I've made my decision," a long pause, "Willie is living the life I prayed for him to live. He is happy, has loving parents, and is ready for college. It would be selfish of me to interrupt his life. I'm so grateful to be blessed to have you as family."

***"Giving means extending one's love
with no conditions."
-Jerry Jampolsky- "Love is Letting Go of Fear"***

Our story teller, Granny Rose, paused for a few moments to gather her thoughts, then continued to share with her family her family's journey.

Over the past twenty years, I have tried to write in my journal as much as possible. Strange, when I would have a slight memory of an event I witnessed or was told, as I would start writing, my mind became flooded with more memories.

Bess, whose baptismal name was Jade Nicole Dominican came to live with us when my mother was pregnant with me. She was family, closer than any of the Murphy's, because of her presence in our home and community. She contributed to plans concerning the Medical Center, and also, my father's dream of Harmony Village to become a co-operative. Bess was there for Mother and Father when Mother miscarried. Mother was devastated, but Father reassured her that there would be other babies; but of course, there never were. Mother became very ill about a year later. She died about six months after being diagnosed with leukemia.

James and Annette were vital to our little community. James was full of positive energy; always coming up with something new and exciting. BethAnne, their daughter, and Emmy Johnston were my playmates. We played house and hospital, while her brother played cowboys and Indians. It was a magical time.

My music teacher was a French nun, Sister Therese whose stories kept me mesmerized. She told them as Children Nursery Rhymes, but I've since learned, they were true stories.

I became acquainted with William's Quaker family after he passed. He left his personal items to me, which included the leather journal I gave him for Christmas after our first All County Christmas Musical. I signed it with the same advice my grandfather gave me when gifting me this journal. He said, "Be sure you log in your memories while they are fresh, before you forget the way they made you feel."

I was determined after completing high school to attend college, not a women's finishing school. My father finally surrender to my request by giving me a challenge "If you can find a college that will accept women, I will be happy to send you there." I searched diligently until I found an advertisement in the Dayton newspaper about a Quaker College in Wilmington, Ohio seeking to hire a teacher for the arts. I just knew I was qualified. I spoke three languages, read Greek and Spanish, could do Calculus, Geometry, Advanced Algebra and played piano and violin. I begged Father to take me to Wilmington, just fifty miles away, to apply for the position.

"The committee was most kind, but I didn't qualify, because I didn't have a degree. However, they would be happy to enroll me as a freshman student for the fall semester. Father happily enrolled me and paid a years tuition with books and supplies. I needed to find a place to live. The following week, I hired Frank to drive me to Wilmington. I was fortunate to find a part-time job at the Huffman Mercantile two days a week, and they had two rooms upstairs the mercantile I could rent. Thus began, my long love affair with Wilmington College, the town of Wilmington and Mark Twain, he had such common sense."

Brock Burns Home

Cincinnati, Ohio

Jenny was daydreaming about a family they had adopted that were living in a lean-to by the dump. The father lost their small farm to the bank because of a two year draught. Due to their inability to grow crops, they were unable to earn the money to buy grain to feed their animals. His wife had been a teacher before birthing their two children. There were no jobs available for either parent. Her parents lived in Philadelphia, and his were deceased. Brock had discovered them one winter Sunday morning; cold, hungry, and depressed. He asked them if they would come with him to his church's shelter. They were embarrassed, but he reminded them of what Jesus taught, "Blessed are the poor in spirit," Each weeping when reminded of Jesus' teachings. "First, my friends, allow me to introduce myself. My name is Elder Brock Burns and to whom do I have just been blest to have as new friends? "My name is Jefferson Clooney, folks call me Jeff, my wife is, Amanda,, our son is Adam, and our daughter Tamerah Grace. Thank you sir, for helping us."

"My wife, Jenny and I feel honored to be able to help and share God's many blessings. Hop into the buggy, we'll be there soon for a hot bath, clean clothing, and a nutritional meal."

The shelter had a sign on the door that read, **_Come as you are, You are welcome._** As the door was opened, Gunnar greeted the new guests, directed them to the restrooms, shelves with towels, wash cloths, and soap.

He then directed them to a large room filled with racks of clothing, shoes, and coats. An elderly woman welcomed and encouraged them to seek her help, if they couldn't find what they needed. An hour later, the Clooney family emerged sparkling clean with smiles and growling stomachs. Jenny, Gunnar, and Brock sat at the long bench table and explained the process that they will enjoy. The children will attend a school run by the church, each parent will be interviewed for employment, groomed in proper interviewing, and housing. They will reside at the shelter until such time they are gainfully employed and can afford an apartment. Brock explained they had a lawyer to help sort out any legal issues they might have. They were both appreciative and eager to do what was necessary to regain a happy and normal life.

The Clooney family kept their area spotless, was on time for all their meetings and classes. They even attended Sunday School and Church services and donated their time to serve in any capacity they could. Jeff kept the lawns mowed, Amanda cleaned and dusted the church sanctuary. In time, they became very good friends with Brock and Jenny. They had a little apartment about two blocks from the Burn's and enjoyed giving back to the Shelter in anyway they could.

On the first day of the fall semester, Gunnar came bursting in excited that he got all the classes he wanted. "Well, my son, looks like you've got things all planned out. By the way, I've not heard you talking about Serena lately, anything new with her? Is she going to college?" "No, she's getting married this Christmas to some rookie cop. That's so stupid! Her daddy never liked me ever since I wrote the article about the Emancipation Proclamation. My stand that Negroes are still not free, angered him. She told me her father didn't want her to see me anymore. Broke my heart for about a minute." Laughing out loud. "What's for dinner?" Jenny thought how relieved she was that he wasn't seeing her anymore. Her parents were quite disturbed by the amount of money the church was spending on assisting the homeless and needy in their community. She thought to herself, "I bet they would have a heart attack if they knew my time with the Underground Railroad! Thank you Spirit for your many blessings."

Brock entered carrying the mail. "Sweetheart, they're is a letter from Bess. Do you want me to leave the room while you read I?" "No, please stay with me. I feel much stronger with you close by." "Jenny, you are a very strong, compassionate and loving woman. Please do not discredit yourself, I won't have it." Jenny opened the letter with tears in her eyes,

Dear Jenny, my friend,

I arrived at my decision by talking long hours with God.

By what you have shared, Willie has a loving home, is happy, and prepared to go to college. All of these are things I've wanted for my beloved Son. I have no right to stand in the way of his happiness or his life goals. You need not worry, I am letting go to God's guidance, and am grateful for your friendship in taking care of my son. I will not do anything that might harm him. He can continue to believe his Mam and Pap " did not make it.

I love you always,

Your friend and sister,

Bess, aka Jade Nicole

"Oh Brock, she is so brave, humble, and a kind soul. I miss her so much." Brock held her, kissed her, and whispered, "You did the right thing. I love you."

OBADIAH BAILEY FARM

WILMINGTON, OHIO

Papa was in the barn when Will arrived home from his first day of college. He loved his diverse classes and interesting professors. Dr. Allen, his English professor, was in a wheelchair, but no one seemed to notice. He was organized and precise in the manner he gave assignments. He explained that there would be four essays and a term paper required to pass his class. This frightened Will, as he'd never written an essay in high school and didn't know if Mama could help him. He stayed after class to be sure he understood his assignment. Dr. Allen was very kind and assuring, "Will, you will do fine. Use the librarian as a great resource. She is patient and loves helping students. I encourage you to write about things you love. Young man, have faith in yourself, you come from a wonderful Quaker family."

It never bothered Will to dress plain. He recognized a few students on campus that were Quaker and rode a horse to campus. He worried a little about learning the campus jargon, but he knew in time he'd get it. He loved his Agriculture classes. The instructor was from Sabina, Ohio, raised on a dairy farm. Will could tell he loved his job, and wanted his students to love their future as Farmers for America.

"Papa, do you need me to help you? It looks like you're almost finished."

"Will, thee are home. Was thee on time for classes?" As Will headed to the washstand outside the barn, he paused, to brush, and feed his horse. "Yes, Papa, I was right on time."

"Thee got a letter from thee brother." It's on the table waiting thee." "Papa and son walk side by side into the back door. Mama looked up from chopping vegetables, wiped her hands on her apron, and rushed to hug Will. "Oh Will, did thee like college? Of course, thee did." Answering her own question. "If thee would like, I will tell thee all about my experience before dinner. Both parents smiled and nodded. "The campus is beautiful, full of maple, ash, oak, and cedar trees. The dairy barn is enormous! We milk the herd of jersey cows with hand run milkers. Professor Whitacre says that when electricity becomes cheaper, we will be milking with electric milkers. It's so much more than I can imagine!"

Dinner was eaten in quiet solitude. Will loved their manner in celebrating the Lords blessings. After dinner was completed, dishes were done and the animals put in their stalls for evening, Will and his parents gathered around the table to read Gunnar's letter. Will read it out loud.

Dear Brother Will,

I love college. My prof's are really smart and interesting. I was able to talk my advisor into letting me take Math classes my sophomore year. I hope I can come for the summer to work & build my muscles. I'll tutor you, in English & you can tutor me in Math. Love Gunnar

Will thought, for an English major, he sure didn't write a very long letter "Is it okay, Papa for him to come work for the summer? He loves working on the farm and going into Wilmington to watch the baseball games. I'd like to show him our campus and the huge dairy herd. And, I admit, he can tutor me in being a better writer." "Of course, Will. Thee needs a tutor. College English is different from King James version, no thee's or thou's." "If I may be excused, I have some lessons to do, and I'd like to write Gunnar to let him know he can plan on spending the summer with us." "Yes, Son, thee needs thee rest, good night."

The boys freshman year flew by very quickly. Will was asked to join an all county Christmas Musical Concert to be directed by the choir director from the Presbyterian Church. His parents looked forward to attending the performance. Papa had never seen a concert. Mama, as a young girl played violin in an orchestra. Gunnar and family planned to attend. They were invited to stay at the Bailey Farm during the event. Gunnar was still working as a journalist at the Cincinnati Newspaper. He wrote a daily article, called Gunnar's Gutsy News and Opinions. Most readers did not realize he was a college student, they thought him to be a well seasoned journalist.

Will received a standing ovation singing Ava Maria in Latin. Everyone was excited for Will, as he enjoyed singing and praising God with his voice.

That Spring, Obadiah fell and broke both his right leg and right arm. Will took him to the doctor in town, but the infection had already entered into his bone. The doctor advised them to take him to Cincinnati to see a specialist, but he also warned that the trip might do him more harm than good. He lived only one week after seeing the doctor in Wilmington. Will was now the man of the house.

Mama was frail, trying desperately to do the chores she had always done. Will hired a Quaker lady to come three days a week to help with gardening, canning, and laundry. After a long two days of pouring down rain, Mama caught a chill, was put to bed with hot stones for her feet and back. By the time the doctor arrived, her temperature was 110 degrees, her lungs were filled with fluid. She called Will to her bedside. "Will, thee has been my beloved son. Everything we have, is thou's. Thee has given us much joy. I now go with Thine Father. I love thee always my son."

Martha Jane Bailey passed away in the presence of Will and Dr. McBride. She was laid to rest beside Obadiah on a little hill behind the horse barn. Will withdrew from college, met with the judge who signed his adoption papers. He explained to Will his parents last will and testament. Will would now be a moderately wealthy young man. He rode home, lost and lonely. With pen and ink, he began to write in his journal the feelings he pondered, the fears he often felt, and his dream to contribute to his community.

Be kind to one an other,
tenderhearted, forgiving
of one another
As God in Christ has forgiven you.
Ephesians 4:32

Harmony Village

Dayton, Ohio

D r. Chad went outside to call LilyRose in to wash up before dinner. She loved her playhouse that Frank Mitchell, the handyman built for her. She loved her animals, the bunny rabbit, the blue birds up in the tree, and all the beautiful flowers. She talked to all of her animals, plants, and the fairies. She was so excited, because today, she was going to help her mother greet patients at her father's medical clinic. Some of the patients brought eggs, vegetables, and even animals for payment. She hoped someone would bring a goat. She'd love to have a baby goat or maybe a duckling.

Just then she saw something moving in the grass under the big elm tree. Carefully she crept closer until she saw laying next to the big tree root, a scrawny baby bird, barely alive. She whispered softly, "Don't worry baby, I'll get Father, he'll fix you up." Just then she saw Bess and Sister Therese coming down the street. She ran to them crying, "Please, please come and help me. There's a baby bird and I'm afraid she's dying, please Aunt Bess, please help me." Bess rushed over to where Lily was standing and immediately took charge. "Lily, ask your mother for some feather down to make a bed for the baby bird, and we also need a basket to make a nest, and some worms and insects to feed it."

Lily returned with her father who went around looking for worms and insects. Bess explained that mother birds feed partially digested worms for their baby birds to eat. LilyRose made faces as Bess crushed worms to feed the baby bird.

An hour later they came in to ask permission to bring the nest inside to rest beside the stove to keep warm. Mother offered a little piece of lambs wool, believing it might feel like a mother bird. They all agreed it was worth a try. That evening, after dinner, LilyRose became so distraught because she felt like a killer taking the life of the worms and grasshoppers. Bess assured her this was natures way to maintain balance and harmony. Something sacrifices its life so that something may live. "LilyRose, the apple you just ate understood its purpose. Their delicious tasting meat feeds us, but the seeds return to the earth to make more apple trees. That's the way it works. It's called the cycle of life." Lily remarked sadly, "I sure hope this baby bird makes it or it will be food for something else, right Aunt Bess?" "Oh my goodness, you certainly are a bright one. Yes, but I failed to explain why we bless our food. Everything is connected, and when we show gratitude to plants and animals for their gift of feeding us, everything multiplies." "Oh, Aunt Bess, I just love my grateful prayers, talking to all my animal and flower friends it make me feel so good."

The next morning, LilyRose ran downstairs to check on the baby bird. She had decided that it was a girl and named it Caroline. "I'll call her Carrie until she is big enough to be called Caroline." As she approached the wood box, where the bird's nest had laid, she screamed. "Mother, Father, Aunt Bess my baby bird is missing!" First to arrive was her father, he had found the bird dead and had taken it behind the wood shed. He felt it was his paternal duty to shield LilyRose from finding the baby bird dead, which would break her heart. Next to arrive was Bess from her room next to the kitchen. Her mother was trying to cover herself with a robe to rush to hug LilyRose. "Honey, please don't cry, everything will be okay."

"But where is she?" Her father stepped forward, with pain on his face, "Princess, baby bird was just too weak, it died, and I was about to bury it." "You were going to bury her without me present. Where is she?" Slamming the door sobbing. Bess intervenes, "Dr Chad, may I go to her? I think I can help her since it was her first great loss. She'll be okay, but give her some time, this is her first witnessing losing something she loves. You know, I understand how it feels to love something so much, and the pain in giving it up." Bess walked out the door as Dr Chad, yelled, "The bird is on the ground behind the outhouse, dear God, I hope you can help our precious angel."

It was in that moment, Chad saw the ugly dark bruises on Mary Maud's shoulders and arms. Startled and with fear in his voice, he asked, "Sweetheart, how did you get those bruises?" "I don't know, I have them on my stomach and my legs." He began to examine her closely. He checked her finger nails, pupils of her eyes, and the color of her tongue. Touching her forehead, he asked "How long has your energy been low? Has working at the clinic exhausted you?" "Yes, even my monthly has stopped. I prayed I was pregnant."

"Oh, my God, I must get you to bed immediately." Picking her up, he realized she was as light as a feather! He carried her to their bedroom, covered her up with the wedding quilt her mother had made, he kissed her, "Sweetheart, you rest, I'll make some tea for you, then you must sleep."

Closing the bedroom door, he rushed to fill the tea kettle and lit the fire. "Father, Aunt Bess says we can have a funeral. I want Carrie to return to nature like she is suppose to do. May I have one of your handkerchiefs to wrap her in? Where's Mother?" "Mother is lying down. She is not feeling well, we must talk softly so that she can sleep. Of course, you may have this handkerchief, I just put this clean one in my pocket." "Thanks Father, you're the best!"

His mind wandered to his grandfather, Chadwick Nicolas Somerset I, and grandmother Victoria Amelia Campbell, their English tea set he he was using to prepare Maud's tea. "Someday, this tea set will be given to LilyRose on her wedding day." Back to the present moment, he worries and prays: "Oh God, I'm at a loss as to how to help my beautiful wife. Please, please ease my fears, she is your beloved precious child, please heal her."

Bess opened the door with Lily close behind. "Father we had a lovely funeral, Caroline Somerset is at rest."

LilyRose waited for the water to flow as her father pumped water into basin so they could wash their hands. She began to sing a little ditty Father taught her to sing while washing her hands. He emphasized that it is important after coming in from taking care of animals and doing garden work, to wash properly. She began to giggle as she sang,

Big red rooster crows loud and strong

Old Bossy moo's to be milked,

The morning birds sing a long song,

to encourage Miss Henretta to lay eggs.

Still giggling, she dried her hands on the hand towel her mother embroidered with her name. Bess invited her to help gather eggs for their breakfast. At the chicken coop, Bess announced that Lily would be going to the clinic while her mother rests.

"Oh, that will be such fun! I hope I find a double yoker. I love the way they look like big yellow eyes starring at me." "I'm going in to start breakfast while you gather the rest of the eggs. Okay?" "Yes, 'cause I'm a big girl." Bess rushed in the house so that she and Dr. Chad could talk. "Dr. Chad, what is going on with Maud? She must be really sick to miss Saturday's Poor Clinic." "Yes, I am very concerned about bruises all over her body, weakness, loss of energy, and signs of anemia. I've read of a new discovery of a fatal blood disease of which, at this time, there is no cure. I am writing to my former Harvard instructor to get his help in what I can do. I'd like to keep this confidential for Maud and Lily's sake. I've fixed bacon, can you make biscuits?" LilyRose returned with nine eggs. No double yoker's, but hungry just the same. She began her handwashing ritual singing softly.

"Lily, how do you want your eggs? Scrambled or sunny side up?" "Scrambled, I'm starved, Farm work makes me hungry. I'll set the table, a cup for Father and Aunt Bess' coffee, a glass for my milk, three forks, spoons, and knives, three plates with two biscuits on each plate. Did I miss anything?" "No, Aunt Bess answered? do you want your biscuit's buttered?" "Yes please, let's eat." Father placed his napkin over his shirt collar, then offered a prayer. "Heavenly Father, God: on this beautiful Saturday morning, please look over Maud as she takes this day to rest and heal, be with Bess, Lily, and myself as we minister to those less fortunate. Guide us to do the best we can for our patients and our neighbors. In gratitude for this loving meal, Amen." When breakfast was finished, they put their dishes in the big dishpan to soak. They wrapped the remaining biscuits in tea towels with a crock of honey to eat at the clinic. Father gathered his leather bag, then went to hitch the horse to the buggy. Passenger sang as Father drove to the free Saturday clinic.

The clinic was located in a two story house Dr. Chad purchased when he first arrived in Dayton. It was quite run down, but in a neighborhood that had a lot of poor and down trodden immigrants. Little by little Frank Mitchell, Dr. Chad's handyman, made quite a lot of improvements. He turned the kitchen into a lab where Dr. Chad and Bess experimented with herbal-medicinal poultices and remedies. Hanging from the ceiling were many plants drying and on the shelves were pots of freshly planted seeds.

Dr. Chad recognized Bess as the expert in plant medicinal therapy. He prayed they could find one that would help heal his beloved wife.

LilyRose was dusting the waiting room and found the sign-in sheet to place on the table by the treatment room. A gentleman opened the front door, looked around the room, greeted by LilyRose , asked to sign the sheet and take a seat, he rudely exclaimed, "Little girl, I don't have time for this nonsense. Where is the doctor?"

Dr. Chad hearing the commotion, came into the waiting room and asked how he could help him? "Me Peggy is overcome with sickness. Ye must help her!" "Sir, please bring your wife in, then you are to fill out the sign-in sheet with both yours and wife's name. My daughter will help you while" Just then, before he could complete his instructions, he was startled by the appearance of a very disheveled pale, stooped over woman carrying a baby, trying her best to get to a chair before passing out. Dr. Chad reached for her before losing control and fell. He took the baby, "Bess, please prepare the examination room for this patient." Bess returned to take the patient to be examined. Dr. Chad laid the baby in the father's arms. He closed the door. Dr. Chad reached out his hand, "I am Dr. Chad Somerset, now what is going on with your wife?" "Me wife is very sick. I need her to take care of the family. I work at the stables and farm." "What's your name, sir?" "Tim O'Brian and she's Tillie. I need her fixed up so she can come home. Dr Chad a little irritated, "I'll do my best, now you'll need to take care of the baby while we examine your wife to see what can be done."

He entered the examining room to find that Bess had already prepared the woman for an examination. She'd put a clean gown on her; in doing so, she saw the filthy, starving condition the woman's body was in. The poor soul was breathing hard as she held her stomach trying to fight back tears. Dr. Chad spoke gently to her, encouraging her to please tell him where she hurt and for how long? She opened her teary eyes, showing both pain and fear, so quietly one could hardly hear. "Me baby's birth was hard! She's the tenth. I lost blood, my insides are falling out. I can't do my wifely duty." then began to sob uncontrollable.

Bess washed her face with cool water, promising they will take good care of her and baby. Dr. Chad addressed the patient. "Mrs. O'Brain, I'm sorry, but I need to examine your private parts so that I can see what I can do for you. I will be as gentle as possible." Lifing her gown up, he immediately knew the problem. He motioned for Bess to come to his side to witness this woman's female parts. "Mrs. O'Brian, you are a very sick woman. You need rest, medical care, and healthy food. My medical assistant, Bess will be with you as I speak to your husband.

She sobbed and prayed, "Mother Mary, please help me." as her husband barged into the room yelling, "What are you doing to Tillie?" Dr. Chad gently but firmly tried to calm him, but when he saw Bess tending to his wife, he began to shouting! "Get that nigger away from my wife" raising his arm to strike Bess, Dr. Chad at least six inches taller than he and about fifty pounds heavier, grabbed him by his neck and pulled him out of the room. He dragged him out to his wagon filled with children and junk. holding him tightly and with a warning, "You will not treat my assistant as an unworthy piece of trash. My wife is Irish and her family has certainly been treated like trash; he paused to straighten up his prisoner in order to look him in the eye, "So let us get this straight. I will not tolerate this behavior. Bess is my assistant. She is highly qualified to do the work of a physician. She knows herbs better than I do, and is excellent in diseases of women. Now you listen to me, your wife is very ill and could die. She needs to be taken care of. Her female parts are falling out because of your neglect. Making her have sex when she was not able to do so, is a sin against God. I will give you fifteen minutes with your wife, to tell her sweetly that she needs to stay in my clinic, and that we will take care of her and the baby while you go home to your farm and family. Mr. O'Brian, am I understood? Or do I need to call my friend, the constable to take over? I'm sure you will find his jail comfortable."

Mr. O'Brian stood up to his regular height. Then with a crooked smile he asked, "Are ye truly married to an Irish Lass? Are ye Catholic?" "Yes, my wife is Irish, we are Catholic, and Miss Bess is personal friends with the Prior and Sister Therese. So, get in there, be nice and polite!"

Dr. Chad took the crying baby from him, then guided him into the waiting room, filled with waiting patients where little LilyRose was acting like a true receptionist. While Dr. Chad was having a little talk with Mr. O'Brian, Bess gave her patient a bath, sponged her long, matted hair, then combed out the knots. She was still in pain, but the medical and compassionate care helped to soothe her emotions. Dr. Chad handed the baby to Bess with the instructions to bathe, fix some goat's milk mixed with water as Tim O'Brian, very gently walked to his wife's side. She had her eyes closed anticipating his anger, but instead he said sweetly and gently, "Tillie, doctor here and Miss Bess are going to fix you up. You and little Maggie are going to stay until you finish his medical treatment. I'm leaving you right now so I can get home feed the children and the animals."

Absolutely astounded by his change of behavior, she whispered, "Thank ye, Timmie, I want to get well." Tim looked around embarrassed that others witnessed him in an intimate moment with Tillie. "Ye get better, Thank ye Miss Bess, to take care of wee Maggie."

After he left, Dr Chad continued his examination. He checked her eyes, ears, and asked her to open her mouth. Noticing she had lost some teeth, he asked, "Tillie, how old are you?" "On my birthday, I was thirty, I was a pretty lass when I married. I had just turned fifteen and Timmie was eighteen."

"Mrs. O'Brian, you are suffering from neglect, poor nourishment, and the results of having too many children in a short time. Your bladder, the bag that holds your pee and your uterus, the bag that holds a baby before it is born, are falling out because of neglect. I believe we can help you, but it is going to take a lot of patience and faith on your part to trust in us to do so. We will begin by making sure you eat the right food to build back your body, and you will need to stay in bed until your body begins to heal, and your organs hopefully, will begin to reattach in their proper manner. We will keep your legs raised to assist in the healing. Miss Bess will stay here with you so that you do not have to get up to take care of your baby or use the toilet. You are on complete bedrest until I see great improvement. Miss Bess is an excellent nurse and medical assistant. I trust her with not only my life, but the lives of my wife and daughter. Little Maggie will begin to thrive with goats milk and tender loving care. Your milk will return as soon as your body has recovered. Do you understand everything that is expected of you?" "Yes, I think I do, but Doctor, what did you say to Timmie to make him be nice to me."

"I told him the truth. I told him I expected him to treat my assistant and you, his wife with respect, dignity, and appreciation. He is an intelligent young man, he understood truth when he heard it. Believe me, by the time you are ready to go home, Mr. O'Brian will know the true meaning of appreciation and will demonstrate it to you and his fellow human beings. And by the way, your body cannot endure another pregnancy. It's up to you to learn the means to prevent another pregnancy. Good evening, I must tend to my waiting patients."

Miss Bess whispered to Tillie, "Don't worry, God made the perfect herb to prevent more children than one can bear." "Oh, Miss Bess, I hope I can learn to be smart, I've always been so dumb." "No, no Tillie, there is a difference in being dumb and ignorant. Dumb means unable to learn, ignorant means not made to understand or being aware. You were not aware of anything except what your husband told you. You are now smarter and more aware of your beauty and intelligence. Now, little Miss Maggie is clean and ready for Mama to hold her."

Dr Chad's surgical skills were needed to sew up a cut lip on a twelve year old for fist fighting after school, a mill worker's cut his index finger. Dr. Chad did not quite believe his story as to how it happened. He gave greenbriar salve for heat rash to a concerned new mother and some herbs to an old man for a sore back after two days of hoeing in his garden. LilyRose proved herself to be most helpful. She did not get sick watching her father clean up a filthy open wound, nor was she bothered by a young mother pleading her son's case to be an emergency.

LilyRose tallied up the days payment. One loaf of homemade bread, four brown eggs, a bag of mill ground flower, and three large red tomatoes. When there were no more patients, LilyRose straightened up the waiting room, took out the trash to the barrel in the back to be burned and watered the plants. As she and father left for the day, she could smell scrambled eggs that Aunt Bess was fixing for her patient's supper. Aunt Bess gave Dr. Chad a list of items she needed from home while tending their patient to get well.

Back home, Maud had awakened at about noon. She struggled to the outhouse then found the note Bess had left. Feeling sad because she was unable to do her job at the clinic, she began to weep. Deep within her soul, she knew what Chad suspected. She was very ill and he was without the knowledge or skill to heal her.

She laid her head on the kitchen table, looked up at the crucifix hanging on the wall, with her hands together, she prayed for strength and wisdom to fulfill her love for Chad and precious Lillian Rose. After a moment of contemplation, she felt renewed and eager to start dinner. She took out the cooked chicken in the ice box, peeled potatoes, carrots and onions to make a stew. She had just enough strawberries to make a shortcake. How Chad loved shortcake! After everything was put together, cooking on the stove and in oven, she put on a pot of water for tea. While the tea was brewing, she cleaned herself up. Observing all the bruises and how thin she had become. She knew deep within, whatever the disease, it was serious enough that she could die. Shaking off that thought, she heard the buggy arrive. She was excited to see her family and for them to know she was alright.

LilyRose was the first in the door. She had picked wild flowers for her mother and was eager to present them to her. She screamed with joy when she saw her mother all dressed, wearing her pearl earrings with happy and sparkling eyes. "Here mother, these flowers are for you. Do we have a vase?" "I believe we do, thank you sweet girl, I love you." "I'm starved, what do we have for dinner? I know, Chicken stew! I can smell it! Oh how I love it!"

"Chad, my love, how did the free clinic go today?" "We were so busy with emergencies, especially one case, a thirty year old and her six month baby girl. LilyRose just jumped right in doing the job she witnessed her mother do, as if she had been doing it since birth." Her mother squeezed his arm and said, "Our little girl is growing up to be a very intelligent, talented, and responsible young girl."

"Oh Mother, I'm not as good as you are, but I'm learning and it was fun! It helped me to let go of little Carrie Bird 'cause that's the way nature keeps balance. I learned this from Aunt Bess who has to eat scrambled eggs while we get to eat Chicken Stew." Maud picked up the ladle, "Well, allow me to fill your plates, Miss Somerset and Dr. Somerset." After taking a bite, Dr. Chad declared, "Why, Mrs. Somerset, I think this is the best Chicken Stew I've ever eaten." "Do you mean better than the stew I made a couple of weeks ago?" Chad grinned and threw her a loving kiss. After all had eaten the stew and homemade rolls, Chad got up to get the dishes for their dessert. "Strawberry shortcake, one of my favorites. These little dessert dishes have been in my family four generations. Someday, LilyRose, you will serve dessert to your children on these very same dishes." "Father, please be careful not to break my someday dessert dishes." As they ate the beautiful strawberry masterpiece, LilyRose exclaimed, "Mother, you must teach me how to make Strawberry Shortcake, 'cause my someday children will be quite angry if I can't make shortcake like my mother."

"You have a point, let's put that on our to-do-list. Maybe next week, okay?" Having completed their dessert, father and Lily gathered the dishes advising Mother, she cooked they clean up. Mary Maud left the kitchen to go into the parlor where the baby grand piano waited for her to play. As she warmed up, Father found his violin and LilyRose, her flute that her grandfather sent her for her birthday.

Father was a little concerned for Maud's energy level, but her eyes shined so brightly, that he had to allow her the joy of making music. Mother gathered her sheet music, while father opened his old leather violin case. He shared, "LilyRose, this was your great grandfather's violin and the piano was your great grandmother's piano. The instruments traveled across the Atlantic Ocean to find their home first in Philadelphia, and now, here in Dayton, Ohio. Someday, they will reside with you and your family."

"Father, I know their names! Great Grandfather was Chadwick Nicholas Somerset the first, and Great Grandmother was Victoria Amelia Campbell-Somerset. She came from Scotland." "Goodness, you surprise me!. I don't think I knew their names until I was a grown man. They were very happy for their son to come to America because they believed everyone deserved to be free to choose their life."

Mary Maud started their family concert by playing a little Irish love song to warm up. Chad joined in on the last verse. Lily was still a little shy playing her new flute. Sister Therese felt she would easily pick up the mouthing and tonguing with daily exercises. Lily practiced daily, along with her piano lessons. She could play some military marches that were in the beginner's book by heart. She longed to play an Irish Jig to surprise Mother. Mother loved classical music, but was still an Irish Lass at heart.

Chad's father began to teach his son to play the violin when he was about seven. He joined a string quartet with his father when he was twelve. It is was one of Chad's greatest and fondest memories. When he graduated from Medical School, his father gave him the gold watch that his father had given him when he graduated from Oxford. Someday, he thought, maybe LilyRose will have a son who will be proud to carry his great, great grandfather's pocket watch.

"What will it be, my love? What is your favorite?" "Oh, Chad, you know I love Thomas Moore's songs! Addressing LilyRose, "Lily, your Uncle Tommy sang a beautiful song at our wedding. I found the music, shall we play it for Lily?" "If I mess it up, you keep on playing alright?" Standing behind his wife, he placed the violin to his chin, as she played the introduction to, "The Last Rose of Summer." They played the song through twice and on the last chorus, Maud's beautiful lyric soprano voice brought tears to Dr. Chad's eyes as she embraced his heart with the memory of her playing the grand piano on their honeymoon in New York City. For their last number, they asked LilyRose to play, "The Sheep Herder's Lullaby on her new flute. When finished, she took a deep bow as both parents cheered.

"Well, my dear family, it is time to retire for the evening," as Maud began to stand, she fell forward, collapsing on the top of the magnificent instrument. Passing out, she hit her forehead causing a loud bang with a lot of blood flowing. Dr. Chadwick quickly laid his violin down, then yelled for Lily to get some clean cloth and water in a small basin. Putting his arm around his wife he pleaded, "Please Maud, wake up, please wake up." She began to moan, then said, "Please, I'm going to be sick! Oh, God I'm so weak!" Lily arrived with cloths and basin filled with water. Chad asked her to put it down and to hurry to get the trash bucket. Just then, Maud emptied her stomach of her dinner. Chad starred into her eyes, while wiping her mouth with the cold rag Lily had given him.

"My Darling, I'm afraid you over taxed yourself. You need to relax, but I will put these cushions behind your back. I do not want you to lay down until I'm sure you don't have a concussion. Maud started to sob, "Oh Chad, I'm so sorry I spoiled our evening. I am just so weak," again fainting. Dr. Chad, at a loss as to what to do, held her, wiped her brow, as Lily handed him the strong smelling salts. "Sweetie, I'm afraid they are too strong for her. We'll just let her smell a tiny bit." He saw that her eyes were dilated, a sure sign of brain concussion. He knew that he must keep her awake through an all night vigil. He asked Lily to please gather some linens and quilts to make a bed for her mother on the divan. She ran like crazy to gather the linens and quilts, and tried her hardest to make the bed covers smooth. Her father picked up his wife, carried her to the divan and placed a pile of cushions behind her back and head. Lily said to herself,"I wish Aunt Bess was here. We need her help."

"Lily, please take the bucket to the kitchen. Sweetheart, you are a wonderful nurse. After you're finished, please go upstairs, wash up, say your prayers, and get some sleep. I'll need your help in the morning. I love you LilyRose.

Lillian (Lily) Rose will remember this day as her last day of being a child. Needless to say, her mother was never able to teach her to make strawberry shortcake. Her days in her playhouse were cut short because she was needed at the clinic or to help with chores in the house. Sister Therese still came for her piano lessons, but she never played her flute again. Life is interesting, everything can turn upside down in a blink of the eye. And of course, it did.

Her beautiful mother passed away nine months later in Philadelphia. She wanted to die in the place she grew up, around her family, and in view of the beautiful rose garden her mother-in-law planted. Lily stayed with her grandfather for a few months, then returned to be with her grieving father. It was difficult for her to remember how to play and daydream; but so easy to feel pain and loss.

Surprising to most residents, Baby BethAnne slept through the whole night. During the day, she was carried on her mother's breast by a long flannel thin blanket wrapped around and fastened in front. Mother's in the village were intrigued and found it to be a mystery to be unravelled.

A middle aged mother, who lived with her widowed daughter-in-in-law, had many questions for Annette. As a mother of three, she was told by her mother that children needed discipline and babies should learn early that crying would not get them what they wanted. She decided to visit Mrs. Black and find out what she could about how she acquired her mothering skills. She knocked on the Black's front door. Annette was surprised when opening the door.

"Mrs. Black, I'm Laura Thompson, I live with my daughter-in-law, widow Laura Thompson. Am I interrupting anything? I'd like a few moments of your time, if I may?"

"Nice to meet you Mrs. Thompson, come on in. Would you like a cup of tea while we visit? Since I'm nursing, I drink only herb tea. I have two brands, Camomile and a Berry combination. Would you enjoy a cup?"
"Thank you, I'll have whatever you are drinking."

"That will be Camomile, it is very calming to both me and my baby."
"Our home is rather messy as Frank, the handyman is still working on our

addition. Follow me, We'll have our tea in the kitchen, it's nice and cozy." Mrs Thomas followed, amazed at Annette's calmness and ease of motion with the baby attached to her bosom. She accepted the seat next to the ice box. She noticed that when Annette opened it, it held many crocks and bundles of fresh greens.

"I'll put the water on for tea. I made some oatmeal molasses cookies with walnuts. James has a sweet tooth, so I keep a jar full of healthy cookies. All made with molasses, maple syrup or honey. He eats one a day, usually for his lunch. Mrs Thompson, what is it that you'd like to talk to me about?"

"Rumor is that your baby doesn't cry, is very content, and you are a very happy and joyful parent. What is BethAnne's schedule?" "It's not BethAnne that is on a schedule, it is James and myself"

"How does that work? Especially when BethAnne doesn't choose your schedule?" Annette poured two cups of tea from the old ceramic tea pot. Filled a small dish with cookies, along with cream in a small pitcher and placed a honey crock beside the butter.

"Mrs. Thompson, James and I were not around many children living on his father's river boat. I ran away from the tribe when I was very young; however, I have wonderful memories observing Indian children being constantly carried by their mothers and aunties. There were always someone to hold and nurture all children of the tribe, and most especially, no child was ever punished by spanking or made to feel inferior. When a child misbehaved, whom ever witnessed the behavior, took them aside, showed the child the error of their actions, and allowed the child to help decide what should be done to correct their behavior. Children are taught to love, honor, and respect their elders. They learn that regardless of the problem, they can go to an elder for wise counsel. They are taught that The Great Sky Spirit loves all its Creation and that Mother Nature sends the rain, wind, snow, and fire to provide food and shelter for all plants, animals, two legged, four legged, flying, crawling, and insects. Each have a great purpose in the balance of creation. It's our job to honor all life. Sacred ceremonies demonstrate the necessity for gratitude."

"I'm sorry, I've ambled on trying to give some background as to why James and I have chosen to live the way we do." "Does this give you some insight or just confuse you more?"

"No, Mrs Black, I'm just stunned. I've been here for almost an hour, the baby has awakened a few times, cooed, but not once cried. How do you perform your daily chores with her attached to you? By the way, your cookies are delicious! I'd like the recipe if it's not a secret." "Nothing is a secret here. Of, course I'll give it to you."

Annette paused," Attached is an interesting adjective. We all grow and expand when it is our time. A baby knows its mother immediately after being birthed. We are its security blanket, They cling until they desire to learn something more. Then curiosity takes their full attention. At this time, detaching does not feel fearful to them, because they feel free to explore. In just two months, I can already feel BethAnne wanting to explore, but she can't do it, if I don't allow her. That's our job. It's a parent's job to help her feel secure enough to be brave and curious.

"Do you mind sharing your living and child care situation with your daughter-in-law? I ask this, not to be nosey, but to understand and to maybe be of some assistance. "No, you've been so kind, I feel I can trust you. My son fought in the Civil War. He died at the Soldier's Home Hospital of complications from being shot in his head. He deteriorated very quickly. His memory was lost, he never recognized either his wife, Emory, or myself. He was in and out of a coma for three months. Dr. Chad came to visit him often. My grandchildren are too young to remember much about their father. I moved here from Lima, Ohio to help Emory with the children. She is working at a restaurant four days a week, so I have the children most of the time. The oldest is Derick, five and Emmy, three. They are out of control, pitch fits when not getting their way, and will not eat anything but what they want. Emory is exhausted when she comes home from work and cries most of the evening. Today she is home, so I told her I needed to take a walk and do some shopping. I just don't know what to do." Laying her head on the table, she wept silently.

"I can feel your anguish." Pausing to further contemplate on what she just heard, "First of all, you and Emory need to be a team. Your first priority is to define what you believe is your prime purpose as Mother and Grandmother. How old is Emory?" "She's just 23, married too young and became a mother too soon."

"Some people mature faster then others. Do you believe she would consent to meet with Bess, Medical Assistant to Dr. Chad? She is a wonderful healer of women's problems and has had many life challenges herself. Mrs Thompson, I also, feel you would benefit by having a physical checkup as well. Have you been through the change? It's a most difficult time for most of us women. Maybe Emory would consent to see Bess if she first talked to you."

"Yes, I finished my monthly about a year ago, but I have episodes of heat and cold that almost drives me crazy." "There are some herbs that help with those symptoms. Bess is excellent in the knowledge of herbal medicinal healing. How do you think I could approach your daughter?" Mrs Thompson pondered for a few moments, "Do you think you and your husband could come for dinner on Friday evening? Nothing fancy, maybe liver and onions, if that's something you'd like?" "I'd love it. I'll check with James to see what his schedule is. I can let you know tomorrow, how would that be?" "Wonderful! Emory works from 9-4 on Friday's. She'll be tired, but not frustrated by the children's demands. Do you believe the children will be a bother to you and James/" "No, we can handle most anything."

"I'm sorry to have taken up most of your day. But I too, must get home to relieve Emory from their fights and fits. I appreciate you, Mrs. Black." "Please call me Annette, and honestly, everything will be okay." Mrs. Laura Thompson walked out the front door with a little more enthusiasm in her step then when she walked in. New friendships were on the horizon!

James was becoming an excellent cook. An astute child at the feet of his mother, he tasted every dish she prepared, and was appreciated for his many intelligent questions, and denied nothing. James was preparing a Russian Beef Stroganoff for dinner. His mind kept wondering to the stories his mother told of her life

in France.

She was Russian born. As a young child, her family fled Russia to avoid war and starvation. Her father, an excellent horse groom, found employment in France when a wealthy French aristocrat observed him working at a stable. He'd stopped to have his horse fed and groomed. His keen instinct told him that this man could become very useful to his stable in the Normandy region. He bred, sold, and showed the famous draught breed, Percherons whose lineage dated back to the Roman conquest. He immediately offered the Russian groom a position in his stable. The position included a little house, garden, and shed for his own horse. The Duke was quite surprised to learn both Peitry and Sonji Kiselev spoke perfect French and that she was with child.

James interrupted his wondering mind to ask? "Honey, do we have any bay leaves? I also need some allspice. Mom's receipt calls for three kinds of mushrooms, but I can substitute." Annette responded, "I'm sure I have bay leaves, but I don't know about allspice? I think I gave the last I had to Maud." "Could you check? Noodles I made yesterday, they should be just about right." Immediately, James mind returned to his mother's story of life in France. Sonji delivered a baby girl two months after Peitry was employed by the Marcone' Stables. They named her Gena Daphene' and christened her in the ancient abby, Mont-Michal. She was adored by the Duke's wife, Helene, their servants, and merchants in the small village for Gena's sweetness, laughter and joyful nature.

"James. How can you daydream and cook at the same time? Yes, I have both herbs, I hope there's enough allspice? How much do you need?" "Four whole seeds." "You're in luck, I have five seeds. What have you been daydreaming about?" "Just thinking about my mother's history; living in France. Someday, I

want our family to go visit Normandy where she grew up." "I'd love it! "So when will this masterpiece be done" "In about four hours. So eat a snack, because this is going to be an elegant Russian meal."

That evening, the Black (Bambozini) family sat down to a table spread with a dark red table cloth and napkins, his mother's gold plated candlesticks and beeswax candles, crystal glasses filled with rich red wine, and with her delicate china and tableware. He ladled each a big helping of homemade noodles, with chunks of beef, mushrooms, and rich sour creme sauce. As a side dish he prepared lightly steamed spinach with crisp crumbled bacon and hard boiled egg. For dessert, he surprised her with black walnut stacked cake between layers of ripe sliced peaches and cinnamon topped with rum sauce. Baby BethAnne was seated between her parents in the high chair made by Frank. She was cooing and clapping her little hands, delighted with all the festivities. On the floor all around her and under her chair was placed a blanket to catch her food droppings. Her parents each took one of her tiny hands, bowed their heads while James said Grace. "Thank you Holy Mother, for this food, our family and your love, Amen."

BethAnne delighted in eating and playing with the noodles swimming in sauce, with a chunk of bread and butter. She was still nursing, but wanted to drink from a glass. James put water in a glass for her to sip, while they sipped their wine.

"Our little princess is growing very fast. She'll be prepared for fine dining when we take our trip to France, right Mama?" "Right Papa." As Annette took Beth Anne to be changed and nursed before putting her to bed, James meticulously cleaned up, carefully washing the precious table settings, and putting them away. After BethAnne was sung to sleep, the couple sat on the porch, holding hands while he told her of his dream to become a chef. Listening intently, she kissed him on the cheek, and said lovingly, "I'm not surprised, I'm just happy we are the dress rehearsal before grand opening night. I love you James, always have and always will." "Annette, my only love, God certainly blessed me to have you consent to be my wife. Hummmm, I think my body feels a little need right now. How about yours?" "I'll race you, last one to bed has to blow out the candles."

The following day, James and Annette were delighted to be guests of the Johnston Family. They dressed casual, prepared BethAnne's diaper bag with toys and crackers. Annette warned, "James, Mrs. Johnston is a very proud grandmother, but very concerned about her daughter-in-law and grandchildren. We need to demonstrate, patience and understanding." "I understand sweetheart. What we've learned about forgiveness, judgment, and patience was not an overnight awareness. We'll do fine, I feel it."

James knocked on the door. They could hear the children's whining and screaming. As the door opened. Emory stood red faced, motioning them to come in, then started to apologized. James quickly introduced himself, "Mrs. Johnston, I'm James, you already know my beautiful wife, Annette. No need to apologize."

Stepping inside, Annette handed her a dish of homemade soft walnut cookies. Emory placed the dish on the table in the hall. Derek grabbed for the dish, dropping cookies all over the floor, then started to scream.

Annette, squatted down and said, "Derek, as she picked up the cookies, these cookies will be for after dinner, and my sweet boy, your cries and screams do not bother Mr Black and myself." Taking his hand, "Now you can take me to the kitchen to help Grandmother." He looked up at Annette and proudly announced, "This is my Grandma, she takes care of me!" "Thank you, Master Derek, your grandmother is lucky to have such a nice gentleman for a grandson." Mrs. Johnston stood wide-mouth, James followed with both smiling girls in his arms. Emmy had two wrapped gifts. "Emmy, now is the time to give your brother his special gift." James sat her down on the floor, Emmy walked over to her brother, and said, "It's yr gft, sa thnk u." Surprising everyone, he took it and said, "Thank you. Both sat down on the floor ripping off the paper. Finding two beautifully hand made bean bags, his was a dog with big ears, and hers a kitty with whiskers, they both laughing joyfully. In the dining room, Emma asked if she could sit next to him, pointing to James and not to be outdone, Derek asked if he could sit by Mrs. Black. Before either grandmother or mother could say a word, both Annette and James took their charges by hand to the dinning room. The meal was delicious. When the children complained about any part of the meal, Annette reminded them, "Now Young Lady and Young Man, your screams will not bother any of us adults. Instead, we will understand, that you prefer to go to your room without any food until you awaken tomorrow morning. Do you understand correctly? It, is your choice, eat now or wait until morning. Both sobbing, the children nodded their heads as they sat at the table imitating the adults. They ate a small portion of the meat, all of their mashed potatoes, some of their spinach, and ALL OF THEIR PEACH COBBLER. After all of the adults congratulated them on how grown up they were, Annette encouraged them to play games with Mr. Black in the living room while the women cleaned up the kitchen. Little Miss Emma announced proudly, "em bg grl, me hlp."

Annette pulled up a chair, put a towel around her like an apron, handed her a drying towel, then said, "Miss Emmy, you certainly are a big girl, you get to dry forks and spoons."

And this is my prayer;
that your love
may overflow
more and more with
knowledge and full insight.
-Philippians 1:9

Jenny and Brock Burns Home

Cincinnati, Ohio

It was a hot and muggy July evening when Jenny approached Brock in his office. "Honey, I'm concerned. We haven't seen Gunnar for over a week. I know he has been working on something for the AP that has taken him traveling around the state."

"He's a very resilient young man. He moved out so you wouldn't worry about his everyday activity." "I know, I know. but I've been writing a letter to Will. Since losing both his parents, he has been struggling to find himself. I don't think he has returned to college to finish his program. Writing to him, makes me think of Gunnar and how close they are. I'm sure Will misses him."

"Dinner is almost ready, It'a kinda skimpy. I just made baked beans and smoked sausage and fruit salad." "That sounds good to me, Have you heard from the Clooney's. I haven't seen Jeff for over two weeks."

"Yes, they decided to take their children to visit her parents. They felt it was necessary that they try to heal their relationship. I hope things are going well."

After dinner Jenny and Brock took a little walk in their neighborhood. The weather was just too hot to go their regular two miles. When they got home, they both took showers, Brock read the newspaper, while Jenny finished her letter to Will.

Dear Will,

We are so sorry to hear of your loss. Your parents were beautiful and loving parents and devoted friends. I trust you are taking care of yourself as you take care of your beautiful farm. Gunnar told me you do a lot of volunteer work at the church for the little folks. Little one's need a lot of good guidance and sharing the beauty of God's natural setting is truly a beautiful gift.

We loved attending your concert. Your voice is a magnificent gift. Your choir director seems to be quite devoted to teaching her students to a higher degree of excellence. You are very fortunate to have such a musician in your community. We've tried to start a choir at our church, but we have not been fortunate to find a teacher.

Hope we will get to see you this year. Maybe later this fall.

Love and Blessings,

Jenny and Brock

The next morning while Jenny and Brock were having breakfast, someone knocked heavily on the front door. Brock went to the door. Standing there were two Cincinnati police officers. Brock welcomed them, "Good morning officer, how can I help you?" "Are you Brock Burns?" "Yes," "Is the Misses here?" By that time, Jenny came swiftly to the door. "What's going on?" "Madam, could we come in? My name is Officer O'Neal, and this is my partner, Officer Smythe." "Yes, please come in, What's happened?"

"Madam, we're sorry to inform you that your son, Gunnar was murdered in Kentucky sometime last week. His body was found in a creek just outside of Louisville." "Oh my God, No! No!" As she fell into Brocks arms sobbing, Brock asked, "What happened, where is his body?"

"He's at the morgue, we had a difficult time identifying him, but we finally found in the inner sole of his shoe, your name and address should anything happen to him." Jenny passed out, Brock immediately found a wash cloth to wipe her face. The officer handed him their card and informed him they can go to the morgue to make a positive identification. They left quickly through the front door. Brock helped Jenny to their bedroom. She sobbed hysterical. He laid beside her, stroking her back, allowing her to grieve, knowing her heart is broken. After a few hours, Brock said, "Sweetheart, we need to let your father know, and if you are ready, to go to the morgue before they do an autopsy. I know this is difficult, but Sweetheart, it has to be done." "I know, I think I felt something was wrong, but I just kept putting it into the back of my mind. Do you think his investigation caused hm to be murdered?" "I don't know, but we need to find out. I'll be ready when you are."

They drove to tell Rev. Sterling about his grandson. Distraught to learn of the horrific story of his grandson's death, he wanted to go with them. He felt he wanted to hear exactly what the officials knew. The three drove in total silence. When they arrived, both men walked on each side of Jenny to make sure she felt protected and had the strength to go forth. The body laid on a steel table. As the mortician removed the sheet covering his body, they all gasped!

His face was beaten so badly that his eyes were smashed in, and there was evidence he was tortured before he died. Two of his fingers were cut off. When they went upstairs to the police department, they were shown what was found on his body. There was a piece of leather that had writing on it, "Nigger lovers get crucified in Kentuck!" There were rope burns around his neck, and arms. Also, there was the last addition of his weekly article in the Cincinnati Newspaper.

"Well, I'm convinced, he was getting too close to criminal activity in Kentucky." Jenny whimpered "His gold cross is gone. May God strike them dead!" "Come Jenny," said her father, "we need to leave this place to pray. Gunnar's soul is fine, his murders are lost." "I hope the police are making this murder a number one priority" replied Brock as he helped Jenny to her feet.

They drove to Rev. Sterling's home. Jenny ran upstairs to her old room and that of the boys when they first came to Cincinnati. She wailed, and wailed! Brock's eyes were filling with tears. He pleaded to Rev. Sterling. "I don't know how to help her, what can I do?" "Just what you are doing. Loving her, being by her side, allowing her to go through grief by expressing her emotions. She's going to be angry and fearful, do and say crazy things. She may rant that she wants to die, or she may say and do things to you she doesn't mean." And Brock, you're grieving as well, but Brock try your hardest not take any of this personal, we need to stay present for each other."

And so, began the long and painful journey to reconcile why a mother lives and her son had to die. She talked of going to see Will, but was afraid to tell him of his brother's death. Finally, she asked Brock to take her to Will's farm. As they drove the road to the farm, she practiced what she would say to Will. When

they arrived, Will came out of the barn to greet them. She fell to his feet crying. "Gunnar was murdered in Kentucky. I'm so sorry Will, I'm so sorry." "Brock asked if they might come in, have a cool drink of water so that he might share with Will what happened. Will was patient as Brock told of what they knew. Finally, Will said, "Miss Jenny, you are a wonderful and caring mother. Gunnar was blessed to have you. You did your best to raise him. Gunnar was a seeker of justice. He wanted to see the wrong's corrected. He died doing his life purpose. I'm happy I had him in my life, even for such a short time. And Miss Jenny, you were my mother when I was alone and lost. You helped me find my Papa and Mama. I was blessed to have them as long as I did. Life is a gift, no matter if its long or short. Thank you Elder Burns for loving Miss Jenny."

They sat in silence as the noon sun moved to the west. Then when spirit spoke to Jenny she said, "Thank you God, for blessing me with Gunnar. Amen"

Will brought out some ham he had in the smoke house. He had some fresh greens, onions, and sweet buttermilk. He had baked a large loaf of sourdough bread that Mama had taught him to make. Will opened the conversation by asking, "When will you have a funeral for Gunnar?" "Probably next week. They had to do an autopsy, which is probably done by now. So the sooner the better. Do you think you can come?" "If I can get a friend to tend the farm for two days, I'll come." "Then, I'll plan on having it next Friday. I pray you can make it. Will, seeing you, has helped me so much. You are such a wise and gentle soul, I love you dearly. We must be heading home so that we can get there before dark. Thank you for everything, and God Bless." Brock pulled the buggy up, Jenny climbed in waving goodbye to Will.

The funeral was held at noon on the following Friday at the Presbyterian church. The sanctuary was filled with Gunnar's friends from church and the newspaper. Will spoke of their brotherhood and loving friend-ship. His body was laid to rest on the hill behind Rev. Sterling's home. There was another soul buried there, Rev Sterling's wife, Jenny's mother that died when Jenny was born. The church ladies had prepared a lovely reception afterwards, but Will said he had to leave to return home. But before he did, he went to visit the wishing well that had his and Gunnar's initial carved on it. "So long, Brother, may you rest in peace." He climbed on his horse and slipped away. Riding down the road, observing God's magnificent tapestry, "Gunnar, I will, with God's help, create an outdoor sanctuary of beauty in honor of your devotion in trying to find peace and harmony."

In the beginning God created the heavens
and the earth.
The earth was formless and void, darkness was
over the surface of the deep and the Spirit
of God was moving over
the water.
God said, "Let there be light. God saw that the
light was good, and
God separated the light from the darkness.
God called the light Day.
And the darkness he called Night,
So the evening and the morning
were the first day.
Then God said, "Let there be an expanse
in the midst of the waters, and
let it separate the waters
from the waters, which
were under the expanse from the waters."
So God made the expanse and separated the expanse
from the waters which were above the expanse.
God called the expanse Heaven, So,
The morning and evening were the second day.

*Then God said, "Let the waters under heaven be
gathered together into one place, and
let the dry land appear," and it was so.
God called dry land, earth, then gathering together
water, He called Seas. And God saw it was good.
-Hebrew Bible, Genesis 1:1-4,*

HOLIDAYS IN WILMINGTON

September in Wilmington is magical. The maple, oak, and elm trees turn yellow, orange, red, and a magnificent purple color. The crisp cool air invites a playful time to roll in piles of leaves, destroying the hard work it took to rack them for burning. And yet, fall prepares us for winter, a time to hibernate, to contemplate, and then recharge before Nature's explosion of Spring and Summer.

Lillian Rose Somerset aka Miss Lily, is busy preparing for the annual All County Christmas Concert. She is going through the sheet music on display in the Huffman Mercantile where she works part time. She is also the choir director for the Presbyterian Church that practices every Wednesday evening. Looking out the big front window, she is struck by the big Oak Tree standing in front of the building. It is changing colors and is now filled with yellow and orange leaves. She wondered to herself, what songs she could use for Sunday service that would announce Fall, the beginning of Winter. As she shuffled the sheet music, the bell hanging on the front door chimed.

She is surprised to see Martin, walk in. "Well, Good Morning, Martin. What brings you out so early on a Wednesday?" "You, I wanted to see you." "That's interesting, since you just saw me after class yesterday. What's so important today?" "This!" as he handed her a red velvet box. "It's too late for my birthday?" Speaking rather gruffly, he said, "Just open it!" She opened the box "A ring? What's this all about?" "Yes, a ring. I want you to marry me?" Closing the lid on the box she handed it back to him. "Martin, I'm not ready for marriage. Thank you for the thought anyway." "It was my parent's idea, this is Mom's mother's ring. They want us to get married."

"Wow! this will certainly takes some thought." Just them a customer entered, LilyRose went to help her. "How can I help you this morning?" "I'd like to look at your calico fabrics. I'm redecorating my kitchen." "That must be fun, please follow mea" As LilyRose helped the customer, Martin left with a scowl on his face and the velvet box in his pocket.

After closing the shop, she climbed the stairs to her small apartment. She ate some soup and a grilled cheese sandwich as she thought about Martin's uncouth manner in which he proposed marriage. "Can you believe it? It was his parents idea!" Looking at the time, she brushed her teeth, then gathered her coat and sheet music, to head down the back staircase to ride her bicycle to church. On the way, she saw William tying his horse to the Churches front hitch. She wondered, "Would he propose marriage to his girlfriend in the manner that Martin did? Of course not! William is a kind and selfless gentleman and a Quaker!"

She entered the church vestibule, hung up her coat, and walked down the aisle to open the top to the piano. She was both pianist and choir director. The song she chose was, " Morning has Broken." The choir consisted of sixteen members; four soprano's, altos, bass, and tenors. A very balanced choir. After about an hour of practicing the various music used each Sunday for the liturgy, she decided to spend the next hour on their anthem. In the midst of practice, she had an idea, pausing she asked, "William would you please sing the second verse as the choir hums in harmony behind your voice?" Nervously, he nodded affirmatively. After just one run through the whole song, the choir applauded William's voice and interpretation. When asked how he could sing this song as if he'd sung it all his life, he responded, "The words are truth, they speak of God's glorious announcement of Love."

They rehearsed the song a few more times, then LilyRose dismissed the choir. She asked William if she might speak to him for a moment?" "William, your voice is absolutely beautiful!. I hope I can count on you to sing in this years Christmas Concert?" "Yes, Miss Lily, I'll be honored to do so. Also, Miss Lily, I am writing in my journal as you encouraged. Thank you again for the lovely gift." Turning away red faced and obviously very nervous. "See you next week, William. It makes me happy you enjoy your journal."

LilyRose only worked in the Mercantile on Wednesday and Saturdays. On this cool and cloudy day, Martin came in kind of out of sorts. Lily feared he would bring up his proposal, but was relieved when he asked, "Where do you keep the sherry wine? I need two bottles." "It's beside the bottles of vinegar. Does your mother need it for Shabbat?" "Yes, put it on my tab. Have a good day." as he left the store. "Wow, Oh Wow was that rude?"

After closing up for the day, Lily decided to visit with the Huffman's. She thought it was appropriate to visit after six p.m. At least she hoped so. When she arrived, Mr. Huffman greeted her with a huge smile, "LilyRose! What a nice surprise, Mother will be thrilled to see you." "I hope I'm not interrupting things on your holy day." "No, your just fine." As he led her to the parlor where Mrs Huffman was knitting. She held her arms out for a hug, exclaiming, "LilyRose, it is always good to see your lovely face."

"I was hoping I could maybe get some clarity about something very personal," she sighed, "On Wednesday, Martin came into the store with your grandmother's ring to ask me to marry him. I told him I was not ready for marriage, then he said it was his parents idea. Then this morning he came in to buy two bottles of sherry for Shabbat. He looked unkept and was very rude. I think he is angry with me and I hope you two are not angry as well?"

The Huffman's looked at each other, surprised and disappointed, then Allen said, "LilyRose, there is nothing that would make us happier then to have you and Martin joined in marriage, but we did not pressure him to propose, Maybe, because he's twenty-six and feels he needs to settle down. We'll talk to him. Please don't worry your pretty little head.

They invited her to tea, then she left wondering why Martin wasn't home? The family had agreed he was to work at the mercantile on the days that Lily was not there. However, she could tell by the books, he showed up late, and closed early and that not all items were logged into the books. She didn't know how to address this matter. "Maybe I should talk to Martin after he calms down. Plus, I think I should follow my own advice, by writing my feelings in my journal regularly."

After LilyRose left the Huffman Estate, Mrs. Huffman went directly to her antique china cabinet. She opened the drawer below the glass shelves where she kept her valuable family items. As she pulled the drawer open, she immediately noticed that Great Grandmother's Huffman's platinum ring box was missing along with her Russian Orthodox religious icons that traveled the ocean almost a hundred years ago. "Allen please come here." "What is it my dear? What is distressing you so?" "My grandmother's ring and the Russian Icons are missing. Oh, what are we going to do about Martin? He's a liar, a cheat, and we don't know what else?" Angry, Allen said, "When he comes home, we will confront him. This behavior must stop!" Mr Huffman never told his wife that he had paid off Martin's debt to a gambling syndicate in Cincinnati. He was too shocked and embarrassed to tell her about their son, spoiled so badly from the day he was born, and was denied nothing. Martin returned late Sunday afternoon, hung over, dirty, and starved. He went to the kitchen to find food, when his father approached him to talk. He yelled that he did not want to talk. Allen answered that it didn't matter what he wanted, the free ride was over. He would not be given an allowance, only the money he earned working at the mercantile. He was not to run a tab for alcohol, if he did he'd talk to his friend, the sheriff and have him arrested for stealing. "Don't be silly, Papa, you wouldn't do that? What would people think?" "No more than what they are already think and know. They see you drunk, running up debts, and not working a day in your young life. This is stopping now! Don't test me Martin, because I mean it, and don't plead to your mother, she is heart broken because you have stolen from her family history and lied about needing sherry for Shabbat." Allen walked out of the kitchen, and could be heard soothing his grieving wife.

Two days later after Martin sobered and cleaned up. He went to see LilyRose at her apartment. He climbed the outside stairs, knocked gently on the door, he asked, "LilyRose, may I come in? She opened the door, then said. "What do you want? I'm not interested in your lies, and your sob stories." "No, LilyRose, I don't blame you. I've had a good talk with myself. I know I've been an egotistical bastard, excuse the adjective, but that is a good description of my addictive behavior. I'm sworn off alcohol, I want to be a good citizen and will work off my debt at the mercantile. I am truly sorry for my inappropriate behavior, and I hope someday you can forgive me. Thank you for listening to me, and I hope I've not spoiled the rest of your day. Good day." He opened the door, then closed it.

"Well we'll just see." As she left for college to tutor a student, she could see Martin in the mercantile taking care of customers. "It will take a lot more than a days work to convince me you've changed."

Weeks go by, LilyRose is immersed in preparing for the Christmas Concert, teaching vocal students, working her days at the mercantile, and playing piano and directing church choir to even come up for a breath.

The newspaper's are full of the possibility of war between Spain with the sinking of the warship, "The Maine."

It was Wednesday, her day in the mercantile, when the door opened by Mr & Mrs Huffman. "Well Good Morning, it is so nice to see you." Mrs Huffman hugged her and handed her an invitation to their 35th wedding anniversary party in two weeks. "We hope you will attend. Some of our family from New York will attend plus Allen's uncle that is a Rabbi will officiate the religious part. We understand your feelings about Martin, but we think he will be quite a gentleman and appropriate in all ways. Please think about it. We love you." Mr. Huffman tipped his hat on their way out the door. Speaking to herself, "Well we'll see. That is the date Father is planning to visit me."

Dr. Chad Somerset arrived in the early afternoon on the day he and LilyRose had planned. He drove his one horse buggy with a small valise and his medical bag. LilyRose heard him coming up the stairs and had the door open when he arrived at the landing. "Father, Oh, it's so good to see you! I've missed my favorite man in all the world. Hugging and kissing him on his cheek, "LilyRose, you'd make any father proud to have a daughter like you. I know you are a busy lady with college, tutoring, working here and choir directing, but when you do you have time to breathe?" "Well Father, I think I learned this behavior from the greatest teacher, you!" "Yeah, I'm guilty as charged. What have you got to eat? I'm starved!"

"Nothing, I thought I'd treat you to the best little cafe in all of Clinton County. Beside the best country food around, they have wonderful ice cream. Their milk shakes and banana splits are, as the kids say, "to die for." "Let's go, banana splits, for heaven's sake what are they?" "I don't know, but they claim it's there creation. College students love them.

As they descend the stairs, LilyRose could see Martin giving William his change. "Father, that young man has the most beautiful voice you've ever heard, If you'll attend church with me Sunday, you will hear him sing." "You know, I think I'd enjoy doing just that. Where's that cafe? You've tempted my appetite."

Father and daughter were met by many towns people in the cafe. They sat at a booth by the window where they watched the Saturday evening promenade of families, dogs, and horses. LilyRose approached the subject that was on her mind since she left Dayton. "Father, now tell me the truth, how are you doing alone at the clinic without Bess and Mother?" Her father, took a deep breath, then reached for his daughter's hand, "Honey, I confess, I'm an old lonely man. I miss your beautiful mother, the love of my life, and pray you will find such happiness, and I miss Bess, but who is now a novice at the convent. She is the best medical assistant and know's more about most women's health issues, than any medical doctor I know."

"Our friends, the Blacks are very comforting, and Frank Mitchell, I don't know what I would have done these many years without his help and counsel. But I miss you and your Mama, nothing or no one can take hers or your place.in my heart. I'm so sorry to be so melancholy, but you started it."

"Father, I miss you, too. But I know you want me to soar, to find my own niche. Please, promise me you'll let me know if and when you need help?" "Oh course baby girl, I promise, if you'll promise me the same thing."

The chicken fried steak with mashed potatoes was excellent, but the banana splits with chocolate syrup were divine. They walked the college campus, found her favorite professor in his office where he raved about LilyRose's study ethic and musical talent. They then opened the door to the Quaker Friend's Meeting Room. No one was there, but they sat in silence for about a half an hour. Leaving the campus, her father exclaimed, "Your campus is nothing like Harvard! But I can understand why you love it here. There is a peacefulness that grabs one's soul. Harvard is also a beautiful campus, filled with so much American History and Intellectuals; where one can challenge the norms of society. I loved my time there, but try as I might, through all their medical breakthroughs, they have not yet, found a cure for leukemia that took my Mary Maud.."

"Father, the Somerset's always taught to count our many blessings. I'm most fortunate to be your daughter, a Somerset, and a woman entering into the 20th Century where a woman will have the right to vote, be a doctor, or even the president of the United States. I believe that Father, and I'm working to realize my vision." "God Bless you, may daughter. I love you to the moon and back." "Yes, Father, even that's a possibility."

On Sunday Morning, Dr. Somerset escorted his daughter to the Presbyterian Church for Sunday Services. It was the first time he was ever in a non-Catholic Church. He found it very moving, especially the music. He loved watching LilyRose at the piano, preparing to direct the choir. She began with an intro as each choir member was focused on her nod to begin, fully in charge of their voices. Fantastic! Then when they sang the anthem, with the young Quaker boy in a Presbyterian robe, whose voice was so angelic it brought tears to his eyes and joy to his heart. He could feel Mary Maud's presence beside him applauding their daughter's accomplishments and the ecumenical celebration of God's Love. He was surprised when the minister announced to the congregation that Miss LilyRose Somerset's father, Dr. Chadwick Somerset was visiting that day. He was asked to stand, as they applauded his attendance. Afterwards they dined at at the small Bed and Breakfast he was staying. After returning LilyRose to her apartment, he embraced her, his heart communicating to his precious daughter how much he loved her. "Sweetheart, you make your Father proud, always follow your heart, be happy." "Father, thank you for coming, be careful and write me when you get home.

Father and daughter were consistent in their weekly correspondence. He promised to come for the Christmas Concert and bring the Black Family. He didn't think Frank Mitchell and wife could make it as she was having difficulty with circulation in her legs. But, he felt sure James, Annette, and BethAnne would attend. Much to LilyRose surprise, Martin was true to his word. He worked faithfully at the mercantile, did not drink a drop of alcohol, not even at Shabbat. He often attended church services, when afterwards he invited LilyRose to Sunday dinner at the Huffman Estate. His parent'a were very supportive of his change in behavior, but stuck to their resolve, Martin needed to be held accountable for his own actions.

LilyRose's weeks were filled with her own responsibilities. She had college work to do, student's to tutor, her jobs both at the mercantile and at the church and a father to keep in touch with. The last Sunday in October, Martin invited her to dinner at his parents home. They had a lovely dinner of roast duckling and stuffing with pears and walnuts. His parents served wine, of which neither she nor Martin drank. After a few games of chess in the formal parlor, Martin asked her if he might speak to her about something very personal. "Miss LilyRose, I am very fond of you. Your personality is most inviting, and exciting. I feel I have fallen in love with you. It is my desire to be a loving husband and lifetime partner to you. Will you marry me?" "Oh, Martin that is so sweet. Right now, I'm so busy with college, the concert, and my two jobs. I'm afraid now is not the time for me to make a commitment. I hope you understand, but I've not had time to even think about love. I'm sorry. "Miss LilyRose, I hope you will consider my proposal, and give it some deep consideration. We will entertain this sometime in the near future." "Yes, Martin, of course. I'm flattered and will certainly give it great thought." He held her hand, pulled her close, and kissed her on the lips. She was startled, but no fireworks! She stood up, then announced, "I need to be going home, I have an eight o'clock class in the morning. Thank you for a lovely evening, I must thank your parents, as she quickly left the room to find his parents in the dinning room playing a game she never heard of. "I must leave now, thank you for such a delicious meal, and no matter how hard I tried, Martin beat me in every game of chess we played. Thank you, I certainly enjoyed visiting with you."

The ride home was very quiet until Martin remarked, "LilyRose, I know courting and kissing is very new to you. I hope you'll grow to like it. I'm happy to teach you." So embarrassed she could cry, LilyRose thought is this how love begins? She did not wait for him to walk her up the stairs, she just hopped out and said, "Thanks, had a good time," Up the stairs she flew like a bat out of hell.

LilyRose realized she had no real friends. No one she could talk to about dating and being kissed. Every-thing seemed to be trial and error. She felt she was trying, but she also knew she was making lots of errors. On Saturday before Thanksgiving, Martin wanted to take her skating to Lake Cowan. The lake was frozen solid and the locals were cutting ice for their iceboxes. She knew how to skate, in fact she was quite proficient, but she still was concerned about the courting game and what all it entailed. Martin and another fellow found a sleigh to rent with two horses to drive there, as the roads were icy and snow covered. She finally agreed to attend. She dressed in her heaviest coat, gloves, boots, and knitted cap. As they drove through the fields, they sang Christmas Caroles. Martin was a horrible singer, off key all the way. They arrived at the lake. There were other skaters with fires burning, laughing and having a good time. She put on her skates and found the ice to be just perfect. Martin wasn't a very good skater, trying to hang on to her for balance and support. She tried to be nice, but she finally gave up, "Martin, I'm cold, How about some hot chocolate?" "Yes, I'm miserable, I'm no skater, but I can warm you up." She brought out the jug of hot chocolate milk his mother made, the molasses cookies, and the blanket they covered themselves while in the sleigh. "Let's sit by the fire, I see a log we can use." As they drank the warm hot chocolate and munched the cookies, Martin began to cuddle a little closer to her. With his left hand, he pulled her chin to his and said, "I'd like show you how to kiss, if I may?" Drawing her close to his lips, he opened his mouth and stuck his tongue into her mouth. She gagged, and pushed him away. "If that's how you kiss, I'm not interested," then took a sip of her drink. "Well I'll be damn, I'm sorry, you just surprise me by how ignorant you are. I guess you truly have never been kissed. May I have another cookie please, if our friends are ready, I think we need to head home." Lily thought to herself, "I can't wait to get home to talk to Annette to give me some pointers on courting and kissing. I'm such a failure!"

Thank goodness, the roads melted the day before she was to leave to go to Dayton for Thanksgiving Holiday. She had Thursday through the following Thursday before she had to report to her classes on Friday. After Thanksgiving dinner at the Black's, with the Mitchell's and Thompson's also in attendance, she learned that James was due to start his new job in Columbus after the New Year. LilyRose asked Annette if she could have some private time with her to discuss a very important matter. At around seven that evening, she and Annette sat down to talk.

"Annette, I need advice on courting and kissing. I'm a failure in both areas." "Gosh, girl I was never courted in my life. James and I grew up together. When I was about sixteen and he was eighteen, I think he noticed me for the first time. He had a long talk with his mother and then he asked if he could walk with me by the river. We threw stones, looked for frogs, and stopped for candy at a store by the dock. He took my hand, and told me that he felt a little different about me since I was maturing. He asked if he could kiss me, I said yes, then he touched my face, looked into my eyes, kissed me so tender and sweet. I knew then, I loved him. And I've never had a day where I've doubted it one moment. Why, have you met someone at college?

"Yes, and I'm not sure I'm ready for this stuff." Lily went on to share what she had experienced with Martin, and how it made her feel kinda dirty. "Well, I'm no pro by any means, but for my money, I don't think this guy is for you. I think we aught to talk to James, he'd give you good advice,"

"Oh, no, I can't do that. Thanks anyway. Why is BethAnne not home for the holidays." "She is staying on campus to take part in some experiment her professor is paying her to be part of. Something to do with hydrogen and oxidation, whatever that is, James could explain it. She's an A student, I'm so proud, although most of the time I can't pronounce what she's studying let alone spell it." "I'm sorry she's not here, hope we can connect at Christmas." "Thanks Annette, I miss having my mother to talk to, Father is wonderful, but don't think I could approach him with my challenge. And Bess is now a nun!" "Yeah, I miss her so much."

One evening, LilyRose and her Father were doing an inventory of the supplies he had in the medical clinic. He said there were some things he needed to talk to her about that concerned her. He poured them both a cup of hot coffee. "I've been doing a lot thinking about some property that I own. Father's estate in Philadelphia is vacant and in need of a caretaker. My Father, Mother, and Mary Maud, are all buried in Mother's Rose garden. Someday, I hope that my ashes will be laid beside your mother. Since Bess is now a nun along with Sister Therese, I believe I would like to offer them the estate to be used as a home for widow's and children of war veterans. Bess is an excellent medical assistant and nurse, Sister Therese a wonderful teacher. I would put it in a life trust for them in honor of my father and mother. How do you feel about this? Do you think the sisters would enjoy this kind of service."

"Oh, Father, you are so generous. And yes, I believe they would go for it." "Then we will speak to them and get it taken care of while you are here. And, another matter. You are almost twenty-five years old. You stand to inherit a lot of money and property. Selfishly, I would like for it to stay in the Somerset line. Hopefully, someday you will marry, and your children will become heirs to your fortune. I am going to set up a trust for you, that will give you a monthly stipend and when you are 35 years old, you will inherit the entire estate. It will be stated that whom ever you marry, will not receive a dime of the fortune. I know you're not the type to talk about what you have or don't have, and believe me LilyRose, that is smart. There are many men who marry a woman just for that reason. I'm attempting to get around these crazy laws that say women are property of men. Are you with me?"

"Yes, Father, I've seen evidence of this already. A girl in college parents were killed in a house fire. Already guys are trying to get her to marry them. I'm afraid one is about to succeed. He's a terrible leech. Everyone is talking about it, It's the biggest gossip on campus."

"Then my sweet daughter, I'll take care of this matter immediately. What would you like to have for dinner?" "Have you got any good milk-shake cafe's around here?" "As a matter of fact, we do. Grab your coat and hat, we'll go for a burger and shake at Forest Park. I'm not sure where it is, but we'll find it."

LilyRose returned home to Wilmington on the Thursday before class on Friday. Her father turned right around and drove back to Dayton so that he could take care of some bank business. Sister's Jade Nicole, formerly Bess, and Therese Anne were very excited with Dr. Chad's offer. They decided they would start their own convent in Philadelphia and began to brainstorm ideas for creating a home and school for widows and orphans. They did not want to be limited to just widows and children of veterans. They decided to call it "Maggie Somerset, Home and School for Mothers and Children." Dr. Chad was delighted. He set up an account for them with Sean Murphy as trustee. This way, their energy could be focused on developing the home and school, not worrying about balancing books. He knew Patsy, Mary Maud's sister would have her hands in it, of which he was so pleased. The more he got involved, the more he felt Mary Maud's presence. His next project was to line up guests for LilyRose's Christmas Concert. He knew he needed to make plans with James about sharing transportation to Wilmington. He hadn't heard yet, if BethAnne was planning to come home or stay at the University to work on her experiment. She was dedicated to unfolding scientific discoveries. He disclosed to himself, "I admit, I'm excited to show off my little musical genius,"

As luck would have it, it did not snow the week of the Christmas Concert. The streets and country roads were all clear. Saturday, December the 21st proved to be cold and shiny. All participants in the Concert were nervous, but very excited. LilyRose was eager to share this years additional performers on the program. New was an orchestra consisting of piano, violins, viola, bass, flutes and chimes to accompany the choir and soloists. She had kept a surprise soloist from the church, and performers until their final rehearsal practice. Twelve year old Amanda Dee Denlinger would play a piano duet with LilyRose. Lily had discovered her one Sunday after church picking out tunes on an old up-right piano in the basement. She immediately felt Mandy had a talent to be nurtured. She met with her father, whose wife had passed away when Mandy was ten years old. She needed to acquire permission to give Mandy private lessons. He quickly informed LilyRose that he was in no position to purchase a piano or to pay for lessons. LilyRose explained her agreement with the church and her personal intent.

"Mr. Denlinger, the church pays me to teach choir and to give musical lessons to members who are committed to learning to sing or play an instrument. Your daughter has great potential. She can practice here at the church, but I would like to give her lessons at my friends home, Mr and Mrs Huffman, on their baby grand piano. I believe she deserves to learn on a beautiful instrument. I will personally take responsibility in scheduling her practice sessions and music lessons if you will give me permission"

"Miss Lily, we don't take charity, I work hard to pay the bills." "Sir, this is not charity. All teachers feel honored to take on a pupil they feel has both talent and desire. I personally was taught by a French nun who was a concert pianist before becoming a nun. She would take no money. She just wanted the honor to help me be the best I could be. Believe me, Sir, Mandy has great potential and I want to see her following her dreams." "Well, Miss Lily, If what you say is true, I'm honored for Mandy to be given this opportunity. Her mother played the piano, but we never had one. Then she became ill, so little Mandy never got to know her mother loved to play and sing. Thank you deeply for your generosity." "Sir, May I bring her in so you can tell her the good news?"

Mandy was invited into the music room of the church. Her father explained their plan. For a moment, she had a hard time believing what she was just told. "Daddy, Daddy is it true, I'm going to learn to play the piano from Miss Lily?" "Yes, Mandy, Miss Lily says that you have talent. But you must remember your schools lessons and your home chores must come first. If you neglect them, no more piano lessons. Do you understand this, Mandy?" Jumping up and grabbing him around the neck, she screamed, "Daddy, I promise, I won't disappoint you, then turning her head to look at Miss Lily she said, "Miss Lily, thank you so much, I promise you I'll do what ever you want me to do." "Mandy, the only thing you need to do, is pay attention to the lesson, practice, and follow your heart. God gave you a beautiful talent, don't waist it, and Mr. Denlinger may I call you Don, and please call me LilyRose."

Mandy never missed a practice session nor one of her lessons. She fell in love with Aunt and Uncle Huffman, which is what they begged her to call them. Each week, when they arrived for her lesson on Thursday right after school, Mrs. Huffman always had a cup of hot chocolate, tiny little sandwiches, and cookies for them to eat. She exclaimed, "You need to keep up your energy to play such a big instrument." The Huffman's always sat in the next room to listen to her progress, but never once did they say anything but encouraging words, "Oh Mandy, that was beautiful, you bring tears to our eyes."

Miss Lily asked Mandy if she thought her father might want to come to observe her lessons. "Miss Lily, Daddy would love it, May I invite him next week?" The arrangement were made for Mr. Denlinger to attend Mandy's lesson. He came dressed for church, nervous, but smiling proudly. Mrs. Huffman greeted him at the front door, escorted him to the adjoining room where they could already here the music class in session. He whispered silently, "It sounds like they are both playing the piano." "Yes, they are practicing a duet, the number is called "Clare de Lune" by the French composer, Debussy. Lily is basically playing chords behind Mandy's expert solo. This is quite an accomplishment for someone to play after such a short time taking lessons. Sir, I know you feel as proud, as we all do." Tears were in his eyes as he whispered,

"Mrs Huffman, I am most grateful for your kindness and generosity. I've not seen Mandy this happy since before her mother passed." "They're almost finished, then we'll have some refreshments before you leave. You honor us by allowing your daughter to share her sweetness and talent."

Lily hired her dressmaker to make her gown for the concert. They agreed on a green velvet jacket and grey long skirt. She wanted Mandy to wear a long dress using the same materials. She told Mandy, "This is our secret, we're going to be dressed like twins. The orchestra will wear black suits and long black dresses, the choir will wear their black robes with red and white stoles for Christmas. She asked the women to please wear their hair in either a bun or french twist. She also purchased William a Green Swede Leather Jacket to go with his standard choir black trousers, white shirt, and black tie. She made sure the grand piano was tuned, and that all music was placed in black folders. No one must ever know, that she over extended her budget, and donated all monies needed to create a professional musical concert with all of its proper trimmings. Mr and Mrs Huffman were kind and generous to allow her to borrow their piano, plus they insisted on paying for a professional mover to set it up and have it tuned as well. LilyRose knew they were very proud to be a part of her musical dream team. Even Scott Stationery Services donated their labor to print the program. All she needed to do was supply the silk paper stock. Her father was very happy to donate in any manner needed to enhance a Lily's desire to present a professional musical.

The program was printed on a very pale beige silk paper with green Old English print. On the back of the program was the names of all those who volunteered and donated in some manner. When opened, on the right side listed the event's program, soloist, and composer. On the left side listed names of all the participants. It looked absolutely beautiful and very professional. LilyRose prayed she did not forget anyone. The tickets had been on sale at the local newspaper's office. All participants were given two tickets for family or friends, the remaining seats were sold for $5.00 for adults, $3.00 for students, and children, $1.00. There would be a free nursery for babies and toddlers, compliments of the Women's League of

Wilmington. LilyRose was looking over the program when a voice said, "Miss LilyRose, the day is almost here. You've spent every moment these last three months working for this event. How may I be of service?" "Oh, Martin, how nice of you to volunteer. Let me see, if I could depend on you and a couple more volunteers to hand out these beautiful programs at the concert. I would ask that you have them dressed appropriately with smiling greeting faces. What do you think?" "At your service Madam, but on one condition, that I have you on New Years Eve to celebrate the new year." "Okay? Yes, I'd be happy to celebrate the new year with you. But until then, I'm still on duty," . "Thursday night is dress rehearsal and I'm still pulling up some loose strings." "I get the hint, I'll see who I can find to assist me in welcoming Clinton County elite." Laughing as he left.. LilyRose once more scanned the program.for possible errors.

Clinton County's Third Annual Christmas Musical Concert

Closing the mercantile, LilyRose breathed deeply, "at last, I feel a bit more peaceful."

Dr. Chad, the Black's including BethAnne arrived on Friday before the concert They chose to stay at an historical Bed and Breakfast on the main route from Dayton to Wilmington. It was a beautiful old estate, now owned by the children of wealthy corn and hay farmers. They raise miniature horses they show at county and state fairs. The barn was filled with trophy's and ribbons of every color. The pictures hanging on the walls were of champions no bigger than a large dog. Annette and BethAnne were enthralled, '"No", said James, "We are not going to buy you another pet we will need to take care of!" "Ahh, gee-whiz, Dad, you're not any fun!" Annette laughing hysterically

"They're ringing the bell for suppertime. Wonder what we'll have to eat?" The group of five arrived to find another couple who were from Oakwood, a wealthy village on the outskirts of Dayton. He was an executive of a new corporation that had just moved on the edge of the city limits. They were friends of the Huffman's, who invited the Patterson's to be their guests for the musical concert. This was James opportunity to announce that the father of the director of the concert was right here in their midst, "Allow me to introduce, Dr. Chad Somerset, of Harmony Village, Dayton,

Ohio." Dr. Chad blushed as he said, "Yes, I'm proud to admit, LilyRose is my beautiful and talented daughter."

The conversation for the rest of the dinner was centered around the fabulous meal. Served buffet style, they enjoyed Roasted pheasant with apple dressing, Baked pork ribs smothered in sauerkraut, Prime rib with roasted petite potatoes and onions, Cranberry-pineapple jellied mold, and a Slaw seasoned with horseradish sauce. Dessert was a four layer Banana walnut cake with rum/butter icing. James, the expert on fine dining exclaimed, "I don't believe I've ever had a meal with such exotic flavors, This slaw is magnificent! Horseradish, how unique and delicious!"

Everyone agreed, then Mr. Patterson brought up the subject of weather patterns. He found it quite interesting that Dayton built their town around two rivers; modeling European architecture. Dr. Chad responded, "I recall Paris and many cities in Germany and Austria that followed the same pattern, very interesting." Then BethAnne introduced the need for the United States to design a system forecasting weather patterns to prevent human disasters. She sighted how India has a rainy season, where thousands die annually because they are not alerted to a monsoon's appearance." She continued, "Science is my great interest. I spend every waking hour while I'm at the University in the science lab working with my prof and other science majors."

"Young lady" responded Mr. Patterson, "I certainly support that sort of research." The waiter arrived carrying the beautiful banana/walnut four layered cake with rum and butter icing. Some of the ladies had stated they couldn't eat another bite, but when the dessert arrived, Mrs Patterson said, "Well, maybe, just a tiny slice." Mr. Patterson smiled lovingly. Then after everyone had enjoyed their dessert and coffee, Mr. Patterson adjourned the dinner with, "I believe we all have a long day and evening tomorrow. I think we'll meet again for breakfast, before we head down the road to

Wilmington. It was nice meeting all of you. Good Night." Dr. Chad and party followed When Dr Chad arrived in his room, he found it had two big beds, "Good, LilyRose can sleep here after the concert."

As he lay in bed that night, he reflected on Mr and Mrs Patterson. Rarely had he ever met such a man with a vision for social change. "I will make it a point to meet with him privately this coming new year."

Lily was already busy following up with last minute details when her father and Black family appeared .at the church. Surprised to see BethAnne, Lily blushed. "BethAnne, I'm so happy to see you are able to attend!" Both hugging and giggling like teenagers. "So far, this trip has been so much fun and even interesting. I look forward to your concert. Your daddy is certainly pleased and proud of you!"

"I hope no one attending is disappointed, I've tried to think of every detail. Oh, please excuse me, I need to speak with one of my soloist." As William entered the backroom of the churches large sanctuary, BethAnne caught herself starring at the very tall, handsome gentleman. She thought, "If he's the calibre of men here with talent, I think I am truly going to enjoy this." Annette was amused at her daughter's reaction, then said, "Did you think Wilmington to be so back woodsy that the men wore only overalls and chewed tobacco?" Smiling while giving her daughter a hug, "Not exactly, but the scenery is proving to be quite interesting."

A flashing light indicated the concert would be starting in a few minutes. They all took their seats. Dr. Chad sat on the end aisle seat, ushering the others politely past him to take their seats. He thought to himself, "I might appear selfish, but by golly, this is my daughter 's concert."

The minister of the Presbyterian Church, Rev. Tad Gillesby stood by the podium on the far right of the room. He smiled proudly. "Ladies and Gentleman, on behalf of the Church Session, I want to welcome you to Clinton County's Third Annual Christmas Musical Concert. We know some of you have traveled many miles to be here, some are residents of Clinton County, and of course, a great number are family and friends of the performers. We are pleased there is standing room only, demonstrating the popularity of Miss LilyRose Somerset's creative and artistic teaching and directing abilities. Your program beautifully details this evening's program. Set back and enjoy tonight's prelude to Christ's birth and celebration." William stepped forth to light a large candle, then began to read a prepared text, as a soft piano accompanied him.

"In the beginning was the Christ, and the Christ was with God, and the Christ was God, Eternal Life is in Him, and His life gives light to all humankind. His life is the light shining through the darkness, and the darkness can never extinguish it. The Bible speaks of "the true light that shines on everyone coming into the world." This candle symbolizes the Christ, the Eternal Light, which is forever present in the world. The Christ is God expressing through all people. It is the birth of Christ in Jesus that we celebrate at this season, and we celebrate it because Jesus was the Way Shower, demonstrating the Truth that God is forever expressing through all life, through your life and mine."

The orchestra began with the choral introduction to "Oh, Holy Night." being directed by Miss LilyRose Somerset, standing on the Director's box, with full attention by her choir members. When given their cue, all voices began to sing...

Oh, Holy Night, the Stars are Brightly Shining,
This is the Night of Our Dear Savior's Birth

Lily's unique interpretation of the beautiful lyrics allowed each section to bring forth their resonate quality as the rest of the choir hummed harmonically in joyful support. The audience could see and feel the merge of director, choir, and orchestra as one Holy Instrument of God's Heavenly Voice.

Then Miss Lily began to read: "And it comes to pass, as it must some time for all people, that there is sent out a decree from the heart that all the world of effects be examined. And all must go each into his or her own city, where none other may enter; the realm of the human mind, which is Bethlehem, crowded with random thoughts, confusion and questions, where there has been no peace, no room to give birth to the Christ Consciousness. But it is meant that your days should be accomplished, and so with Joseph, your inner strength, and Mary, your soul of love, carrying the infant knowing of your Christ potential, you enter the din of Bethlehem, and seek shelter in the stable, your Center of Light. In this Holy, complete Light, you bring forth the first born knowing, your Christ potential and your heart becomes a manger to nurture the power of Truth born for you this night."

The violin section stood and began playing an intro to O'Little Town of Bethlehem, then the whole orchestra joined in to finish the Carole. The audience enthralled by their musical experienced, was surprised when little Mandy joined Miss Lily at the grand piano. Miss Lily played an intro, then Mandy, confident with Miss Lily beside her, played French composer, Debussey's Clair de Lune, Moonlight No. 3. The audience was spellbound with her mature piano technique and interpretation. When finished, they stood and cheered her for a few minutes. She bowed, then left, returned, bowed again as they cheered her on.

Miss Lily returned to the conductor's box, raised her baton as she con- ducted the intro to "Ava Maria" by composer, Schubert in its original Latin. William stepped forth, having removed his black robe, wearing a beautiful emerald green swede leather jacket. His 6ft 2 inch height and physical muscular build, with perfect voice control, created the perfect image of humanity's prayer to Mary, Mother of Jesus, to intercede for the world's pain and suffering. William's baritone voice along with his dramatic interpretation created for the audience, regardless of religious belief, an intense feeling of love and compassion. When finished, William took his place in the choir. Then suddenly the whole sanctuary burst in applause. People were wiping their eyes and cheering, Bravo! Bravo! Bravo! Lily motioned for William 'to take a bow. He too, was shedding tears. Once again, LilyRose stepped upon the conductor's box for the evening's final number, "Silent Night." by Franz Gruber. She tapped her baton on the music stand, raised it to begin the introduction for the choir, The soprano's started by singing,

"Silent Night, Holy Night, All is Calm All is Bright
Round yon virgin, mother and child,
Holy infant so tender and mild,
Sleep in heavenly peace, Sleep in heavenly peace."
Then the whole choir harmonized the second verse. For the third verse,
Miss LilyRose turned to the audience, motioned for them to rise, hold
hands, while singing the last verse.
Silent Night, Holy Night, Son of God, Love's pure light,
Radiant beams from Thy holy face, with the dawn of redeeming grace,
Jesus, Lord at Thy birth, Jesus, Lord at thy birth."
Little Mandy stepped forward to gently blow out the flame. Darkness! A Moment of silence to feel the Holy Presence, then the lights came up. Miss LilyRose, took William's hand to her left, and Mandy's to her right and they all three bowed, then motioned to the choir to bow, and finally the orchestra stood, Suddenly a tinkle of tiny bells, rang so softly, God's Holy announcement, "Peace on Earth, Goodwill to All."

Everyone was enjoying the moment, no one seemed to want to leave, all desiring to speak to LilyRose, William Bailey, and Little Miss Amanda Denlinger. The first to grab Mandy was her father. He picked her up, swung her around, complimenting her on how wonderful she performed and exclaiming, "You're Mama was watching from Heaven. We're so proud!" He then stepped back to let the audience honor his little girl. Many shook his hand, saying he must be proud. What an evening!

But it was far from being over. The Huffman's were having a reception for all the soloist, LilyRose family and friends, Penelope, their employee who was about LilyRose age, and James and Katherina Patterson. The caterer's had the dining room table decorated for the holidays, and a Christmas Tree was in the corner with a Star of David on the top. Lily asked Martin if that was okay? She was concerned the Huffman's might be offended, "Silly Lily, no, they ordered the tree and the decorations. They are ecumenical, as they say in Washington." Under the tree were gifts for all the guests and helpers. The performers received beautifully embroidered scarves with *Christmas Musical Concert*, date, and soloist' name. The other guests received boxes filled with Belgium candy, nuts, and Christmas hanky The men's were white with their initials, women's were white lace with initials. LilyRose wore on her jacket lapel, the hand carved red rose that William had given her. She and William exchanged gifts before the concert. He felt proud she wore the pen he made, and would treasure the New Year leather journal with his initials and date of concert engraved on it. Miss Lily gave Mandy at gold neckless with a gold angel charm. All were thrilled.

Martin saved his gift for LilyRose until last. As she opened the silver box tied with a red ribbon, all eyes were fixed on her. Relieved, inside was a beautiful bottle of French perfume and a sachet silk bag to hang in her clothes closet. She kissed him on the cheek while guest's cheered. As the party came to a close Lily gave Mr. and Mrs. Huffman a gift of an autographed framed picture of Mandy playing their baby grand piano. They were thrilled! The Huffman's motioned for Mandy to come receive her gift. She squealed with delight, It was a pair of ice skates, a muffler and cap made by Mrs. Huffman. Lily presented Martin with a leather diary with his initials engraved. She had written inside, *May each entry be filled with joy and happiness LilyRose, Christmas 1890*

The Patterson's, a delightful couple, affirmed the whole evening was the perfect way to start the Holiday Season. Lily noticed Penny was enjoying Donald Denlinger's attention, and BethAnne was engrossed with questioning William about his Children's Nature Center. "Hmmmm, thought LilyRose,"

Father pulled the buggy to the front door of the Estate. James stepped up in the front while the ladies rode in the back seat with a fur blanket to cover their bodies. By the time they arrived to the Bed and Breakfast, LilyRose was fast asleep. Father awakened her by whispering in her ear. "Hey, Daddy's little girl is not so little anymore and Daddy is getting too old to carry her, so please allow me to help you to your feet and up the stairs." As soon as they arrived to their room, Lily flopped on the bed, but Father made her change into her night clothes. After brushing her teeth, she climbed in bed and was out like a light in just a few minutes.

The next morning they all met in the dining room for a Christmas Buffet. There were little sausages, ham curls, bacon bites with cheese, scrambled eggs, fried potatoes and biscuits and gravy. There was also a fruit mold, and fried apple pies, hot coffee, tea, and orange juice. LilyRose reminded everyone she had to be at church for the late service to play the piano. The choir was excused until Christmas Eve services. "I can't eat another bite. Father is dropping me off at the church and turning right around to pick you up to head back to Dayton. I'll see you at Christmas break. I'm so pleased you came, and BethAnne, I hope you

decide to come home for Christmas. We're having Christmas dinner with the Mitchell's. James remarked, , "We are as well. See you then, LilyRose your concert was the most beautiful concert I've ever seen. You are brilliant!"

LilyRose jumped into the buggy. Her father reached for the fur blanket, then said, "Finally I have you alone. Sweetheart, I've been wondering, when did you decided to introduce those spiritual readings and where did you find them?" "The night before. I wrote them and asked William that morning if he would read his part. He agreed. I felt the creative process bubbling up, it was awesome, Father!" "You're Mother could do just as you did. Come up with something at the last moment. On the last night of our Honeymoon in New York City, she saw a European Grand Piano on the second floor of St. Nicholas Hotel. She ask the manager if she could play it before dinner on the main floor. He agreed, told some of the guest that she was going to entertain at four pm. About ten people arrived, they sat in a semi-circle around the piano. She played two classical pieces, an Irish Love Song, and finished with an Irish Jig. I was so proud! It took courage for her to ask management, and then to perform in front of an audience when all she expected was me to be there."

"Oh Father, I remember our one and only family concert. Sometimes I can still hear her playing so beautifully, and then she passed out, never to be well again. Oh, Father, I'm so sorry, I know how much you miss her." "But she was with us at the concert, I could feel her. Did you?" "Yes, I believe when William lit the candle, I felt her standing beside me." "She was with us just a short time, some folks never had what we had. Love is eternal, and someday, I will be with her, for ever and ever. We're almost at the church. I'll be here to pick you up on the Wednesday before Christmas. Please be packed and ready to go. Pray the roads will be clear. Bye, Sweetheart, I love you." "Bye Father, and I love you, too."

The roads were clear when Dr. Chad picked up LilyRose all packed and ready to go. Mr. Huffman, her landlord and employer greeted Dr. Chad with a hardy hand shake and a gift from Mrs. Huffman. She knew they would be pressed for time, and had packed a big picnic basket to eat on their way.

"Your beautiful wife thinks of everything. I know we'll enjoy every little tidbit. I have a couple of apples I thought would hold us until we arrived home." LilyRose hugged Mr. Huffman while her father carried out her bags. She asked "Please, thank Mrs. Huffman for us, she's so special. I love you both."

A customer came in just as they were leaving. Mr. Huffman wiped his eyes, then lumbered to assist the gentleman at the tool counter. "How may I help you?" he asked, "I got a broken door on my shed. I need three large henges and screws. Noticing the gentleman was a seasoned farmer, boots, heavy coat overalls and that he'd not ask for credit, but instead, paid by cash. He carefully counted out every penny, Mr. Huffman thought to himself. "If more of us, followed his good common sense, there would be less foreclosures." "Thank you, Mr. Huffman. That little lady that usually works here, is always so helpful to the Misses. We attended the Concert. She is a treasure, I hope she stays around after she finishes her schooling. Goodbye, thank you and have a good Christmas." "Yes, we hope she stays around as well. Have a nice Christmas."

Even though the Huffman's were Jewish, they felt supportive and loving kindness to their neighbors. All religious were about caring for each other. He looked at the big clock on the wall, thinking. "Eva will have dinner ready, a log in the fire to welcome me home this cold evening."

Lily was in such a hurry to leave, she forgot to ask about Martin, who she felt for sure would arrive to say goodby. She knew one thing for sure, he'd arrive on time for dinner at the Huffman's. Eva made it very clear, If you're not here at dinner time, there will not be any food available until the next meal. "No snacking in the kitchen!" was her mantra.

Dr. Chad was having some of his own personal thoughts as they rode along. "Why did Martin's father have to fill in for LilyRose? At that exact same moment, LilyRose was having some disturbing thoughts "I thought Martin would be working the mercantile, why did Mr. Huffman fill in? I wonder? As the silence continued, LilyRose reached in the back for the lunch basket. Taking out two large napkins, a steaming hot rolled towel with pieces of roasted chicken, two still warm baked potatoes, two hard boiled eggs, and a round of homemade bread and butter.

"Father, I think we've hit pay dirt, this here is pure gold. It's my turn to feed you like a child, hand me your open hand, here's a big fat leg wrapped in a linen towel. After you've eaten the chicken, I'll fetch you a hot po-ta-ter." Both enjoying her little comedy theater. they finished their meal with a jug of fresh apple cider.

"Now Sir, please wipe the lip of the jug with your sleeve before you pass it on." Again both laughing out loud, Dr. Chad amused but serious at the same time. He loved his daughter and her ability to be spontaneous with laughter and humor. He affirmed, "Christmas is going to be the best since she left to go to Wilmington. She has earned this little vacation. I will do whatever I can to make each day be filled with joy and happiness."

Martin arrived at the Huffman estate right on time. Penelope, the housekeeper greeted him on her way out. He hung his overcoat in the hall closet, took off his boots, and headed to the nearest lavatory to wash up. His mother heard him come in, kissed him on both cheeks, then said, "Was your meeting fruitful? You're a very talented young man, I think they too, will see your potential." "I'll need to meet with some members, it's a joint effort. I'm trying not to get my hopes up too high. Hello Dad, did you get the Somerset's off to Dayton? "They were in a rush, we didn't have much time to visit. They wanted to get back before it got dark. Eva, the dinner smells delicious! LilyRose and father were very grateful for your kindness in preparing a picnic basket. I can imagine how difficult it must be to eat on the run, but LilyRose will make it enjoyable. I'm sure of that."

Martin immediately took over the conversation. He explained what he was learning about politics. Governor James Campbell is attempting to put together a campaign for his re-election campaign. There is to be a Democratic headquarters in all the large cities with small town delegations to campaign farm to farm around their perimeter. Martin felt if he were given the responsibility to cover Wilmington and Clinton County, it would open the door for him to be elected or appointed to the city counsel. His future dream was to go Washington, DC as either a representative or a senator. His father asked, "What about your education? Don't you feel you should finish your degree? I would think that might be a requirement?" "Come on Dad, a degree's not everything. Look at Lincoln, he was self taught and he became a very fine president." "Yes, there were no colleges in his back door, and Lincoln worked hard, came from a poor family, and never allowed anything to distract him. I hope you'll do the same, what's next?" "Another committee meeting to interview me, then they decide. I'm going up to my room to study up on Gov. James Campbell. He served in the Civil War on a gun boat, just a schoolboy, got sick, almost died, then got sent home. Think I'll go to the library first, do you still have the most recent newspapers?" He left the room, never asking to be excused, not thanking his mother for the delicious meal.

"Oh Allen, I'm so hopeful he's found his perfect career. However, I fear I must continue to remind him of his poor manners. It's as though, he never heard Please, Thank you,I or may I be excused. I'm afraid I spoiled him, it all falls back on me. I was too lenient." Dropping her head in shame. "Eva Stein Huffman, you're no more to blame than myself. We were overjoyed to finally have a child, an heir to our long hard work. But Martin does not even pretend to care about the store, the responsibility it requires to manage it, nor does he develop trustworthy friendships. Our recent demands to hold him accountable to amend his debts has proven he can do it, but I'm afraid his heart is not in it. I think he just enjoys playing the game?"

As Eva stood to clear the table, Allen witnessed her red eyes and shaking hands. "Come on my beautiful bride, we'll do this together, just like the old days, when we lived in New York. We worked hard as a team, and we may be getting old but we're still a team regardless of our grey hair."

While she washed the dishes, he carefully dried each plate, cup and saucer, then gently returned them to the china cabinet. He thought of his Rabbi Father, who every evening would put on his prayer shawl and sing,

"Hear Old Israel, the Lord God is One." In old Yiddish dialect. How I loved to be with him as the men of the community gathered around to impart his learned wisdom."

"I'm sorry Allen, did you say something? I was daydreaming." "I too, was day dreaming. Thinking about Papa, the Rabbi, reading from holy texts, the Torah, Talmud, or Qabbalah, as his feeble bent over body would come joyfully alive. I am so grateful we had those times with our parents and family members to appreciate God's grace in showing us the way to live , give, and to prosper."

Dr Chadwick Somerset's Home, Christmas 1890, Harmony Village.

Dayton, Ohio

LilyRose is in the kitchen looking for a spatula, called out, "Father, where do you store your spatula's? I'm making pancakes with apples, I need a spatula. Will you come to my rescue?" "I'll do more than that, I'll help you." In a drawer by the kitchen sink, he pulled out two, a large and a small. "Mistress, what suit's your culinary skills the best?"

"Whoooooo, I'm a beginner, haven't done much cooking for about six years. I hope my apple pancakes will be edible, cause my belly is on strike for food!" As she continued to whip the lumps out of the batter, her father is busy beating eggs and cream for scrambled eggs. "Do you want bacon, ham, or sausage to go with your pancakes?"

"Let's make it easy, What is the quickest?" "Ham, it's already cooked. Only needs to be carved. How many slices do you want? "One and a half, if my pancakes are decent, that should fill me up."

After the first two pancakes, LilyRose got the hang of frying, flipping, and stacking the crisp apple pancakes. She made twelve about the size of a saucer and devoured four covered with warm butter and maple syrup. She ate her ham with her scrambled eggs. She was always picky about food running into each other. Father had no problem with meat, eggs and pancakes dancing together. He ate five apple pancakes, two chunks of ham with half of the eggs he scrambled for the meal. He enlightened LilyRose with a math problem,

"If you and I ate all the eggs, covered the ham back up to preserve it in the smoke house, and there were twelve pancakes made, you ate four and I ate five, how many are left for the poor dog and cat?"

"Father, I'm amazed you made it through Harvard, if this math problem has you stumped! Why, I've already wrapped up three left for a snack when we go visiting your patient. The correct answer is: NONE GOES TO THE ANIMALS!"

Father grabs a towel, wraps it around her neck, kisses her on the forehead, "Lily, I must say, you always have kept me on my toes. I'll bet a prima donna hasn't had as many hours "on toe" as your dear old dad." "Is that another one of your math puzzles?" And kisses him back.

Father had two patients, both men and both suffering from arthritic conditions. One, a farmer who had been pinned under his hay wagon for about an hour until a passerby saw his wagon overturned and horses making strange noises. His left side was pinned down causing him to have some numbness in his left leg and

continuing pain. "Herbert, how's your body treating you these days" "Doc, I'm eighty-one, no spring chicken anymore. I sleep with hot stone on my leg when it's cold, soak it in the tub when I can heat the water, but mostly, I pay no attention to it, the work's got to get done"

"Let me check you out, any swelling or numbness you haven't had before?" "I don't rightly think so? Now let me think" as Dr. Chad listens to his heart and breathing. "Yes, I've noticed I'm like the best weatherman, I can sure tell if it's going to rain or snow. I think we'll get two inches of snow tonight. Is you're clinic going to be open tomorrow?"

"It is, but I can walk there in a few minutes. Herb I can hear a new sound in your heart, have you been having any chest pains, or exhaustion?"

"Sometimes, I get right poorly before I get my chores done. But if sit down a bit it goes away. Milking is a pleasure, I relax when milking, but mucking out the barn tires me out. "Is there anyone that can help you with that chore?" "Nope, I ain't rich, My son is in the Army, daughter lives too far, and my wife is not strong enough. Nope, if I drop dead mucking manure, then it's my lot in life."

"I've written my recommendations for both you and your wife. Please drink at least a half gallon of water a day, DO NOT PUT SALT on your food. It's hard on your heart, Try to eat more vegetables than meat, take a little nap everyday, and try not to worry. Okay?"

"Why so much water? I drink lots of coffee." "Try drinking twice as much water as coffee. Water flushes your system of bad germs, too many minerals in the kidneys, and helps you digest your food properly." "What's today's doctoring gonna cost me?" "What's you got you can spare?" "I've got a bushel of unshelled corn or peck of dried apples, take your pick" Dr. Chad turns to LilyRose, "Thank you, we'll apples so Father can show me how to make fried apple pies." "You'd grow'd up to be right pretty and smart, telling daddy what to do." All three laughed at the truth in Herb's words.

As father and daughter approached Eugene's run down three room home, their conversation was about Lily cleaning out her mother's closet. Her mother's personal items had never been touched since she had died over twenty years ago. Lily told her father, "Only if there was time and they could do it together,".

As they pulled into Eugene's snow covered yard, they spotted him rocking in one of the two chairs on the falling down porch. "Good afternoon Eugene. Aren't you cold out here?" "Warmer out here then inside. My neighbor's wife is sick and he's not cut any wood of late." "Where is the wood located?" "Behind the old shed, I can't swing an ax and sawing takes two people."

Dr Chad and Lily help him into the cold house as they surveyed the conditions in the house. Water bucket was half full, cabinets had potatoes, carrots, onions enough for a week, enamel commode was full, covered with newspaper, and just about everything was filthy and needing repair. "When did you last eat Eugene?"

"Yesterday, I had some tater soup. My hen stopped laying so I killed her about a week ago. She made me some fine eating." "How's your arthritic back doing?" "It's freezing, I cover up in everything I got. Still can't get warm. I've been drinking snow, can't make it to the well, it's got to be primed."

After some soul searching and deep thinking, Dr. Chad said sternly, "Eugene, here's the deal. You can't stay here alone. Your starving and freezing to death. My daughter and I, along with Frank Mitchell will get you some groceries, chop fire wood, and clean this place and you up. You will need to contact your family for help and a place to stay. So your job right now is to gather your clothes, put everything in a pillow case because you're coming home with me and my daughter. By the way, this is my daughter, LilyRose, she is visiting me for Christmas, she lives in Wilmington, Ohio." Eugene immediately took notice, then said, "My daughter lives close there, she lives in Sabina with her two children."

"Is she married?" "I know what your thinking, she can't take care of me, her worthless husband took off about four years ago. The Lord has helped her by finding her a job as a maid for a preacher. She has the basement for her and the children. It takes everything she makes to feed and clothe those youngins. I can't believe the law won't do anything in finding him and make him pay."

LilyRose very quickly responded, "I'm afraid it is about inequality. Someday, we'll get our rights and things will change, until then women will continue to be treated as property to men, with no rights." Dr. Chad said, "Amen, Now let's get going here, you understand?" Eugene nodded, feeling a little helpless.

Frank and Dr. Chad did the ugly part, cleaning up Eugene's house, cutting wood, while LilyRose saw to washing and repairing his clothes and discreetly getting rid of what could not be salvaged. She made him take two baths until her eagle eye was satisfied with his ears, finger and toe nails were sparkling clean. He complained during it all. Finally, she raised her right hand, pointed to her left hand and said, "Mr. Eugene, I know under that filth, crust, and orneriness, there is a kind and clean gentleman. Believe me, I will not rest until I see him. Here' a brush, clean your teeth with this soda and believe me, if they are not clean, I'll show you how and it won't be fun!" "Miss LilyRose, I like your spirit. Why aren't you married?

"Because, I haven't found a man whose one-tenth the man my father is. He raised the bar for being kind, compassionate, loving, and unselfish. Not sure I even want to entertain marriage with what I've witnessed in the playing field."

Eugene could be seen brushing and brushing his teeth, over and over. Lily was smiling to herself as she boiled his clothing in the copper galvanized tub on the kitchen stove. She was making a big pot of ground beef and mixed beans. She made a big pan of corn bread and thought her fried apple pies were not perfect, but still good. She found herself looking forward to eating dinner; it had been a new and interesting day. Just then Father and Frank arrived home. "Well, will you look at our friend Eugene. You look like you've been under my daughter's command. Why, I know she doesn't fear nothing or no body." "Yes Sir, She makes me think of my General during the war. He said, he did not like to lose and we didn't.

Miss LilyRose is the tallest woman I believe I've ever seen. Why, I think her height and red hair tells a man she means business. She's also very sweet and pretty as a china doll. Thank you Miss LilyRose , I hope I passed muster." Everyone joins in praising LilyRose, she then said, "Why, shucks fellers, I know you love me 'cause your hungry, get cleaned up, 'cause my recruit and me are hungry as bears."

As they sat down at the table, Eugene surprised them by offering to say grace, "Lord, this here family have hearts of gold. They live your teachings, thank you for sending them my way. In Jesus name, Amen/"

Frank complimented LilyRose on her chili. He explained that in Texas Territory, they eat a lot of beef and beans. They add hot peppers, then call it chili. You've added a buckeye state flavor; lots of onions, garlic, tomatoes and parsley. Eugene filled his bowl twice with two big pieces of corn bread with butter and honey. Dr. Chad warned him to go slow, when your stomach has shrunk and you fill it too full, the results may not be pretty. LilyRose brought out the fried pies and hot coffee. The perfect ending for a day filled with hard work and conversation.

LilyRose spent most of the holidays looking through her mother's clothes, jewelry, hats, shoes, and dresses.. Her mother was very short, maybe five foot, and Lily was five feet nine inches tall. They both were blessed with beautiful auburn red hair and slender bodies. Surprising to LilyRose, is that her mother's clothing all fit her except for the length. Nine inches will give a dressmaker quite a challenge in altering them. She decided to take them home with her and see what could be done. She loved her mother's wedding dress. It was made of pure silk and Irish lace. She wasn't keen with the low off the shoulder bodice, but could see it altered with more lace and white velvet. "What am I doing?" she thought, "I'm not ready to marry, I have too many things to learn and do before I settle down to marry." Just then her father knocked on the door, "Come in Father, I've been trying on Mother's dresses. They all fit my body but they are way too short. I think I can get them altered. My dressmaker in Wilmington is a genius. She'll jump at the opportunity to create something new in the process."

"Your mother's wedding dress? I'm so happy we were able to have her portrait painted in it before she got ill. Do you think you'd like to wear it when you marry?" "Yes, but Father, that's going to be down the road, I've got a lot of things I want to learn and do before that happy event. I've picked this royal purple gown to wear New Year's Eve. Martin is taking me to a New Year's Eve Ball at the Bed and Breakfast we stayed in when you came for the Concert. I've made our arrangements, I feel it to be good sense to stay the night there because of a possible blizzard. My room is on the second floor and Martin's is on the first floor behind the ballroom. He said it wouldn't bother him as he sleeps like log, whatever that means."

"Your mother wore that gown the evening she played the grand piano at the St. Nicholas Hotel. She was so beautiful, poised, and accomplished. The audience of about ten, gave her a standing ovation. You are so much like her, but your height takes after the Somerset's. I feel honored to claim that little bit of your beauty and talent."

"How's our guest doing?" "Father, Eugene is such a sweet person, I think he lost himself after his wife died and daughter got married. He never let his daughter know how bad off he has been. And Father, he fought at Ft. Donelson under General Grant. Isn't that amazing? I asked if he remembered a medic called Jeb, he said there were thousands of troops and a whole lot of snow during that battle."

"The Black's have invited us for dinner, can you be ready in fifteen minutes? "That I can do. James is an amazing chef, They leave for Columbus after the new year."

Dinner was a Sea Food Delicacy. Shrimp cocktail, served in crystal glasses with bits of pineapple, pimento, and water cress, to be followed by dollar size crab cakes with black mushrooms, and tarragon on a bed of mixed baby greens. The main course was grilled salmon stuffed with toasted honey mustard Russian dark toasted bread with minced onion and garlic served on a platter surrounded by sliced sweet potato and winter squash toasted to a dark glazed sheen. Every dish was presented, as if in an elegant establishment for formal dining. And of course, it was. In just a few weeks, Chef James Black will be serving those who appreciate the great art of food preparation and service.

The chef joined them for coffee, tea, and an orange liquor from Spain. The dessert was beautifully presented in crystal dishes and to the guest's surprise, never before eaten. James had labored to create a famous Italian dessert to perfection. Italian Lemon Gelato, an ice cream dish that cleansed the palate of any unappreciated taste or odor. LilyRose exclaimed! "Forgive my vulgar exclamatory response, But damn, this is to die for!"

"LilyRose, that's the finest compliment I've ever had, especially coming from a novice in vulgarity. Laughter followed

The ladies all met in the kitchen gossiping while doing the dishes. BethAnne was anxious to return to campus and her science research. Annette was concerned if she would be able to complete the house packing by the time the movers came in a week, and LilyRose was thinking about final exams when she returned after holidays. Everyone hugged and promised to stay in touch. But of course, they didn't. Life in general, just got in the way.

Many Daughters have done excellently,
but you surpass them all.
-Proverbs 31:29-

Man has falsely identified
with the pseudo soul of ego,
When he transfers his sense
of identity to his true being,
the Immortal Soul,
he discovers that
all pain is unreal,
He can no longer
can even imagine
the state of suffering.
Sayings of "Paramahansa Yogananda"

WILLIAM LINCOLN BAILEY FARM

WILMINGTON, OHIO

Will arrived home from the Concert and Huffman Reception at about one in the morning. Shep was waiting eagerly for him. Shep was the third canine Will owned since he was adopted by the Bailey's as a youth. He didn't have the heart to name any new dog differently. Shep number one, was a border collie; all those that followed, just showed up a few days after the previous Shep passed. The second Shep was a badly starved and abused German Shepherd. It took Will weeks to get her to trust him, to learn she was not to chase animals, and let FurBall, the old mixed cat cuddle up close to her for protection. She was also pregnant, with constant, nutritional food, warm bed and loving care, she delivered three babies, one died, but two lived. Will's farm multiplied with rescued animals. He loved all animals and they adored him.

Shep number three was found in the corn field. A careless hunter shot him in the hind legs. Will took him to a Vet who suggested he put him down, but Will refused. After patching up, Will brought Shep home to be cared for while he healed. Miraculously, Shep healed without amputation, but Will did have to splint his legs until their shattered bones healed. He fed him a good healthy diet, with natural herbs in his water and food dish. When he removed the splints, his left hind leg was paralyzed. Will told him, "Shep old boy, I'll think of something to help you be as good as new." This he did.

He went to the dump regularly looking for wooden boxes to make chicken nests. One day, he spotted a broken dresser with four tiny rollers at its base. Will believed these rollers had great possibility. He asked at the gate, "Sir, is a dollar enough for these four little rollers?" "Yep, more than enough," "Keep thee change, and good day to thee." Realizing he hadn't used any of plain jargon in a very long time.When he got home, he immediately sanded down a piece of wood about the size of the length of Shep's foot to the joint. After the wood was smooth, he screwed the roller to the wood from inside of the wood to the outside. He wrapped the roller and wood on Shep's leg tightly, making sure his back legs matched. All the while Shep lay very still, sensing Will was doing everything to help him walk. As it was, he could walk and drag his foot, but this would help him to roll faster. It worked, but Will knew their had to be another way, just be patient, as Rome wasn't built in a day, as they walked around the property posting NO HUNTING!! and ANIMALS & PLANTS ARE PROTECTED signs all around the property.

William was feeling a little disjointed. The concert was more than he ever expected. The reception at the Huffman Estate was also very nice. All the guests were very polite and complimentary, but inside, he felt a little lost, like in baseball; he was in left field, without a glove and the ball was heading right to him.

He found his new journal. Last year's journal that Miss LilyRose gave him was filled with stories of his past life, before becoming William Lincoln Bailey. They were stories of his memories as a slave boy, living with his Mam and Pap, Miss Jenny and his brother, Gunnar.

Today, he thought, "I begin a new year. I will write about my thoughts and memories from this day forth." With a new fountain pen purchased at the mercantile, he began by addressing both a date and salutation.

December 25, 1890

Dear William,

The snow is falling, heavy and thick flakes the size of a silver dollar. I find myself thinking about the first Christmas over two thousand years ago.when Mary and Joseph were looking for shelter because she knew the baby was about to be born.

Today, I feel that I'm about to be born new, with greater possibilities than I can ever image. I listened to conversations around me at the reception. I wondered what does any of this mean to the greater meaning of life? Then I realized my thoughts were filled with judgment. Was I comparing myself with those nice caring people? Or maybe feeling sorry for myself because I've lost so much in my lifetime. Today, I am alone, no one to share my thoughts and my heart with. I admit to having private thoughts and dreams about Miss LilyRose. Sometimes I feel as though she is reading my thoughts and can tell what I am feeling. It scares me to have these feelings because it appears like she is going to be promised to Martin in the near future. Why does that bother me? Honestly, because I don't feel he's good enough for her, and that certainly makes it look like I think I'm better than he is.

No, no! Erase that! I don't think that is what is causing my distress. It's her eyes, they don't dance and sing like I've seen them do when playing or directing music. When she reached for my hand to take a bow, I felt my heart beating so fast I thought I'd faint. Then when she opened the rose pen I made for her, she had tears in her eyes when she said, "William, this is my best Christmas present." I could feel she meant it. She never says something she does not mean. I'm sure of it.

She is in her home in Dayton for Christmas with her wonderful father. He reminds me of my Papa Bailey. They are hardworking, giving and caring souls who love God and their family. I must remind myself how much God blessed me when he sent me to be Martha and Obadiah's son. I want to always be grateful when I have these moments of melancholy.

My goodness, It's feeding and cuddling time! My animals all want to be cuddled and sense so do I. God's abundant natural environment awaits to be celebrated on this most Holy Night as the Stars are Brightly Shining, 'tis the Night of our Dear Savior's Birth. .

Be kind to one another,
tenderhearted, and
forgiving one another,
as God in Christ has forgiven you.
-Ephesians 4:32

Sabina, Ohio visit. Huffman Mercantile

Wilmington, Ohio

It was still terribly cold when Dr. Chad brought LilyRose back to Wilmington after the holidays. While unloading her luggage, he announced that he was not staying for lunch. He thought this would be a great time to visit Sabina to meet with Eugene's daughter. Then he'd stay the night at the Bed and Breakfast before heading back to Harmony Village.

"Father, you are such a good and caring man plus devoted father. I wish more of our citizens paid attention to the document this country was founded on!" "Honey, I'm sorry that these past generations have not lived up to that most perfect document's principle! I have faith in your generation to weave into our citizen's daily lives, a tapestry woven with kindness, respect, and acceptance." "Oh, Father, you're so poetic and right on. I'm going to write what you just said in my journal to remind myself; one person, can inspire greatness, by doing the best they can."

After hugging his daughter, Dr. Chad immediately headed to Sabina, a little town east of Wilmington to meet with his patient, Eugene's daughter. When he arrived at the church parsonage, he found two children playing in the yard. He asked if they would tell their mother that Dr. Somerset would like to talk about her father.

They opened the door and shouted, "Mom, some doctor is here to talk to you about grandpa." She opened the door, as Dr. Chad handed her his calling card. "Ma'am my name is Dr. Chad Somerset of Dayton, Ohio. Your father Eugene is my patient. May I have a moment of your time?" "Yes, of course, is there anything wrong with my Dad?" "Yes, and No." Pausing a bit to formulate his words. "His physical health is not too bad for a feller his age, but his Vet's pension does not cover his daily expenses, and his stubborn pride won't allow him to ask for help."

"Where is he? I'm so busy taking care of my two children and the church parsonage, I'm afraid I can't take on my father at this time." Starting to weep, motioning for the children to stay outside and play. "Ma'am, I understand your situation." She lead him down to the basement where she and children lived.

She continued, "I get the basement and twenty-five dollars a month. It doesn't include food or doctor bills. I barely get by. I clean the parsonage, set up any meetings the Pastor has, and fix his meals. I'm very happy here, I feel safe, children love their school, and we all attend church and Sunday School."

"I see. Does the church have a yard man, janitor, or handyman?" "No, the preacher works in the yard, volunteers clean the church." "Do you mind if I speak to your minister? I'd like to make an offer to him? Your quarters in the basement are large, is there a place for your Dad, if needed?" "Yes, but I can't feed or take care of him if he's sick. Yes, I'll get the pastor."

Rev. Lionel McBride followed Bella Joy Hicks down the basement stairs to her little apartment she shares with her children. Dr. Chad stood to greet him as he descended down the steps.

"Rev. McBride, I'm so happy to make your acquaintance, I'm Dr. Somerset, Mrs Hick's father's physician. I'm here to make you an offer to both assist your church, Mrs Hicks and her father." "Go ahead, I'm listening" "Eugene Hicks is a veteran of the Civil War. He own's a little piece of property in Dayton, but cannot meet his financial obligations due to his small pension and his arthritic condition. I went to visit Eugene last week for a check up. I found him, almost starved and freezing without either food or chopped wood for his stove. My daughter and I brought him home to nurse him back to health, wash up his clothing, bathe his filthy body and shave his beard and wash and cut his hair. Mr. Hicks now looks, smells, and feels much better about himself." "So Doctor, how does all of this affect or include me and my church?"

"I took the liberty to look around your church property and found you need a gardener, a janitor, and a handyman. In about a month, Eugene can provide all those services to you and your congregation. I'm suggesting that Mrs Hicks allow her father to move in with her. This basement is quite large, in return he will give his services to your church for a fee of about twenty dollars a month. Because I have total faith in Eugene's work ethic and ability to meet all requirements needed here, I will donate fifty dollars as seed money for the first two months."

"Dr. Somerset, I'm a good Christian minister and can't figure out for the likes of me, why you'd do this for Mrs Hicks father and for a church you've never attended." "Rev. McBride, you ask what is my motivation? Matthew 3:3-16, Blessed are the poor in spirit, for theirs is the kingdom of heaven, Blessed are they that mourn, for they shall be comforted." Shall I go on? This morning I brought my daughter back to Wilmington so that she can complete her sophomore year. Then God spoke to me, "Go see Eugene's daughter." "I've learned to follow God's guidance. I'm a man of means, I invest in God's creation, and God's greatest creation is humankind, don't you agree? This is my offer, Mrs. Hicks has my address, contact me if you agree that it is God's promise of unconditional love."

"Dr. Somerset, is Miss LilyRose Somerset your daughter? The reason I ask is we took about six members to the Christmas Concert. It was magnificent"! "Yes Sir! Lily's my daughter, only loaned to me by God,

I'm so blessed." Climbing the basement stairs, Rev. McCloud promised to follow through: "I must take this to the Church Board of Trustee's for approval. It will be probably be about two months before we will have a definitive answer."

"That fine with me. It will take about a month to six weeks to get Eugene back on his feet. We have a medical plan he will need to follow. During this time, he will be staying in my home, gaining his strength back by assisting Frank, my handyman in making repairs on the barn, shed, and tearing down Eugene's cabin to be used for pasture until which time he chooses to either sell or lease. I'm a man who loves to see families be close to each other. Mrs. Hicks and her children need Eugene and he needs them. Do you have a family Pastor?

"No, I lost my wife two years ago during childbirth. She and baby died the same day." It's hard to lose a loved one, I still miss her."

"I understand, My wife died almost twenty years ago, and I miss her as if it were yesterday.. If it hadn't been for Lily, I might have died of grief. She's my sunshine and my rainbow. Good Evening Sir, God Bless."

Today, I begin again,
grateful for the light of God
within, that inspires my thoughts and actions
and directs me towards new paths
and new beginnings.
-Eugene Hicks, a grateful Dad and Grandad-

New Years Eve, December 31, 1890

Wilmington, Ohio

Martin and LilyRose arrived at the Bed and Breakfast at about four in the afternoon for the Christmas Eve Dinner and Dance. They were led to their individual rooms, his on the first floor, hers on the second floor looking out to the open fields still heavy with snow. They both bathed and changed into their evening attire. They met at the foot of the winding staircase, promptly at six p.m.

"LilyRose, you look beautiful in that gorgeous gown. Is the color a lilac or purple?" "Purple, lilac is a very pale shade, more often worn in the spring and summer months. This was my mother's gown, she was barely 5 feet tall. We are same size, with the exception of height. And I might add, Master Huffman, you look quite stunning this evening, as well."

The maitre' de escorted the couple to a table overlooking a decorated Spruce tree on the back patio. Every room was beautifully decorated for the holidays. There were three items to order from the New Year's Eve menu. Prime Rib with mint/horseradish sauce,, Seared Salmon with petite onions/garlic, and Roast Pork and Dressing. Both agreed on the:

Prime Rib with mint garnish

Scalloped potatoes

String beans, baked crescent rolls.

Baked Apple Pie w/raisin sauce for dessert.

When the waiter offered red wine with the meal, the couple both declined. As they were finishing their dessert, Martin and LilyRose could hear the band begin to play their New Year's Eve Musical Program. The first song they played was a Viennese waltz. The couple rose to find a table in the Ballroom. As they entered, Martin was very aware of the approving eyes of most men in the room. He smiled thinking, "Too bad, Old Chaps, she's mine." as he helped LilyRose to her seat, he remarked, "My Lady, the men in this gathering are both admiring you and envying me." "Martin, you are so kind, it's my mother's gorgeous gown that is the grand attraction. Mother wore this in New York on their honeymoon. The dressmaker did an excellent job in extending the length don't you think?." He nodded smiling.

The evening was remarkable. The couple enjoyed watching other couples do the most recent dances. One couple said they were visiting his maiden aunt for the holiday. Her Christmas gift to them was this Bed and Breakfast New Year's Eve Dinner and Dance. They were from New Jersey and knew all the latest dances and styles. She admired LilyRose's gown; wanting to know the designer's name. LilyRose shared the gown was her mother's, purchased in New York over twenty years ago. Her admirer couldn't quite believe it! The couple's exchanged partners for the next dance. Martin remarked later, "I was terrified I'd step on her feet! I felt like a country pumpkin who awakened in the arms of a Princess with no place to run." Lily shared, "He was such a learned dancer! He made me feel like I was floating instead of dancing. Thank you Martin, this evening has been just wonderful!"

"I agree." Especially when I feel the envy of the other men." "Oh, you silly goose, I believe you are playing with my emotions." The waiter's were handing out New Year's Eve paper streamers, noise makers: horns, and bells. On cue, the countdown began, letting go of the old year to cheer in the New Year.. The couple had a balloon and a couple of noise makers when the counting.started. "Ten, Nine, Eight, Seven, Six, Five, Four, Three, two, and One. A loud gun blast! The Band started playing, Martin grabbed LilyRose, kissed her passionately, then looked her into the eyes and kissed her again. She thought, "So, this is what a passionate kiss feels like? Well, it's kinda nice."

They danced a Viennese Waltz, pleading her feet were hurting. Martin got down on his knees, removed her ballerina type satin slipper, then massaged her feet. Embarrassed, she said jokingly, "Prince Charming, the shoe fits, but the feet are tired." He stood up, it was then she realized Martin was the same height as she. As she looked around the room, he was the shortest gentleman in the room. She thought, "Does it matter? Does it really matter?? Maybe not, but it feels strange." He escorted her to the top of the stairs, then kissed her goodnight. She flowed down the hall to her room, while he kinda skipped down the stairs to his room.

Breakfast was served at ten a.m. Most guests were in attendance. Some slept in. Martin and Lily were packed to leave right after breakfast. Disappointed, the New Jersey couple were not in attendance. Lily and Martin boarded their buggy that arrived at front door on time.. They offered goodbye's to the staff, then started down the road to the Huffman Estate where they were expected for dinner at five.

On the trip to his parent's home, Martin noticed LilyRose wearing a green velvet traveling suite, he commented, "LilyRose, that's an elegant travel ensemble you are wearing including fur hat and fur muff."

"Again, Martin, this is one of my mother's. The dressmaker had a difficult time matching the velvet, but found it in the little town of Coldwater. She purchased the end of their last bolt. Two yards! Just enough to extend the length of skirt. I'm happy you like it, The cape and bodice fit perfect. "Do you know if your mother had a dressmaker? Or did she make it herself? "Father wasn't sure, but all the Murphy women were talented dressmakers." "It's amazing that after twenty years, and they are still in perfect condition."

"When Father built our home, he had all closets lined in Cedar paneling." "He is certainly a smart gentleman." Martin said. "Not just smart, but wise and frugal. We Somerset's know how to stretch a penny. That's how I've been able to live in Wilmington, my scholarship did not include living expenses, just tuition and books. I've been fortunate to have three jobs and to have the apartment above the mercantile."

"You mean your father isn't paying for your education and living expenses? "No, because I proved to him I can live independently and I love it!" "I'm stunned, and a little disappointed in the man I greatly admire!" "And I'm stunned you think he wouldn't pay for my education. Martin, my Father would deny me nothing. But I told him Wilmington is my decision, and I'd like to pay my own way. My father is tremendously proud of me, but being proud means he respects my own decisions. He does not buy the old senseless law, that a women is personal property to a man, and I truly hope you understand this, because if you don't, we can not go any further in this relationship." "Of course, LilyRose, I'm a modern man, but wasn't aware your father was. The time has flown, we're almost at my folks. I don't know about you, but I'm beginning to feel the pains of hunger."

"Sounds good to me, do you know if they have invited other guests?" "God, I hope not. I'm kinda tired and would enjoy a little relaxation." "But, we must always honor your parents, they are respected and looked at as a pillar of this community." Helping LilyRose down, he replied, "Of course, that is true, if they've invited guests, I hope it's someone from the City Council," as he handed the reigns to the family groom for grooming. LilyRose waited for him to escort her into the front entry hall. The aroma's were deliciously smelling with happy chatter among them. Martin called, "Mom and Dad, we're here. The roads were clear all the way."

Both Allen and Eva Huffman proudly greeted their son and LilyRose. "Dinner is ready and so are we. Oh LilyRose your cape is beautiful! Martin please hang your cloak and LilyRose's cape in the hall closet.

LilyRose, please follow me, I have something I'd love to show you."

As they entered the dining room glowing brightly, stood a beautiful gold menorah. This candlestick is called a menorah. It means lamp, a symbol of light. Jews used oil in their lamps to represent the Light of God. Someday when we have more time, I'll tell the whole story of Hanukkah, sacred holy days in the Jewish calendar. I wanted to share this beautiful menorah that has been handed down in my family since the fifteen century. It is made of gold and used at this time of year. Tomorrow Allen will return it to our lock box at the Wilmington Bank." "Mrs Huffman, I mean Eva, I love family heirlooms and traditions. I'm eager to learn yours and to share mine. Thank you for showing me this beautiful sacred piece of art."

Dinner conversation was all about the New Years Eve Ball, LilyRose's mother's garments and how Mother Nature had blessed them with roads clear for traveling.

Mrs Huffman and LilyRose cleared the tables, rinsed and stacked the dishes to be washed in the morning. Mrs Huffman was adamant that they were to gather together for conversation after dinner, not do dishes.

"Well, my family tradition is the women have a gossip gab fest while doing dishes. Gossip is not injurious, but whose getting married, having a baby, going to college, and that sort of thing. But, if you insist on enjoying our conversation, I'm afraid you might be disappointed as Martin and I are very tired. New Years Eve was very full of laughter and joy."

"Of course my dear, we'll have a New Years toast of cranberry punch, and send you on your way home, unless of course, you'd like to spend the night." "I'm sorry, I am needing my little bed. After unloading my bag from the weekend, I need to write a paper for my final in Music Composition."

After everyone was given a long hug, Martin and LilyRose headed to the mercantile and her little abode upstairs. When arriving, Martin gathered her over-night bag and followed her up the stairs. She opened the door, the handyman had lit the fire to warm the rooms. Martin carried the bag in, then sat down at the

table. He reached into his coat pocket, motioning for LilyRose to please sit for a minute, he said,

"Miss LilyRose, I love you with all my heart. You are not only beautiful, you are intelligent and talented. I want to marry you, be the father of your children, and to grow old with you wherever you'd like to live. Please marry me." After a few moments to think, LilyRose said grinning.

"I might regret this in the morning, but Martin, I think I'd like to marry you." After putting the ring on her finger, he kissed her long and tender, Then said goodnight, "I must tell Mom and Dad, they'll be thrilled!" then he left. "What in the world did I just do? I said Yes to Martin's proposal!"

Love has no other desire but to fulfill itself,
But if you love and must needs have desires, let these be your desire:
To melt and be like a running brook that sings its melody to the
night.
To know the pain of too much tenderness,
To be wounded by your own understanding of love;
To bleed willingly and joyfully,
To wake at dawn with a winged heart and give thanks for another
day of loving
To rest at the noon hour and meditate love's ecstasy;
To return home at eventide with gratitude;
And then to sleep with a prayer for the beloved in your heart
and a song of praise upon your lips.
Kahlil Gibran, "The Prophet"
"Love" pages 13, 14

Dr. Chad Somerset Home, Harmony Village

Dayton, Ohio

The mail was early this morning. Dr. Chad was just leaving for the clinic when he saw the delivery man turn the corner. He waited, then he tipped his hat at the mailman and saw he had a letter from Lily-Rose. He was expecting a letter from Rev. McCloud in Sabina, Ohio, but he was thrilled to hear from LilyRose so soon after the Christmas holidays. He ripped it open to read,

Dear Father,

I'm sure you didn't expect to hear from me so soon. No, I didn't flunk my exams, No, I didn't lose any of my jobs, and Yes, I am engaged to be married. I still don't believe it. After the New Years Eve Ball and having dinner with his parents, he drove me home and just popped the question, I said yes, so now there is to be a wedding.

I need to know your schedule this June. I'm taking the summer semester off, and feel it might work to be a June Bride. I plan to be married in Mother's Wedding Dress. My dressmaker is thrilled to have the challenge to keep Mother's style and incorporate my conservative image. We're thinking white velvet covered buttons and velvet box pleats for the length.

I've told Martin he still has to get your permission, so expect a visit any day. If you say "no" I'll understand your decision to be the wiser than mine. I love you, so take care of yourself, I still need you to walk me down the aisle.

Your one and only daughter,

LilyRose Somerset

descendent of all the

Chadwick Nicholas Somerset's

past and present.

Dr Chad just stood and read the letter one more time. Folded it, then returned it to envelope, wiped his eyes and said out loud, "LilyRose, Martin better be what you believe him to be, 'cause I still have my doubts, but then that's how all Father's feel, no man is good enough for their daughter. But, my LilyRose is so special, Maud what do you think?" then a voice from deep within: ***I will instruct thee and teach thee in the way which thou shalt go; I will guide thee with mine eye. Psalm 32:8-***

The next day a letter from Rev. McCloud arrived. It was very short and to the point.

Dr. Somerset,

Our Board of Trustees are in favor of your offer. God Bless,

Rev. McCloud

Sabina Christian Tabernacle

"I must have a long and serious talk with Eugene, and do it today." Dr. Chad arrived at the clinic with a few patients waiting in the unlocked waiting room. They had followed instructions, signed in, and were waiting patiently. "I'm sorry for being a little late, I received a letter from my daughter and took a few moments to read it." "Good news, Doc?" "Yes, she's still in school, has three jobs, and a place to live." "I think that's pretty good news," answered a young woman who had signed first on the sign-in-list. Dr. Chad opened the treatment room for her. "First of all, may I ask what's your name?" "Alice Bledsoe" "How old are you, Alice?" "I'm almost nineteen. Next month is my birthday." "So, what's going on with you?"

"I think I'm pregnant, and my boyfriend is in the Navy on the Great Lakes." "Does he know about your situation?" "No, and I don't want him to know, I'm afraid it will break up our relationship." "So, you plan to have the baby in secret? Thinking no one will write and tell him his girlfriend is pregnant, maybe fooling around on him, is that it?"

"No Doctor, I want to get rid of it!" "Excuse me, you-want-to-get-rid-of-yours-and-his-baby without telling him?" Alice began weeping, then sobbing, "I can't have a baby without a father to take care of me and baby."

"Young lady, you are asking me to murder your baby, to keep your pregnancy from him, and think you don't have any responsibility to baby, boyfriend or me? You need to write him, tell him the truth, give him a chance to make things right, either marry you or support baby, but for God's sake, don't keep it from him."

"Junior is a really good man, I believe he truly loves me, but, Junior's last name is Michell? She starts really crying "I know Junior Michell, he's a good and honest chap, he'll do the right thing."

Alice wrote Junior a long letter explaining her circumstances. She said she'd not let her daddy know who the father was, so that he wouldn't be made to marry her. She shared that at first she was so scared that she wanted to get an abortion. She found out it was illegal, and that he had a right to know he was having a son or daughter. "Please write back with what you think. I love you always Junior,

Your Alice PS, I finished all my studies for graduation. Dr. Chad said he'd make sure they give me my diploma."

When Junior Michell received Alice's letter, he asked his commanding office for an emergency leave to go home. His girlfriend was pregnant with a wedding planned as soon as he could make it. He was granted leave, but first he had to stand at attention while his commanding officer gave him a lecture on what is

expected of a junior officer. Junior humbly said, "Yes, Sir!" and then he was dismissed to catch the next train heading to Dayton, Ohio. He arrived home in eight hours due to late and discontinued passenger trains. He had to take the last 20 miles on a freight car filled with coal. He arrived at Frank Mitchell's home filthy with coal dust and starving for anything he could find to eat.

"What happened to you, Son? Did they throw you out of the Navy?" "No, Pop, I took leave, I'm getting married to Alice, we're going to have a baby." "Oh, I guess that's kind of an emergency. Go get cleaned up. Is she expecting you? "No, I plan to surprise her and her dad with my proposal. I bought a ring, not precious gold, but I'll buy her another one on our first anniversary."

Mildred Grace Mitchell came into the room asking, "Is that Junior, did I hear we're going to be grandparents? Oh Frank, I'm so thrilled! Alice must come live with us until Junior can be stationed where there is housing."

""I want to go see Dr Chad. I'm sure he knows of the girl's pregnancy, but I'm sure he doesn't know Junior's intentions." Frank arrived at the Medical Clinic just as Dr Chad was closing. He smiled greeting his friend, "Frank, good to see you old friend," "Dr. Chad, Junior just came home." Dr. Chad said, "I knew it, I just knew it, I told her Junior had a right to know, when's the wedding?" "I don't know, but I'll be darn, I can't tell you news, you don't already know!"

Eugene struggled with Dr. Chad's news about his daughter in Sabina. He was certainly feeling a lot better, had gained 30 pounds and was getting stronger. Working with Frank had help put some muscles where flab used to lay. Dr. Chad had offered to lease his land for pasture. Frank and Eugene had torn down all of the cabin, carefully removing all nails and stacking the lumber in the shed. Dr. Chad thought someday in the future, Eugene might want to rebuild. But for now, his daughter needed him to help with the children, and the little church could certainly use a handyman. Frank and Eugene got to talking at break time when Junior's furlough was mentioned. Frank shared there was to be a wedding in the chapel this coming Friday evening. Her daddy's preacher friend would do the honors, and until Junior was stationed where military housing was provided, Alice would live with he and Mildred. Mildred was already knitting baby clothes and planning a baby shower. "I declare, women are the funniest creatures, there's nothing like a wedding, a birthing or a burying to get them motivated." "I'm not planning on a burying for a long time. Do you want to come see Junior tie the knot?" "Yes, I believe I do, then Mildred and Alice can plan a "going away" party for me, I'm going south to Sabina, Ohio to live with my daughter." "Well, I be dang, if life ain't funny."

And then, if that was not funny enough, a month later Dr. Chad announced that LilyRose was marrying her boss and landlord's son in June. No one wanted to believe Miss LilyRose Somerset was getting married. It just didn't seem possible, why it was just yesterday you could look up and find her setting on a limb at the top of an Oak tree, or playing make-believe that she was a doctor , not a nurse, delivering her cat's babies. The poor cat just pretended right along with her. It made everyone in Harmony Village feel old to think Miss Lily was getting married.

Dr. Chad delivered a healthy baby girl to Alice and Junior Mitchell. They named her Susannah Diane Mitchell. She was so tiny, but with the biggest feet! Her daddy commented, "Honey, you're gonna have to feed Suzi a whole lot of your good milk for her to grow into those big feet." "Hush your mouth, she's got feet just like her daddy's, aren't they cute? With brown curly hair like her Mama's, and a big smile like her Grandpa."

After everyone staked a claim to Suzi, her daddy kissed her and Mama goodbye 'cause the Navy was calling him back to sea. Tear's flowed as they let go.

And this is my prayer,
that your love may overflow
more and more with
knowledge and full insight.
-Philippians 1:9

MARTIN AND LILYROSE WEDDING DAY - JUNE 19, 1891

WILMINGTON, OHIO

The wedding of Martin and LilyRose was to be held at the same Bed and Breakfast that her father made reservations to stay. When Dr. Chad arrived and was checking in, the man at the desk asked him was he related to the bride. It was then he realized he'd be staying at the same establishment his daughter would be enjoying her honeymoon night. "Yes, I am her father." blushing like it was to be his wedding.

"They have the second floor suite reserved for their wedding night, then they will leave the following day for their honeymoon cruise on the Ohio and Mississippi River to St. Louis on the Mississippi Delta Queen. Isn't that just so romantic?" "Yes, very." as he offered for the bellboy to take him to his room, and for the bill to be sent as well. He was committed as father of the bride, to pay for wedding, reception, and guest's lodging. It just hadn't dawned on him, his daughter would be staying there on the first night of their wedding. "How Naive of me?"

Dr. Chad came a day early. He planned a day for quiet contemplation and serene sleep, of which he found impossible every since he learned of LilyRose intention to marry Martin Huffman. He did everything he could think to stop this negative rhetoric going on in his head. He called Mother Superior, she told him to go to confession, he did, and then he went to Mass. For about three hours he felt better, then it started again. Maybe getting away a day earlier would do the trick? Now here he was just one floor below his daughter's honeymoon suite. "Oh, God please help me. Whose going to give LilyRose her pre-marriage help and instructions? Maybe Eva Huffman was giving her some motherly advice. He crawled in bed, prayed for guidance, and fell asleep.

The next morning, he drove to Wilmington to pick up LilyRose for the great event. She was still packing when he knocked on her door. She opened it crying, "Oh Father, I'm having my monthly, I don't know what to do?" He held her in her arms, to command his mind to stop flying and his heart stop racing, Finally he said, "LilyRose, this happens to a lot of brides. The groom will understand, he will be patient. How long have you been on your period?" "I started last night, I usually go only four days, but it is heavy, then I just stop. I want to be sure I do not stain Mother's wedding dress. I'm packing every pad I have, and that's a whole lot."

"You'll do fine, and Martin loves you and will understand." "Father, after we leave the Honeymoon Suite, we will ride to the Huffman's to leave the wedding gown, and then we will go on to Cincinnati to board a riverboat down the Ohio River. I've got to have enough supplies. Women are cursed. I just don't understand why?"

"Let us get going. On the way I will explain why women are the stronger sex." Father and Daughter rode for about fire miles before either said a word. Finally, "LilyRose, In my fifty five years, I've observed both sexes during life's adversity and also, in moments of tremendous joy. Some day, women will birth children in a more sterile and humane manner than I've observed during my practice. During pregnancy, women's bodies need nutrition and more nurturing. Nutrition because foods that are grown where one resides have what it takes for the body to receive the vitamins and minerals necessary to fight infection and disease, Nurturing is imperative because a women's body is changing dramatically to prepare for birthing. She may have ups and downs emotionally, but that's why having a baby is not just one sided, it is a team effort. The husband needs to stay tuned in to her mood swings and always let her know how much she is loved:." "But Father, I'm not having a baby, I'm trying to have a honeymoon!" "Oh my darling daughter, I apologize for going to Texas to get to New York! Now, I've said women are the stronger sex; however, that doesn't mean physically it means, emotionally and mentally when faced with challenges to their survival and those they love, A woman is capable of seeing the bigger picture, generally a man sees only what's in front of him. An example: The mortgage is due, he has not earned enough to pay it. He starts to lose his sense of balance, becomes argumentative as he cannot see an end to the problem. Generally, women know how to humble themselves to ask for help, or for more time, and are patient in the best way to present a possible path to accomplishing the goal without letting it look like charity. Charity threaten's a man's perception of his manhood because that's what he's been taught. She has the ability to nurture his manhood by presenting facts he never thought of. Your mother, who never worked a day in her life for anyone else, knew exactly how to present a possible solution to me, that I never dreamed possible. While going with me to see my patients at the Veteran's Home, she mentioned Annette's Steam Hut as a possible way to help these men to relax, and then at that moment, my training in medicine triggered a procedure for cleansing the body of infection, bacteria etc, was by sweating the toxins out of the body. I've always thought the feminine aspect of a relationship to be the cheerleader, whose vision could see the end results. We all have moments when we feel we'd just like to quit. But when love is the common denominator, the team member in pain, will be supported and cheered to help her or him to see the light at the end of tunnel. I know you might be thinking that all of the women in our family died young. Your great-grandmother, Victoria died as a result of filth in the water., your grandmother, Mary Margaret died of a stroke, and your own mother, died of leukemia, all very young by today's standards. Preventive Health Care, proper nutrition, pure drinking water, cardiac

exercise, and living your purpose is changing the life expectancy of men and women today. However, women are living longer by a slight margin, but it will increase because the average man is stubborn, does not want to change his behavior or diet. So, my darling daughter, If this sounds like a sermon being preached to change you, absolutely not. I already see you living your purpose, eating properly and enjoying the out-of-doors, and breathing fresh clean air."

"You are now beginning a new life challenge called marriage. Follow your intuition, take one step at a time, and communicate your hopes, dreams, and misunderstandings." "Oooops, we're here and you haven't said a word. I'm so sorry."

"Don't be Father, I heard and felt every word you shared. Yes, this monthly can not be overcome, but my fear and need to be in control, has awakened me to do what I can do, and just let the rest go. Thank you Father, I love you so much."

The wedding was beautiful, not religious but spiritual. LilyRose wanted to honor both traditions, Jewish and Christian. She wore her mother's gown and Eva's beautiful shawl she wore on her wedding day. However, LilyRose wore it as mantilla, from a picture she saw in a magazine. Her father walked her down the aisle, Martin's father was his best man, Amanda was her maid of honor, and Eva was given the honor of inviting guests to sign the Wedding Book. LilyRose gave both father's a book of Rumi's poetry. Rūmī was a beloved Sufi Mystic whose poetry was spontaneously recited. She asked that both fathers choose a poem that spoke to their heart to read as a blessing of wisdom of unconditional love to their beloved child.

The officiate was the newly appointed judge from Wilmington. Before the judge pronounced the couple, husband and wife, Allen read, from an English interpretation of Rumi's poem, *Love is Reckless,*

Without cause God gave us Being: without cause gave it back again.
Gambling yourself away is beyond any religion.
Religion seeks grace and favor, but those who gamble these away,
are God's favorite, for they neither put God to the test
nor knock at the door of gain and loss.

Again, from the same poem, Dr. Chad cleared his throat, took a deep breath, and spoke clearly,

Is it possible for the bodily eye to see You? Can thoughts comprehend Your
laughter or grief? Tell me now, can it possibly see You at all?
Such a heart has only borrowed things to live with. The garden of Love
is given without limit and yields many fruits other sorrow or joy.
Love is beyond either conditions: without spring, without autumn, it is always
fresh

Judge Malcom Hendricks finished the ceremony: "Martin Stein Huff-man and Lillian Rose Somerset, by the power vested in me, by Our Heav-enly Father, the Great State of Ohio, and the City of Wilmington, Ohio, I now pronounce you Husband and Wife. You may kiss your bride.'"

The kiss was short, but sweet. The guests all cheered. LilyRose threw her bouquet. A surprised waitress caught it. She was embarrassed, as she looked to her boss. LilyRose rushed to her side, then removed her garter, threw it to the manager, whose shock did not permit him to say a word to his waitress.

The wedding party was escorted into the dining room for a beautiful dinner. The couple had chosen to have a buffet with various entree's and desserts. The wedding cake was made by Eva Huffman. It had three tiers with yellow and pink roses around each layer's edge. The cake's base was a carrot cake, middle layer strawberry, and the top layer was pineapple. Everyone oooed and ahhed as they were served a piece on glass crystal dessert dishes. The couple chose a sparkling cider for the toast. Eva and Mandy were asked to offer the toasts. Eva's was eloquent and spiritual: "May God in His Infinite Wisdom Bless you both as you begin your married life. Everyone takes a sip of the cider punch. Amanda's toast was full of love, joy and innocence.: "Mr and Mrs Martin Huffman, my teacher Miss LilyRose, you both look happy and beautiful. , Let us drink a toast for prosperity and babies." Everyone drank and cheered the happy couple, thinking, *Out of the mouths of babes."*

The couple graciously thanked everyone for attending and for their gifts that will be unwrapped after they return from their Honeymoon Trip on the Mississippi Delta Queen to St. Louis. Due to the dangers of driving at night, Dr. Chad had graciously reserved rooms for all guests which included a breakfast buffet in the morning. Dr. Chad's mind wondered? "Lily had no music? I can't imagine why?" He gave his daughter a goodnight kiss, shook Martin's hand and then went to settle up his bill with the owners of the establishment. Mrs. Huffman generously gave the remaining cake to the servers then she and Allen kissed the couple a loving goodnight kiss and hug. LilyRose reminded them they would see them at breakfast and then leave immediately for their home to store gifts and wedding attire before leaving for Cincinnati. The Mississippi Delta leaves promptly a seven p.m.

The couple, holding hands, climbed the stairs to the Honeymoon Suite. LilyRose thinking to herself, "Oh please, I hope I haven't soiled Mother's gown." Martin thinking, "Finally, it's legal, now I see what she's got for me." As Martin opened the door, Lily said, "I'm sorry, I'm in need of bathroom. Please excuse me" "Sure, first after you, comes me." He began to undress. He took off his black jacket, tie, and was about to remove his shirt when she opened the door. "Oh, I'm sorry," then turns around so that she is not watching him undress. "Hey, we're married, you have permission and a right to see what is about to happen."

"Martin, I can't. I started my monthly yesterday." Embarrassed with head bowed looking at her bare feet. She had removed her stockings and shoes when using the toilet. "Oh for Christ's sake!" "Martin please don't curse!" "Don't curse? LilyRose I've been patient, waiting for a year to make love to you, then on our wedding night you announce you can't do anything because you're on your "monthly." Well there are other parts I can fondle." as he continued to undress, throwing his clothing on the floor as if his personal servant would be picking up after him. Stark naked he opened the door to the bathroom, entered, then slams the door. LilyRose quickly puton her cotton gown. He came out, standing at the foot of the bed and said, "Okay, let me see your breasts?"

"Martin, please trim the light, I'm nervous." "I want to see what you have. Is that too much to ask?" She begins to weep. "Oh pleeeeeeze, if your father and my parents weren't down stairs, I'd rip that granny gown right off of you." He climbed in bed, then unbutton's the gown only to see she has a chamise and pantaloons on. He pulled the chamise down, took a strong hold on her right breast, the nipple stood up, "Good to know you aren't dead! Surprisingly, you do have some sexual urge. He sucks on it, then the other breast, all the while massaging and licking her neck, ears, and breasts. He forces her to hold his penis. She moans and cries, convincing him he is turning her on. "Okay Sweetheart, we can wait a few days for me to take you to those exotic places. He kisses her, said goodnight, then turns over to fall asleep.

LilyRose prays pleading silently, "Dear God, help me to be a good wife. I'm not sure I love Martin the way a wife should. I need help, please guide me, I feel so foolish and juvenile. Thank you, I am your devoted servant, Amen."

The next morning, she and Martin arrive at the Huffman Estate about 20 minutes before dinner time.. The groom unhitched the horse, then carried the luggage into the front hall. LilyRose was beet red, Martin tried hard to smile. LilyRose immediately looked for Eva who was upstairs changing from her traveling suit into something more comfortable. She knocked on the door. Eva opened the door, LilyRose immediately confided that she was on her monthly and needed some more rags to take on their trip. Eva took her into her arms and shared, "My beloved LilyRose, I'm so sorry, I hope Martin was understanding." "Yes, but I'm not sure I'm prepared. I was terrified I would soil my mother's wedding gown, then when I told Martin I felt so guilty because this happened. It just now occurred to me, that I don't want to take any valuables on the boat. Could I please leave my mother's pearls, and your ring to be placed in your bank's vault?" The dress will need to go to the dressmaker for her to clean and box for storage. I have a wedding ring I found in a field behind my father's home. I'm not sure it is valuable, but I kinda like it.

"Of course, my dear. I plan to take the Menorah for safe keeping, as well. Let me find you some necessary supplies and when you are able to take part in the sexual act, use this salve I'm going to give you. It will help lubricate you the first time, afterwards, you will begin to enjoy making love. I still enjoy Allen, but when my body started the change, it hurt, until a friend in New York sent me this salve. I ordered a case of six, fearing it would go off the market. I will give you two jars. Don't be afraid to use a lot. I love you. You are the daughter I always longed for."

LilyRose changed into her mother's emerald green traveling suit. She just couldn't justify in her mind, purchasing another just because Martin had seen her in it before. Her hair needed to be combed and put into a bun at the base of her neck, for ease in traveling. She took off the platinum wedding ring, put on the little gold wedding band, then removed her precious strand of pearls and earrings from her overnight bag. She didn't understand why this little act, brought such peace to her heart. Eva came in with rags folded in a towel. She had a bolt of white cotton that she quickly cut and folded for LilyRose. Lily handed her the jewelry. Eva hid it under the mattress at the foot of their bed. Placing her finger to her lips, a signal that this was their secret. The two women left the room to give Allen a big hug, and thank him for their generous gift of a honeymoon cruise package. As always, Allen Huffman was a humble and caring soul. He loved giving and he loved both his son and LilyRose. They once again climbed into their buggy with a fresh horse, some snacks, and their trunk for a seven day cruise on the Ohio Mississippi Rivers.

"Be careful and safe, and enjoy your cruise, as Eva waved goodbye. You don't need to write, but do be careful, Love you two," Allen, with tears in his eyes, thought, "I surely hope we've done the right thing."

The couple arrived at the Cincinnati dock a half an hour before the boat was to leave. Martin had the horse and buggy boarded by a friend of their groom. As they sat on the bench waiting their boarding, Martin asked, "Are you still on your monthly?" LilyRose nodded and said, "Your mother gave me more supplies which is a relief." "How many more days?" with an irritated and gruff voice?" "Maybe one more, I hope." "I will be playing cards this evening if there's an extra for the game." LilyRose looking very sad and not understanding, "I thought maybe you and I could stroll under the stars. The sky is going to be clear and a full moon, it should be lovely." "Not my cup of tea." He answered as he stood up to follow the steward to board the ship. He never offered to help LilyRose with her carpet travel bag. The crew loaded their trunk.

"Do you know where the Honeymoon accommodations are located?" "No, but I'm sure we will be led to them upon boarding. You sound like a nervous imp, are you afraid of the water?" "No, I was just wondering."

"At eight o'clock they were given the boat's schedule, along with dishes of fresh fruit, cheese, veggies, fresh petite rolls, coffee, tea, and bottle of Champaign for the Honeymoon couple. LilyRose started to tell the waiter they did not drink, when Martin snatched the bottle and put it on a galley shelf. Surprised, she said nothing. She continued to read: Breakfast at 9, binoculars issued at 10 for those choosing to gaze at the sights along the shore, lovely homes, animals grazing, and birds in the air. Lunch at 12 noon, with cards, chess, and puzzles in the lounge at 2 p.m. Dinner at 7 with dancing until midnight. LilyRose said, "Martin maybe I will finally get a chance to be beat you at Chess. You're so good and very competitive." "I don't think so, I've got other plans." "But, Martin it's our Honeymoon!" "So what, you've already messed that up." He grabbed the bottle of champaign, his leather pouch, and left the room. She did not see him again until around three in the morning. Staggering and grumbling as he crawled into bed. The next morning the first thing he said to LilyRose, "Where's your money? I need it." Looking around for her traveling bag he said, "Come on, where's your money?" "I didn't bring much money, Allen told me everything was taken care of." "How much did you bring?" Looking into her boot, she brought out some bills that amounted to about $25.00. "This is all I have, what do you need it for?" "None of your concern." Then said, I'll see you at breakfast."

LilyRose spent the day lounging on the deck, watching the parade before her. Ladies wearing the latest fashion, hat and all, Men smiling proud peacocks as they spoke to one another. Martin was not at breakfast, she saw him briefly at lunch with some men she judged as "dandy's." He ignored her, so she acted as though she never saw him. He showed up around midnight, with just one question. "Are you still bleeding? She answered half awake, "Not exactly." "So I take that to mean, everything is a go?" He undressed smelling of alcohol and cigar smoke, then climbed in bed" "You're still wearing that granny gown? Where's the silk one you promised? " "Martin, I've not seen you all day, then at midnight you arrive and expect me to be all excited you decided to recognize me." "You're right, my darling bride. Now's the time for you to learn who has all the Aces, and it's not you. Get undressed and put on the silk one."

She went to the bathroom and put gobs of the salve Eva had given to her. Wearing the purple silk negligee, she very quietly entered the room. "Come here, let me have a look." "Shhhhh, these walls are not thick,"

"I don't care, but if you do, then you won't be yelling." He smelled so badly, LilyRose wanted to vomit, he fondled her breasts, then stuck his middle finger into her women's part, and said, "So, you're all greased up, smart girl, so here goes, as he jammed his penis into her vagina. She whimpered as she felt him go in, then held on to the side of the bed as he mumbled and yelled,   "Yes, Yes! Not that bad was it? Let me rest, then we'll do it all over again."

As he rested, he began to snore. She very quietly got out of bed, wrapped her heavy robe around her, opened the door to the deck, and walked out, to pray. "God, I really did it this time. I'm trapped, and he knows it. Please help me to find a way to get away from this monster. He's evil, what did I do to earn this?"

Have confidence in your Father today,
and be certain that He has heard you, and answered you.
You may not recognize His answer yet,
but you can indeed be sure that it is given you and will yet receive
it.
Try as you attempt to go through the clouds to the light,
to hold this confidence in your mind.
Try to remember that you are at last putting your will to God's.
Try to keep the thought clearly in mind that what you undertake
with God must succeed.
Then let the power of God work in you and through you
that His will and yours be done.
A Course in Miracles, Workbook for Students
Part I, Lesson 69, Paragraph 8

William Lincoln Bailey's Farm

Wilmington, Ohio

William was working on his strawberry patch when he heard a buggy pull in. He picked up his weed basket, when he heard screams and laughter coming from the front of the storage shed. As he turned the corner he saw Mandy and her father petting his dog as they talked about picking strawberries. "Hello there," called William, "Mr. Will we'd like to pick some of your strawberries. May we?" "I mean to pay, I've heard your berries are the best." "I'm happy for you to pick some. There's so many, I can't keep up with them. There five cents a small quart baskets, if you pick, If I pick, there fifteen cents a quart."

"We'll pick, Mandy wants strawberry shortcake, so I told her I'd pay, if she picked about four quarts." William asked, "Did you bring your baskets?" I've got a few if you need them."

"I've got a bucket, we'll measure out four quarts when she's finished." "Come, have a seat, while we watch her work." He gave Don a cup of cool water from his well. "I guess you've heard the news? Miss LilyRose and Martin were married a couple of weeks ago?" "Yes, I was invited but was not able to attend. Did your family attend?" "Yes, Mandy was a bridesmaid and was asked to offer a toast of apple cider for the couple. She was so excited, that's all she talked about. We haven't made this public yet, but Penny and I are getting married just before school starts. I'm been called by the church to be a pastor. I'm excited and humbled at the same time."

"Oh, Don, I'm so happy for you. You will be a great pastor." "Thank you Will, your affirmation means a lot to me, I truly respect you and what you are doing with your farm. I pray someday, you meet a wonderful lady to spend your life with. You deserve the best."

"Daddy, Shep showed me where to pick the biggest berries. He's so smart. Is this four quarts?" showing her bucket that is half full. Mr. Will took out a quart basket, started measuring, then said, "You're as good a berry picker as you are a piano player. You have just a little over four quart, but the rest are on me." She hugged him and said, "I was in Miss LilyRose wedding. She also asked for me to give the toast with fresh apple cider. I'm sorry you weren't there? There was no music/ I thought there would be lots of music."

"No, I had chores to do and produce to sell." "Thanks Will, will we see you at church this Sunday?" asked Don. "Yes, I plan to be there. Until then, God Bless and keep you safe." As they left, Will picked up his bucket of weeds and placed it on his compost pile, added some water to the pile, then washed his hands at the well. He looked up at the sun and realizes he hadn't eaten any lunch and it is almost dinner time. "I think I'd better eat some of these fresh strawberries with cream, and maybe I'll scramble some eggs and tomatoes to make a sandwich with a hunk of the homemade yeast bread."

The choir did not sing during the summer months. He had decided to not attend both the Quaker Meeting and the Presbyterian service as he normally did. He'd decided on the quiet Quaker Meeting, not fooling himself, he knew he didn't want to be around the Presbyterian's complimenting Miss LilyRose and Martin on their wedding. He fought with his negative thoughts, "If only I believed he is good enough for her. She deserves to be happy and treated like the special soul she is."

After eating his supper, milking the cow, and feeding the stock, William decided to work on the memorial he was making. It would be cooler just before sunset, and he felt inspired to do some more weaving of the two inch strips of pine that was to be a wall for climbing honeysuckle and crepe myrtle. The bench would be engraved with *Martha & Obadiah Bailey on it's back,* then on the front of the seat it would have Gunnar Sterling, Brother & Friend, and on each end would have Mam aka Bess, and on the other end, Pap aka Jeb. On the back, he planned to engrave Angels blowing horns, and the seat, little children of all nationalities and races holding hands in a circle, dancing together. He promised himself to work on it a little each day. The strips of wood had been soaking about three days, and should be just right. William found it very easy to bend and weave them into a five foot piece about a foot wide. His pattern was unfolding nicely. When the pieces were all done and dried, he would put together the wall, which he decided he would name,

"Wall of Peace, God's Love and Beauty shines through"
The Peace I seek is within me.

Dr. Chadwick Somerset's Home, Harmony Village

Dayton, Ohio

Frank and Dr. Chad were gathering the last of the garden vegetables for canning. It was September and Dr. Chad hadn't heard from LilyRose, and Frank said Alice hadn't heard from Junior since he left after baby Suzi was born. He had told Alice he was tired of being called Junior and wanted to be sure the Navy knew his legal name, Lukas Franklin Mitchel. He said he'd like to go by Luke for short. Besides taking care of baby Suzi, Alice kept herself busy writing him letters and calling herself, Mrs. Lukas F. Mitchell. Dr. Chad was amused with her zest for life and her joy in being a mother.

"You know Doc, It's going kill us if she leaves to live with him some where near his port. I know, I know it's selfish, but dang it, we love her and Suzi." "I know how you feel. Lily hasn't written since she married, and I'm just worried to death about her. My mind goes crazy with what if, what if." As they were walking in to the kitchen with all the garden produce, they saw the mailman delivering mail. Frank handed Dr. Chad his basket and said, "I'll go see if Alice got any mail. Maybe you have some, too." Both men went high-tailing to their mail boxes as fast as their legs could take them. Dr. Chad was closer to his box, but Frank was running like a teenager, both made it to their boxes about the same time.

"I got a letter," shouted Dr. Chad. "So did Alice," waved Frank. Dr. Chad could hardly wait to to find his reading glasses and open his letter. He used a kitchen knife to slice the envelope open.

Dearest Father,

By the time you get this letter, I will know for sure, but I think I am pregnant. I haven't had my monthly since the day of my wedding. I'm sick every morning until about three p.m. Then something happens, I feel like I could eat everything in sight, especially dill pickles and pancakes. Doesn't that sound pitiful?

Eva is going crazy with the idea of being a grandmother. I hope you'll be pleased and will take a trip down here to check me out. The local mid-wife is kind and knowledgeable, but I'm afraid I'm a wee bit prejudice, I think my Father and Bess are the world's best. Too bad Bess is in Pennsylvania and not available.

It's 2'30 and the postman is due, and it's about time for my daily feed, please bring jars of pickles, make sure they're dill.

Love you,

Your Lily

Dr. Chad just grinned and grinned. "Well, I be, can you believe that? I'm going to be a grandpa. What do you think of that Maud? I sure miss you, especially in sharing the joy of being grandparents."

The door swung open with Frank standing and panting like a worn out race horse. "Hey man, take a seat before you have a heart attack. Look's like you have good news? "My grandson is now Ensign Lukas F. Mitchell. I was in the Army, what rank is an Ensign?" "An Ensign is an officer. It is equal to a second lieutenant in the Army." "Oh, my goodness, wait until I tell Alice and Mildred. Oh, I'm sorry Doc,

did you get any good news? "Naw, just that I'm gonna be grandpa"

"You old coot, I know you're excited. Are you headed down to Wilmington any time soon?" "As soon as I can get the fall chores done and saddle my horse. That is if I can find help from one grandpa to another? Any suggestions?" "We might have to put an add in the paper." Patting Dr. Chad on the back while heading home to spread the good news and thinking to himself, "My grandson is an officer in the United States Navy. Why it's not been that long since he was a sassy snotty nosed bully that needed a tough hand and loving heart."

Two days later Dr. Chad arrived at the mercantile in Wilmington, Ohio. Loaded with medical supplies, and medicinal herbs for pregnant women. Of course, he brought fresh produce, jars and jars of pickles, and a smoked ham. He opened the door to the mercantile and found LilyRose, not Martin tending the store.

"Where's Martin? He asked. "He's out of town, talking politics. Oh, Father I'm so happy to see you. It's eleven in the morning, and my belly won't hold any nourishment." "Have you tried soda crackers and soda water? It seems to help?" "The store is out, our new shipment is due this week. Yes, along with my pickles, that's all I've eaten. Let me see if Josh is finished stocking so he can relieve me to visit with you upstairs. Josh is a senior in high school, working for the summer. He's so much help." Dr. Chad shook Josh's hand, then said. "Young man, learning to be independent at an early age will serve you as go forward with your career. Thank you for helping my daughter." "It's my pleasure, Sir." Dr. Chad and his tired daughter climbed the stairs to have a long and nurturing chat.

"Father, there is coffee in the cabinet, but I have to warn you, sometimes the smell makes me sick to my stomach. It seams there is a conspiracy to make me give up." "Give up what?" "I mean, I don't know what I mean." "Why isn't Martin helping you? And what's this business about politics?"

As he started to boil water, he asked, "Does tea bother you?" "No, not to smell, just to drink."

"Honey, we've got to get some food in you, I believe you've lost 10-15 pounds since I last saw you." "I don't know, but nothing fits right anymore." She began to cry, then laid down on the bed, covered her head then sobs. Dr. Chad finishes making his tea, then went down to his buggy to bring in the produce, herbs, and ham. He asks Josh if he would continue minding the store that Miss LilyRose is not feeling well. "Yes sir, I'll be glad to. I'll stay after we close to stock the shelves. Happy you're here Sir, she needs you." Dr. Chad thinks to himself, "I'm going to get to root of this, something is drastically wrong and I aim to find out what.it is."

After putting away the food, he brewed a cup of Chamomile Tea. He told LilyRose that he asked Josh to mind the store so she could get some rest.

"Now, try to sip a little of this tea, until you have drunk it all. Then go to bed and try to relax." She did as told, surprised the tea stayed down, finding herself so relaxed, she fell fast asleep. Dr. Chad crept down the stairs to help Josh run the store. About half an hour later, Eva and Allen Huffman came into the store. He asked them if he might be able to speak to them alone." They walked outside to the bench in front of store."

"Eva, Allen it is so good to see you." "What's going on, Dr. Chad, is there something wrong with LilyRose?" asked Eva nervously. Dr Chad, thinking just how to answer her question, he responded. "As you already know, LilyRose is pregnant. I've not had a chance to examine her, but since you are here, Eva, maybe you can assist me in the examination? Her biggest problems is she is over worked and under nurtured. It appears Martin is not taking her pregnancy serious, and is out talking politics. Now if that sounds harsh, it is meant to be. LilyRose is my daughter and I swore on my wife's death bed to raise her properly and to protect her with my life. Do you see where I'm coming from?"

Allen answered with a voice both sad and angered. "Yes, I hear you, and I am ashamed it is my son whose the cause of LilyRose pain and fear. Believe me, I will take care of this immediately. I now understand why she has not been to our home for some weeks, we've been stopping by the store to check on her, but she always was perky with that endearing smile."

"What do you plan to do?" "Martin will no longer live the privileged life of a spoiled brat. No more money, no account at the mercantile, he will be banned from our home, of which Eva gasped, yes Eva, he had his chance. From now on if he wants a family and if he want's to be a part of ours, he will earn it by making amends to his beloved, pay his debts, and get a job that pays him a salary to live on."

"I believe we, you as his parents, and me as Lily's need to speak to her so that she understands we know what has been behind her masked face, and understands we are here to love and protect her. Do you agree?"

"Absolutely!" remarked Allen. Then Dr. Chad faced Eva. "Eva, believe me I know how you feel, you are in the middle, a son you love but don't like, and a daughter-in-law you love and respect. But if we don't

stop this abuse now, he will have no chance to change, and my daughter may be damaged for life. Do you understand." Sobbing she responded, "Yes, I do, one minute I'm so angry at him, and then I pity him. Let us go up to see LilyRose now while Josh is here and Martin is gone."

Both parents as a united front walked up the stairs, opened the door and found LilyRose at the table drinking some more tea. She asked,"has the crackers arrived yet?" Dr. Chad shook his head, "Sweetheart, you have guests." She smiled and stood to give a hug.

Eva began the conversation. "LilyRose, you do understand how much Allen and I love you as our own daughter?" LilyRose nods. "Then you will understand our concern for you and the baby. We are going to take you to our home, for the duration of your pregnancy and the celebration of your child's birth. Allen and Dr. Chad will explain our concerns."

Both men took turns in sharing the facts and their fears. Allen said that he would run the mercantile until the appropriate man could be hired. The apartment would be bolted up until he found a proper renter . That Martin was being put on notice that he was to be responsible for himself without any privileges as a husband and father until such time, he proved himself capable and reliable. Lily quickly stated, "But I need my job here," Dr. Chad responded, "LilyRose, you can still lead the choir and teach students, and you do have your own money to use, if you need or want it. We love you, this is how it's gonna be. Your in-laws are wonderful decent souls, I trust them and so do you."

It was two days later that Martin climbed the stairs to the apartment to find it empty and boarded up. He stomped down the stairs and walked into the store, surprised to find his father, who said, "Good afternoon Mr. Drunk Politics" as he handed him an envelope with the letter outlining in detail his new LIFE COMMANDMENTS as Martin stood, totally stunned, he started to shred the envelope.

"I anticipated this," said Allen, "but I made several copies, all signed by the UNITED FRONT father and parent's-in-law with a copy in the Sheriff's office. So, my son, I advise you to read it through and begin to abide by your new life commandments." Martin, totally under the influence of alcohol, started ranting and raving. When Mr. and Mrs. Donald Denlinger came through the door with Mandy, he suddenly stopped, then looked directly at Allen. "You're not my father, I always knew I didn't belong here. Goodbye."

Mr and Mrs Denlinger, and Mandy just stood very quietly, then Mr. Huffman said, "This is an old Jewish custom. A child must learn to take responsibility for their actions, and if the lesson is not learned by age of 12-13 it will once again be taught in their 20's. A child is given two to three chances. Martin is having a rough time accepting his consequences."

Mr Denlinger cleared his throat, then nervously wondered if Mr. Huffman was in need of a store manager and someone to rent his little apartment, he stated, "The church has given me a call to the ministry. This has always been my dream. However, it will cost a lot of money and take some years to accomplish. We figured if you would allow us, Penny and me to run the store, rent your apartment upstairs, we could rent our home out and save money. My wife is a good accountant, and I've got a good back for heavy work when needed."

"You know Don, the Lord said, "Ask and you shall receive." "Mr and Mrs. Denlinger, God was mighty quick in giving me what I asked for. Could you and family come to our home this evening about seven pm so that Miss LilyRose can fill you in on what is required as manager, and for us to negotiate your salary and rent?"

"Yes, Sir, we'll be there. Miss Mandy shouted! "Oh boy, I get to see Miss Lilly, I've missed her."

*Let Go
and let God,
trusting in
New Beginnings.
-Allen Huffman-*

WILLIAM LINCOLN BAILEY

WILMINGTON, OHIO

As William was unloading the produce he brought for the mercantile to sell, when he noticed Penny at the register. Wondering what was going on, "Good Afternoon Penny, I was surprised to see you working here." "William! It was a miracle from God. We were making our plans for Don's future ministry, and Mr. Huffman needed new managers, so we rented our home, moved into the little apartment, and are delighted in how everything is working out."

"Is Miss LilyRose sick?" "Kinda, if you call having a baby sick. She does need bed rest, so she is now with her in-laws." Then bending to whisper in his ear. "Their son, is banned from this establishment, I don't know anything else."

"Can you tell me how many more quarts of berries you look to sell? And if you see Miss LilyRose, tell her I'm praying for her and the baby. Oh, and if you would, please make out my check to The Presbyterian Children's fund, so they can buy more supplies for their crafts and nature trips." Noticing that William seemed rather disturbed, Penny asked again, "What was your first question?"

"How many berries do you need? "Let me see, it is coming fall, folks like their berry cobbler, how about 12 quart because I'm buying two myself, the family wants a cobbler, Hey, how about you coming for Sunday dinner after 2 p.m. We'd love to have you." William thought for a minute, then said, "I'd be much obliged to accept your invitation. What should I bring?" "How about some lovely flowers for the table?" "This I can do. Have a great day Penny. Tell Mandy I said hello."

William felt the pain increasing by thinking about LilyRose being ill. He was so conflicted with his head and his heart. He always ended up feeling guilty, for what? He didn't understand. After doing his chores, having a little bite to eat, he decided to write in his journal. Seated at his little table that acted as his desk, he began to write,

September 30, 1891

Dear William,

It will soon be October, the leaves already beginning to turn colors, but the most drastic change is in the temperature. Nights are in low 40's and days barely make 70. All of my garden produce is gone with the exception of pumpkin and squash. Black berries are still plump and will make delicious jam. I'm still carving on the bench, sometimes it makes me feel happy, but then there are days just remembering makes me feel sad and guilty. I keep praying to be washed of my feelings of jealousy and distrust.

Today I heard Miss LilyRose is with child and sick. I immediately felt a bit of anger at Martin, then Penny justified my anger by gossiping about him being banned from the store. A good Christian would not listen to gossip let alone celebrate in it. There I go again, judging Penny. I've decided, I love Miss LilyRose but lusting on another man's wife is a great sin. I keep asking for God to take this lust from my heart, but instead it grows stronger.

We begin choir practice the first Wednesday in October. Maybe I should drop out, but I'm too much of a coward. I love her and fear for her safety with Martin. I have a paper due on Monday for my Agriculture Class. I am writing about bee's and how badly we need them. I wish I could talk to Gunnar, he was the writer. I miss him so much. Just knowing he was in Cincinnati, not too far to visit, eased my heart of loneliness. He wrote beautiful poetry, I wrote this the other day, *I am alone, but not lonely, for my solituede is joyously reinforced at the junction of all our being.* Who am I trying to fool? I wrote this after longing for LilyRose Somerset, not honestly thinking of Brother Gunnar. God rest his soul.

I guess I've written enough for this day, dear diary. I think I need to spend more time praying.

Penny opened the door to William after climbing the long stairs to the apartment. "Welcome Will to our little abode. Mandy is eager to show you something she has been working on for school music class." Will handed her his coat to hang on the peg. Mandy came from behind the newly built wall beside the

kitchen blocking one of the windows.

"Mr. William, I'm writing a song for class, do you want to help me? I'm stuck." " Okay, let's see what you have written already." She handed him her notebook with the words written, some crossed out, other's not.

"Flowers bloom all year round

But not always in our little town

Some are red and some are blue

Bringing happiness, all year through

"It seems to me, all you need is a chorus to complete the song. How about?

"I sing, we sing,

joyfully bringing love to everyone,"

How's that?" "It's so perfect." "Will adds, "The chorus could have a little Latin beat," " Oh, thanks Mr. William, I just love it. I'll write the music when I take my lesson with Miss LilyRose. I know she'll just love it, too."

Knowing William's custom of eating very little meat, a lot of vegetables, and some dessert, Penny prepared a Chicken Stew with all kinds of vegetables, a big round of sourdough bread, and Strawberry Shortcake. She fixed hot coffee and tea to go along with the dessert. Don was thrilled to have William as their first

guests in their new little home.

"Will, I'm so pleased you joined us for dinner. We're still getting organized and if you don't mind, I'd like to ask your opinion and suggestions on Mandy's room that is in progress. It is only 10 by 10. Knowing your Quaker heritage and how they utilize space, I think you could be most helpful." "I'll do my best. First of all, Mandy what do you need to feel organized and also creative?" "I need bookshelves, desk, closet, and of course a bed." "If I could barrow a pencil and pad, I'll make some drawings as we look at your room." They entered her room that has a cot for sleeping, a produce box for a lamp table and books, and pegs on the wall for clothing.

"Is there anything in here you feel you can't live without?" "Just my books and clothing." William began to draw a diagram of the room, door and window. He added a built-in-desk with bookshelves under the window, and bookshelves built over the window and down the side. The shelves on the side could hold her folded clothing, underclothes, socks, scarves, gloves, and hats. On the far end of the room would be her bed with a trundle bed under for girls overnight visits. The wall above the door could have a high shelf, and the wall beside the door could have anotoher shelf with a rod underneath to hang dresses, etc the other side of the door would have pegs for coats, on the floor would be a wooded box lined with tin for wet boots and shoes to be cleaned daily if wet. Handing his drawing to Don with Mandy looking on, "Oh Daddy it's perfect, everything neat and in place. Mr. William you are a genius." Blushing, Will said, "When something has a place, it likes to be in that place when not being used. That's the Plain Folk Philosophy."

"Will, do you have any idea of how much it might coast?" "Not too much, I've got the trees to be cut for the lumber. I'd say the cost of paint, hinges, and a door. Mandy can do the painting. You and I will chop a large tree, cut the lumber, build the furniture. We must plant two trees to replace the one that we cut. If we start soon, we'll be finished in a month. Saturday's are good if Mandy will take care of my customers." "I sure will! This is going to fun!" "Hard work is always fun, when we work together. Do we start next Saturday?" Yes, Will, if Penny can manage the mercantile while I'm away." "Of course, Don, this is our first family project. I'm excited."

The first Saturday, Will and Don picked the tree, cut it down, cleaned the bark off, then used the cross saw to cut boards to Will's specification. The boards needed to lie flat for a week to dry out the moisture from the live tree. They loaded the planks into the shed and piled everything they could find on them to keep them flat.

Mandy was quite a salesperson. She welcomed every person who came to buy produce and flowers with a big smile. She had to periodically ask Mr. William the names of the flowers she did not know. But mostly, buyers were happy with the sales person, produce and flowers. The produce was mostly pumpkins, squash, dried beans, dried fruits, and herbs, and some canned jams.

The following Saturday, Will and Don began very early to start building the desk, bookshelves, bed frame and trundle. Will also suggested, if they had time, to build flower boxes for all windows in the apartment. By 6 pm, the men were finished, exhausted and starved. Penny had prepared two meals. Lunch was sandwiches of ham and cheese, apples, and cookies. Dinner was fried chicken, baked potatoes, home made rolls, and pineapple upside down cake with cinnamon and brown sugar glaze. Mandy set the table, heated the food, and called the men to eat. She too, was tired, because this was a trophy day in sales. She sold every pumpkin, most of the squash, and all the beans, and dried fruits. She showed Mr. William the cigar box that was full of coins and some bills. "God is so good to us. Thank you God, as they ate the delicious food."

Will explained to Mandy, the hard part was yet to come. "Mandy, your father will not have my help putting it together, He's a master carpenter, but he will need your help. After it's together you will need to paint or varnish the wood to preserve it. It has been such fun working with you and your father. Enjoy your new room. I love my home, I call it my sanctuary."

"Thank you for the biggest sale day I've ever had. We now want to count out God's portion, 10% to go to where God inspires us. Suggestions?" "The poor people by the railroad tracks, They need food and clothes." "Then Mandy, you need to figure out how to spend this and deliver to the people."

"I'll have my friend Ruthie, help, She lives in a tent by the tracks and is in my eighth grade class, She wants to be a teacher." "That's a great idea."

*It will be a healing
for your flesh,
and a refreshment
for your body.*
Proverbs 3:8

Huffman Estate

Wilmington, Ohio

As she promised, LilyRose wrote her father every week. Sunday's after her choir, she gave a piano lesson to Mandy for one hour. Then before dinner, she would write to her beloved father. This week she was overcome with joy learning William was helping Don and Mandy fix up her little room in the apartment above the mercantile. Mandy was so excited to tell how ever item was being made to fit snugly into the small space. After Mandy left, LilyRose took out her beautiful diary and began to write:

Dear Diary,   October 7, 1891

I gave Mandy a music lesson today. She brought a little lyric she had written for her music class that William helped her with. We set it to music, and in doing so, I felt so close to William. I'm not embarrassed to tell you that I am in love with William Lincoln Bailey. I have been since the first time I heard him sing. Why I failed to let him know my feelings was because of stupid learned social behavior that doesn't allow a woman to say what she wants.

Here I sit, feeling sorry for myself for being so stupid. Martin is not near the man William is or will ever be. As I've said before, William is so much like my father. He's tall, he's big and I like tall, big men because I'm tall and used to looking either into their eyes or up to their eyes, never looking down at them. Everything about Martin is small, his character, his build, and his talents. Forgive me God for making comparisons, but that's how I honestly feel. I don't want him around my child ever!!!! I know I'm having a little girl. I'll name her Mary Therese after my mother and grandmother and my beloved music teacher, Sister Therese Anne. I should probably allow the Huffman's to contribute to her naming, but she will be caring their surname and that's enough. If I have a son, I will name him after my father, Chadwick Nicholas Somerset Huffman.

Father has promised to be here one week before the baby is born to assist the midwife in my delivery. When he and Eva examined me, he said he figured I got pregnant the third week of my marriage. What a horrid honeymoon that was. It was certainly not honey filled. All Martin needed was a set of horns and a forked tail to set the tone for his style of love making. He loved it when I screamed. If I told my father what he did, I'm truly afraid my father would kill him. I will never cause my father to go to hell because of what I've had to endure. After all, I said yes when I could have said no. God help me forgive myself for my offensive behavior. How ignorant!!! Diary, thank you for listening, no one must ever know my ignorance and abuse.

On March 16, 1893, LilyRose delivered a baby girl with the most beautiful black curly hair, just like her grandmother Eva. Her skin was so white the little veins stood out when she cried. When put to her mother's breast, she looked up into her Mother's blue eyes as if to say, "Look Mother, I'm different, I've got green-hazel eyes instead of blue, and black hair instead of red." "Yes, sweetheart you look different but you've got the Somerset heart."

"She was christened Mary Teresa Rose Somerset-Huffman in the same gown her mother, grandmother, and great-grandmother's were christened in. Grandparents joined in a group picture of mother and child that would be painted by Grandpa Huffman's artist friend. Eva proudly shared her baby portrait taken in New York when she was six months old. Everyone said Mary Therese was her double. Eva just smiled approvingly.

As the years went by, Mother and Daughter were like two peas in a pod. She could play "Twinkle-twinkle Little Star" on the piano, but like her mother, she loved trying to climb trees, dig in the dirt, and play with bugs. Eva would frown as LilyRose and Allen laughed.

Dr. Chad brought LilyRose's doctor kit she played with as a child. But Mary Therese absolute favorite gift was her white pony, Mickey, Grandaddy Chad brought to her for her fifth birthday. She never wanted to leave Mickey's side. Begged to sleep in the stable with him. She was a natural horsewoman, just like her mother. Her grandmother Eva was proficient in riding side saddle, but Mary Therese wanted none of that. She rode Mickey both bear back and on saddle. She was told she was responsible to take care of Mickey, feeding, watering, and brushing down. She wanted to muck the stable, but both grandfathers said they'd do that until she was older.

Grandaddy Chad was taking Mama and Mary Therese to visit in Dayton, Ohio. Mary Therese said she would not go if Mickey couldn't go. So, Grandaddy Chad had horseshoes put on Mickey so that he could walk behind the buggy on their trip to Dayton. At one point Mary Therese said, "Grandaddy, can't you hear Mickey calling for me to ride him?"

And so, for the last ten miles Miss Mary Therese rode majestically into Harmony Village entrance with all the children's eyes aglow with envy. She jumped down and announced, "All children will be given a free ride while I'm here visiting Grandaddy Chad."

Their visit was for the rest of the month of March. Then on April 5th, they headed back to the Huffman Estate. LilyRose seeing how spoiled her daughter was getting to be, decided when back in Wilmington, some changes needed to be made.

To follow under all circumstances,
the highest promptings within you;
to be always true to the divine self;
to rely upon the inward Light, the
the inward Voice, and to pursue your
purpose with a fearless and restful
heart believing that the future will
yield unto you the reward of every
thought and effort; knowing that
the laws of the universe can never
fail, and that your own will come
back to you with mathematicalexactitude,
this is faith and the living of faith.
James Allen, "As a Man Thinketh"

Huffman Estate

Wilmington, Ohio

Eva and Allen announced to LilyRose they were going to visit their friends Katharina and James Patterson in Oakwood, Ohio for a few days. They hoped she wouldn't mind being left alone for that time. Lily-Rose secretly desired this time alone with her daughter to correct some of her misbehavior.

"Absolutely not! "I'm thrilled you are giving yourselves some time with your friends. We'll be just fine!" The groom packed their luggage into their two horse buggy. Eva began to instruct Lily that she had prepared all types of food for them while they were gone. "Eva, I can cook." "I know dear, but I want you to be able to just relax as well."

As they started to leave, Mary Theresa again, ran to give them another hug and kiss yelling, "Grandpa and Grandma, have a fun vacation." throwing them kisses.

"Let's you and me have some lunch. Would you enjoy a grilled cheese sandwich?" "Yes Mommy, please can we play checkers after we are finished?" "I think that's a wonderful idea. But first we need to go and tend to Mickey's feed, water, and brushing." "I didn't forget, I just didn't think it it was time yet." "It will be after we eat and clean up our mess."

After the kitchen chores were finished, they grabbed their coats to head to the stables. The groom, Henry had already taken care of the horse

LilyRose generally rode. Mary Therese carefully measured out Mickey's feed, water, and was brushing her when Henry came into the stall.

"Ma'am, could I speak to you please?" LilyRose went out the door to speak with him. "I don't want to frighten you, but I've been hearing noises around the barn and stables. Just please lock your doors tonight for safety. Okay? Mr and Mrs Huffman would be upset if anything happened while they were away."

"Thank you, Henry, I appreciate you telling me, I'll lock the doors and check all windows to see if they too are locked. When Mary Therese is finished, we'll say goodnight to you." When Mary Therese was finished they walked to Henry's sleeping quarters to say goodnight. Then they went in to the house, locked all doors and windows then took their evening baths. They were just getting ready to drink their hot cocoa when LilyRose heard something. Then she convinced herself it was just the wind blowing a tree limb against the window. She found some sliced chicken in the ice box and some apple sauce. She made a sandwich for she and Mary Therese to divide. She added cinnamon and brown sugar and a peanut cookie..

They ate their dinner, washed their dishes, then went upstairs to climb in bed. LilyRose read a favorite story to Mary Therese then knelt beside her bed to say her prayers.

"Dear Jesus,

Thank you for Mickey, for Mommy and Grandaddy Chad, Grandpa and Grandma and Henry. I love you Jesus, Amen. She kissed her mommy goodnight, then hugging her toy bear, as she fell asleep.

LilyRose went to her room, combed and brushed her hair, then cleansed her face with cream, put on her warm gown, and crawled into bed. A couple of hours later she was awakened with someone staring at her,

"Whose there?" "Just little old me, you're long lost husband" "How did you get in?" ""With my key. Now, just make this easy for us all. Where is your jewelry, Mom's Menorah, your furs, and anything of value. I need money."

"Martin, you always need money to buy more alcohol and to give to your lady friends." He slapped her hard on the face, she grit her teeth. "If you're going to make this hard, I'll show you what hard is if you don't tell me where they are."

"Your mother took everything to the bank to put in their vault. The furs are in her closet, I know of nothing else that is of value." "Where's your money?" She started to get her purse, when Mary Therese walked in carrying her teddy bear.

"So this is the product of my seed? Come here little girl, give your daddy a big kiss." She ran to her mother crying, "Mommy whose that mean man?"

"I'm your daddy, you stupid kid! Now let me see what I can find. He opened LilyRose stocking draw then pulled them out and told Lily to sit on the vanity chair. LilyRose started hitting and kicking him. He hit her in the head with the silver hair brush, blood starts to stream down, as he tied her legs to the leg of the chair and tied her arms in back of her. Mary Therese came in screaming, "Leave my Mommy alone," he took off his belt, and said, "You need some daddy discipline," then started beating her with the strap. Finally, he left her alone as she continued to cry. He grabbed a pillow case to load up anything he believed of value. After loaded with all he could carry, he left the house.

LilyRose asked her daughter to please try to untie mommy. After many tries, she is successful in getting her hands untied. Quickly LilyRose untied her legs, then looked at Mary Therese's back and legs to find huge red bruises already turning black and blue. "He'll pay for this, as God is my witness, he'll pay for this."

Holding hands, Mother and Daughter slowly go down the stairs, to find he was no where to be seen. They go to the stable, to find LilyRose's horse is gone, then to Henry's room where they found him tied and gaged with a rope from the barn. He is so upset with himself, but LilyRose said, "Henry, stop it, this couldn't be helped. Tomorrow, we will go to town to see the sheriff, to report this. Martin is a drunk, he has resorted to being a common thief to feed his habit. He is dangerous, I will file charges against him for beating me and my daughter. You are my witness. Now, you come in the house, we'll have some hot tea and get some sleep. Tomorrow will be a long day.

The next morning with only little Mickey to pull the buggy, they drove into town to report the assault and theft. The sheriff said he would let all officers of the law in Ohio know about a warrant for his arrest. He also planned to have a deputy stay guard at the Huffman Estate until Allen Huffman returned home.

LilyRose also wanted to tell Don and Penny at the mercantile what had happened and to be on the look out for Martin. The sheriff also put a man at the mercantile. They both went to see the local doctor to be examined. He said they were both fine, but Mary Therese's bruises needed to have some salve and cool compresses to reduce swelling. She was brave and did not cry. "Mommy, is that mean man really my father?" "Yes, sweetheart, he is a very sick man. Alcohol is his god. He is so sick he even hurt his little girl to get what he wanted. The sheriff is going to protect us from him. Don't worry my sweetheart. Mommy loves you."

When they returned to the Estate, LilyRose and Henry did a quick inventory of what they believed he had stolen. He had taken Allen's shot gun, his bottles of wine and sherry, Eva's costume jewelry, gold dresser set, perfume bottles, and mink stole. He would have probably taken more, but he only had a pillow case and her horse to get away on. She thought, "What a disgusting piece of human flesh. Not only disgusting but dangerous as well. How do I tell my father what Martin has done? God help us."

You, O Lord will protect us,
you will guard us from this generation forever.

WILLIAM LINCOLN BAILEY FARM

WILMINGTON, OHIO

It was cloudy October day, William was busy working on the woven wall for the Memorial Garden. He heard Shep barking to the west, when he looked up to see LilyRose's mare CupCake grazing with something hanging on her saddle. He laid down his carving knife, called for Shep to stop barking, then carefully walked towards the horse. He called her name, she raised her head in recognition. It was then he saw a sack tied to the saddle horn. Concerned and becoming fearful, he took CupCake's reigns when realizing she needed water. He guided her to the watering trough and began to talk to her.

"CupCake, sweet girl, where's LilyRose?" He saw in the sack, a ladies gold hair brush, mirror and comb, and a mink fur stole. He knew then, something bad was about. He said to himself, "As soon as I water the mare, I am going to ride out to the Huffman Estate to see what has happened." He did not feed the mare but just one pan of grain, as he had no idea how long she had been without food, but knew if she ate too much after being starved she could become sick. He saddled his horse, Buddy, then took CupCake's reigns and started down the road towards Wilmington. He hadn't gone far when he saw a horse heading his direction. It was a deputy! He stopped, the deputy and William knew each other.

"Hey Will, where did you find Miss LilyRose' horse." "In my back pasture, grazing with this sack hanging." "I'll take a look at that bag, her husband got into the house, abused her and little girl, looking for jewelry. Because she had all her valuables at the bank vault, he got real mad and took whatever he found in this here pillow case. I'll need to take the case for evidence." "Deputy, I was just heading to the Huffman Estate to take CupCake to Miss LilyRose. Is she and baby okay?

"Yes and No. She was tied up, he whipped the baby with a belt and tied Henry to a horse stall. He's a drunk and mean as a snake." "Thanks for the information, I'll head on out, feel free to look around out there for more clues, he couldn't go too far on foot."

William rode towards the Huffman Estate, all the time thinking, his mind racing with negative emotions toward Martin and loving concern for LilyRose and child. As he pulled into the long driveway on the property, he was stopped by a deputy. William stated, "Deputy, I found CupCake in my west pasture this morning. Deputy Kyle has the evidence he found on her. He's at my place now looking for more criminal activity and evidence. Martin can't go to far on foot, the sheriff should send a posse to look for him."

"Do you think I can leave my post to notify the sheriff?" "If you feel you can trust me, I'm happy to stand guard while your gone." "Yes, Will, I know I can trust you. I'll be on my way."

LilyRose saw William leading CupCake. She ran out to meet them crying. "Oh CupCake, I'm been so worried." The mare was nodding and leaning close to LilyRose, as Mary Therese came yelling, "Mommy, Mommy CupCake came home." looking at Will, she declared. "Mr. William is a nice man to find CupCake." Will could see the ugly bruises on her legs and arms. He thought, "Oh God, what an evil man!" LilyRose asked frantically, "William, where did you find her?" "In my back pasture. We need for Henry to look her over, get her some water, and if you don't mind, I'd like for us to go inside to talk." "Oh, William, of course, I'm sorry, I've been frantic for her safety." Henry took the two horses to tend to while LilyRose, William and Mary Therese entered the door to the kitchen.

"He came through this door. He had a key. I think the Huffman's forgot to change the locks. They're in Oakwood, Ohio visiting friends. Should be home to tomorrow. This will absolutely break their hearts." "Well it breaks my heart to know you and Mary Therese were abused and robbed by your husband and the child's father." "I know William, but it is going to take's some doing, she paused to ask Mary Therese to go to see if Henry needed any help at the stables, after she had left, "I plan to divorce him, get an order of protection, and I swear, I will kill him if he ever lays a hand on my child again." She started crying as William put his arms around her. She immediately fell into his embrace. He held her for a few moments, then feeling very embarrassed he said. "Miss LilyRose," she interrupts him, "Please William, do-not-call me Miss, I am your peer, when you call me that I feel dirty, like some person who is above you. Please, please don't do it, just call me LilyRose, Lily, I prefer Lily," "I was just going to say you don't really mean you'd kill Martin."

"William, my beloved William, I'm afraid you are wrong in your opinion of me. I'm a mother bear when it comes to those I love being hurt or harmed in any way. I would die for those I love, and you are included."

She kissed him on his cheek, then turned her head towards the door. As she did this, she said, "Please remember my words, for they are truth so help me God." Will's eyes were completely filled with tears as he turned loose of LilyRose. He had no words to respond to her exclamation of love. He only knew he was a coward and so afraid of his feelings, that he must get away. He also realized he was too much of a coward to run, and so much in love he would stay until knowing she was okay. Seeing some riders coming up the path, she said, "I believe we have company, I think they're a deputy's posse sworn to find Martin."

They both walked out the door to greet them. Yes, the Sheriff had hired a posse of local men dedicated to finding Martin and arresting him for assault and robbery. One of the men was to stay guard at the Huffman Estate, the rest would leave. They all carried rifles and ammunition on their belts. William felt sick to his stomach, violence of any kind made him feel ill. Some people felt that was the coward's way out, but he felt violence created more violence. Remembering Lily's strong feeling about being a "mother bear," he asked himself, "Could I kill if I believed someone was going to hurt LilRose? "Oh Dear God, I can feel that question attacking my soul?"

After the Deputy's left, they went to the barn to find what Henry found concerning CupCake's condition. "Miss LilyRose, she's had some trauma to her body and to her emotions. He used a whip on her. There were many stones and burrs in her horseshoes, her mane was tangled from running in and around trees, and she definitely was defiant to the rider! I believe she knew he hurt you, she might have even thrown him."

"Poor CupCake, thank you for being my loyal friend," hugging her neck. Patting Buddy's neck Will thanked Henry for grooming him along with CupCake.

"Mr. William, you need to thank Mary Therese, she took care of Buddy." He turned to the child, "Why thank you Mary Therese, how'd you reach him to groom?" "Mr. Henry got a stool to help me. I had to stand on my tippy toes because Buddy's too tall. He's such a good horse." "Is there something I can do for you in exchange for your groom service?" "May I come to the farm and plant flowers and play with Shep?"

"You certainly may, the farm is for children, you are welcome anytime." Will saddled his horse, tipped his hat to all, and rode out down the lane feeling more confused than ever. "I believe I need to do two things as soon as possible, Write in my journal and talk with God."

I thought I had life all figured out,
then life threw me a curve ball.
William Lincoln Bailey

*Only in relationship can you
know yourself, not in abstraction
and certainly not in isolation.
The movement of behaviour
is the sure guide to yourself, it's
the mirror of your consciousness:
this mirror will reveal its content,
the images, the attachments, the
fears, the loneliness, the joy and
sorrow.
Poverty lies in running away
from this, either in its
sublimations or its identities.
-J. Krishnamurti-*

Dr. Chad Somerset's Home, Harmony Village

Dayton, Ohio

Thinking to himself, Dr. Chad observed the natural signs predicting a cold fall and even colder winter, "I will need to fill both barn and shed with enough hay and oats to feed the animals if this comes about. Best be prepared, I'll go talk with Frank to get his take on what he thinks the weather will be this fall and winter."

As he is walking down the lane to the Mitchell home, he saw the postman arriving. He waited by his mailbox, tipped his hat to the postman as he handed Dr. Chad a letter from LilyRose. He started back to his home, with each step he was tearing open her letter,

Dear Father,

You know I'd never ask for help if I could handle this myself: but Father, I can't do this alone, nor do I even know how to start. I want to divorce Martin!!! Three days ago, while the Huffman's were in Oakwood visiting their friends for four days, Martin arrived with his own key, opened the door, assaulted me, beat my baby with a strap and forced me to allow him to ram sack the house for anything of value he could find. He became even more angered when he learned his mother had taken all valuables to their bank vault. He assaulted and tied Henry to a stall in the barn and then fled on CupCake. The next day William Bailey found CupCake in his pasture, traumatized and in deep despair. I notified the Sheriff and a Posse is now out searching for Martin. The Huffman's arrived home yesterday and both are depressed and ashamed to have a son such as Martin. I told them I wanted a divorce. They agree and have hired their attorney to assist me. However, Father I don't believe a woman in this country has much chance in doing what I want done. I believe only you can accomplish this, and I feel ashamed depending on you to find the answers.

I want a divorce that states Martin cannot come near either myself or my precious daughter. I no longer want the Huffman name, nor do I want my daughter stuck with the name he has used to do his criminal life. I do not want anything from him, no support for either of us, and I never want to set on eyes on him again.

Please Father, help me. I know you had grave misgivings about me marrying Martin, but my arrogance caused me to make the biggest mistake of my life. Nothing good has come from it except my precious Mary Therese. I married the wrong man, .and now I'm paying the price.

I love you, Your LilyRose

Conversing with himself, Dr Chad pondered what he needed to do before leaving Dayton. "I hope Frank can and is willing to handle the chores here. I have no one to take over the Medical Clinic. I'll talk to Mother Superior if she can open it for the poor. My beloved LilyRose is hurting and needs me. Oh Maud, I truly wish you were here." He immediately went to Frank's home to find they had heard the day before that Lukas, their grandson, was going to be stationed in Boston and that there is housing close by. Alice and baby would be leaving soon.

"Frank I'm so sorry, this makes me afraid to ask you what I need to ask of you. LilyRose needs me, she is divorcing Martin and it's a mess. Here, read her letter." After both Frank and Mildred Grace read the letter, they said, "Dr. Chad we'll do our best to take care of things for you. When do you plan to leave?" "Tomorrow, if I can get things handled. I've got to talk to Mother Superior if she wants to open the poor clinic, my other patients, I'll just have to tell them to go to the new doctor in town."

Martha Grace said she'd be willing to go talk with Mother Superior and Frank said he'd be willing to take letters to his patients notifying them he would be gone for an undetermined amount of time." "I'm so grateful to you two," as he broke down, so emotional, he couldn't continue to speak. Frank patted him on the back and said, "Doc you'd do anything you could to help us, so get on home and get packed, I'll hire some help to get more hay and feed in for winter, now get!"

After arriving home, Dr Chad made himself a cup a tea, ate a sandwich, then made a list of things that only he could do. Number one was to write a sample letter for Mildred Grace to copy for Frank to take to his patient's. He signed eleven blank sheets on his letterhead and placed them with his confidential medical book of patient's names and addresses. He thought, "God, if I can't trust those two dear friends, who can I trust?"

The next morning he loaded his buggy with his favorite horse who was well trained, stocky, and dependable. He took a smoked ham and bacon, and a well seasoned hind quarter of beef. He knew the Huffman's didn't eat pork, but both he and LilyRose did. He didn't know where he would stay, but knew he'd find something close. The weather was icy cold, the road would be dangerous, but he had faith in his ability to drive safely. He also took both rifle and his hand gun wondering if he even had any ammunition for the hand gun. His personal items were few, but the crocks filled with butter, honey, and cider weighed heavy on the load. He left just as the sun was peaking over the horizon. As he drove in silence, he thought about being a parent to LilyRose was the greatest joy in his life. His emotions were still very raw. He knew strength came from being able to allow your emotions to come forth, to feel the pain, and then to take action to what needed to be done. He understood LilyRose' need for his presence, She was a very strong and intelligent woman, but knew she needed Father's grounding.

Life's fulfillment finds constant
contradictions in its path; but
those are necessary for the sake of
its advance.
The stream is saved from the
sluggishness of its current by the
perpetual opposition of the soil
through which it must cut its way.
It is the soil which forms its banks.
The Spirit of fight belongs to
the genius of life.
-Rabindranath Tagore-

Huffman Estate

Wilmington, Ohio

Everyone was at the breakfast table on this sunshiny fall day. Since the incident the Huffman's have insisted that Henry sleep in the maid's room off of the kitchen. They no longer employed a maid since LilyRose moved in. She insisted that she could help with the cleaning of the large home and doing the laundry. Most of their laundry was sent in town to be done by a new establishment run by a Chinese family. They did a superb job. Allen always paid them more then their bill, he exclaimed, "When persons go the extra mile in service to their clients, they deserve to be rewarded and appreciated. I learned today, their little girl will start school this week. The misses told me her daughter would be a little behind, but I'm sure she will catch up, language being her only real problem."

"Grandpa, do you think she will be in my class? I'd love to have a new friend." "If she's five, she probably will be." Mary Therese was in the first grade because she already knew her numbers, the alphabet, and could already read some of the sentences in her Mc Guffy's Reader.

During the meal, LilyRose announced that she is expecting her father to come either today or tomorrow. He will need to make arrangements for his clinic and farm animals, but will be here as soon as he can to help us all out." Allen quickly responded, "He can certainly stay here, but Don and Penny Denlinger are back east attending seminary. Mandy is going to college, living with her best friend. That means the apartment can be cleaned up, so your father can have his own place for as long as he chooses to stay." "Oh, Papa Allen, that is so sweet of you, you're the most generous man. I love you." Mary Therese piped in. "My Grandpa is the best! So is my Grandaddy, I'm lucky, I've got two!"

After the meal, all the ladies cleaned off the table and gathered the dishes to be taken to the sink to be washed. No one touched the silverware, as it is Mary Therese job, and she takes her job very seriously. She consciously places each item in the hot water pan, one item at a time; careful not to burn her hands. She asked, "When I'm six what will my job be in the kitchen?" "I guess we'll have to study on that question, but I'm sure what ever it is, you will be able to do it."

Mornings are for fresh starts
Evenings are for soft landings,
In between, we simply do our best.
Anonymous

WILLIAM LINCOLN, BAILEY FARM

WILMINGTON, OHIO

The memorial garden was almost finished. William was very happy with how it was unfolding. He had stained and varnished the "Wall of Memories" and the bench was almost finished. The carving of the Angel had taken a little longer than he anticipated. He was now using a fine paint brush to paint a darker color in the grooves of the carved etchings. He heard footsteps coming up the path, he turned and was surprised to see LilyRose dismounting her horse, CupCake.

"William the bench is beautiful! What are you creating?" Smiling he said, "It's a garden within a garden?" "How lovely." William just sat there, not knowing what to say, then he found his voice, "I decided to do a memorial for my lost loved ones. When I lost my brother Gunnar, I realized how much I missed talking to him. We could share everything."

"I never knew you had a brother, how old was he, when did he die?" "Lily, he was my half brother, we had the same father, different mother's." "Wait a minute, I'm confused, your parents were the Bailey's, did Mrs Bailey have another husband?"

"Lily, this is going to take some time to explain. Do you have the time? Won't they be worried about you?" "Yes, but William, I want to hear the story, will you come by this evening so we can talk?'

"Don't count on it, but I'll try. I've a few things I need to finish." "Tomorrow my father will be here. I wrote him about what Martin did.

I don't know when we will be able to talk privately after he's here. Please try to come."

Lily mounted her horse and threw him a kiss. William's heart just pounded. He is so conflicted as to what he can share and what he can't. A voice within adviced, "William, the truth is always appropriate."

As he was picking up his tools and supplies, the Sheriff rode in asking, "Will, have you seen or heard anything since we last talked?" "No, nothing. However, I've been thinking that he could have hitched a ride on a farmer's hay wagon without the farmer knowing. If he got to Cincinnati, he could get lost among the homeless, there are plenty of them there."

"Or, he could have jumped on a river boat heading to St. Louis. We'll catch him, he doesn't have many options as to where to stay hidden. He's addicted to alcohol, them boys are really dangerous, because they need it! They go for days not eating, just drinking. We've got a deputy watching the railroad tracks, he might have jumped a train. If you learn anything, let us know."

Running, running, running
no place to go
The soul is lost
Falling lower, lower, low.

*Be very very still
and allow every new
experience to take place
in your life
without any resistance
whatsoever.
You do not have
to do anything,
you simply have to be
and let things happen.
-Eileen Caddy-
"Footprints on the Path"*

Huffman Estate

Wilmington, Ohio

Henry, LilyRose and Mary Therese were in the stables mucking out Buddy and CupCake's stalls when William tapped on the door, calling, "Is there anybody here?" Both mother and daughter came running to let him in. "Will, I'm so happy you came to visit. Let us finish our job, then wash up so we can visit properly on the veranda." "Mr. Will, Mommy said we will bring Grandaddy Chad to see your Garden. Grandaddy Chad is suppose to come tomorrow. I'm so excited. He's so much fun, and I've got a new girlfriend, she's Chinese her name is Linn with beautiful eyes."

"Little Miss tell-it-all is all wound up. We're almost finished, go have a cool drink at the pump while we finish our job. Henry will tend to your Buddy. Come on Miss Mary Therese." .

They all sat on the rattan chairs on the veranda. They could see the sun about to go down. Mary Therese laid her head on her mother's lap, her eyes began to flutter, a sure sign of being sleepy. "Sweetheart, let's go in, I'll askGrandma Eva if she will get you ready for bed while Uncle Will and I visit. Is it alright for her to call you Uncle Will? Mister feels so formal?" "Yes, of course, Uncle Will it shall be." "Night Uncle Will," as they both left Will sitting on the veranda drinking a glass of tea with mint watching the sunset.

"Grandma Eva loves it when she can read a story and say prayers with Mary Therese." Feeling sad for the both Huffman's, Will thought, "Their only child is an unappreciative and a lost soul. God Bless them."

"So, now William, breaking his silent thoughts, I would like to hear the story." "My story began in Kentucky on a farm owned by an evil man, much like Martin. His wife Jenny is a beautiful soul. His name was Jack Jones and he was a slave seller. He captured my Mam and Pap, who were run-a-way slaves from Mississippi and took them to his farm where he raped Mam in front of Jenny and Pap. Mam got pregnant with me, Miss Jenny was already pregnant with Gunnar."

"That's how you and Gunnar are half brothers?" "Yes we all escaped from Jack. Pap and Mam ran away first. Miss Jenny believed she could pass me off as her deaf daughter, if the Rebels caught us. We crossed the Ohio River and went to live with her father, Rev. Sterling in Cincinnati. Then a Quaker family adopted me, and that's why I'm a Bailey.

"Oh, William, that's quite a story." "The reason I'm so white is that Mam was a three quarter white house slave and Jack was white, so I have just a drop of Negro blood in me. Mam was tall like you. I believe she was almost 6 feet tall, very fair with jade green eyes. I loved listening to her tell stories of her life on the plantation. She gave me a Buckeye Nut, which was my Lucky Charm, with instructions to find a Quaker to help me to freedom. I found Obadiah and Martha Bailey who loved me, taught me, adopted me, and willed me their beautiful farm. I'm a very lucky man."

Lily sat quiet for what seemed forever, then she asked, "William, how do you feel about your life in general with all that you've been through?"

"Like I said, I'm very lucky, but sometimes, I feel very conflicted. I know I'm free, but not as free as you, and Gunnar. Gunnar was a journalist for the Cincinnati News, he deplored slavery and everything it entailed. He was murdered while uncovering White Supremacy that was running the city government, sheriff's office, and churches in Kentucky. They tortured him, burned him alive, and threw him in a river while he was still breathing." "You see, Lily, the Devil is still controlling folks by teaching fear. We must teach our children about love and living together in peace and harmony." A total silence and then Will said, "I think I need to be leaving, it's getting late." "Will, I meant it when I told you that I love you. It doesn't matter to me what kind of blood you have, it's your character that I love and admire. The worst mistake I made in my life is not telling you how I felt, and instead I married the most evil man I ever met. Don't try to hide from me, I know you have feelings for me, so some day," Will interrupted, "Lily please, It just isn't done. Goodnight."

He went to the stable, mounted his horse, and left without turning around to wave goodby. Lily said under her breath, "William Bailey, you've not heard the last from me, I promise you that." She picked up the glasses, dropped them off at the kitchen, then climbed the stairs to her room. After preparing for bed, she took out her diary and began to write.

Dear Diary,

Guess what? I am totally in love with William. His life before being adopted by the Bailey's was horrible. But, I made a big mistake by marrying Martin, I will not deny love again. Tomorrow Father will be here. I know he will support me in my desire to wipe Martin from mine and Mary Therese's life. I still believe in miracles!"

Let all that you do be done in love." 1 Corinthians 16:14

Dr Chad arrived at around noon the following day. His daughter and granddaughter were so excited they couldn't eat much breakfast, so now they were starved. Lunch would be lavish, true to form, being Eva's kitchen and her desire to serve those she loved and admired.

Dr. Chad was loaded with foodstuffs that had to be put away. They had ridden all morning on a bed of ice from his ice box and now needed to be wiped down and stored. After this was done, Dr. Chad and his mutual admirations society washed their hands just before the lunch bell rang. Eva had prepared lamb chops with rice, green beans, and hot rolls. For dessert she made a bread pudding that smell divine with cinnamon, raisins and maple syrup. Dr. Chad was asked to bless the food, "Father, bless this food so lovingly prepared by a loving heart, your beloved servant Eva. We are grateful to all be together in love and friendship. In your name, we say, Amen."

Sharing was very loving with lots of appreciation shown to each person. Henry was still not comfortable being in his employer's home, but was beginning to appreciate their individual personalities. When introduced to Dr. Chad, he was pleasantly surprised to find him to be a very calm and an easy person to talk to. "Henry, tell me, what is your favorite part in working with animals?" "I love their individual personalities. Buddy, the pony is a little show off, he loves to play hide and seek. He thinks if he can't see you, you can't see him, Mr. Huffman's horse, is very quiet and observant of who and what is around him, and CupCake is a lover. She knows instantly who she can trust and is very protective of Miss LilyRose.

I love all animals." "That Sir, I believe is a prerequisite for all grooms. If a groom only works for money, then your animals will not be served well."

The subject finally got around to what Dr. Chad's plans were while in Wilmington? "I'm here to serve my daughter in any manner that I may be of service, I may be here a month, six months, or even a year. Time will tell. I'm looking for a place I might rent, furnished preferred." Allen responded immediately, "The apartment over the mercantile is available. The family moved out of town and if that suits your needs, it's yours for getting it back into shape, and cleaning it up."

"Why Allen, that's most generous; however, I certainly can pay rent." "It will be a comfort to know someone is in there I can trust with the situation as it is. There might be squatters who will try to move in. if you get my meaning?" "Yes of course, I can certainly get it in shape while I'm getting in shape."

Father moved into the little apartment, and was there for almost a year. Both lawyers assisting in the divorce proceedings advised: It was impossible to keep a man from his child for a lifetime. The court believed a man could be rehabilitated. So, it was agreed that LilyRose would still be LilyRose Somerset-Huffman until Mary Therese married and changed her name, or if LilyRose remarried and changed her name. LilyRose would be granted a divorce with out receiving any financial benefits from Martin Stein Huffman who was not there to speak for himself.

What LilyRose did not know at that time, was that Eva and Allen had already re-written their will to make LilyRose and her heirs, beneficiaries of all monies, properties, and investments. Lil Rose would be a very wealthy woman.

The years flew by. Lily went back to college to get her degree in Music Education, William Lincoln Bailey still sung in the church choir and performed in the All County Christmas Concert, he completed his Children's Natural History Center of which, he led guided tours for elementary schools in the county. However, the Memorial Gardens was not part of the tour. It was off limits, his private sanctuary.

Mary Therese became fast friends with both Linn, her Chinese friend, and Ruthie her friend who lived by the railroad. Eventually, Ruthie's father got a job in a factor and her mother worked as a dressmaker. They rented the apartment above Huffman Mercantile, that had been sold to another department store chain. Life was changing quickly.

Dr. Chad decided to retire. All home owners who joined the co-operative, accounts were closed out by he issuing them all deeds to their property. After having all family heirlooms, and Lily's mother's baby grand piano stored in a warehouse in Wilmington, he gave Frank and Mildred Grace Mitchell the deed to the big house. He told Frank that he earned it both by his friendship and his labor of love over all these many years. Dr. Chad decided he wanted to move back to Philadelphia to be close to Mary Maud's grave. He thought maybe he could volunteer at Maggies Home for Mother's and Children as a medical doctor.

Then one evening, Martin showed up filthy, and deathly ill with what appeared to be a flu.. Neither LilyRose nor the Huffman's had the heart to throw him out. Lily went to work sterilizing everything. She demanded Martin stay in the maid's room by the kitchen, She hired a young woman studying to be a nurse to tutor Mary Therese since all schools were closed. They stayed in Mary Therese's room upstairs and the Huffman's stayed in their rooms, except to help with the chores and during meals. Martin was getting worse, all she knew to do was give him herb teas, keep him clean, and to burn his clothing and diapers in the burning barrel. She boiled his clothing, sheets, blankets in vinegar water. Then, Allen came down sick, and Eva demanded she would take care of him, then in two days she became ill, Martin died, and she had to call the coroner to take the body away because he was still a "wanted criminal'." Allen passed a day later, and Eva followed begging LilyRose to bury them together in pine boxes underneath the big oak tree on the knoll in the far corner of their land.

Eva told LilyRose where their vital papers were, the code at the bank, and where the keys to their lock boxes were. LilyRose felt like her head was swimming, with so much to do and remember.

Everyday she made sure that Mary Therese and her nurse and teacher were not sick nor showing signs of being sick. She wore a mask and rubber gloves while doing any of her house chores. Their meals were all kinds of soups and teas. Henry stayed in his room at the barn, went in town to purchase necessary items, and did exactly what LilyRose advised him do to prevent sickness. By the end of the month, the four surviving residents were still free of any signs of illness.

She had heard from her father that he was well, but that she had lost a couple of her Murphy cousins. After once again sterilizing the whole house, burning all linens, and clothing worn during the ordeal, she ordered new clothing for everyone by a mail order store. They arrived in ten days, and all were thrilled to feel as if they were once again alive. Lily and Mary Therese decided to take a ride to William's farm. They arrived wearing their new riding clothing and bringing Uncle Will a some homemade sourdough bread and ginger cookies. He was delighted to see them, and told how he felt ill for a day, but drank lots of herb teas, rested and prayed for guidance.

They returned home to a flyer posted at the mailbox, that school would start back the following Monday. When Mary Therese returned home after her first day, she was depressed because her friend, Ruthie and her dad had died. Her mother was struggling as a seamstress to make ends meet. She had not worked all the time her family was sick. She just had her son, and he was hoping to find work to help his mother. Life was hard for everyone. This terrible disease did not pick and choose; every family was affected in some manner.

LilyRose decided to teach music part-time, and to start a trust fund to help families in need of help. She imagined that if there were no jobs available for the type of skills they had, then she would pay for them to learn a new skill that would provide employment. She always knew there was a need for nurses, so she thought of a program to be developed in high school, where young ladies could learn the beginning skills to be a nursing assistant, then when the classroom academic part was completed, they would be assigned to hands-on-work in a doctors, dentist, hospital, senior care center. After graduating, if they didn't want to go on to college or to a certified nursing school, they could be employed as aides in doctor's offices or care centers.

Mary Therese graduated a year early and was now going to Wilmington College to study Animal Psychology. Then as a complete surprise, Lily-Rose had a nervous breakdown. She felt as though the life and light just left her. She stayed in bed, did not want to eat, and then her sweet daughter said, "Mom, please get out of bed, I don't want you to leave me, too. Mom please, I need you." It was like someone had shocked her with an electric wire! She fixed herself and Mary Therese a big breakfast of bacon and eggs, pancakes, and orange juice. Mary Therese smelled the bacon frying, came into the the kitchen, hugged her Mom and said, "Thank you Jesus, I have my Mom back."

After Mary Therese left for college, she asked Henry to saddle her horse, that she would be gone for about three hours and that there was some bacon and scrambled eggs if he wanted to eat them." He smiled seeing LilyRose was feeling better. He was getting worried about her zest for life.

She rode directly to William's farm. At first she couldn't find him, but after looking in the house, the shed and barn, she asked the new Shep where William was? Waging his tail, he started running to the orchard. She found William pruning apple trees and singing to the top of his lungs. She started laughing, then he looked down at her, embarrassed being caught doing what he loved best, singing. "Hello Will, remember me?" "Well let me see, are you Ethel, or maybe Mable? Oh, I remember, you're the doctor's daughter,

LilyRose,"

"Get down from there this very minute, I need a hug! He slowly me-andered down the ladder, dried his forehead with his handkerchief, then walked over to Lily and embraced her. She looked into his eyes, as they kissed, and kissed some more. "Oh William, I've missed you so much, can we go into the house, it's so hot out here in the sun?"

They enter the kitchen, he opened the ice box to get the ice tea, as LilyRose wrapped her arms around him, and began to kiss once more. They found themselves lying on the couch as she unbuttoned his shirt. Will asked, "Are you sure this is what you want? I have nothing to prevent making a baby," she covered his mouth with hers, and began to undo her riding pants. They both were so anxious: he nervous, she excited! When totally undress, her breast right in front of his face, she finds his penis, began to massage it as he moans, she continues harder as he sucked her breast. Lily made a bold move, she sat on top guiding his penis in, he cried out!, "Oh, Lily I love you so much." "And I love you Will, with all my heart." Then with a boost of energy that sent them both into ecstasy, he spilled his seed all over both of them. He suddenly is horrified with what they have done! "What If you get pregnant? "Then I will be thrilled! I'm probably a little too old for that, but if I do, I'll be happy to have your baby. Nothing would pleased me more." "Lily you're so beautiful." "Your love makes me feel beautiful. Let's take a shower or are you up to doing this again" He pulled her down whispering, "You know this was my first time" "Awe, shucks, you could have food me big boy, let's have it again." This time it was slow and easy until nothing could hold him back, he mounted her with everything he had, and she yelled and screamed with such delight it brought tears to both of their eyes.

"God, I wish I could stay right here, fall asleep in you arms, but Mary Therese will be home and I need to fix some dinner and try not to sing so she thinks something is amiss with her Mom.. I love you Will, where's your shower,

"I'm afraid there is no hot water, only cold, but we'll do it together, then it will be fun. I'll probably shrivel up like a little stick." "But I bet I can make it grown again. Let"s be at it.

So began, LilyRose and William Lincoln's love affair. They saw each other at least once a week and maybe more, if their schedules permitted it. Then Lily missed her period. She was never on time, so she decided not to tell William until she missed another one. She had missed her second period when about two weeks before she should start again, she had severe cramping, then passed a huge glob of blood that looked suspicious. Heartbroken, she knew then that she had miscarried. She cried all night. She opened her diary,

Dear Diary,

Today I lost our baby, I named it Lincoln Somerset Bailey. Tomorrow I will ask William if we can bury it in his Memorial Garden. I'm so sad. I feel certain it was a boy, but if it was a girl, I'd would have loved her too. I've decided it's time for us to get married and live like normal lovers. I know Will is scared of what people might think, I don't care and he should not either.

The next dayLily rode out to Will's farm with the little china cup of Love. She hoped they could bury it today, and he'd make a cross with his name on it. Some day when Mary Therese is old enough to understand, she will tell her about her little unborn brother or sister. I pray when we marry, I can have another baby. It would be wonderful to have a child with Will who would be a wonderful loving and present father.

Goodnight dear diary, Lily

LilyRose found William resting in his recliner on his porch. She silently leaned over to kiss him. He immediately awakened. "Hello my sweet William." as he reached up to kiss her, she noticed that his ankles were swollen. "William, why are your ankles swollen? Have you been eating a lot of salt? " He raised up to a sitting position, "I don't know why they are swollen, I felt tired so I decided to rest a bit."

"This concerns me. We need to take you to the doctor." "Lily, what do you have wrapped in that towel?" "Our baby, I miscarried yesterday, I know it's a boy. I named him Lincoln Somerset Bailey. I want us to bury him in your Memorial Garden."

"Oh my darling Lily, I'm so sorry, are you doing okay.?" "Yes, I had missed two periods, and thought I was starting my monthly, when severe cramps, took me to the bed with a hot water bottle, Then I felt another great pain, when I got up to check, there he was, a glob of love. I put it in a china cup that be

longed to my great-grandfather in England. I thought it would be a beautiful casket. Do you think I'm foolish?"

William raised to put on his shoes, his ankles were so swollen and he does not feel well. Concerned for Lily and her desire to bury the baby has his heart troubled. "Could we do this another day, we can put it in the cooler? I'm not feeling well and I do not want you trying to do it alone." "Yes, my sweet William, but only if you permit me to take you to the doctor, swelling feet and tiredness is not a good sign. I can hitch your buggy and drive you to the doctor." Will started to move, then began to faint. Lily grabbed him, then helped him back into his recliner. "That settles it, we're going to the doctor. I'm hitching up the buggy to my horse, what do you need?

"I need to wash my face and brush my teeth." Lily went inside to gather a pan of water, his tooth brush and soda William feeling a little embarrassed "Lily, I'm so sorry, do you want to place the cup in my ice box?" "Yes, you don't think I'm foolish?" "No more than when I showed you my memorial garden, You showed compassion and understanding .I'd like a glass of water to sip while you hitch up the wagon. Thank you for being here and taking me." "I love you Will, I'd do anything for you." She handed Will a cup of water, then went to hitch the buggy. When she came in, his coloring was a little better, but he still needed help walking to the buggy. After he was seated with a blanket around him, they headed down the road.

The young doctor was located in the new medical office located in the old mercantile. Lily knew nothing about him or his hours, but she knew Will needed to be seen. When they arrived at his hitching post, the sign said,

Steven Miles, M.D.

Hours 8-6, Sat 8-12

She went into the waiting room to ask for assistance in walking Will in. He's a big man and it would be better if I had another person. The doctor heard her walk in. Lily stated her challenge as he went out to help walk Will in. He immediately took Will into the examining room. After a through physical exam, he said. "Mr. Bailey, I believe you are suffering from congestive heart failure. What that means is your heart is literally being surrounded by fluids, the left ventricle is not working properly. We need to relieve you of some of this fluid. Are watermelon still available at the market?" "I'm not sure, I grow them and they are all gone. I have cantalope, will they do? I have a few of those left."

"Mr. Bailey, I need to make you aware of the seriousness of your condition. I want to prevent you from having a heart attack. You must have complete bed rest for a week with your legs propped up higher than your heart. Drink fluids, absolutely no salt, meat, and as many melons, squash, fruits you can handle. I can see you have been a very strong hard worker, but I'm afraid this must stop. Are you able to hire a worker to do your daily chores? "I'm not sure, but I'll try."

"And another very important thing you must understand., Try to alleviate any stress in your life. Try to find enjoyment in slowing down. Next week, when I see you again, I will have a medical plan for you. Also, I'm a Harvard graduate with privilege to their resources and latest medical treatments. Lily asked, "Have you ever heard of my father, Dr. Chadwick Nicholas Somerset, he graduated from Harvard."

"Dr. Somerset is your father? He's written many scientific medical papers I would love to meet him, does he live around here?" "He moved back to Philadelphia about a year ago, but if you would like to contact him, I will give you his address. He loves the art of healing."

There was no other way, William realized he could avoid Lily's help. He could not live at his place, do the chores, etc with out help. He agreed to her proposal to live at her home, talk to Henry about who and what he knew about finding the right person to help William manage his farm and Children's Nature Center.

When she arrived home, Mary Therese was home from her visit with Linn, her new Chinese friend. She came out to greet her mother to find William in the buggy, pale and week. Her mother asked her to get Henry to help bring William into the bedroom behind the kitchen. She then asked Mary Therese to check to see if the room had fresh linens with water pitcher and mug By time they were able to get William inside and to the bedroom, Mary Therese had everything arranged in the room. She found the linens were all clean, she filled the water pitcher with cool fresh well water, and had fluffed up his pillows. He had no pajama's, but she found a big shirt in the drawer that belonged to her Grandaddy Chad when he visited last.

Henry helped him undress, then he supported him as he got into bed. Lily brought more pillows to put at the foot of the bed to raise his legs. She asked Henry to bring a chamber pot from the storage room. By the time all of this was done, LilyRose started to make a list for Henry to purchase in town. As this

was Saturday, the stores would close by five pm; they would need to hurry.

At the top of the list was personal items for William. Shaving kit, tooth brush, hair brush, comb, nail file, four pair of white stocks size extra large, 4-6 pairs of men's large underwear, a pair of house slippers, size extra large, a bathrobe, extra large, large warm cap, and a large felt hat.   The rest of the items were groceries and supplies. She suggested that Mary Therese go along to find the groceries while Henry purchased the personal items.

It was after seven when Henry and Mary Therese arrived home. Lily-Rose had made a pot of soup with vegetables they had on hand. No salt or meat. The soup had plenty of carrots, potatoes, celery, squash, corn, onions, and garlic. She recalled that Bess had said that watermelon, garlic, and onions were God's natural healing foods. You can't eat too much. She found she had a big round loaf of bread she picked up on Wednesday before choir practice. And a big hunk of cheese; that should fill up the family. There were always home made cookies in the pantry, but not for William, his food will be bland, but she hoped to make it tasty with fresh herbs. After eating, Henry said he'd ride over to tend to Will's animals, gather the eggs, and milk the cow. He said not to worry, he'd let her know when he returned home. When she went in to get Will's dinner tray, he was fast asleep. After returning the tray to the kitchen where Mary Therese was washing dishes, she returned to empty the chamber pot. His urine looked very dark, she knew that after eating a good diet, it would clear up. "Dear God, take care of precious William, he's always done for others, it is now time for him to be taken care of."

Will went home two months later loaded down with his medical plan, some medicinal powders that Dr. Chad and Dr. Steven agreed upon. He was given a cane, a diet and exercise plan, But what pleased him most, was Henry agreed to be the manager of the farm and Children's Nature Center. William would oversee the operation, but Henry was in charge. Henry hired two employees, both part time. They worked two days a week, alternating days until harvest. They were farmers themselves, but farming just didn't pay enough to make a good living.

Henry hired a new groom for Miss LilyRose. A young man studying horse breeding and management. He loved mechanics and always had his nose in a book studying how things work. His name was Jonathan Young from Cleveland, Ohio. He did not have the same privileges on the estate that Henry had. Jonny needed to sleep in the Groom's quarters, cook his own meals, and take his laundry to the Chinese Laundry in town. He was responsible for three horses, CupCake, Buddy, and a gelding called Lightening. He fell in love with Lightening, love at first sight between horse and young man. Lightning's coat was jet black, had a star on his forehead. When Jonny walked into the stables, Lightening would raise his head to get his attention.

It was Mary Therese's graduation year. During her senior year, she attended Wilmington college, but would graduate with her high school classmates. An exceptional student, she was far ahead of her fellow students with exception of Linn. Both student's grades were above 4. GPA.

Linn wanted to study math at MIT, Mary Therese' wanted to be a Psychologist treating children with mental and physical disabilities. She planned to do her undergraduate courses at Wilmington, then go to Stanford for her Master's and PHD Degrees. They each felt they were on the best path forward. Linn received a full scholarship to MIT. She could begin her classes in the Spring Semester, beginning mid January. Mary Therese received a full scholarship for music and psychology at WC. She too, would begin classes in mid-January. Both young ladies would march with their senior class, Valedictorian for the class was going to be between these two friends. After their points were added up, grades were considered the greatest measure; however, the faculty believed being a balanced student also merited points to be added to final score. Their GPA's were exactly the same, 4.5. The faculty wanted the girls to be a part of the decision making process. Their extra curricular activities could be the deciding factor. The girls met in the Principles office. He shared their results with the decision that the girls should make the final decision. Mary Therese said, Linn it's your choice. Linn replied. "Since I'm Chinese and we like to gamble, let's flip a coin." Linn won, Mary Teresa was relieved

Mary Therese went two years at Wilmington. In her third year she and Jonny Young got pregnant and married. She finished her third year while pregnant, with baby Lily Kai. They lived in the Groom's Quarters. When baby Lily Kai was two months old, the couple decided to visit his parents's in Cleveland, Ohio for his 25th birthday, leaving baby Lily Kai with her grandmother, LilyRose. His parent's purchased him the gift he had been begging for since he was twenty, a bi-plane. The couple went to the nearest airfield to learn to fly the plane. Jonny's mechanical skills helped him to understand the mechanic's of the plane, but aerodynamics was a bit more difficult. After a month's visit, the couple decided to fly back to Clinton County's new air strip. There were a couple of barnstormer's preparing for an air show. They promised to give the couple some pointers.

When they arrived at the Huffman Estate, they found LilyRose had hired another groom, and the living quarter's were occupied. LilyRose, not knowing what their plans were, and needing a groom, hired a young man to help her around the estate. The couple had left her with the baby, which she loved, but it presented quite a pull on her time, trying to keep up with all of her responsibilities, of which number one was taking care of William.

She placed their clothing, etc. into Mary Therese' room. When they surprised her by showing up, filthy with oil and grease on their clothing and body, she asked, "How did you two get here from Cleveland?"

"Mom, Jonny's parents bought him a bi-plane for his birthday. We took some flying lessons there, then we flew into Clinton County's new air strip where we met some barnstormers who have promised to teach us more about flying."

"Slow down, you just got here! Did I hear you say you flew here? Are you planning to leave again?" "Yes, Mom we want to learn while we have the chance from some authentic barnstormers. There is going to be an airshow this weekend at the air strip, we've got six tickets, do you want to go?

"Well maybe, that sounds like it could be fun. Right now, I have errands to run. Are you able to take care of Lily Kai, she is the best baby, while I'm gone for about three hours?" The couple looked at each other, than Jonny said, "Can you be back in two hours, I'd like to go watch those barnstormer 's practice." Then Mary Therese added, "Mom this is once in a life time opportunity, can you please be back in two hours?"

"No I can't, but I'll take Lily Kai with me, she's such a sweet baby. Will you- please take he now? Get her some diapers, bottle of milk, and a rattler? I need to gather some things and get the groom to hitch up my buggy." She thought to herself, "Mary Therese is acting like a moonstruck teenager, not a married woman with a baby who needs her Mommy. What happened to her?" I must find some time to talk to her, she's not acting like the daughter I raised and love dearly." Then LilyRose had a flash back at the time when the Huffman's all died during the flu epidemic and she bounced into William's home and flew into his arms, professing her love. "Oh My God! Things are piling up, and I feel so lost." "Dear God help me, I wish I could speak to my father, it has become so difficult having him living in

Philadelphia. The last letter I had from him, Bess had died of a stroke, and Sister Therese Anne decided to return to France to make amends with her family. The Home for Mother's and Children was in good hands since they started their own convent. Last report, there were eleven nuns living there, teaching, nursing, gardening, and even building little cottages for the mother's and children who were still together. Grandfather's trust had grown, thank God for the Murphy Family's loving watchful eye. The baby started to whimper when Mary Therese handed her to her GrannyRose. But as soon as the buggy was moving, it seem to rock her to sleep. Her first stop was to check in to see how William and Henry were doing. Being in his own surroundings with some sort of purpose, was certainly a healing balm to his heart. Father told LilyRose if William lived five years it would be a miracle. She thought every moment was a precious wonderful miracle. While he was still at her home recovering, she went to his home to dig a hole in the Memorial Garden. She dug down about three feet, and placed a silk hanky around the china cup, then asked God to invite him or her to be a member of the Angelic Heavenly Choir. Today she will show little earth angel, Lily Kai her uncle or aunt who chose to stay in Heaven to help guide us along our way. Please be with Mary Therese, she is in need of guidance and direction."

She knocked on the cabin's door. Henry opened the door smiling. He said they had just eaten, but if she needed anything, he could whip it up. Then he saw Lily Kai, "What a beauty! She's got your red hair and blue eyes, William will be happy to see you." She carried Lily Kai to where William was seated at the table. She sat down by him, to allow him to see her. Lily Kai reached out for him to take her. LilyRose said, "I'll let her stand on your lap, then you won't have to pick her up. I believe she already knows you. Look she is loving being in your presence.

Will, I'm very upset with Mary Therese and Jonny. They just got home from Cleveland visiting his parents for his 25th birthday. They bought him a bi-plane, I believe that is what they called it. They are at Clinton Co. air strip as we speak, learning to fly from some barnstormer's. They just expect me to take care of Lily Kai at the drop of a hat. I can't believe my daughter has become so irresponsible, not thinking ahead, just jumping into the moment as though she were a teenager. Lily Kai is so precious, she loves everyone, but I'm concerned for her precious little emotions, I never saw Jonny kiss her or hold her, not even once."

"She is adorable, thank you for bringing her to see me. Henry and I are doing quite well. I've been cooking because it's mostly sitting down. Today I made loaves of bread and a pot of lima beans. How are you doing aside from the daughter's drama? Have you heard from you father?" "Yes, one of the nuns died of a stroke, and Sister Therese Anne went back to France to make amends to her family that she ran away from about 45 years ago. They now have eleven nuns at the Mother and Children's Home."

"Henry is such a help with the Children's Center. We had a group here on Monday from one of the county schools to learn about Nature's Water Cycle. He's a quick learner and very good with children." Lily Kai did a big jump and William asked Lily to please take her. He was concerned he might drop her.

"William, I loved those days and nights I cared for you. I felt like we were married and I was doing what any loving wife would be doing for her husband after a busy day in the fields. I know, I know, "It Just Isn't Done," and because I don't want to cause you any stress, I'm trying to be a big girl by just letting it be. But every night before I go to sleep, I write in my diary, I tell you how much I love you, that you are in my prayers, then I kiss my pillow, wishing you were there with me." Then changing the subject, she asked?

"Do you and Henry think you'd like to go to the air show on Sunday afternoon?" We have six tickets, I'll pack a lunch, we could sit in the big buggy and watch the barn stormer's do their tricks, and I'm sure I'll have Lily Kai. We could just stay for about two hours, I'm sure I will have my fill of bright sunshine, loud cheering, and daring pilots doing acrobats in the air. "What time would you be going?" "I would think about 1:30 would bring us back by about 4 pm. We could return any time we wanted. Okay?" "If it's okay with Henry, we'll be at your place with the two horse buggy. She kissed him on the lips, and once more said, "I love you my William, from here to eternity and beyond. See you Sunday." Will took a drink of water, and said to Lily, "I love you too, always have and always will." LilyRose holding Lily Kai's little hand waved goodbye.

MaryTerese and Jonny spent every day at the air strip while the barn stormers were still in town. They came home each evening laughing and excited by what they learned. He had his bi-plane stored in a hanger at the air field. Then about six weeks later, they announced that they planned a trip to the west coast. They wanted to see the Pacific Ocean and to learn from the pilots they heard were living and flying around San Francisco, Santa Cruz area. LilyRose was shocked, angry, then depressed. They were just going off without any concern for their little baby. I must talk to Mary Therese. Finally one afternoon while Jonny was in town buying supplies, she called Mary Therese to the kitchen. "I need to tell you, this adventure you two are planning has me nervous and scared. You're going off, leaving Lily Kai: what if something happens, and I can't find you?"

"Mom, I'm 23 almost 24, this is a once in a lifetime opportunity. It is so much better for us to leave lily Kai with you as a baby. then to try to do it when she is a toddler, in school, or older. I know you will do the absolute right thing for her in every situation. I would not leave her with her other grandparents, they seem rather flighty to me. Please understand, we are not abandoning you or Lily Kai. Jonny plans to open his own mechanic's garage when we return and I will finish my last year of college so that I can fulfill my dream of working with kids and horses. I love you Mom, but if not now, when?"

LilyRose, William, Henry, and Lily Kai drove to the air strip to see them off on their adventure. LilyRose could not stop crying, she was so afraid for them. Will, taking her hand, looking into her beautiful blue eyes said, "Lily, this is when there is nothing you can do but have faith You've raised her to be a risk taker, to be creative with her time and talents; now is the time to let go, trust and have faith in Our God Almighty. We can't know what the future has in store for us, but we can take one day at at a time, doing the best we can, moment by moment."

"Yes, you and this precious baby are my inspiration. I guess it's time to go, Lily Kai needs to be changed, and we need some nice cool cider. Life goes on.

Most gulls don't bother to learn more

than the simplest facts of flight

how to get from shore to food to back again.

For most gulls, it is not flying

that matters, but eating.

For this gull, though,

it was not eating that mattered,

but flight.

More than anything else,

Jonathan Livingston Seagull loved to fly.

-Richard Bach, "Jonathan Livingston Seagull"- page 12

The St. Louis Daily Newspaper reported that On March 21ˢᵗ, 1918, A bi-Plane caught on fire, crashed and burned, the two passengers did not survive. If anyone has any knowledge of their names and where they are from, please notify the St. Louis Sheriff Department.

On April 4, the editor of the Wilmington paper saw an AP about the air accident in St. Louis. He wrote an editorial about the Air-Show at Clinton air-strip and added the news bulletin to his article. Henry saw the article. He thought, "I know of no easy way to tell her, she must be told." He showed the article to William hoping it didn't cause his blood pressure to go up. "Henry, we must go to LilyRose before someone else gets to her. "They immediately got in their one horse buggy and arrived about 35 minutes later. She was outside hanging up diapers when they arrived. William motioned for her to please come to the veranda. She hung the last diaper, then headed to the veranda. "Lily, I'm afraid we have bad news," as he handed her the newspapers. She started wailing, then sobbing, then nothing. She walked out to the stalls and got a whip and began striking the clothesline post. With each wack, she said something that was not understood, then when she was totally exhausted, she fell to the ground, breathing deeply. Slowly, but determined, she stood up, walked to William and Henry and said. "They were following their dream, life must go on, I have a child to raise and I'm so grateful she wasn't with them. I must find out how to get her remains. I appreciate so much that you told me, before anyone else" Bracing herself she said, "William, as you have shared many times, we only have this moment to live and to be the best we can be. My precious Mary Therese is no more, but she will live in my heart forever. I must find her and bring her home. Will you help me? I mean, help me by giving me strength when I falter and to remind me love is eternal?" He reached out to hold her hand, then brought it to his lips. "As long as I live, I will be your unfailing strength, maybe not of body, but of heart and soul." Then kissed her finger tips.

She notified the sheriff that she believed the bi-plane was the "Spirit of Lily Kai" and wanted any of her daughter's remains returned to her. A week later she received a box filled with ashes, a skeleton of a left hand with a melted ring on her ring finger. Also in the ashes, miraculously was found, a puppet clown with just a bit of its red yarn hair singed.

"It is good to have an end to journey towards,

but it is the journey that matters in the end.

"Ursula Le Guin,

"The Left Hand of Darkness"

Jonathan Young's ashes were sent to his family in Cleveland. They never contacted LilyRose concerning Lily Kai nor did LilyRose send her condolences. It was as if, neither family existed.

Mary Therese Somerset-Huffman-Young was buried beside her beloved grandmother Eva. On the other side of her grandmother was her grandfather Allen, and next to his father, was Martin's ashes. LilyRose thought of her daughter's beauty, both inside and out. How she never wanted anything to suffer. She would give anything she had to a poor soul who needed it. Her friend Linn, now a senior at MIT, spoke of her friend's generosity. "I remember eating in the lunch room, when Mary Therese saw a student with nothing to eat. She said, "Come on Linn, let's go share our abundance with her, she looks so lonely." "I guess we youth think we'll live forever." She then placed a wreath of red roses and white lilies on the grave, then handed little Lily Kai a long stem rose. Lily Kai held it up high, then looked up to the sky as a white dove flew over. "Yes, Lily Kai, Mommy just flew by to let you know she'll be watching over us."

That night LilyRose took out the picture album she had of her daughter. Her radiant black curly hair was always so striking. Her green/hazel eyes were very piercing and magnetic. She was so serious about everything she did or witnessed. She was a tom boy, who owned dolls, but never played with them. She said she loved the smell of manure in the barn and would prefer to live with her horses then in her fancy bedroom. She was eclectic in her style. She loved learning new things, and wanted to study her Jewish heritage. When she was ten, her grandmother Eva took her to New York so that she could attend a Jewish Temple and experience Hanukkah. She hated the game of "Cowboy and Indians" because it was about killing the Indian's. And when she was fourteen she spent the summer building her own treehouse, where she placed a telescope through a hole in the roof so she could watch the stars and dream of going to the moon. She closed the album then put Lily Kai to her mother's bedroom. It was almost eight o'clock when she heard a knock on the door. She looked out the window and saw her wonderful father standing there with a white lily in his hand. She opened the door crying, he embraced her saying, "I'm so sorry sweetheart, I got here as quickly as I could. I had to change trains twice. But it beats the wagon."

"To be upset over what you don't have is to waste what you do have."
-Ken Keyes, Jr-

Father stayed for almost two weeks. He was a comfort and also a joy. By the time he left, they were into doing their crazy dialogues and impersonations. They visited William and Henry a couple of times. As he examined William, he would do some of his silly antics to get the patient to relax. William would play right along. On the last day that he visited William, as he was putting his leather doctor's kit together, he took Williams hand to read his pulse, he then said, "William, I owe you a bit of gratitude. You have been a grounding force in my daughter's life. She is a very strong woman, but like all of us, we need those persons we can trust with our heart and soul. Thank your for being just that. We both know you are very ill, but your strong will is evident in the manner that you love. When our life's purpose is for the higher good for all humankind, we can rest knowing we did the best we could."

"I've enjoyed meditating in your Memorial Garden, walking the land you so beautifully honor with grace and gratitude. The children of this city and county are eternally blessed by your gift of love. I will be leaving in a couple of days. I will not see you again on this side, but we will meet again, and in doing so, we will rest in peace knowing we did our best to leave the world a little better than when we found it. God Bless You My Son and Eternal Friend,"

Dr. Chad went right to the buggy and paused, as he prayed. "I know neither Will nor myself will be here much longer. Guide LilyRose as she stands firm in raising Lily Kai to be a loving and grateful soul. Thank you Father, for blessing me with LilyRose as a daughter, Amen."

As her father boarded the railroad coach, she threw him a goodbye kiss. She knew she would never see him again. He died two weeks after returning home. Her cousin Peggy Murphy found him in the rose garden, laying beside Mary Maud's grave. LilyRose traveled by rail coach with baby Lily Kai to be with her cousins in celebrating the lives of both her parents and Bess Dominican. When she left Philadelphia, she brought back, her mother, father, and Bess' journals. Also, she went to the Pennsylvania Bank to empty the safety deposit box. She found in it, her mother's wedding ring, a diamond in the middle with an emerald on each side in honor of her Irish ancestry. She found her grandfather's St. Christopher's medal and chain, and her grandmother's crystal rosary, also, her great-grandfather's copy of Benjamin Franklin's Auto-Biography, her father, grandfather, and great-grandfather's college diploma's, certificate from Medical School, Law School, Oxford, and Judge of Philadelphia. All blessings from those who have gone before. May each rest in peace. The next day, she and Lily Kai boarded a train to Wilmington and in William's arms. She was eager to share her Somerset heritage.

Henry picked her up at the train station. He told her that William was very weak and believed he was living just long enough to see her. She told him that when they got there, she would wanted him to officiate their spiritual wedding. She said whatever, you choose to share as the ceremony will be appropriate for us to be married in the eyes of God. Williams concern that he has repeated over and over these many years, "Lily, It Just Isn't Done" referring to that drop of Negro blood he has in his body, never stopped me from wanting us to marry. Love is not bound by societal norms, it is a God-given blessing. I'm sorry you never had the fortune to have a love in your life."

"But I did, Miss Lily, we grew up together. Then when I got conscripted to the war, she wrote me every week. Then I heard from my mother, that she took ill and died. Before she died she left me a letter begging me to find love, that I deserved it. I never found another I could love like my little Franny, she was so beautiful and kind. I hope I can do a good job for you." "Life is a challenge, I'm so sorry you lost dear Franny," "She's still in my heart, Miss Lily"

Lily Kai awakened just as they arrived at William's farm. When she saw where she was, she started jumping in LilyRose arms. "She loves William. But who couldn't love that wonderful soul?" Henry opened the door, went straight to his room to get his Bible. Lily found William very, very week. She took his hand and could feel his very slow heart beat. She said, "Sweetheart, I brought some of my Somerset heirlooms. My number one, is my mother's wedding ring. Look at it. It has a diamond for eternal love and two emeralds for her Irish ancestry. I've asked Henry to perform a Spiritual Wedding Ceremony. We don't need a legal document to be married in the eyes of God. All we need is Love and that is what we have. Is that okay with you?"

"Yes, Lily I love you. So will you marry me?" "Oh yes, I thought you'd never ask.

She took out her grandfather's St. Christopher's medal to put around his neck as her commitment to their love. Henry began.

"Dearly Beloved, we are gathered here in the presence of God, for the Holy Sacrament of Marriage, between William Lincoln Bailey and Lily-Rose Somerset. William Lincoln Bailey and LilyRose Somerset the Eastern poet, Kahil Gibran said this about marriage: "You were born together, and together you shall be forevermore, You shall be together when the white white wings of death scatter your days. And you shall be together even in the silent memory of God. Give your hearts, but not into each other's keeping. For only the hand of Life can contain your hearts. And stand together, yet not too near together: For the pillars of the temple stand apart, And the oak tree and the Cypress grow not in each other's shadow." "If you, William Lincoln and you, LilyRose accept this to be true marriage, please respond together by saying "We do." With joyful tears, they both said, "We do." "What tokens of your love do you have to offer. William held up the ring, "May this ring be a reminder of the love you two share, You may place the ring on Lily's left ring finger." William smiled as he slowly placed the ring on her finger. "What token do you, LilyRose offer," Lily took out the medal from the box, "LilyRose, may place the medal around William's neck. "Now, By the Power of the Living God, whose love and joy abide's in you both, I now pronounce you Husband and Wife, From Now unto Eternity." "You may kiss your bride." They kiss, so lovingly and tenderly, Then Lily bent to whispered in his ear, "My darling, I let go, so now you may Go Home, God's Light will carry you home to be with Mam, Gunnar, Papa and Mama, Father and precious

Mary Therese, and our baby, Lincoln. The Heavenly Choir is waiting for your Beautiful Voice of Love." Will once more, struggling with one more breath, said, "Lily, I love you always" and then he was gone. Little Lily Kai was out doors playing when she suddenly burst through the door shouting," "GrannyRose, I just saw Uncle Will fly away." "I'm so happy you saw him go., isn't it grand? He doesn't have to suffer anymore."

Henry said he'd call the mortuary, as he requested to be cremated, then they would have him laid to rest in the Memorial Garden. "Ma'am, I truly honor you, you're the strongest woman I've every met. Thank you for including me in your service, I hope it met your expectations." "Thank you Henry, it was more beautiful than I every expected. I must leave not,but I'll be back in a few days to help with his things."

As they rode home, Lily Kai chatted about Heaven and Uncle Will going to see her Mommy. LilyRose thought,"Children truly do see only beauty and truth that we adults so often fear.

That night, after dinner dishes were done, Lily Kai was bathed and read to, LilyRose poured herself a glass Shabbat wine that had been in the china cabinet for many years. As she poured the red liquid, she realized that her emotions were calm and serene. She thought, "Is this what it means to let go and let God? I know my Beloved was ready to leave; not me, but to move on to his next assignment. I feel sadness, but not pain or hurt. Will touched so many lives with his loving kindness. His gentleness calmed all who were around him. Father loved him. He knew that Will and I had what he and Mother had: pure unconditional love. But

Will's insistence, that "It Just Wasn't Done" was his way of protecting me from the evils of the world. Someday, Oh God, someday may this prejudice and abused be erased, never to be seen again. She climbed the stairs to her room, put on her nightgown, and picked up her Diary.

Dear Diary,

Will has moved on. He died peacefully after Henry officiated a Spiritual Wedding Ceremony. It was beautiful. He used a passage from Kahlil Gibran's poetry. I will try to remember to have him give me the passages to enter into my diary. Tomorrow I will go through his things, do whatever I can do to complete his estate. Funny, we never talked about that part of our lives. I'm not sure he had any idea of the wealth that I incurred. Between my grandparent's, my parents, and the Huffman's, I know I am a very wealthy woman. My goal now, to be sure I find the most perfect way in which I can serve humanity without enabling them. With God's help, I'll be told. I also am blessed with Lily Kai, I think she'll keep me young for a while. She is so much fun and so smart!

Goodnight diary, Lily

The next day, after breakfast, the two Lily's drove to William's farm. Henry was already stacking his clothing to be given away. He was delighted Lily came, thinking she would take a few days to grieve before heading out to help. She brought some homemade ginger nut cookies and jam. He had coffee brewing so they decided to have a cup before getting started. Lily Kai took a cookie as she went out to play in the sandbox. Will built the sand box for children to play in while visiting. He always sifted it and kept it clean because of his cat. But the cat died about a month before, so hopefully it would be clean enough for Lily Kai to play in.

After putting the dishes in the sink, checking to see what they could eat for lunch, Lily said she would begin in William's desk and dresser, his most personal and private areas. The first thing she found was a large envelope address to her. She opened it, then started to read:

"My Beloved Lily,

By the time you find this, I will be gone and you will soon learn I left a lot for you to take care of for me. I'm sorry Sweetheart, I know you understand, I just wasn't able and felt you are the one I can trust to do things as I desire.

Enclosed is a copy of my last will and testament, making you executor of my property and all that it includes. We already set up as nonprofit Nature Center for the Children of Clinton Co. Henry, Don Denlinger, the Sheriff, and you have been designated as member's of Board of Trustee's. If this is not according to how the law requires, I know you will know what to do. As for my personal money, there is fifteen thousand in the bank that I want to see go to the Friends Meeting Association and ten thousand to the college for a scholarship fund for students desiring a career in organic agriculture or environmental science and education.

Also, you will find a box that has my journals, and personal treasures. They are for you to keep and distribute as you see fit. I've nothing to hide anymore. I feared being sent back to slavery for so long, I forgot the importance of faith and trust in our Divine Father and allowed fear to keep me hidden from truly trusting. You taught me so much about love. I want to be cremated and my ashes scattered in the Memorial Garden. If they don't allow cremation, please put my body in a pine box to be buried. I prefer ashes.

I already made arrangements for Henry to be made manager of the farm and Nature Center, to live on the residence and receive a salary. If he doesn't choose to do this, I hope you'll be able to find the appropriate person or persons. Lily, I'm so sorry to ask this of you, but there just never seemed to be enough time when we were together to work it all out. My lawyer, who happens to be your lawyer, told me as executor you could use whatever money it takes to accomplish setting up the Nature Center. I've been trying to find a way to honor Gunnar in the name of the Center, but haven't been successful; again another thing I've left undone.

As I close, I want you never to forget the love and joy you gave to me during our short time together. But Lily, it will go on, as God's eternity never, never ends. I love you always, Your William,

William Lincoln Bailey

In his box was the Buckeye nut, white feather, a Bible, lock of Lily's red hair, his two journals, and a copy of his last will and testament and deed for property. Henry found her crying with her head on his desk. She'd forgotten when Will stopped by the house and she was trimming Lily Kai's hair. He'd ask if he could have some, "It makes good padding for bird's nests." He had kept it, just as she gave it to him with a red ribbon around it. She looked up to see Henry, then said, "Henry, William has made me executor of his will. He hoped that you might enjoy being the manager of the farm and Nature Center with a budget to hire two employees, to pay expenses and also be paid a very good salary. However, it must be something you'd love doing, What do think?"

"I think I'd love it. If Will chose me, then he believed in me, I'd be honored. Oh Miss LilyRose, I'm so humbled and excited." "Please Henry, call me just Lily or LilyRose because we're equals, remember? Now let me see, that's one item I can mark off my to do list."

"I forgot to give you this Lily, I thought you'd want me to take the medal off before the mortuary received the body." "Thank you Henry, yes, I wouldn't want it to burn up or be lost."

She called for Lily Kai to come get washed up before going home. She came in chatting about how clouds make pictures in the sky. "I saw a big bunny rabbit, then it went away." Lily thought, "This child is so much fun! I truly believe she's with me to teach me how to live without her mother, my father, and beloved William."

The new groom was leading Buddy around the ring behind the barn when they pulled in. Lily couldn't remember the grooms name. She was the first groom she ever met that was female. As she got out of the buggy, she asked,

"I'm sorry, but I've forgotten your name. I know you are going to college, but what are you studying."

"That's okay, Ma'am. You've got a lot going right now. My name is Angela Piper, they call me Angie. My undergraduate degree will be in Agriculture, but I want to become a Veterinarian. Do you know, it is harder to get in Vet school then into Med school?" "No, I didn't. My father was a well known surgeon, He went to Harvard Medical School on scholarships. He died this past year, and I miss him so."

Buddy saw Lily Kai and started making a fuss raising his head." "Ma'am, the pony wants Miss Lily Kai to pay him some attention. He misses her." "GrannyRose, can I please ride Buddy?" "Only if you wear a helmet and Angie stays with you." "I will Miss, I won't let anything happen to her."

LilyRose entered the house with William's personal papers, box, and journals. She heated some left over chicken and made a salad and sliced some sourdough bread. She sat down at the table to read one of his journals, when she heard a ruckus outside. She went to the door to find Lily Kai arguing with the groom. "No, I can do it myself," she yelled. LilyRose immediately took action "Lily Kai, get right in the house, now young lady!" "Ma'am she wouldn't let me put Buddy's bridle on him." "That's okay, you're going to have to listen when an adult in charge tells you what to do." "Angie, she will not be allowed for two days to come to the barn to be with Buddy. Thank you. Would you like a Chicken Sandwich, I'll make you one." "Yes ma'am, I'd love one. Thank you." "I'll bring it to you when I have it made, thanks again."

Lily Kai pouted all through dinner. She didn't realize that her Granny-Rose could hold out as long as she did. LilyRose went about singing as they washed dishes, then she motioned for Lily Kai to head upstairs to get a bath. After she had her pajama's on and read a story to her, they knelt to say their prayers. Lily Kai said, "Dear Jesus, help me to hold my temper, be nice to adults, and please tell my GrannyRose I'm sorry. I love you Jesus."

Granny Rose left to take her bath, and was brushing out her hair, when Lily Kai came into the room and said, "I'm sorry, Jesus won't let me sleep until I say I'm sorry." "You're forgiven Lily Kai, but I will have no more disrespect to adults or any one, and there's one more person you need to apologize to, tomorrow's the day. Now just whom might that be?" "Angie. Now can I ride Buddy tomorrow?" "No, Lily Kai, you are not being punished, but you do have to suffer the consequences for your mistakes. You did the right thing to apologize, but you still have consequences for your inappropriate behavior."

"You know GrannyRose, sometimes you just aren't any fun. Goodnight." "Goodnight, and yes Lily Kai, sometimes life is not all fun and games. Lily Kai, GrannyRose loves you to the moon and back." "And I love you to the moon and back, too."

Grabbing a cup of tea, Lily Kai took William's first journal to read. She sat up most of the night reading about his terrible life as a baby living with a mentally ill, egotistical maniac. Then suddenly things began to connect. His Mam's name was Bess with jade green eyes three quarter Negro, Bess Dominican was fair and part Negro, both women were very tall. She jumped up and said, "I must read her journal! I just wasn't up to reading hers and my parents journals after arriving home from Father's funeral.

She opened the closet and brought out the traveling bag that contained Father's medical and personal journals, Mother's diaries since she was 12 years old, and Bess' diary. Mother considered Bess her best friend and had given Bess a beautiful leather diary for Christmas the first year she came to live and work for them. After digging deep, she found the diary. Pretty well used and full of letters, recipes for making herbal teas, women's pain med's, and one to purposely miscarry a baby. She said to herself, "I had no idea?"

She began to read the first entry. "Miss Mary Maud gave me this very beautiful diary. She said that it helped her to deal with situations if she could write about them. I've not revealed my real name. Jade Nicole Beaumont, but it was changed when Jeb, aka Desmond Lafayette Beaumont and I got married. We were both Beaumont's because our Master Father's were brother's. We lived on different plantations. We ran away because his half brother, Phillipi tried to rape me. We changed our name to Dominican after we were married at the convent in Memphis While on the Underground Railroad, we chose slave names. because house slaves were more valuable if caught. We became Jeb and Bess Dominican.

The nuns help us to get on the Underground railroad, but one night Jack, a slave seller caught us, took us to his home, made Jeb and his sweet wife, Jenny watch as he raped me. She was already with child and I became pregnant with Jack's child. Jeb said he'd love the child because it was part of me. Miss Jenny had a boy she called Gunnar, and a couple months later I had my son, Willie. They loved each other and looked almost like twins, except, Willie was always a little bigger than Gunnar. One night Jack came home so drunk that he beat Miss Jenny and Gunnar until she lost her baby. Gunnar was trying to stop him from beating his mother. He beat the child with everything he could find. LilyRose stopped reading, laid the diary down, and began to weep, "Jenny suffered just like I did when Martin beat me in front of Mary Therese" LilyRose wanted to stop reading, but just couldn't stop. She began where she left off.

Miss Jenny waited until he passed out on the bed, she tied his arms and legs to the bed posts and used his shotgun to shoot him right into his hateful ugly face. She sent Gunnar to the barn to get us, he was too little to use the big key to unchain us, so he gave it to Jeb. By the time we got there, she was already bleeding, but it didn't stop her. She screamed for us to throw Jack into the outhouse pit. We then burned the bed sheets. Jenny went into labor, delivered a still born baby boy. We buried the lifeless baby behind the garden,   I'll never forget when we wrapped Jack in the bloody sheet covered in his bloody brains, she said, "throw him in!" As we threw him, she said something like, "Lord, Jack Jones was a mean evil devil. He hurt me, he hurt and killed one of my babies, If I'm to go to hell, help me raise my son to be a good and decent man. The Lord giveth, and the Lord taketh, I just help the Lord. She then threw her wedding ring in on top of him. She turned to me, and said, "He took mother's wedding ring to sell for moonshine, that one was fake."

LilyRose laid the diary down. She now knew how the pieces of the puzzle fit. Bess Dominican aka Jade Nicole was without a doubt, William's mother. Will's mother was living in Dayton, Ohio working with my Mother and Father, and even more strange, Will's beloved LilyRose, had endured the same type of abuse as his mother did. "Oh My God!"

It was in that moment that GrannyRose interrupted her story to say:

"Lily Kai, did you, while growing up ever think or image the kind of abuse I was exposed to?" "No, GrannyRose, I barely remember Uncle Will or Grandaddy Chad. At times I could feel your sadness, but I never in my wildest days, believed you to have been treated so badly by my Grandfather Huffman. I, of course, do not remember anything about my mother and father. I was too young. But your love for my mother and me always made me feel safe."

GrannyRose wiped her eyes, "I'm happy to have protected you and helped you feel safe. She then turned to address her great grandchildren. "Jody and Joey, you-are-not-too-young to be made aware of prejudice and the types of abuse it breeds, especially sexual. Women have endured sexual and incest secretly because society has been unwilling to see women as equal to men. At this time, in your lifetime, women and children all over this country and world, still suffer abuse because the root cause is prejudice. Because I have these journals, news articles, and pictures to verify the cruelty experienced by me and our ancestors, I felt it was a necessity to share, before I die, stories both negative and positive our ancestors experienced. These journals and diary's will verify what I've just shared and will continue to share.

I'm not ashamed to admit my love for William Lincoln Bailey. It did not matter to me or my family that William had Negro blood, but his fear for how I might be treated did not permit us to be a married couple. He would say over and over, "LilyRose, "It Just Wasn't Done," "Our death bed marriage was in the eyes of God, and I've never taken off this ring, since William placed it on my finger breathing his last early breath.. It originally was my mother's wedding band. The symbology of this ring is sacred. The diamond is for eternal love, and the emeralds are for Irish simplicity and humbleness. Wiping tears from her eyes, she then continued: You children are fortunate to have a loving father who came from a different culture." Turning to look at Ardon, she asked, "Ardon, have you shared your story and native culture with your children?"

"No, I haven't, and hearing you tell your story, has made me realize how much I've failed my family by not sharing the rich culture of my native ancestors. Right now, I make a commitment to you Jody and Joey to take you to Arizona this coming summer, to visit my family on the Hopi Reservation. With GrannyRose permission, after our break, I will share a short version as to how "Morning Star" became Ardon Joseph. Our time together, has excited my soul to revisit and enjoy the beauty of Northern Arizona, the Hopi Culture and the Sacred Mountain."

The kitchen table was laden with fresh fruit, crackers, cheeses, and cookies. After the bathroom break, a walk around the garden a couple of times, the family was ready to listen to their father tell his story of how he got to have a Hopi Mom and to end up at Sinclair Indian School in Pennsylvania.

My story began with two young girls from Connecticut, who after finishing their private residential school in New York, boarded a train at Grand Central Station, to go across the country to see the Pacific Ocean. As you can imagine, they both came from wealthy families, their father's both worked on Wall Street. This trip

was part of their graduation gift. When they stopped in Flagstaff, they decided to stay a couple of days to see the sights, then head on to California. They stayed in a Bed and Breakfast. While having their morning breakfast, a member of the school board heard them speaking Eastern English dialect. He interrupted the

girls to introduced himself. He boldly asked them if they could teach proper English? They both laughed and said, "Of course, we're very proficient in the Kings Language." The gentleman asked if they would like like a job teaching. Flagstaff needed both an English teacher and one that could teach basic Arithmetic. He said if they would like to see the school, which was empty because of summer break, he'd like to show them. They walked about a mile to find a little red school house with two rooms. A classroom, and living quarters for the school teacher. One of the girls decided she'd like to stay. Her friend was angry with her because she didn't stick with their agreement. She went back home to Connecticut. The girl who stayed, spent the summer visiting the various sights, learning about the culture, and writing letters home that she was enjoying studying about the natural habitat and the native cultures.

As she explored Flagstaff, she noticed a young native boy sitting on his blanket, right outside of the train station selling his native art. He could not speak much English, but she finally figured out that he was Apache from a reservation farther North East. Then one day, she saw that he had a black eye and blood on his clothing. He told her some Cowboys were trying to pick a fight with him. A few days later, he wasn't at his regular place by the station.

She remembered that he had shared that he spent the nights in the woods by two big Aspen trees that connected as one. She searched into the woods where she found him badly beaten up. She helped him to walk to the office of the old Doctor she had gotten to know. He was afraid of white man's medicine. Finally he hurt so badly, he allowed the Old Doc to help him. The doctor was a very kind man, and could speak a little Apache, Navajo and Hopi. The Doctor told him he had two broken ribs, and some bad cuts. He sewed him up, and bound his ribs and told him to stay out of trouble. The girl paid his bill, then told him she was the new school teacher, that she'd hide him in the school house until he got well. After some months, they fell in love. She knew her family would not approve of him, after all she was a descendant of Pilgrims, and they all know what they gave to the Indians; cheap beads, liquor, small pox, and stole their lands.

By early fall, the young girl knew she was pregnant. Her Indian lover was thrilled and wanted to get a job to take care of mother and child. He found a job cleaning the railroad station and the saloon. One night he didn't come home. The next morning she found out he had been murdered behind the saloon. She went to the Sheriff to report the murder. The Sheriff laughed, told her to go back where she came from. This was the west, "we don't like our women messing with Indians and if Indian's mess with our women, we hang them. So, you best be careful, you might end up like your boyfriend."

"Scared, she went to see the doctor and his kind wife. Giving his full attention to her story, he sat her down to give her a fatherly talk. But when she told him her parents would disown her if she was having a baby out of wedlock, he asked her just what did she propose to do? She said she planned to hide her pregnancy with heavy clothing, and teach until it was time to have the baby. She wanted her baby to be raised in a native culture. All she knew about the father was he was Apache, twenty-three years old, and a beautiful artist. He could paint, do leather engraving and silver jewelry. Doc told her he'd see what he could find out.

A couple days later, he came to the school during lunch period. He told her he knew of a young Hopi girl who just lost her baby. Her husband was killed while out hunting. He said the Hopi culture is beautiful, they are family and clan oriented. Everyone in the village is considered a relative. If you'd like, we can visit the reservation on Saturday to meet with she and her family. She said she'd love that.

The Hopi family was happy to take the baby on one condition, that the girl must live with them until the baby was born. The doctor agreed to deliver the baby, but after the delivery, she must agree to give the child to the Hopi family. The girl only asked that they name the baby, Morning Star. The Hopi family wanted to know why? The girl shared that every night she dreamed the baby was a Morning Star and that she would love her baby forever.

The Hopi family felt that was a good sign and agreed that at the naming ceremony, he would be called Morning Star if that was in agreement with the sacred signs they would be given. The doctor came up to Hopi Land about a week before she was due. He stayed with a family whose son he was treating for multiple mysterious injuries. When asked how they happened, all were tight lipped.

When the baby was born, he was handed to his Hopi mother, as his biological mother wept softly. She returned to Flagstaff with the doctor, stayed with he and his wife until she was well enough to make the trip home. About six months later, the doctor received a bank check for $200. No return address, nothing written. He promptly delivered the money to the Hopi family.

Morning Star grew up learning the Hopi Way of Living, spoke the language perfectly, then when he was twelve he was taken by the U.S. Government to a Native School in Carlisle, Pennsylvania. The school was to train the children to be Americans. They cut their hair, was not permitted to speak their language, and were punished severely if they did not obey. He was given the Americanized name of Ardon Joseph. When Ardon turned eighteen and had finished his schooling, he was prepared to return to Arizona when he decided to stay long enough for the school's annual arts and craft show.

Persons from all over the east coast came to buy native art and crafts. Ardon's work was greatly admired. A curator from an Art Gallery in Manhattan, New York offered to display his work and give him a job at the gallery. He had no idea what he was agreeing to, but wanted to get as far away from Carlisle, Pennsylvania as he could.

One day, Lily Kai Somerset, on a break from Harvard Law School, walked into the Gallery. Ardon took one look at a gorgeous tall woman with radiant beautiful red hair, with a determined stride, and knew instantly, where ever she was going, he wanted to go with her. So now my children you know your daddy's past, and this summer you'll visit a beautiful native culture called, "the Hopi Way."

Their mother, added to the story. Lily Kai stopped off at New York on her way home from Harvard for the summer. She invited Ardon to visit her home, meet her GrannyRose, and the town she loved. They visited the college campus, where he was offered a full scholarship with a room on campus. She left in the fall to return to Harvard, he stayed to finish his degree in Fine Arts. They married before she finished Law School, holding up her native wedding ring made by Ardon with various precious natural stones circling the ring. "And then one day, they got lucky, they made two beautiful babies, Joanna Dorene and Jonathan David, named after their dear friends. in New York. They affectionately call Joanna, Jody and Jonathan, Joey. Do you happen to know them? If you don't, do, because their terrific. Both kids started clapping and cheering.

GrannyRose said, "And I agree 100%. So folks, I think we need to eat this beautiful meal that has been waiting for us the whole day. Then GrannyRose is going to take a hot soak, and go to bed. The old gray mare she ain't what she used to be! We'll continue tomorrow after we've all had a good night sleep."

The family all pitched in to clean up, the twins said they would spend the night with GrannyRose, and fix a big breakfast of blue berry pancakes and sausage. The parents were instructed to arrive in the morning, no later than 9:30. Gathering their coats, Ardon and Lily Kai left to stay in their own home to feed their animals, a rescue mutt and a squatter cat.

They arrived right on time, Joey said that GrannyRose was still getting dressed. Lily Kai climbed the circular staircase to her grandmother's room. She was still in her dressing gown. "GrannyRose, are you not feeling well?" "Just dragging my feet a little this morning. If you'll help me find something comfortable to wear, I don't need to shower, I had a soak last night."

Soon, they all arrived to the kitchen breakfast table. The twins were all thrilled with the fine meal they had prepared. Blue Berry Pancakes, Scrambled Eggs, Sausage Patties, Orange Juice, and Hot Coffee and Hot Tea. GrannyRose sighed, "I don't believe I've had such a wonderful feast in my 93 years." "Awh, Granny Rose, you told me that once when I came home from college and treated you to corned beef hash and poached eggs." "Ooops, as the kids say, "I just got busted."

Two months later, just after her 94th birthday, GrannyRose died in her sleep. She had taken off her wedding ring and St. Christopher's Medal, and placed them on a note that said,

"To my precious great-grands: Jody, the ring; Joey, the medal. I love you."

Common experience teaches that
when great demands are made upon us
if only we fearlessly accept
the challenge and confidently
expend strength,
every danger or difficulty brings its own strength
As thy days so shall thy strength be."
-J D Hadfield-

Summary, Wilmington College Convocation, Five Years Later

The president of the Student Body of Wilmington College stood at the podium to introduce the speaker for Convocation, a weekly opportunity for students to attend lectures from prominent citizens, alumni, social, or economic institutions. It is a Quaker principle to thrive and worship freely and to honor and cooperate peacefully with all of God's Creation.

"Students, faculty, and guests, on behalf of our Student Organizing Committee, I want to welcome our speaker, an alumnus of WC, graduate of Harvard Law School, devoted law professor, world traveler for Peace and Collaboration, author and wife to Dr. Ardon Morning Star Joseph and devoted mother. Will you join me in welcoming Lily Kai Somerset-Joseph to our podium today?" Audience stands and cheers, while Lily Kai walks to the podium, humbly waving for them to be seated as she begins.

"Wow!" as she wipes the tears from her eyes, "You know how to soften an old soul, but rest assured, I intend to speak my allotted 30 minutes. Audience laughing as she steps away from the podium to stand directly in front of the audience. "My title for todays talk is, "What you focus on, will expand."

I'm not the originator of that statement, many scientists, philosophers, and spiritual leaders have been studying that simple statement and have declared it a fact. Philosopher's, scientists, and theologians have explored it in their writings, and spiritual leaders are proving it by their daily lives. They teach that all humankind at the moment of creation was seeded with a spark of the Divine; a Soul. What we think, we become. We were given free will and as a result, we reap what what we sow by our choices. So the statement, "What you focus on expands," is indeed a fact, a principle we live by whether we are conscious of it or not.

Right here in this great institution, there is a library full of the writings of the greatest men and women in history, politics, philosophy, space exploration, medicine, and natural science. Any good student of life practices the "art of observation." John Muir studied nature. He documented what he observed and came to some conclusions. Thomas Edison failed over one thousand times to find the element needed for the incandescent light bulb. Dr. Stephen Hawking, a present day Math genius, all though he has not been able to use any of his bodily functions due to a diagnosis of ALS at age twenty-three , twenty years later he spends his days in his lab working on the mathematical equation for "The origin of the Universe." He said he learned what didn't work, and now focuses his mind, that works beautifully. Edison when asked how he found the courage after failing so many times said, "Why, I never failed, I just learned what didn't work."

I invite you, to open your mind, to observe, explore, and question everything that is around you. Questioning is not judging, it is the art of observing all aspects of life and living. Humankind is a very complex, yet simple creature. We love new things, but when we feel we understand it, we start to search for another challenge. Often times things are discovered, when looking for something else. Artists work long hours painting, writing, studying in order to feel they did their best. And of course, they did. Because in that moment, which is all there is, we all do the best we know how. The next moment is a whole new beginning. A whole new opportunity to move forward to learn something else. Life is exploration, and how we live it is intentional, whether we are aware of it or not. Our Internal Guidance System will keep us on track if we but learn to listen and trust Its Guidance.

Today I am presenting to this assembly, a radical point of view. One I've developed by my own exploration, observation, and Inner Guidance. I would like to introduce this by asking you to raise your hands if you believe there is peace today in any part of the world?. "Young man, in the green shirt on the front row, you raised your hand immediately. Do you mind sharing where you know there is peace in our world today?" The gentleman answered very confidently, "There is peace right here in Wilmington College." "Would the rest of you agree?" "Mumblings and whisperings can be heard with a few who shouted, Yes! "Is there anyone with a dictionary handy that could look up the definition?" A few minute pause, "Could the young lady in the back with her hand up, please read what she has found?" "Peace is the quality of being calm, quiet, serene." "Thank you, does anyone else have a different meaning? Would this be your consensus as the true meaning of peace?" The audience responds affirmatively.

My next question is: "Can we see energy?" The majority of the assembly shout, no! "So how do we know it exists?" Someone shouted, "We see the evident of it."

"Yes! yes, we definitely see the evidence of this thing we call energy. We blow up a balloon, we can't see the air we blew into the balloon, but the balloon grows in size, that we can see. Now that I have set the tone for my radical statement, I will introduce to you what I believe, by what I've observed and experience.

THERE IS NO PLACE ON PLANET EARTH THAT IS EXPERI-ENCING PEACE NOW because each of us, are creating our experience by our thoughts. Our thoughts are energy, the energy I think is expressed in waves that are felt by those in my environment, and travel world wide. When I judge myself as being inadequate, I create an energy that affirms what I put out, and thereby my actions match my thought. I lack self-esteem and confidence to live life the way my heart desires." Lily Kai pauses for her words to sink in.

What I have just shared is a Scientific Principle, called Cause and Effect. Most of you know this already. It is nothing new. It's been around since Creation. But what is new to most of us, is the fact that our thoughts determine our experiences, and we can CONTROL OUR THOUGHTS. If I spend my every waking moment fearing something or someone, my fear energy will draw them to me. If I take charge of my thoughts by affirming "I am guided by love and kindness, nothing can harm me." Then I am creating a positive uplifting energy that supports life and harms no one. To be present to the moment, by being aware of your thought in that moment, affords you an opportunity to make a conscious choice as to what you want to bring forth in your life. It is written, "To Thine on Self be True," which means when we consciously examine our own lives, what we are thinking and be totally honest with ourselves, we cannot ever plead victimhood. The only person we can ever change is ourselves. To try to change others without changing yourself is to promote being a "False Prophet."

As I shared in the beginning, I love reading. When I was in the library in London, England, I came across a philosopher from California, named Ernest Holmes who wrote a book called, Science of Mind. The title caught my attention. His premise is, Change your Thinking, Change your Life. The book awakened in me some things I've always believed, but had no way of validating myself. This book opened the door for me in serving my clients, writing legal proposals, and understanding my own thoughts and beliefs. Dr. Holmes said, "If you understand how your mind works, you will be a better Catholic, Jew, Christian, or Muslim."

It has certainly helped me to be more compassionate to myself as I brought forth those things I feared and was afraid to heal.

My parents died flying their bi-plane when I was just a toddler. As a result, I was terrified of flying, and until I could change my constant negative thoughts about flying, fear of dying as they did, I could not heal. I was stuck with the story of their death that was repeated in my family throughout my life. My husband was instrumental in helping me change my negative thoughts. Fear is the root of all pain and abuse, until we can take charge of our thinking, we will continue to be run by FEAR, False Evidence Appearing Real.

Five years ago, my Grandmother, LilyRose Somerset invited her only living family members to her home, PEACE AND SERENITY CENTER formerly known as the Huffman Estate to share the history of our Somerset Family. She had with her a stack of journals and diary's. She said it was her desire to share the stories that had never been told before, some positive and others, not so positive. She used the phrase. "It Just Wasn't Done" as a societal norm that basically controls our society.. It took three days for GrannyRose to tell her many stories, share letters, newspaper articles, photographs, portraits, deeds, and trust from over more than a hundred years. GrannyRose firmly believed that until the Truth could be told, then the past would stay hidden in closets, and never be healed for generations.

She died just two days after turning 94 years old. When I returned to my Political Science Class that year, my students asked if I would share some of what she told us. At the end of the class, there was a consensus that I should write a book about my family's history. That is the book I have with me today. It's title is, "It Just Wasn't Done." I've written the story just a GrannyRose told it. It is the story of three families, from very different backgrounds: English Aristocracy, Northern American Abolitionists, and Southern Slavery

as their lives journey to end up in Wilmington, Ohio to question the evolution of the Declaration of Independence and the Constitution of the U.S. and its current application in the lives of all of those who reside here. Did you know Wilmington was a station for the Underground Railroad, that Quaker's were conductor's, and Wilmington College graduated their first class in 1870, right after the Civil War. Did you know that William Lincoln Bailey was a run-away-slave from Tennessee? You may know of the beautiful

Natural Science Children's Center just west of Wilmington. Will was adopted by Obadiah and Martha Bailey when he was fifteen. Will was a graduate of WC, and soloist for the well-known All County Christmas Musical Directed by my grandmother, LilyRose Somerset-Bailey. She and Will were married in a Spiritual Ceremony as he laid dying from Congestive Heart Disease. He coined the phrase, "It Just Wasn't Done," because he feared in marrying my grandmother, it would cause her harm to marry a slave boy. On

his death bed, he confessed that his fear caused him to miss out on having children, being married to his one love, and to make a living statement to the injustices suffered by slavery."

I can see by the clock, I've accomplished one of my goals, I used up my 30 minutes. My second goal is that I hope I planted a seed for you to take time to examine your own life and to remember what you think about expands, and thirdly, as you leave the hall today, the ushers will give you a ticket with a number on it. A member of your Student Council will draw ten numbers for a free copy of my book. Also, on the table there are coupons for any student wanting to purchase the book for $10 which includes shipment from the publishers. Students began standing and giving a standing ovation as she leaves by the side door, she said,

"Have a beautiful day, you've been a wonderful and affirming audience. Blessings"

"If you genuinely love
or at least send kind thoughts
to a thing, it will change
right before your eyes."
John & Lynn St. Clair Thomas-
"The Eyes of the Beholder"
and so it is.

EPILOGUE

You are probably wondering what happened to those character in the book that played a great part in the story. The story ended with the death of LilyRose Somerset after her ninety-fourth birthday which was in the year 1952. I'll do my best to bring forth the characters as they continue their journey.

The **Beaumont Brothers:** Louis Phillipi Beaumont, after learning his god-son Phillipi Beaumont, son of Jean Michel Beaumont had tried to rape his slave daughter, Jade Nicole, and after he found Phillip tied in the boat shed with a note by Jade stating Phillip tried to rape her, and that she and Desmond were running north to freedom, he chose not to interfere with their plans for freedom.

Jean Michel Beaumont, when learning his son tried to rape Jade, and that his slave son, Desmond had tied Phillipi up, stripped him of his clothing, and Jade chose to run away with Desmond, decided to punish Phillipi by making him take part in the day-to-day plantation activities. Phillipi ran away to join Rebel Army. Rebel Army invaded both Beaumont Plantations, killing and stealing slaves, food, and destroying anything they could not use. Jean Michel found his beloved Rochelle, slave mother of Desmond, nailed to a wall dart board, with darts thrown into her body by a game they played until she died. When the brothers found out from General Grant that Phillipi and Desmond had died at Ft. Donelson, through their grief, Louis was determined to make amends to Jade Nichol.

Jean Michel could not find a way to reconcile his grief. His brother, Louis found him dead by suicide. After burying his brother Louis found the money he had hidden, and took off north to find if Jade Nicole made it to freedom and if possible to make his amends to her.

Franklin, Mildred Grace, and Junior, aka Lukas Mitchell: When Dr. Chad left for Philadelphia he deeded his big home to Frank and Mildred. After about three years, Mildred passed from complications from a circulation problem. Frank deeded the big house to Mother Superior for a Convent House. He left to live with Alice and the children in their new home close to Boston Harbor. Lukas had five more years before he could retire.

James, Annette, and BethAnne Black: James had a very successful career managing an elegant dining establishment in Columbus, Ohio. He retired after 20 years due to health problems. He was obese, about 200 lbs. He died a year after retiring. Annette, always a lover of French antiques went to Paris, France to study art and antique tapestries. She came back to Columbus after six month, opened a tiny shop in Columbus that catered to those who were serious about French imports. BethAnne married her college professor and lives in Alaska where they have a grant to study the polar ice cap and tundra.

Dr. Chadwick Nicholas Somerset III died in Philadelphia on a fall evening beside the grave of his beloved Maud. He felt he had done what God had sent him here to do, and was extremely proud of his only child, LilyRose Somerset who lived in Wilmington, Ohio where music and family were her passion.

Bess aka Jade Nichole Dominican became a nun, moved to Philadelphia, PA where she and Sister Therese Anne opened Maggie's Home for Mother's and Children on the old Somerset Estate. She died of a stroke.

Sister Therese chose to return to France to make her amends and run her family winery.

Chadwick Nicholas Somerset I and wife Victoria Amelia Campbell are buried in London England. He was a barrister for the Crown, and she a descendant of the Campbell Clan of Scotland.

Chadwick Nicholas Somerset II and wife Mary Margaret Shaughnessy immigrated to Philadelphia where he became a judge and she a great support to orphan children and the Catholic Church. They are both buried on the Somerset Estate.

Mary Maud Murphy-Somerset wife of only ten years to Dr. Chad and mother to LilyRose died of leukemia and is buried on the Somerset Estate in the Rose garden she so loved.

Allen Moses Huffman, wife, Eva Stein Huffman and father to only son Martin Stein Huffman all died during the epidemic. They were the owners of the Huffman Mercantile in Wilmington, Ohio

Mary Therese Somerset-Huffman-Young and husband Jonathan Young were killed in a bi-plane accident near St. Louis, MO leaving behind their infant child Lily Kai Somerset-Young in the custody of her mother, LilyRose Somerset.

Jenny Sterling, daughter of Rev. Henderson Sterling and wife of Brock Burns, are all buried in the cemetery in back of the Presbyterian Church of which they all served.

Gunnar Sterling, son of Jenny Brock, and half-brother to William Lincoln Bailey is buried in the Memorial Garden on William's farm.

Desmond Lafayette Dominican, wife of Bess aka Jade Nichole Dominican perished on the battlefield, at Ft. Donelson, under Gen. U.S. Grant.

Obadiah Bailey and wife Martha Jane were Quakers and conductor's on the Underground Railroad. They adopted Willie, renamed William

Lincoln. They both are buried in the Memorial Garden William built behind their homestead, now known as the Children's Natural History Center of Clinton, County.

Lily Kai Somerset-Young, graduated from WC and Harvard Law School. She was a strong advocate for Peace, appointed a Federal Judge for Wilmington, married Ardon Morning Star Joseph, famous Native American artist and Art Professor, birthed twins, Joanna and Jonathan. Both Ardon and Lily Kai lived long full lives and are buried at the Peace and Love Center's Memorial Garden.

William aka Willie Lincoln Bailey, biological son of Jade Nicole aka Bess Dominican, adopted son of Obadiah and Martha Bailey, creator of a Children's Natural Science Center on the farm he grew up in. He died of congestive heart failure and is buried in the Memorial Garden he designed and built to honor his brother, Gunnar, his slave mother, Jade Nichole, and his adopted Quaker parents, Obadiah and Martha Bailey. He died in the arms of his beloved spiritual partner LilyRose just moments after saying their spiritual vows as husband and wife.

Lillian Rose Somerset-Bailey: daughter of Dr. Chad and Maud Somerset, mother of Mary Therese Somerset-Young, grandmother to Lily Kai Somerset-Joseph, great grandmother to Joanna Dorene Joseph, and Jonathan David Joseph died just a few days after her 94th birthday. She gathered her family together to share her family history and to acknowledge the love, joy, and compassion they had enjoyed and the abused that needed to be revealed so that it could heal. After sharing her story, she felt she was completed and was ready to return to her creator. She is buried in the Memorial Garden next to her Spiritual Life Partner, William Lincoln Bailey with an inscription that reads: Two Hearts + One Love = God's Eternity.

Joanna Dorene (Jodi) Young-Riji, graduated from WC with a degree in Child Psychology, married Reza Riji at a Bahai Meditation Center in the Adirondacks in Northern New York. They set up a Yoga studio above Ardon's Art Museum in the old Huffman Building. She birthed a daughter, with red hair and green eyes. They are presently expecting again.

Jonathan David (Joey) Graduated from WC with a degree in pre-medicine. He was in Veterinarian School studying large sea mammals. While surfing in Maui, a shark turned his surf board over and took his leg off. He died as two dolphins were seen pushing him to shore. He was still wearing his great grandfather's St. Christopher's Medal. He is buried next to his parents at the Peace and Serenity Center. His twin sister, Jodi plans to name her expectant son, after her beloved twin brother, Jonathan Morning Star.

The Poet Jalāl ad-Dīn Muḥammad Rūmī said,
I was a mineral, and a rose, a plantation
I died as a plant, and became a beast,
I died as a beast, and evolved into a man.
Why should I fear that I will lose by dying?
Once again I shall die as man to join
the holy company of angels, But I must
Soar above them too,
"Everything must die Save His Face,"
When I have died as an angel,
I shall be that which is just beyond the mind's grasp
let me die to myself, for the ego's death Declares,
"To Him we return."
SOURCES USED"
Magazine, Newspaper, Professional Articles
LIFE MAGAZINE, Fall Special 1991,

Bill of Rights,200 year history of Turbulence and Triumph

RIGHTS UNDER THE CONSTITUTION,

by James A. Moss, 1053 Edition

THE CONSTITUTION of the United States,

by ACLU of New York

US Department of Justice, Civil Rights Division,

Voting Section Act of 1965

Back to the Basics of Citizenship, *A Law Related Education Statewide*

Conference

Sponsored by AZ Bar Foundation, October 10-13, 1995

TEEN Vogue, 8/27/22

"When Did Women Get the Right to Vote?"

AMERICA'S STORY, Book I, by David C. KIng

VANDERBILT LAW REVIEW

Law and Disorder in Nineteenth Century KY

by Robert M. Ireland

Articles taken from Internet

Wikipedia, Free Encyclopedia

John Henry Patterson, NCR owner

The Menorah: A Symbol of Light

Getting the Story Wright, by Bishop Milton Wright

CONVENTS: Encyclopedia of Greater Philadelphia

History of Wilmington, Ohio

Presidency of Ulysses S. Grant

World of 1898: International Perspective on Spanish-American War

Great Dayton, Ohio Flood

The Quotable Mark Twain

Christmas Candle Lighting Service, Rev Dr. Bob Henderson

The Smithsonian, October 2022 Edition,

We The People, U.S. Dept of Education 1987

BOOKS

Federal Textbook on Citizenship, by U.S. Government

LIFE, The Story of the United States

Battle Cry of Freedom, the Civil War by James M. McPherson

The Last Full Measure, by Jeff Shaara

Killer Angels, by Michael Shaara

The Prophet, by Kahlil Gibran

Thoreau: Walden and other writings, by Joseph Wood Krutch

Tao Te Ching, Lao Tzu, translations by D. C. Lau

Selected Poetry by: Rainer Maria Rilke, by Stephen Mitchell

Foot Prints on the Path, by Eileen Caddy

SPIRITUAL TEXTS

St. James Old and New Testament, Holy Bible

The Supernatural Bible

A Course In Miracles, Foundation for Inner Peace

Science of Mind Textbook, by Ernest Holmes

Kabbalah

The End of Sorrow, by Eknath Easwaran

A Guide for the Advanced Soul, compiled by: Susan Hayward

"Freedom is not a state; it is not some enchanted garden perched high on a distant plateau where we can finally sit down and rest. Freedom is the continuous action we all must take, and each generation must do its part to create an even more fair, more just society."
John Lewis, "Across That Bridge"

AUTHOR'S COMMENTS

The book that I have written is a novel, the facts are historical, the characters came through me by dreams and contemplation. From my point of view, I know they lived, but with different names, colors of skin, and social economic status.

I awakened one morning five years ago to a title being shouted at me. "It Just Wasn't Done! It Just Wasn't Done," kept going through my mind. I got up shaking and with tears running down my face, as if I just returned from the story's full drama. I felt out of sync the whole day. Thoroughly exhausted, I did something I rarely do, I took a nap. Again, the characters were telling their story in full technicolor. When I got up to start dinner, I found myself talking to Victoria with a Scottish Accent. She said, "Just relax and allow the stories flow through you, because we want our stories to be told." I realized I was creating obstacles and excuses because I did not believe I had what it took to write a novel.

One evening, I had a couple over for dinner. After dinner, we gathered in my living room with a glass of wine. Ken asked if I was writing my book. I timidly admitted to have written a couple of chapters. He asked if I'd share a chapter. I read the first chapter to the book. When finished, Ken said with tears in his eyes, "Betty, this story must be told." I had goose bumps because those were Victoria's exact words she said in my dream. I felt the energy affirming me, I was given this task and I must do it!

Since that day, the writing has been a labor of love. I found myself crying during some of the scenes, and laughing hysterical in others.

Thank you for giving yourself a personal visit into the lives of our kindred ancestors that our souls know most intimately.

b.b. Campbell, author

QUESTIONS FOR GROUP DISCUSSION

A. The book explores the dynamics of all types of relationships. What caught your interest as you began to read the book?

B. Chadwick Nicholas Somerset I, had a very different philosophy then his peers, concerning life and what is important. Can you share what or who made an impression, in your opinion, to help form his personal character?

C. Lillian Rose Somerset, the main character, in your opinion, what were her strengths and her weaknesses?

D. Dr. Chad had a dream. What were the positive and realistic goals and could you believe they were possible? Why or Why Not?

E. Willie, aka William Lincoln Bailey had a big roll through-out the whole story. Did he appear real, authentic, or what?

F. What was your reaction to Martin's alcoholism?

G. Did Mary Therese willingness to leave her infant child cause you any emotional response? If so, what, and why?

H. Was the ending predictable or a surprise? How do you believe it could have ended. Did the List of Characters and Epilogue add or detract from the story?

I. Did the story keep your interest? Would you recommend the book to others?"

ACKNOWLEDGMENT

I've been blessed to have wonderful souls who have supported me through this project. First of all my family saw very little progress and still lovingly supported me to the very end. I love you Teri, Tami, Tonya, and Chad to the moon and back. To my wonderful techie's, Reza, Joanne, and Cherra who waded the swamp and saw me through it. Deepest gratitude to Reza, my personal life coach who believed in the project and never let me fall into the hole of self-doubt. Marsha, my blessed cheerleader and researcher who found answers I had no idea were there. Bev, my talented artistic friend and illustrator who could sort out my complex thoughts and make them a reality. To my wonderful women friends who encouraged my abstract creative feminine spirit; Joanne, Patti, Janet, Linda, Magnae, Devra, Diane, Sakina, Char, Vivian, Bev, Marsha, Sally, Di, Grace, Eileen, Hollace, Lisa, Marianne, and Deb. My former college students who called me Mom and inspired me by their courage to overcome great obstacles; Michael, Angela, Stefan, Vuthy, Cristina, Loc, Daymara, Dr. Persida, Dunia, José, Eira, Bo, and Badaway. And last, forgive me if I've left anyone out, my dear friend and writer, Dr. Geri who heard the story first and encouraged me to write it. My faithful friend and former college roommate, Mary Margaret, an excellent character actress. Together we have weathered many storms and still believe in light at the end of the tunnel.

I am eternally grateful for all of your love and support. You each hold a special place in my heart. Betty aka Mom.